Other books by the author:
_____

Poetry of Love
Three dates
Three Sisters

Somersaults
in the hailstorm

Tshego Monaisa

Print 978-1-77605-622-4
e-book 978-1-77605-621-7

Layout & typesetting by Janet Von Kleist
jvonkleist@yahoo.com

Published by Kwarts Publishers
www.kwartspublishers.co.za

For Girls
and the women
we become

*For Girls
and the women
we become*

....

This book is dedicated to my cousin,
Mpho and the memories of our friendship
and sisterhood. My parents, Manini and
Lekwane, who framed my world and
gave me the scope and capacity to dream;
and my brothers, Tumelo and Aldrin
who I carry in my heart every day.

....

Prologue

Lerato had never been married, and neither did she want to be. Well, not right away anyway. If there was anything she was passionate about it was shoes. She was standing in her favourite shoe shop right now and she could not for the life of her choose between the bright yellow wedges encrusted with crystals, or the luminous red stripper heels she'd been eyeing for the past month. She'd come in today to buy the red pair, and that's when she saw them – the yellow wedges with crystals.

Lerato wasn't really a wedge heel kind of girl, but how could she resist the encrusted crystals? She couldn't. So she didn't. Right then and there she whipped out her gold credit card, cringing at the thought of how reckless she'd been with it lately, but hey, a girl needed to look good, right? Without any further thoughts that might conjure up the feelings of guilt that she was all too familiar with, she asked the assistant for a size six in both pairs and resolutely marched to the till, the boxes firmly in her hands.

"Lerato," she squealed into her cellphone as she absent-mindedly handed her credit card to the cashier.

"Do you still not check your caller ID?" a tired voice droned into her ear.

"And do you still not wake up before noon?" Lerato droned back.

It was her best friend from primary school – Maki. People could not figure out how they'd remained friends for all these years, but for Lerato it was easy – Maki was a thousand laughs a minute. Her dry humour could crack a whip at any time and any place. In fact, Lerato had often wondered how she could *not* have been friends with her. Lerato may not have been as sharp-witted as Maki, but over the years their bond and loyalty to one another had grown immeasurably. Besides, no one knew better than Lerato did, how Maki needed a makeover every once in a while, and who better to give her a new look than the self-proclaimed fashionista herself? Lerato smiled as the cashier put her new babies in a bag and handed her the till slip to sign.

"What on earth would I be doing anywhere outside my house before midday?" Maki croaked.

"Meet me for lunch at the usual spot?" Lerato chirped, abandoning the issue about Maki not being a morning person. That discussion could – and had once – gone on all day.

"Sure," Maki replied, "give me half an hour to spruce up."

"Look presentable!" Lerato yelled into the phone after Maki had hung up. They'd been friends long enough to not say 'bye to each other. It wasn't necessary, and what was the point of saying bye when they'd be back on the phone with each other within minutes anyway?

Lerato sashayed out the store, her sunglasses perched on the bridge of her nose. The amount that she had just spent on her credit card caused her stomach to momentarily plummet, but like the expert avoider she was, she decided to put that thought aside, march to her favourite sushi bar and resolutely sit at the counter. She ordered sashimi and California rolls with a glass of dry white wine, scrolling through her phone and chatting idly on social media while she waited for her friend. When she realised that an hour had passed she looked up and saw Maki stroll casually through the doors of the eatery, her hands in her pockets. She was sporting a cap, white vest, camouflage army pants and dirty All Star sneakers. Lerato did a double take and almost gagged at the sneakers.

"You're late," she sneered.

"Something you want to say about my outfit?" Maki smiled. She'd known Lerato long enough to know how she felt about her clothes.

"Let's just grab a table," Lerato replied, snatching up her shoe bag and marching past Maki to sit at a table. Maki caught a whiff of Lerato's breath.

"Are you drinking in the morning again?" she sighed, following her impeccably dressed friend.

"It's noon," Lerato snapped. Then, when Maki raised her eyebrows in answer, she defended, "I have to forget about my problems somehow."

"You have to get over your shoe addiction, is what you have to do," Maki replied. When Lerato cast her a stern look, she continued, "Admit it. That's the only reason you're at the mall at the crack of dawn."

"It's the middle of the day," Lerato replied airily. She signalled for the waiter and, as she ordered another glass of wine, added, "And lunch is on you." She threw a wink in Maki's direction.

"Why would lunch be on me when we both have a friend who actually works?" Maki asked without glancing up from the menu. "I called Tebza on my way here."

"You're incorrigible," Lerato smiled, impressed.

"I'm a broke writer, and you, well you're just broke," Maki laughed.

"So, what sushi are you going to have?" Lerato asked, a smile forming on her lips. "Maki?"

"That joke is so old," Maki sighed. Looking up she noticed Tebogo standing in the doorway scanning the place for her friends. "How can Tebza not see us when we're right here?" Maki asked Lerato under her breath.

Stifling a laugh, Lerato waved Tebogo over. "Over here, Tebza," she called.

"Oh, there you are," Tebogo replied, walking over to Maki and Lerato, and sitting down slightly out of breath.

Maki and Lerato exchanged a contented look; their little circle was now complete. Tebogo had joined the duo in high school and they had been inseparable ever since. Nothing had changed in the last 15 years; they were as inseparable now as they were then.

But they were also typical. Lerato was the pretty girl who had come to Joburg hoping to strike it rich as a model, or just by being pretty. If the modelling thing didn't work out she was sure that she'd die, just die. Well, it had been ten years and the modelling thing hadn't worked out. Nor had the TV presenting thing or the acting thing. Lerato just didn't have it in her to face the millions of other people who also turned up at auditions. And even though she was pretty and had great bone structure, so did every other girl who turned up at what Lerato had thought was "her" audition. She'd even auditioned to feature in those overnight success reality shows, but hadn't cracked that either.

However, Lerato was determined to suck it up and stay in Joburg for as long as she possibly could. The thought of going back home to the rurals penniless and with nothing but crushed dreams terrified her, so she decided to get a job at a call centre as a telemarketer. She had no qualifications except for Matric and no work experience or hobbies – apart from shopping – so she figured she could at least try to sell stuff over the phone. But it wasn't all she'd imagined it to be. For the most part people were rude and hung up on her; then there were the sleaze balls who tried to have phone sex with her even though she clearly stated that the phone calls were recorded. She didn't make much, just enough to pay the bills, and she was elated any time she made a sale – that made it somewhat worthwhile for her.

Lerato wasn't the type to hold onto the past, though. So what that the modelling/acting/presenting thing hadn't worked out? Life was too short to be miserable, so she paid for her necessary expenses with her salary, and got deeper and deeper into debt by shopping, partying and eating lavishly – all the things that her salary didn't cover.

Maki on the other hand was trying to make it as a writer. She'd always been the deep thinker of the group, and one of her favourite activities was trying to solve a murder mystery or criminal investigation ahead of the storyline while watching TV detective shows. She'd written a few puff pieces for her community newspaper, but it seemed like she couldn't catch a break as a full-time writer. The young woman had consoled herself that her industry was largely made up of freelance writers anyway, but was sure that one day she'd get a full-time job either at a newspaper or on a soapie production team. Her dream job was to be a soap opera writer, but for now she told herself that she was content as a freelancer because it gave her time to work on what she was hoping would be her bestselling novel.

If there was one thing Maki had tons of, it was ambition, and if she found no other vehicle to house her ambition, she would exhibit her own talent by writing a cracker of a murder mystery that would become a bestseller and catapult her to stardom as an acclaimed author. In the meantime she stayed up late to write, sometimes into the early hours of the morning, and woke up at noon to meet her friends for lunch – on them, of course.

Tebogo had always been unsure of herself. She was unhappy, yet afraid of change. She'd been in her non-committal, not-going-anywhere relationship with Tshepo for years, since varsity, in fact. One would think that, being the most educated of the group, she'd be the one who had her life together. And on the surface she did, but she was stuck; stuck in a boring job in the legal department of an insurance company with boring clients and boring claims. That was all because she'd succumbed to her mother's wish for her to go to law school and qualify as a lawyer, when all she really wanted was to go to beauty school and become a make-up artist and nail technician.

But she felt guilty for wanting what she'd wanted. Tebogo had been raised by a single mother who hadn't had the opportunities that she had. How could she say no to law school when she'd studied hard all through high school and had been afforded a bursary by one of the country's top businessmen? How could she have let him and her mother down to chase her own selfish desires? She wasn't even sure if she'd be any good at that beauty stuff.

She would have asked her friends for advice, but she knew that Maki would try to convince her that she had what it took, even though, she would add, she had let her looks go. Lerato would say that it was because of her boring job that required her to wear boring clothes that she had let herself go. Maki would chip back in that Tebogo's lack of self-confidence was because she felt some sort of duty to Tshepo because they'd been together since dinosaurs roamed the earth. And the conversation would then turn to how she'd managed to stay in a relationship with Tshepo for that long.

But despite what her friends would say, deep down Tebogo knew that she wouldn't be making any changes to her life, because she owed it to herself to stay in her soul-eroding job because it provided stability. And she would stay in her lifeless relationship too, even if just to dull the voices in her head.

***

Lerato wished she could open up to her friends about Seputla, her boyfriend. They'd always known everything about each other, and even though her friends had often judged her harshly for her poor choices in men, she knew that it was because Maki had always been super protective of her – despite the fact that she hadn't had a man in a decade, and Tebza was always sympathetic towards her.

But every time she tried to open up and tell them about Seputla she would think twice about it and stop dead in her tracks. For the first time in her life she was afraid of her friends actually judging her. Seputla wasn't the typical guy that she normally dated, and she'd dated quite a few. Her other boyfriends all had one thing in common: money. Whether they were spoilt trust fund brats, arrogant sugar daddies or tenderpreneurs, one thing was for sure – they all wanted a pretty girl on their arm and would often pay to have her there. How else would she afford all the niceties in life that she deserved?

It wasn't like she was trading sex for the good life. After all, she did like some of the guys that she'd dated, but she got bored quickly so she'd move onto the next. There had been cases where one or two of her exes would demand that she give back the stuff they'd bought for her, but there was a secret to her strategy: never let them know where you live. That had always been her one and only rule, not only because she was ashamed of her place because it didn't quite match up to the standard of how she'd always portrayed herself, but also for safety reasons. Okay, maybe she did occasionally trade sex for nice things, but hey, life was short and she worked at a call centre; do the math.

She let out a small, cynical laugh, catching both Maki and Tebogo's attention.

"What?" she asked defensively, sipping her wine.

"What's wrong with you?" Maki asked.

"Nothing," Lerato replied quickly.

"Why are you acting so weird?" Tebogo squinted at Lerato, creasing her brow and studying her.

"Stop staring at me like that," Lerato demanded.

"What aren't you telling us?" Maki pressed.

"Nothing! Leave me alone," Lerato scolded, shocked once again at how well her friends could read her.

"Have you met someone?" Tebogo asked inquisitively.

"Is this about Jabu?" Maki tested accusingly.

"No," Lerato replied to Tebogo. "And yuck," she added to Maki. "You're both wrong."

"You have met someone!" Tebogo exclaimed, her eyes lighting up. She was a hopeless romantic.

"Well, you could say that," Lerato conceded, taking another huge swig of her wine.

"Oh no," Maki mused under her breath.

"Don't be like that," Tebogo reproached.

"Now you know why I didn't want to tell you," Lerato added, pursing her lips.

"You're not getting out of this that quickly," scolded Maki. "Who is he? An investment banker?"

When Lerato shook head, Tebogo added, "Is he married?"

"No," Lerato replied quickly, and then paused before adding, "at least I don't think so."

"You know you're going to tell us at some point, right?" Tebogo laughed, tired of Lerato's games.

"I'm leaving," Lerato said, quickly picking up her handbag and her new shoes; she left the restaurant gracefully without a goodbye or a glance back at her friends.

"Just like that?" Tebogo protested.

Maki also got up suddenly. "I have to go too – major deadline on the SPCA piece."

Tebogo stared after the trail that her friends had left in the restaurant and picked up her cellphone to send a message on their "Divas" WhatsApp group. "You should've just said that you don't have money. I would have gladly paid the bill," she typed. Then, taking out her debit card and ignoring the beeping sounds from her phone, knowing that it would be Lerato telling her that she loved her, and Maki thanking her, she signalled for the waiter and sighed under her breath, "Like I always do."

Tebogo was twenty-seven but she felt like she had the life of a forty-year-old. She'd been with her boyfriend, Tshepo, for close to ten years and for the most part she felt like his mother. They lived together, and instead of nagging him to pick up after himself, cook them a nice meal every once in a while or even do the dishes at least twice a week, she'd capitulated and had just decided to do everything herself. It wasn't that hard anyway, just time consuming, and she hated confrontation. The inevitable argument just wasn't worth it to her, and she'd long given up the desire to be right. It was ironic given that she was a lawyer.

Truth be told, she wasn't excited about her job. She'd stopped fantasising about going to court and had instead resigned herself to her current job in the legal department at a local insurance company, working on the road accident fund claims. And there were a lot. People were either getting into car accidents or dying. Or both.

After paying the lunch bill she grudgingly got up and walked out the restaurant, slowly heading back to the office. She stopped when she saw Tshepo in the distance. Even though she was accustomed to not feeling excited or having butterflies in her stomach at the sight of him, this time something was different. It seemed like the lack of excitement hit her harder.

Tebogo had told herself that the butterflies-in- the-tummy effect died because they'd been together for so long, but as she stood rooted to the spot observing her boyfriend, she began to realise just how unattractive he was to her. Perhaps it was true that she had let herself go, but so had he. It was no wonder they'd barely touched each other in months aside from the obligatory kiss hello when she got home from work, before she headed to the bedroom to change out of her work clothes and then back to the kitchen to get started on supper.

As she stood there watching Tshepo, something in Tebogo challenged her to either accept her life the way it was, or to change it. And as hard as it was to admit, she knew she couldn't carry on with the way things were. She vowed to make some sort of change, and quickly ran towards the office before he saw her.

Maki had never been depressed but she was pretty sure that this was it. What bothered her most was that her friends hadn't even noticed. "Am I so boring that my friends can't even tell that I have depression?" she thought as she flung her satchel on the couch. The young writer had dabbled in drugs when she was younger and had vowed never to do them again, but the thought of a line of coke washed down with a joint really appealed to her. She threw herself onto the couch. Her life wasn't working out, and she wondered if it was still worth living.

Lerato always laughed at Maki's appearance, but the truth was that what she'd thrown on that morning was the best outfit that she could find in her cupboard. She hadn't been shopping in ages; true, she hated shopping and found it tedious, but she couldn't afford to go shopping even if she'd wanted to. It didn't help that prices were constantly going up and she'd sold everything that she could think of, including her beloved movie collection. That had been hard. All she had left was her laptop and TV, and there was no way in hell that she would ever sell either of those.

She pressed the remote to switch on the TV and when it didn't come on realised that she'd forgotten to buy pre-paid electricity. Maki sighed morosely. "Maybe I should ask Lerato to hook me up with one of her sugar daddies." She laughed sadly at the next thought –that they probably wouldn't find her attractive – and rolled herself into a ball on the couch, too lazy to bother about the electricity. The aspirant writer didn't even reach over to pick up her crime novel as she ordinarily would have. She'd always relied on reading to cheer her up, but this time she didn't think that even that would lift her out of her funk.

Chapter 1

Tebogo flung the plastic bags and their contents onto the kitchen counter, staring icily at Tshepo. She'd prepared a monologue on her way home, and if she was to get through it successfully it would be best if she wasn't in a chirpy mood. As expected, he was slumped in front of the TV, a big bowl of popcorn in his lap and the remote in his hand.

"Hey baby." He smiled in her direction as she stood frozen to the spot in the kitchen, watching him.

Suddenly a knot of anxiety tied in her stomach. At the distressing thought of losing him, she sped across the room and fell into his lap.

"What's wrong?" he asked, concerned.

The words came out in a rush. "I was at the mall today and I saw you but I couldn't speak to you, I just watched you. And as I watched you I began to convince myself that you aren't the one for me and that I've fallen out of love with you."

She literally saw the colour drain from his face. "Have you fallen out of love with me?" he stammered, almost inaudibly.

"No," Tebogo whispered. "I haven't. I'm just unhappy about a lot of things," she continued, plucking up the courage to voice her fears. "Tshepo, things just aren't the same between us. We've fallen into this boring routine where you come home and watch TV, and I come home and cook. We don't talk, we don't laugh and you don't even touch me anymore."

"Whoa, slow down," Tshepo said, putting a finger to her lips. "I thought you were happy?"

She shook her head. "I'm not happy," she admitted softly, tears welling up in her eyes. "I haven't been happy in months." She would've said years, but she didn't want to break his spirit entirely.

"I'm so sorry, baby," he said, cupping her face in his hands and turning to face her fully. "I didn't know that you weren't happy."

"You thought I enjoyed playing wifey to you and acting like an old married couple?" she asked him jokingly.

"Well, yes," he laughed. "Actually, speaking of marriage..." he continued, wiping a tear from her cheek.

Tebogo's heart skipped a beat.

"You wanna do it?" Tshepo asked, scrunching up his nose in anticipation of her answer.

"D-d-d-o what?" she stuttered, her mouth suddenly very dry.

"You know, get hitched?" he asked, a glint in his eye.

"Are you asking me to marry you?" she asked, disentangling herself from him.

"Yes," he answered nervously.

"Well, if that's the case," she added playfully, "I believe you have to get down on one knee, mister." Tshepo slipped off the couch and knelt on the floor with both knees, holding her hands in his.

"Tebogo Precious Seamela, will you marry me?" he asked solemnly, gazing lovingly into her eyes.

"Aaaahhhh!" she screeched. "Yes, Tshepo Trevor Moake-mele, of course I'll marry you!"

Tshepo jumped up from the floor and took her in his arms – popcorn and TV remote abandoned – and spun her in the air. In that moment, despite her elation, if just for a fleeting second, Tebogo couldn't ignore her anxiety, that caused her stomach to plummet.

Maki had been twisting the same strand of hair between her fingers for an hour, lost in her thoughts. She was attempting to edit her puff piece on the recent appointment of the new Municipal Manager, but had read the same line at least a hundred times. Her thoughts kept wandering back to her unfinished crime novel. Finally she gave in, closed the puff piece document and opened up the manuscript that she was typing on her laptop.

She was starting to have a love-hate relationship with her novel. This was supposed to be the masterpiece that would get her out of her funk, but lately she was starting to question whether her funk would ever truly lift. She'd always been a bit off centre and had relied upon the validation of others to make her feel good. Take her friendship with Lerato for example.

Lerato was the cool kid in primary school and everybody wanted to be her friend. The pretty girl hadn't taken to Maki at first and Lerato still did the same thing now that she had done then – judge Maki on her appearance. Except Maki, being the "crazy" one, had taken that in her stride and used humour as a tool to cover her wounds. What Lerato thought of her didn't matter, she'd told herself. But it did. It had mattered since she was eight years old.

Their friendship had eventually formed on the playground after Maki saved Lerato from an encounter with a boy in their class who was trying to look up the popular girl's skirt. Maki stood between Lerato and the boy, having a "your momma" insult session back and forth with him for at least ten minutes. Maki hurled insults faster than Lerato had ever thought anyone could, leaving the boy with a tear-streaked face after he lost dismally to Maki. Lerato had been impressed and, after winning Maki over with sweets and chips for a week, they became bosom buddies, much to everyone's surprise and to the chagrin of Lerato's suitors. Maki played the role of Lerato's bodyguard, and that had carried on for the next 20 years. When any of Lerato's men had become threatening, Maki would step in and find a way to chase them away. She had a number of routines she used for that purpose, including prank calling Lerato's man-of-the-moment and pretending to be his wife, calling a suitor and threatening to spill all the gory details about his affair with Lerato to the media, and even going as far as pretending to be a SARS representative threatening to expose the often high-profile men to the local tabloids as tax evaders. One time she actually showed up at a hotel swinging a cricket bat and threatening to do a makeover on the guy. In all these instances Maki had been Lerato's protector; her guardian angel almost. But Maki was crumbling under the pressure of life's overwhelming responsibilities and wondered who would be there for her when they came hurtling down.

Lerato arrived home with her shoe bags clutched tightly in her right hand. "Seputla," she called out. When she was met with silence she stepped through the doorway and tiptoed across the corridor to her room. She squealed in shock when someone hugged her from behind, and then fell into an uncontrollable giggle, swiping Seputla with her handbag. "You scared me!" she laughed.

"Hey baby," he greeted, turning her around and pulling her in for an overpowering kiss. One thing was certain, the man could kiss. Lerato was gasping when she came up for air.

"You went shopping?" he asked.

Guilt-ridden, she answered, "Yes, I just got a few things."

"Let's see."

But Lerato avoided the request and disentangled herself from his embrace, saying it wasn't anything special, before quickly disappearing into her bedroom and emerging again without the bags. She quickly changed the subject by saying that she would get supper started. Lerato had never really been the cooking type and surprised herself with what she could throw together when she tried. She was equally surprised that she actually enjoyed cooking for her man which was something she'd never even considered before. She laughed when she thought of the number of restaurants where she was known on a first name basis, simply by her choice of date.

A relationship with Seputla was not what she had expected when she met him at the gym. His toned physique was attractive to her, but Lerato had been insulted when Seputla randomly walked up to her and challenged her to increase not just the speed but also the gradient on the treadmill. Lerato ignored him. A while later he bothered her again when she was working on her arm definition. "If I didn't know any better, I'd think you were trying to tell me that I'm not in shape," she'd retorted.

"You're not," he replied drily.

"That's because you body builder types want women with abs as hard as yours. A woman still has to retain her feminine physique," retaliated an indignant Lerato.

He'd laughed and said he wasn't after her physique, but was glad that she'd finally stopped ignoring him. Then he walked away. That's what really upset Lerato; nobody walked away from her. She called him back, and when he didn't turn around, she ran after him.

"Didn't you hear me calling you?" she'd demanded.

Seputla casually replied that he didn't respond to "Hey!" and told her that he would accept a date with her as a way of making it up to him.

"I have nothing to make up to you!" she'd spat out. Then when the realisation struck her, with a small smile on her lips, she'd nodded and said, "I see what you're trying to do." The handsome gym instructor winked and walked away again. Ignoring the voice in her head that told her not to look, Lerato did, and enjoyed the view of him from behind.

That had been three months ago, and she'd loved picking his brain as much as he'd loved making fun of her since that day. Lerato discovered that he was also very affectionate, a trait she adored especially since her exes had never seemed to want to touch her until they had sex with her. That wasn't pleasant either. Most of the time there was no foreplay at all, and the act itself was either rough and aggressive or just plain boring. She'd never understood how one could "make love to your mind" until Seputla came along. Not only did he make love to her mind, but also to every single inch of her, which was something deliciously new to Lerato.

***

Lying on her couch deep in thought, Maki read the last paragraph that she'd written: "Mackenzie was lying. She was not innocent in the death of Molebatsi. She had covered up his murder the same way she'd covered up the last three murder cases she'd had a hand in, and had managed to frame her lover, Collin."

The young author read the lines at least four times; something wasn't gelling. She placed her laptop on the arm of her sofa and picked up her cellphone to make a call. Her plan was rudely interrupted by the annoyingly familiar voice that she'd named Betty: "You have insufficient airtime to make a call. Please load..." Maki hung up before Betty had finished, and stared at her phone in disbelief. Didn't she just load airtime the other day? She did a mental calculation of the days that had passed since she last remembered buying the airtime and her stomach sank when she realised that a week had gone by.

Maki walked over to the kitchen, her stomach groaning loudly in hunger, but she was met with a pungent smell. She wasn't sure if it was coming from the fridge or the pile of dirty dishes in the sink that had been there for at least a week. Bravely she walked to the fridge and opened it. "Yup, smell's coming from the fridge alright," she mumbled before dumping the rotten cucumber and forgotten leftovers in the bin. She sighed. That left only a semi-peeled onion and a bottle of water. She hated sponging off her friends, but what choice did she have? As she sent a message to Tebogo and Lerato on their WhatsApp group, asking them to meet

her for brunch the next day, she knew that she'd have to be
honest with her friends.

Chapter 2

· ·

Tebogo was the first to arrive at the restaurant. After looking around to make sure that none of her friends were there yet, she sat down at a table with three other seats. She glanced down at her new ring. Tshepo had given it to her that morning; it was the most proactive thing he'd done in years. As the ring caught the sunlight, it sparkled and Tebogo smiled feebly. She'd gotten what she'd wanted, right? The man had produced a ring, signalling his commitment to her and their relationship, right?

The waiter who appeared at the side of the table shook her out of her reverie and she hurriedly ordered a Cosmo, at the same time noticing Lerato enter the restaurant. She was sure that at least four of the other patrons looked up as her friend walked in, but Lerato seemed oblivious which took Tebogo by surprise. Lerato was always fully aware of the attention that she got from men – and the looks that those men's wives or girlfriends shot Lerato as a result of the way their men were eyeing her.

Tebogo quickly put her hand under the table as Lerato sat down, hiding her ring from sight.

"Hey, doll," Lerato greeted Tebza, sitting down as a waiter delivered a mojito to the table.

"I ordered a cosmo," Tebogo meekly reminded the waiter who blushed in Lerato's presence.

"No worries," Lerato winked at the embarrassed young man, "I'll drink the mojito, and you can get my friend her cosmo." The waiter rushed away.

"So what's new?" Lerato asked, turning to Tebogo and sipping her drink enthusiastically.

"Well …" Tebogo started before Lerato cut her off.

"How's work? How's that going? It must be stressful, neh?"

"Why would it be stressful?" Tebogo asked slowly as her cosmo was put in front of her and she glanced at the waiter momentarily to thank him.

"Well, I wasn't going to say anything," Lerato added cautiously, "but you've been getting rounder and rounder every time I see you."

Tebogo was dumbfounded. She was about to defend her increasing size and agree with Lerato that work was stressful, when Maki sat down at the table and began rambling about how she'd had a deadline and her car wouldn't start.

"But you invited us here," Lerato protested.

"I know," Maki replied out of breath. "I only remembered the deadline an hour before I had to leave the house, but I'm glad you guys came." She reached for Tebza's drink and took a huge swig as the waiter appeared to take her order.

"Cosmo?" he asked Tebogo.

"Please," Tebogo replied, exasperated as she scratched her head in frustration. Suddenly both Maki and Lerato gasped and stared at Tebogo wide-eyed.

"What?" Tebogo asked.

"Aaahhhh!" Lerato squealed and clasped Tebogo's hand, staring at the ring.

"Were you going to tell us?" Maki asked, curious.

"Of course," Tebogo said, removing her hand from Lerato's grasp. "It's from Tshepo," she added slowly.

"Of course, silly, who else would it be from?" Lerato joked.

"Unless there's something you want to tell us?" Maki laughed.

Tebogo averted her eyes.

"What's wrong?" Maki was quick to ask. "You don't seem happy."

"I'm not!" Tebogo replied, the words tumbling out of her mouth before she could stop them. "I haven't been happy in years."

The waiter placed Tebogo's Cosmo in front of her and distressed, she took a huge swig. "I was at the point where I was tired of pretending to Tshepo about how unhappy I was."

"About?" Maki enquired gently.

"About everything," Tebogo wailed. "And then the other day, just when I'd summoned enough courage to tell him exactly how I felt, he proposed. Can you believe it? The man has hardly spoken to me in recent weeks, he barely touches me, he never takes me out, and the only time we go shopping is to buy groceries. Then, when I start to tell him how I feel, he drops to his knees and proposes!" She looked to her friends for answers.

"When did he give you the ring?" asked Maki.

"This morning," Tebogo sighed. "I'm not even sure if he really wants to marry me or if he was just shutting me up."

"Yeah, I know the feeling," Lerato commiserated. Both Maki and Tebogo turned to her, Maki scolding Lerato with her eyes. "This is not about you!" she was silently screaming. Oblivious, Lerato continued. "I know exactly how you feel. Do you know how many men have proposed to me, only for me to later find out that they were already married?"

"This is not about you!" Maki squealed out loud.

"Just sharing," Lerato defended herself. "Just trying to be helpful."

"Well, you're not," Maki spat.

"And, in other news," Lerato said, as the waiter appeared and she signalled to him that they would have another round, "Seputla has moved in with me."

Maki's tummy growled loudly; she quickly grabbed the menu and started looking through it, silently cursing her stomach. Thankfully none of her friends had heard her stomach's complaint.

"Who?" she asked, as she nonchalantly paged through the menu.

"Seputla. I'm sure I told you two about him," Lerato answered.

"Nope," Maki said, pursing her lips.

Lerato looked to Tebogo for confirmation. Tebogo shook her head.

"Anyway," Lerato said to Tebogo, "I was hoping you'd share some of your recipes with me."

"What?" Tebogo shook her head at Lerato.

"You know," Lerato answered, "What you cook for Tshepo every night."

Mouth agape, Tebogo pointedly stared at Lerato. Maki looked up at Tebogo, the air pregnant with tension. "I just told you that I'm not in love with the man I'm engaged to and you want recipes from me?"

"Well, I just thought ..." Lerato stammered.

Tebogo stood to her feet. "Thanks," she seethed in Lerato's direction. "Thanks a lot." She spun on her heel and left.

Maki turned sharply to Lerato, scolding her with her eyes.

"What?" Lerato quipped, defensive.

Maki put down the menu. "Shame on you, Lerato." She quickly pocketed the sugar sachets on the table and rushed out, leaving Lerato shocked and alone.

"Are you stealing?" Lerato yelled, but Maki was already halfway to the door. Lerato stared at the two empty chairs where her friends had been. Just then the waiter walked towards her with their tray of drinks. Panicking, she waved her hands frantically, indicating that he should cancel their order and return the drinks to the bar, but he placed the tray on the table. "We won't be having these anymore," Lerato said, flashing her wide smile at him. "Can you return them? she asked, batting her eyelids.

"Afraid not," the waiter shrugged. "Restaurant policy."

"Damn it," Lerato muttered under her breath as the waiter turned and walked away.

Maki paced her living room floor. She had no clue what she was going to do. All her money was going towards her rent and the first two weeks of the month's groceries. And now it was the third week of the month. She fell onto her couch, staring at her phone in her hand. Should she send Tebza a "Please call me?" Judging by the way Tebza had stormed out of the restaurant, she wasn't sure if that was a good idea. "Maybe I should send it under the guise of checking up on her," she thought. But she quickly crushed that idea too because she didn't want to seem as insensitive as Lerato. As she sat on her couch, deep in thought, she realised that there was only one thing that would cheer her up – aside from shoplifting at the local grocery store like her main character, Mackenzie, in her novel. She quickly reminded herself that her book was fiction, and shoplifting was not a good idea. Grabbing her car keys, Maki bolted out the door.

Tebogo arrived home after a long afternoon at the office and closed the door behind her. She was surprised by the candle-lit atmosphere, soft jazz playing in the background, and in disbelief as she caught a whiff of the chicken aroma coming from the kitchen.

"Baby?" she called out, alarmed. She couldn't help but smile when Tshepo appeared in front of her in an apron.

"What's this?" she asked.

"A necessity," Tshepo said, taking her hand and leading her to the dining room table. "This evening I will be serving you," he smiled.

Tebogo couldn't help but blush as Tshepo filled her glass with champagne. "Ooh, you got the French champagne too," she teased, impressed.

Tshepo kissed her hand. "Only the best for you, baby."

When Tebogo's fiancé sat down opposite her, his good looks were highlighted in the candlelight. "You know you didn't have to do this, right?" she said.

"But I wanted to," he replied. "What you said the other day struck me and I didn't want you to feel as though I don't appreciate you." He took her hand in his. "And I want to show you that I don't want us to be in the same routine we've been in for years."

Touched, Tebogo lifted her glass to propose a toast. "To always being honest with each other." Tshepo quickly lifted his glass too, and added a quick, "Yes."

"And to loving each other the best way we know how," she concluded, gushing. Tshepo leaned in for a kiss, and as Tebogo closed her eyes and kissed him back, she could not remember the last time she felt happier.

Lerato slammed the door violently behind her, causing Seputla to look up from his books.

"Sorry, baby. You studying?" she asked.

"Yeah," he replied, but turned back to his books. "How was work?"

"Long," Lerato replied, taking out a bottle of still water from the fridge. "And brunch with the girls was terrible. Can you believe that they left me stranded at the restaurant with the bill to pay?"

"Dreadful," Seputla laughed sarcastically, but Lerato wasn't amused.

"I'm being serious," she lamented.

"Maybe if you stopped buying all those shoes you never even wear you could afford to buy yourself and your friends a nice meal," Seputla commented.

Lerato was stunned. "Excuse me?" she demanded.

"Just saying," Seputla mused, and buried his head back in his books.

"No, you're not just saying!" she yelled. "Where did that come from?" Seputla closed his books as she eyed him suspiciously. "Have you been going through my stuff?"

"Baby, we live together," he replied dryly.

"But my stuff is my stuff," she defended.

"When do I get to meet these friends of yours?" Seputla asked, dodging the issue.

Lerato was caught off guard. "What do you mean?"

"I'd love to meet them," he said. "Maybe we could invite them here for a nice dinner."

"After they left me stranded? Hell no!" Lerato snapped.

"Have you even told them about me?" Seputla asked, studying her.

"Of course! They're my best friends; we know everything about each other." Lerato replied defensively, silently grateful that she'd finally scrounged up the courage to mention Seputla to Maki and Tebogo earlier. Suddenly she turned to him with a glint in her eye. "I see what you're doing."

"What?" Seputla shrugged casually.

"Changing the subject. You really shouldn't be going through my stuff," Lerato smiled at Seputla's ingenuity.

"I was looking for a razor," he smiled.

His lazy smile caused Lerato's tummy to knot. He could knock her over with a feather when he smiled at her like that. She walked over to him and sat on his lap.

"Hello," he said, smiling again.

"Hey," she replied, huskily, wondering how she'd been lucky enough to fall for a guy like him.

Lerato kissed him and he pushed the books off the table as he lifted her onto it. As she lifted her leg and put it around him, he whispered, "And I still want to meet you friends."

Maki dashed into the DVD store, then she collected herself and stood in the aisle, closing her eyes to take in the smell. As she slowly exhaled, she opened her eyes and was startled to see a man in front of her, staring at her, unimpressed.

"What are you staring at?" she demanded, attempting to save face in the embarrassing situation.

"You're blocking my way," the man with the waist-long dreadlocks replied.

"Oh, sorry," Maki said, quickly jumping to the side.

The stranger walked past her, but she didn't want him to go yet. "I don't think that's such a good idea," she warned. When he stopped and turned to look at her again, she pointed to his hair. "Walking around like that... your hair could get chopped by off by druggies and sold for thousands."

"Good thing I don't hang around people or places where my hair could mysteriously get chopped off," he mused.

Maki couldn't help but smile at the man's confidence. She surprised herself by extending her hand to him. "Maki."

"Tumelo," he said, smiling in return and taking her hand in his. The young woman held onto his hand for a little longer than was necessary.

"Can I have my hand back?" he asked, "I can tell you're thinking of ways to mysteriously drug me, chop off my locks and sell them for thousands."

Maki blushed and quickly removed her hand from his grip. "You want to get out of here?" she asked.

"I knew it!" he laughed.

"For dinner or something," she quickly added, embarrassed. Maki didn't know what it was about this man, but she felt entranced by him. She was still shocked that she'd introduced herself before he did and now she was asking him out! She was also hungry. Maki silently said a quick prayer that he would agree to have dinner with her. Thankfully he did, and as they left the DVD store he told her that dinner was on him. She smiled widely: Score!

"So what are you doing hanging out in DVD stores?" Maki asked, slurping up her butternut soup. A minute later the waiter placed a rack of ribs and potato wedges next to her and she asked him to wrap them up as a take-away.

"I'm a filmmaker," Tumelo replied, leaning back in his seat to take her in. "And you?" he asked. "Were you just there to sniff the air?" he laughed.

Maki pursed her lips in mock annoyance. "I'll have you know that DVD stores and bookstores are about to become things of the past. I was trying to take in as much of it as I can now so that I could hold onto the memory," she quipped.

Studying her intently, he slowly asked, "Romance or thriller?" There was a mischievous glint in his eye.

"Pssh, that's easy – thriller, any day," Maki replied confidently. Then she jumped into the game. "Film or TV?"

"Ooh, tough one," Tumelo replied, squinting, deep in thought. "I'll have to go with film, but only by a margin."

"Good choice," Maki smiled. "Scorsese or Tarantino?"

"Not fair!" Tumelo protested, throwing his napkin on the table to playfully protest. Then he looked up at her and, with a smile, asked, "Gabrielle Union or Halle Berry?"

Maki was suddenly loving her life. Imbued with a rare bout of self-confidence, she smiled and, with a playful wink, said, "Both." Tumelo laughed raucously and clapped his hands together.

As he walked her out of the mall and towards the parking lot after dinner, he asked her if she was seeing anyone as he wanted to see her again and didn't want to offend her man. "Do you seriously think I'd be hanging out in DVD stores and accepting dinner invites from strangers if I had a man?" she laughed. Then, as she carefully punched her number into his phone, he reminded her that she had actually invited him for dinner.

As flirtatiously as she could manage, she licked her bottom lip and said, "Call me." Turning to walk away, she prayed that he was still watching at her and, with the most confidence she'd ever had, she casually threw her head back to check if he was still looking at her. Maki was shocked when she stared straight into his eyes. She smiled, turned away again and kept walking, elated that he was totally checking her out, and at the same time trying to keep her emotions in check so that she wouldn't trip and fall.

Chapter 3

· ·

The next morning Lerato woke up with her hair a tangled mess on the top of her head. She'd become accustomed to waking up to the smell of freshly brewed coffee. She adored this trait in Seputla, and marvelled at how she'd had the coffee machine for years and had never even used it. Until Seputla.

She'd had a lot of "until Seputla" moments lately. For the most part she was stunned at the woman she was becoming, but her new relationship was also excruciatingly unnerving. For one thing, she was in unfamiliar territory where she wasn't in charge, and she loved being in control. Hell, she revelled in it! It was all she'd ever known when it came to her love life. In relationships one always had to have a strategy, but since she'd met Seputla she felt like she was free falling and she wanted to find something to quickly grasp onto. That probably explained why her need to buy shoes had sky-rocketed in the last month or two.

She felt like she was losing control, and she had this mental image of herself hurtling to the ground, but she also felt as though her parachute was open and she had a strange and overwhelming sensation of freedom. She was struck by how fresh the air was in her new terrain, coupled with the incredibly scenic view. Then she'd curse and lambast herself, because for the first time in her life she was crashing and falling heedlessly in love.

When Seputla walked into the bedroom without a shirt on, Lerato subconsciously bit her lower lip. "Hey beautiful," he smiled, handing her a cup of piping hot coffee.

"Hey," she smiled, sitting up in the bed. It wasn't just that he made her coffee every morning, or that he made it bare-chested, it was also the way he made it. Although she'd begged him to tell her his secret, he wouldn't, insisting that she didn't need to know because he would always make it for her.

Lerato loved that about him – how he eased her worrying mind with comments like that, implying that he saw a future with her. Although Lerato had dated a lot of men, none of them could hold a candle to Seputla. But he was the only one who had the potential to irrevocably break her heart, and that petrified her.

As she sipped her coffee and lazily watched Seputla get dressed, her phone beeped, signalling that a message had come in. It was on the Divas WhatsApp group and was from Tebza. Lerato quickly read the contents to see if Tebogo had forgiven her, even though she hadn't actually asked for forgiveness. The beautiful young woman was used to being forgiven without having to ask for it because she was hardly ever held accountable for her actions. But she'd never seen Tebogo so angry before, and the way that she'd stormed out of the restaurant had shaken Lerato. It wasn't so much that Tebza was angry, she could deal with that, it was that she had disappointed her friend. Although Lerato acknowledged that she was a taker, the one thing that crushed her was disappointing her friends. She had always wanted her friends to think highly of her and was sure that they had put her on a pedestal. Even though they were the best of friends and had seen each other at their best and worst, Lerato had still not said sorry to Tebogo.

The message on the group chat was an invite to dinner with Tebza and Tshepo at their place later that evening to celebrate their engagement. Lerato was deep in thought as she put down her phone and Seputla asked her who the message was from. She told him about the invitation to dinner and Seputla smiled, happy at the thought of finally meeting her friends, but when he asked what time dinner started, Lerato lied and said eight o'clock, when the invite had clearly stated that they should arrive at seven.

Maki screamed out loud in delight as she read the message on the WhatsApp group. Two dinner invites two nights in a row! Score! She reminded herself to take a Tupperware dish for leftovers because Tebza had become militant about her Tupperware dishes and annoyingly accused Maki and Lerato of never retuning them.

Another message from Tebza followed soon after the first: they were welcome to bring dates, but Maki was exempt because they all knew that she didn't have one. Tebza was subtly hinting to Lerato that she'd better bring Seputla so that a) they could meet him, and obviously that meant interrogating him, and b) so that Tshepo, poor soul, would have male company for once. Tebogo had never understood how Tshepo had put up with her and her two best friends throughout varsity and was still going strong.

Maki smirked as she read the message. Feeling pleased with herself, she replied that she too would in fact be bringing a date, and ended her clapback with the "talk to the hand" emoji.

Lerato threw her phone on the bed and fell over laughing when she read Maki's message. Seputla reminded her to get into the shower so she wouldn't be late for work, but instead Lerato picked up her phone again and quickly typed a message, asking Maki who she thought her date would be. She threw out a few callous suggestions before tossing her phone back on the bed and rushing to the shower, ignoring the beeps of incoming messages from her friends.

Tebogo was stumped; she didn't understand how Lerato could continuously be so crass. Was it the pretty girl thing or what? She'd always thought that Lerato would outgrow that annoying attitude, but it seemed to be getting worse. She read with disgust Lerato's message asking Maki if her date was a hobo she'd pay for the night to act the role of her boyfriend, or one of her imaginary characters that she was always writing about.

Across town, Lerato's message didn't have the same effect on Maki. She gloated as she moonwalked across her living room floor because she had actually met a man and had actually punched her number into his phone so she would actually be bringing a date to the dinner party. She kicked her leg in the air and did a Michael Jackson "woo hoo", but then her elation was replaced by a sinking feeling. Suddenly Maki remembered that she hadn't taken Tumelo's number. And a dark and depressing feeling took over at the thought that – even if he did miraculously call her that day – she would still have nothing to wear.

Maki grabbed her car keys and rushed out the door; she had to find Tumelo! She was out of data, so she parked in the parking lot of the nearest shopping centre; it was just a two minute car ride there, but was too far to walk to. After logging on to the centre's free wi-fi Maki scoured Facebook for him. There were a gazillion Tumelos! Thank goodness hers had distinguishable dreadlocks.

After going to the profiles of at least five Tumelos and zooming in on their profile pictures, she was about to give up when suddenly she found him. It didn't help that in his profile picture there were at least five other guys with equally as lengthy dreadlocks, grinning and happily smiling for the camera. He was in the midst of the five guys, but she could tell that it was him thanks to her sharp eye and her phone's ability to zoom in.

Finally her investigative journalism skills had benefitted her personal life. Checking his friend list, Maki saw that they had one mutual friend; and that in total, Tumelo had more than 2 000 friends which said a lot about his popularity – that and his choice of profile picture.

She wondered if she should be wary of him being so popular. Maki had always been more into the shy types, but she'd jumped the man in a DVD store and had asked him to dinner that he had paid for, so she was willing to take her chances. With a coy smile, she messaged him, thanking him for dinner the previous night and asking if he was free to join her that evening for dinner at a friend's. She casually added that he had her number and she didn't have his, so she'd be waiting for his call.

Chuffed, and with a wide and exuberant smile, Maki wound the windows all the way down and cranked up the volume on Unathi Nkayi's *Make me high*. Her loud and happy singing startled the elderly white ladies who were slowly pushing shopping trolleys to their cars. Maki was in such a good mood she had to fight the urge to hoot and wave at the women while sticking her head out the window and yelling that she had met a man and had a date. After all, she didn't want to give the grannies heart attacks.

***

Tshepo had outdone himself. He had set up their small, cosy backyard with a huge spread of sushi and cheeses. Beers were chilling in the cooler box for the guys, there was cider for Maki, white wine in an ice bucket for Tebogo and red wine on the table for Lerato. He had also packed up laughing when Tebogo told him that Maki had said that she would also be bringing a date. When he began to make fun of Maki's date options like Lerato had, Tebogo was quick to defend Maki because she knew what it felt like to be the butt of Tshepo's jokes and Lerato's teasing.

When Tebogo walked in and saw the decor in the backyard, she gasped at the romantic atmosphere that the fairy lights adorning their garden created, and she marvelled at how enchanted the entire set up felt. But try as she might, Tebogo couldn't shake the hint of resentment that Tshepo had never before gone to such great lengths for her. She was a little angry that it was only after he proposed that he suddenly began to be proactive in their relationship. Telling herself to stop being silly, she stood on the patio, breathed in the fresh air and said a small prayer of gratitude, because at least her man had finally stepped up and taken action.

Maki was sure that she would burn a hole in her bedroom floor, but she could not stop pacing. She bit her bottom lip anxiously, on the verge of tears. She'd found a little black dress in the back of her cupboard that she hadn't worn in years and that miraculously still fit – probably because of the bouts of hunger that she had to subject herself to because of her poor career choice. Maki reminded herself that at the time she chose her career it seemed obvious that she would choose her passion, but look where that had gotten her. The silver lining was that she looked good, but unlike Khuli Chana she could not convincingly sing the song, "No more hunger".

She'd been in such a good mood all day that she'd even washed the dishes that had stacked up in the sink in the secret hopes that Tumelo would come to hers after the dinner for a night cap. Her stomach had fluttered in excite-ment-come-nervousness-come-anxiety at the thought. While tidying up she found a stick of vanilla incense and lit it as she sang along to Trompies Magasman, and her heart sank when her laptop died, cutting off the song. She tried to charge her laptop, but when nothing happened she remembered that she still hadn't bought electricity.

As Maki got dressed she convinced herself that Tumelo wouldn't be thrown if she lit candles instead of switching on the lights, seeing as he was a filmmaker and therefore one of those creative types that easily bought into situations. Thinking about him caused her stomach to turn; she'd tried to keep those thoughts at bay all day because he still hadn't called and she was nervous that he would stand her up. Of course she didn't know for sure if he'd even read her message, so she couldn't exactly call it being stood up. Maki cursed herself for telling her friends that she'd bring a date, but it had felt so good to shut Lerato-must-have-the-last-word-Meale up, that she'd got ahead of herself. But now look.

The young writer studied her reflection in the mirror and let out a low whistle, impressed by the way her dress gave her some semblance of curves and caused her shapeless figure to seem grown and sexy. She'd even gone to the lengths of applying foundation and eyeliner; she would have done mascara too, but the damn thing had dried out because it was so old. Come to think of it, Maki couldn't remember the last time she'd used mascara. Thankfully she'd found some eyeshadow at the back of her bathroom drawer and had settled for the smoky eye look. She'd laughed at herself in the mirror, impressed by her transformation. But that was an hour and a half ago and Tumelo had still not called. Maki was also freaking out because she didn't have data to check if he'd left her a WhatsApp message and was too scared to drive to the shopping centre for fear that her make-up would melt in the sweltering Joburg heat. Instead she paced, and cursed, and bit her lip, and cursed again.

At five past six, knowing that she couldn't delay any longer, she strapped on her leather boots and grabbed her black leather jacket, ready to leave. Before checking that the doors and windows were locked she remembered to take a Tupperware container from the kitchen. When she opened her cupboard she saw that she did indeed have at least ten of what used to be Tebza's Tupperware dishes which explained her recent militancy in that department. Ordinarily Maki would have laughed out loud at the situation, but her earlier exuberance at having found Tumelo on Facebook had been replaced by a gnawing feeling of regret. As she headed out the door after grabbing her laptop, laptop charger, handbag with cellphone and charger in it so she could charge them at Tebza's, she prayed that Lerato's Seputla would draw all the attention away from her dateless situation.

Lerato was in her underwear, busy showering herself in perfume after completing her make-up. She'd gone for a golden eyeshadow and matte lip look, complemented by an updo hairstyle that accentuated her cheekbones. She wondered if she was going over the top because she deliberately wanted to look extra good so that her friends would see what a perfect match she and Seputla were. She wasn't nervous about her friends meeting him, because he had such a calming effect on her. If anything, she'd always been afraid of her friends meeting her other married or much older – yet always ridiculously wealthy – suitors. Although they didn't say it, she knew that the other divas felt that she could do better. And she had, she had found Seputla. So what was there to be nervous about?

Lerato's breath caught in her throat as she saw Seputla walk into the bathroom in the reflection in the mirror. She turned around, gobsmacked. He'd gone to the barber to clean shave his hair and she was an absolute sucker for a bald head, but in addition to that, he was in a suit. A black suit with a crisp white shirt and bow tie. She'd never seen him in a suit before and she was utterly speechless.

"You like?" he asked, spinning around so that she could take him all in.

"I love!" she gasped. "But I think the bowtie might be overkill."

She rushed across to him, took off his bowtie and pressed down his shirt collar. "Perfect," she said pecking him on the lips in appreciation. "I've never seen you in a suit before," she smiled.

"I've never met your friends before," he replied with a laugh.

"You nervous?" she asked.

"Nope," he replied, "I just know how much they mean to you so I want to make a good impression." He kissed her long and hard, and when she came up for air he smacked her bum and told her to get dressed so that they wouldn't be late.

Chapter 4

Maki rang the intercom, and as Tebza's voice cackled over the speaker, her stomach plummeted because they would see that she'd arrived alone. As she stepped into the house, Tshepo made her feel even worse when he casually teased her about being the type of guest to never bring the hosts anything, not even a bottle of wine. Tebza quickly pursed her lips at Tshepo while assuring Maki that there was plenty to drink. Maki immediately disappeared to the bathroom to splash cold water on her face, but then cursed her made up face because she had to settle for dabbing it with cold water and a cloth instead. Maki thought of the most believable reason to give her friends for why Tumelo was not joining her, breathed in deeply and exhaled slowly with the doorknob in her hand, then turned it bravely and stepped out of the bathroom.

Tebogo was waiting for her in the corridor. "Is he coming?" she asked cautiously. Maki's disappointment came hurtling back.

"I don't know," she replied, unable to lie to Tebza. "I left him a message."

Tebza smiled a slow, reassuring smile. "No worries," she said. "You're stuck with us."

Maki could have cried. She hugged Tebza tight and followed her out to the garden.

"Whoa," Maki said when she saw the effort that Tshepo had gone to. "Who knew that under all those rolls of fat was a secret charmer boy?" she teased. But Tebogo didn't cringe;

she was used to the way Maki and Tshepo always had to have a go at each other.

"The secret of keeping my woman happy, Dimakatso," Tshepo said happily. "And speaking of people in happy relationships," he added, squinting deviously before delivering his punchline, "where is your plus one?"

"On his way," Tebza quickly replied before Maki could answer. Following Tebza's lead, Maki added, "He's stuck in traffic."

Tshepo was unconvinced but carried on braaing the meat and slurping his beer as Tebogo led Maki to the sushi.

"He really does exist," Maki said in a small voice as she doused her California roll in soy sauce."

"Tell me, tell me!" Tebza eagerly demanded, her eyes lighting up in excitement.

"His name is Tumelo. He's a filmmaker and we met in a DVD store."

"Ooh," Tebza replied. "Sounds fascinating."

Maki wasn't sure if Tebogo was having her on, but then she remembered that Tebza often commended her for having the guts to follow her passion, so she guessed that she was being for real.

"Anyway, we went out for dinner and I put my number in his phone but he didn't put his in mine," Maki added regretfully.

"You mean he didn't call you afterwards to make sure you got home okay?" Tebogo asked, shocked.

"No," Maki panicked. "Should he have?"

"Hmm," Tebza said, pursing her lips, cautious not to hurt Maki's feelings. "I would have wanted him to."

"Damn it," Maki cursed under her breath.

Slowly, Tebza continued. "Does he even know about tonight?"

Maki shrugged. "I found him on Facebook and left him a message. Speaking of which, is it cool if I charge my phone and laptop?"

"Of course," Tebza replied. "But why'd you bring your laptop?"

"Girl, you know how Tshepo's music sucks; I had to bring mine to make sure that we proper turn up to your engagement!" Maki squealed so convincingly she almost believed her own lie.

Tebza had all but forgotten that her engagement to Tshepo was the cause for the occasion, and as Maki turned to go towards the house, she caught a quick glimpse of the ring that imposed itself on her ring finger. Once again she felt the all too familiar sensation of her stomach plummeting.

Lerato couldn't stop tapping her foot. "You nervous?" Seputla asked, giving her a quick glance before fixing his eyes back on the road again.

"No," she replied, but her shaky voice gave her away.

He put his hand on her knee reassuringly. "It'll be fine," he smiled. "There must be a reason you've all been friends for so long."

"Yes, but the last time I saw Tebza she was so angry at me," Lerato swallowed nervously.

"You mean you haven't apologised?" Seputla asked disapprovingly.

Lerato quickly shook her head. "The last time we spoke was when she sent us invites for tonight and I assumed she was fine."

Seputla sighed. He loved Lerato but sometimes her immaturity got to him.

"Well, then I guess this would be the perfect time to bring it up," he said softly under his breath.

Lerato recoiled in her seat. She hated how he'd become comfortable with telling her what to do and how to behave. She hadn't said anything to him but it was really starting to get to her.

"Don't sulk," he added.

He did it again, she silently fumed. But instead of replying to him, she cranked up the volume on the radio and forced herself to focus on the evening ahead.

"Anything I can help with?" Maki asked as she stepped into the kitchen. Tebogo was putting the final touches on the salad.

"Nah, I'm all good," she smiled. But before she'd even finished answering, Maki was focused back on her cellphone which she had connected to the wi-fi in the house.

"I asked Tshepo hours ago if he needed help with anything," Tebogo complained. "He said no, and now he wants me to make the salad and put the garlic bread in the oven!" she lamented. When she was met with silence from Maki's end she turned to see her friend seated on a barstool, the colour drained from her face.

"What is it?" Tebogo asked, panicked.

"He's not coming," Maki replied in a small voice.

"Honey ..." Tebza said sympathetically. Then, after a moment's thought, she asked, "He does exist, right?"

Maki clicked her tongue at Tebza, and her friend quickly added, "It's probably for the best anyway; you should probably get to know him for you before introducing him to all of us."

Maki smiled; Tebogo always knew what to say to make her feel better.

To defuse the situation completely Maki joked, "At least I won't have to feel embarrassed when I pull out my Tupperware for leftovers at the end of the night!"

Tebza laughed. She loved how Maki could add humour to any situation; it was a trait she desperately wished she had.

Just then the intercom rang, sending reverberations throughout the house.

"Is that Lerato?" Maki asked, looking up from her phone. For the first time in ages, she was taking selfies and uploading them onto Instagram, with the caption: feeling myself.

She secretly hoped that Tumelo would see the pics and regret not showing up when he'd see how fine she looked, but she also needed to make the most of the free wi-fi; Instagram did not play nice when it came to data.

Tebza removed the garlic bread from the oven and was about to head to the door, when Tshepo yelled, "I'll get it!"

"Do you think she's nervous about us meeting her new beau?" Maki asked, squishing her nose in curiosity.

"What would she have to be nervous about?" Tebogo asked, unable to hide the annoyance in her voice. She was still peeved at Lerato because of what had happened at brunch the other day.

"You two talk yet?" Maki asked. She was sensitive about Tebza's feelings getting hurt because Tebza wasn't as tough as Maki and Lerato.

"Lerato? Talk?" Tebogo chuckled. "Yeah, right."

Maki and Tebogo heard Tshepo's voice getting closer to the kitchen, and they both looked up to see Tshepo walk in, holding a bottle of wine.

"You see, Maki," he said, deliberately sticking the bottle of wine in her face. "This is what real guests do." Maki just rolled her eyes.

Behind Tshepo, Lerato, looking beautiful as always, walked in, followed by a man who looked – much to Maki and Tebogo's shock – nothing like the men she normally dated.

"Hi, guys," Lerato smiled nervously at Maki and Tebza.

But Tebza's attention was entirely on the mystery man. She was stunned into silence, and Maki's mouth was unapologetically agape, as she stared at him.

"Seputla," Seputla smiled, extending his hand to Maki.

Maki took his hand but didn't say anything. All she did was look him up and down, a smile on her lips and an unmissable look of disbelief in her eyes.

Seputla rescued his hand from Maki's grip and shook Tebogo's hand.

"Hello," Seputla smiled, as he shook her hand.

"Hell!" Tebogo said, taking in Seputla's dashing smile and how good he looked in a suit.

Seputla blushed somewhat and exchanged a questioning look with Lerato, but Tebogo pointedly turned to Maki who laughed raucously, clapping her hands together.

"Beer?" Tshepo asked, turning to Seputla, annoyed that Tebogo was unable to hide how impressed she was with the stranger who had just arrived.

"Please," Seputla said, itching to get out of the kitchen, and suddenly feeling a tad overdressed as he took in Tshepo's shorts and T-shirt.

Lerato cleared her throat after Seputla and Tshepo left. She'd been hoping to have a moment alone with Tebza to apologise for the other day.

"Thanks for inviting us," she said in a small voice.

Maki slapped Lerato on the bum, causing Lerato to squeal in shock.

"Moghel!" Maki shouted. "Out with it!"

"Where did you find him?" Tebogo asked, curious.

Happy that her friends seemed to approve of Seputla, Lerato replied in a small, shy voice: "At the gym."

"And you took his number?" Maki asked, curious.

"Does he own the gym?" Tebogo asked, confused.

"No."

Maki gasped. "He's a trainer? So, he's not bucks-ed up?"

Lerato sighed, exasperated. Turning to Tebogo and ignoring Maki, she asked, "Can we talk?"

Maki was soon distractedly chuckling under her breath and checking to see how many likes she'd accumulated from her selfies. Suddenly realising that the air in the room had become slightly tense, she looked up to see Tebogo and Lerato's eyes on her.

"What?" she asked, taking a swig of her cider. "Oh," she said in realisation, standing up to go. "Let me go socialise with our men," she laughed as she left.

Ordinarily Lerato would have raced after Maki because she never liked it when she practiced her investigative journalism skills on her dates, but this time she had more important things to attend to.

"I'm sorry," she said to Tebza as soon as Maki was out of earshot.

"What about?" Tebogo asked. It was clear that she was hurt, but was trying hard to cover.

"About being obnoxious and rude at brunch," Lerato said.

Tebogo couldn't help but smile. "Lerato Meale admitting to being obnoxious and apologising?" she squealed in disbelief. "This Seputla must be good for you!"

Lerato blushed at the mention of Seputla's name. "He is kind of amazing," she smiled.

"And fine, girl!" Tebza laughed.

"So all is forgiven?" Lerato asked.

"Sure, if you help me take this salad and bread outside," Tebogo smiled.

"Sure," Lerato replied, quick to help and eager to get back to Seputla before Maki unleashed her investigative skills on him.

Tebogo added, "You'll have to settle for the bread, salad and meat though, Maki has finished all the sushi."

Lerato laughed, happy to be in her friend's good graces again.

When Tebogo and Lerato stepped outside Maki was seated on the patio playing Mondli Ngobo and Black Coffee from her laptop. Lerato was happy that Maki had left Seputla to chat to Tshepo and was even more relieved when she glanced over at Seputla and he gave her a small, secret wink to indicate that he was having a good time.

Lerato placed the garlic bread on the table and approached Maki. "Your dude not here?" she asked, careful not to upset Maki too. She hated apologising and it seemed like a prerequisite from her lately.

Maki pursed her lips. "You mean my hobo?"

What Lerato said next shocked Maki and was very unlike her: "I'm sorry about that."

Maki looked up from her laptop. "Say what now? You mean you don't have a witty retort to the hobo joke?"

"Nope," Lerato smiled.

"Woah," Maki laughed. "What did Seputla do to you, my friend?"

"I know I can be an obnoxious brat and I'm sorry," Lerato continued.

"Mm-kay," Maki mused; she wasn't sure if she bought into this whole "new and improved" version of Lerato. Didn't she only meet this guy three months ago?

Reading her mind, Lerato said, "I had to change at some point. I couldn't be the 30-year-old slay queen scared of being replaced by a younger and prettier version of myself."

Maki couldn't help but chuckle. Lerato had always rounded up her age to the nearest ten.

"So you mean to tell me that you're hanging up your tiara, my queen?" Maki joked. Looking into Lerato's eyes, Maki was surprised to see that her friend was tired.

"The pretence of it all is annoying. Fooling yourself into believing it's what you want, but deep down knowing that you want to be someone's number one is exhausting. Seputla and I have meaningful discussions; he is actually into me, you know?" Lerato mused. "This is a first for me."

"And you're good?" Maki asked.

"I'm scared," she replied quickly, "but a good scared. I've never been this person before."

"Well, that's good," Maki smiled. "But don't let him change everything about you. Who would you be if you weren't even the slightest bit obnoxious?"

"I guess we'll have to wait and find out," Lerato replied with a nervous smile.

As Mondli Ngobo's voice reached a crescendo, blasting through the speaker, Tshepo loudly tapped a spoon on a glass to get everyone's attention. Lerato sashayed over to Seputla who happily welcomed her by casually draping his arm over her shoulder. She, in turn, put her arm around his waist and squeezed him close. Their affection was effortless and put Maki at ease.

For the first time that evening Maki had a good look around the gathering and took everyone in. Even though Tebza had put on some weight, she looked good in a figure-hugging, red knee-length satin dress. Although they were in her home, she'd even gone to the effort of wearing kitten heels. If this whole do was in her house, Maki would be in flip flops. Trust!

Next, Maki turned to Seputla and Lerato. He had taken off his jacket, thank goodness, but she had to admit, the brother did look good. And she loved the way he looked so comfortable around Lerato, and she seemed at ease around him. For a fleeting moment Maki saw that the two of them could be together forever, and was immediately uncomfortable. Weren't they here to celebrate Tebogo?

She turned to Tebza and saw her slip a piece of bread into her mouth. There was something about Tebza that seemed incredibly shy to Maki, but in a weird way, as if she didn't want to be at her own engagement dinner party. Maki studied Tebza more intently. It was as if – as she sat there at the edge of the table, secretly stuffing small pieces of bread into her mouth – that Tebza wanted to disappear.

Maki's stomach dropped as she remembered their conversation at brunch before Tebza stormed off. She had said that she was unhappy. Then Lerato had stolen Tebza's moment and that had been the end of that. She could kick herself! She did have to check in with Tebza, and not just for bread and airtime money, but because she actually was her friend. Maki bit her bottom lip, angry at herself for letting her own life preoccupy her so much that she hadn't even bothered to check in on Tebogo. As she watched her worriedly, she promised herself that she would talk to her properly later that evening.

Maki's eyes wandered back to Lerato. The girl could wear a black refuse bag and she would still look good, so when she did her hair and make-up the way that she had tonight, she was drop dead gorgeous. No wonder Seputla had a protective arm around her. Lerato was wearing a champagne gold cocktail dress with spaghetti straps and gold heels. Maki chuckled at how good she was at describing Lerato's clothes even though she'd never be caught dead wearing anything like what Lerato had on.

Tshepo was in the middle of his speech. Maki sighed, bored, then realised that she'd have to stand up to go get another cider. Tshepo was droning on about the kind of woman that Tebogo was and how she meant the world to him.

"That's right!" Maki yelled, and threw her hands up in the air.

Seputla was taken aback by this but Lerato was amused. She knew Maki well enough to expect that kind of behaviour from her. Maki turned again to Tebza; the young lawyer felt her friend's eyes on her and hurriedly took a sip of wine to try to conceal her feelings, but it was too late. A sinking feeling in the pit of her stomach confirmed that Maki had seen her. She shifted nervously. Maki, not wanting to embarrass her any further, averted her gaze, focusing back on Tshepo.

He was like the cat that had stolen the cream. He gloated about the first day he'd met Tebza and how he'd known from that day that she was his soulmate. Seputla smiled at Lerato and kissed her lightly on the forehead. Creasing her brow, now intensely aware of Tebza's unhappiness, Maki studied Tshepo. He did seem a bit showy in praising Tebogo for her characteristics; maybe the poor girl was just tired of living up to everyone's expectations.

Then it clicked; that was it. Maki looked around. If it wasn't for Tebza, Tshepo would be half the man he was. And for the most part, Tebza took care of Maki and Lerato in their little circle. No wonder she'd snapped at Lerato the other day – she needed girl time and Lerato had taken that away from her. She made another mental note to check in with Tebza later. After Seputla and Lerato had left – no doubt they'd want to leave early, couples often did –and once Tshepo had gone to bed, she'd have a sit down with Tebogo.

Tshepo raised his glass to make a toast. Lerato cooed, casting a glance at Tebza who had suddenly perked up and was smiling warmly.

"Tebogo Precious Seamela, you have made me the happiest man in the world by agreeing to be my wife. I intend to live the rest of my life showing you how grateful I am to be your husband. I love you. Cheers."

"Cheers," Lerato and Seputla toasted exuberantly, clicking their glasses with Tebza and Tshepo's. Maki hurriedly went to get another cider from the cooler box and clinked her glass with the others, all the while giving Tebza secret glances in an attempt to comfort her through eye contact.

Tebogo wanted the earth to open up and swallow her – Maki was onto her! She panicked. But then again maybe that was what she needed – a bit of honesty. It was about time. She swallowed nervously as tears pricked her eyes, threatening to spill over onto her face, and she heaped food onto her plate to appear calm and busy.

She was angry that she had opened up to her friends at brunch about her unhappiness and that neither of them had called to check in on her since. She was particularly angry with Maki and she was very aware of her right now busy trying to send her signals through eye contact. Why didn't Maki understand that now was not the time! Tshepo was sitting right there for goodness' sake!

Tebogo had been completely stunned by Lerato's apology, but was very welcoming of it. Lerato was finally growing up. Maybe now she would stop calling Tebogo in the middle of the night to fetch her from strange places because she'd had a fight with a married man who'd left her stranded in the middle of nowhere with no money for an Uber. Lerato had lived quite the dramatic life, maybe now was the time to settle down.

More than anything Tebogo was disappointed in Maki. Other than the fact that she'd been distracted by her mystery guy who clearly wasn't that into her because he hadn't bothered to show up tonight, she had no excuse for not checking up on Tebogo. A simple, "Hey, Tebza, you good?" would have sufficed. But, as usual, it seemed Tebza was good for only two things to her friends – buying them lunch and listening to their problems. She had literally sent an SOS to her best friends and told them that she was unhappy, and neither of them had come to her rescue. So, as usual, she would not say anything and would eat to numb the pain.

Tshepo noticed with resentment that Lerato dished up for Seputla, but that his wife-to-be, whom he had just spent an entire ten minutes praising, was already stuffing her face. Ordinarily he would have said something in jest to make his point, but he didn't want to contradict the speech he had just made. Luckily Maki cranked up the volume on her playlist and the harmonious melodies of Kabomo infused the air.

He took note of the ease with which Lerato, Maki and Tebza chatted with Seputla. He wasn't sure how he felt about the guy; he seemed like the smooth type. Tshepo had never met any of Lerato's boyfriends before and he was trying to figure out why they had to meet this one. He studied Lerato; she seemed softer, less angry. This guy must have some magic quality to make everyone around him feel comfortable, but Tshepo wasn't easily fooled. *All these pretty boy types are the same,* he thought, annoyed. All they had to do was flash their smiles and everyone let their guard down. *Well, not me,* Tshepo thought grimly. He had known Lerato way too long to easily buy into this guy. Tshepo would be watching him; he owed it to Lerato.

Tebogo nervously tapped her glass with a teaspoon and everyone fell silent. "I guess I have to say something too," she smiled.

About time, Tshepo thought, rolling his eyes. When he noticed that Maki's eyes were boring into him he quickly plastered a smile on his face and cleared his throat.

"To Tshepo," Tebogo started slowly.

Thank you for boring me for the past ten years, Maki thought, then she tuned back into Tebza's speech …

"Loving you is easy; thank you for being you." Tebza concluded. Short and sweet.

"Woo hoo!" Lerato cheered.

"Here, here," Seputla chipped in.

That's it? Tshepo thought angrily. *I spent ten minutes talking about her!* But instead of commenting he grinned and stood up to kiss Tebogo who smiled, but secretly squirmed.

"What's going on with you two?" Maki asked Tebza after she'd finally cornered her in the kitchen.

"We're out of snacks; I'm just topping up so we have something to eat while we drink," Tebogo said airily.

"This is not about your damn snacks!" Maki replied aggressively. She wanted to shake Tebogo; she hated how her friend never spoke about her emotions. "I mean you! What's going on with you?"

"I'm fine," Tebza replied dismissively.

"Tebogo, I'm talking to you," Maki wailed. She hated when Tebza put up a brick wall. "And I have guests," Tebogo retorted.

Maki eyed the peanuts, raisins and chips that Tebogo was busy distributing into snack bowls and noticed with a sinking feeling that people her age had snack bowls. "You're not still mad about Lerato asking you for recipes are you?" Maki questioned.

"Gee, thanks for bringing that up again," Tebogo replied sarcastically.

"So you are still mad?" Maki protested.

"At least she apologised. What's your excuse?" Tebza asked abrasively.

"Me?" Maki asked defensively. "What did I do?"

"Nothing," Tebza replied as she sauntered past Maki and out of the kitchen. "That's the problem. You did nothing."

Tebogo rejoined Seputla, Lerato and Tshepo on the patio. She sat on Tshepo's lap, laughing and filling in the gaps of Tshepo's story that had both Lerato and Seputla in stitches. Seputla and Lerato held hands and he had covered her shoulders with his jacket.

When Maki stepped out onto the patio and took in the scene, for once she actually felt like the third wheel or, in this case, the fifth wheel.

Maki was mad. She didn't even know what Tebogo saw in Tshepo. He was fat and his jokes were corny as hell! Plus he was rude – sometimes even directly to Tebza's face. That was why Maki laid into him every chance she got. She was secretly hoping that one day Tebogo would see it too. Maki feared that Tebza actually saw it and was afraid of leaving Tshepo, which was what baffled her. To make matters worse, if she said anything to Tebza she'd be made out to be jealous because she'd been single for so long. To keep the peace she had to go along with Tebogo's unhappiness. But she knew herself well enough to know that she couldn't keep quiet. She would just have to find a way around the situation and be there for Tebza like a good friend should.

Chapter 5

Maki cursed under her breath, annoyed. She was shopping for food – one of her least favourite things to do. The local community newspaper that she wrote for had actually paid her without her having to chase them up this time, and even though she would probably be short on rent, she had PMS so she overindulged and bought lemon cheesecake. As she took it off the shelf she made a mental note to remember to buy electricity and airtime.

Standing in the heat outside the grocery store she punched in the code for the airtime and immediately called Tebza, who, no surprise, didn't answer her call.

"Hey, Tebza, just wanted to thank you and Tshepo for hosting us last night," she said. Then she paused, and after a moment added: "Oh, let's cut the crap. Tebogo, I'm worried about you. I know you're unhappy. Hell, you even said so at our brunch! I'm sorry I didn't check on you. Let me know when to call you so we can talk. I love you."

Maki hung up. She really felt for Tebogo. She never ever said the words "I love you" to just anybody. Then she remembered Tebza stuffing her face with bread during Tshepo's speech, and Tshepo's eye-rolling action during Tebogo's speech, and her stomach knotted again.

As she pushed her trolley to her car she wondered how long Tebogo and Tshepo thought they could pretend for. Her phone rang and she answered quickly without checking the caller ID. "Thanks for calling me back so soon. I'm so, so, so, so, sorry about last night," Maki gushed.

"And I thought I would be the one who'd have to apologise," a man's voice said over the phone.

Maki checked her phone screen; it was a number she didn't recognise. "Who's this?" she asked, pressing her phone to her ear again.

"Tumelo," the man replied.

Maki closed her eyes, dropped her head to collect herself and smiled from ear to ear. "Fancy hearing from you again," she smiled.

"Yeah, I'm sorry about last night," Tumelo said. "Had a hectic client deadline I couldn't get out of."

"I guess it was short notice," Maki mused.

"Anything I missed?" he asked.

"Yes, an entire dinner party," Maki laughed.

"Well, let me make it up to you. A friend of mine has been nominated for a SAFTA and is throwing a dinner party to-night to celebrate. I'd love to take you," Tumelo said. Maki felt her insides melt and she squealed, delighted. "It's a date."

"Good, I'll send you the address," Tumelo said.

"Can't wait," Maki said, ending the call. She could not re-member ever feeling happier.

Maki banged loudly on the door and Tshepo opened it, unim-pressed. "Did you forget your leftovers?" he droned, walking back into the house. Maki decided to let that one go. She was in too good a mood to let Tshepo's unhappiness affect her, and she didn't have time for a grown man's mood swings.

"I'm looking for your soon-to-be-wife. Is she here?" Maki said, stepping into the house.

"No," Tshepo said, flopping onto the couch and cranking up the volume on the TV. "Maybe if you didn't show up here unannounced, you'd actually know that."

Maki wanted to retort, but instead looked around the place. In the light of day it looked nothing like the fairy-lit en-chanted magical garden from the previous night. She paged through a magazine and was grateful when she heard Tebza's car drive in. A moment later, Tebza stepped into the house. She eyed Maki questioningly, then walked over to Tshepo to kiss him.

"Hey, babe," she said, as she kissed him on the lips.

"Hey," Tshepo replied nonchalantly.

"Hey," Maki said eagerly to Tebza.

"Hey," Tebza replied slowly.

Maki cast a look at Tshepo then back at Tebza, signalling with her eyes that she wanted to speak to Tebogo in private. Tebza got the hint and led Maki to the bedroom.

As soon as Maki closed the door, she wailed, "I'm sorry, okay! I can't take this silence and I can't even speak to Lerato about it. I just need to know that you're okay!"

Tebza smiled. "I actually am, hey."

"So why didn't you call me back?" Maki protested.

"Just wanted to see you squirm," Tebogo replied with a smile.

"Dude!" Maki laughed.

"You love me, huh?" Tebza chuckled.

"More than you'll ever know," Maki said, throwing her arms around Tebza. "But dude, you seriously need to talk. What's eating you?"

"Is that a fat joke?" Tebogo asked, defensive.

"What?" Maki replied, confused. "No!"

"I'm sorry, it's just – Tshepo's been making a lot of fat jokes lately."

Maki fumed. "What? Has he seen the size of his fat rolls? He looks like a whale on top of that couch!" Maki headed towards the door to confront Tshepo, "I'm going to give him a piece of my mind!" Tebza quickly stopped her.

"Don't! You'll make things worse!" she yelled.

"Are you serious?" Maki yelled back, turning to Tebza. But when Tebogo didn't meet Maki's eye, Maki softened and, studying Tebza, she gently asked, "Is he abusing you?"

"No!" Tebogo protested. "You see, this is exactly why I never tell you anything. You're either always ready to fight someone or you think the worst of them."

"So what is really going on?" Maki asked, sitting on the edge of the bed.

"We're just two people in love," Tebza started.

"Who spend all their free time together," Maki surmised.

"Precisely," Tebogo added, morosely. "And it's been that way since we were 20 years old."

"So you're bored?" Maki concluded, smiling. She was secretly relieved that it wasn't as bad as she'd made it out to be.

"I guess," Tebogo replied.

Maki cast her a sidelong glance.

"Put on your dancing shoes, baby. If adventure is what you want, then adventure is what you'll get."

Tebogo frowned in confusion, but Maki lapped up the moment.

"Get ready, baby, we are going out!"

Lerato was jealous when Tebogo called her from Maki's car, excitedly yelling that she and Maki were going out. Lerato could not believe it and checked her phone to see that she indeed was speaking to Tebza, her best friend since high school.

"But you never go out!" Lerato yelled back.

"I know!" Tebza continued to shriek excitedly.

"What did Tshepo say?" Lerato asked, suspicious that he might not even be aware of their plans.

"Who cares?" Tebogo blurted, "I haven't been out in ages!"

"Where are you going?" Lerato asked, unable to keep the envy out of her voice.

"Maki's boo is friends with someone who's having a dinner party, so that's where we're headed," Tebogo explained.

"What? He exists?" Lerato yelled in disbelief.

"This is payback for the hobo jokes!" Maki yelled back happily.

"But I apologised!" Lerato defended.

"Sorry, babe, but you're booed up," Tebza added.

"And you're not?" Lerato protested, desperate to understand what the hell had gotten into Tebogo.

"I got ten years in the game, babe," Tebza replied, all the confidence in the world bubbling out of her. "Ten years is nothing on three months," she laughed. "Enjoy your honeymoon phase. We're out."

Tebza hung up.

"We're out?" Lerato stared at her phone. When the hell did Tebogo start speaking like Nasty C? She wasn't sure if this was Maki's influence or if she was just jealous because she'd been left out of their plans. Maki's words rang in her ears: "This is payback for the hobo jokes!" But she'd apologised, hadn't she? What did all these people want from her? If it wasn't Seputla in the gym working late and then coming home to study while she cooked supper for him, it was her friends making her feel guilty. She had turned into a domestic goddess and apologist of note lately, and for what? This adulting business was sucking all the life out of her!

Lerato's phone beeped, signalling a text. She thought it would be Maki driving the knife deeper into her back but her eyes bulged out of her sockets when she saw that it was from Manur. She quickly read the contents of the message, as all the memories came flooding back.

Manur was a sheik she had met in Dubai when she was there with her ex, Aubrey. Manur had been into her, but had respected Aubrey enough not to invade his territory. But since then he'd found her on Facebook, they'd swopped numbers and had stayed in touch. And now Manur was in town on business and wanted female companionship. Hers in particular.

Lerato pondered this, conflicted. She was home alone again, and the scene of cooking for Seputla was getting old. She deserved to be wined and dined, damn it. She re-read Seputla's earlier WhatsApp message. He would be working late again. Lerato decided to send him a WhatsApp message telling him that she was going out with Tebogo and Maki, and that she would be home late too, then she dashed off to shower before he arrived back home.

Walking into Tumelo's friend's place, Maki and Tebza felt like they were transported to another city. The place was overflowing with creative types – free spirits who chatted, carefree and happy, while the house was imbued with the sounds of Moonchild Sanelly. Maki smiled; this was definitely her scene. She glanced at Tebza who seemed in awe of her surroundings. *Poor girl,* Maki thought, *she's been held back by Tshepo all these years.*

They turned a corner and bumped into Tumelo whose face lit up as soon as he saw Maki.

"Hey!" he greeted warmly, throwing his arms up to welcome her and holding her in a tight embrace. Tebogo was impressed! Maki couldn't remember the last time anyone had greeted her with such warmth; it sent tingles all the way up and down her spine. She let go of Tumelo and turned to Tebza.

"This is my friend, Tebogo," she said. Tumelo and Tebza shook hands.

"Call me Tebza," Tebogo said, smiling.

"Welcome," Tumelo said. "Drinks?"

"Yes!" Maki shrieked, and as they followed Tumelo to the drinks table, Tebza made eyes with Maki, signalling that she was impressed. Maki smiled, content. As Tumelo handed Maki and Tebza each a glass of dry white wine, Tebza caught sight of a famous local actor out of the corner of her eye.

"Is that..." she began, then to her shock, the actor approached them and greeted Tumelo warmly. Tebza shot Maki a glance, silently saying with her eyes: "Is that who I think it is?"

Tumelo relieved her of her misery when he turned back to Maki and Tebza. "This is my friend," he said, and the actor shook Maki and Tebza's hands, lingering over Tebza's.

"Pleasure to meet you," he cooed.

"Likewise," Tebogo smiled.

"Congrats on your SAFTA nomination," Maki added politely.

"Thanks," the actor beamed. "Let me take you around and introduce you to a few people." The actor, Maki, Tumelo and Tebogo walked outside and Tebza saw a lot more faces that looked familiar from TV.

"These are my friends," the actor said, "Ofentse and Oatile." Tebogo and Maki shook the actor's friends hands. "Good to meet you," Tebogo replied.

Maki smiled and took it all in. She wasn't sure but she thought she also saw one or two famous producers. *How do I ask them for a job without Tumelo thinking I'm using him?* she wondered.

"Penny for your thoughts," he whispered in her ear.

"Interesting life you live," she smiled, then noticed that the actor had continued walking with Tebza and was introducing her to all his other friends. She smiled; she'd never seen Tebza happier.

"Not quite," Tumelo laughed. "It's mostly late nights rushing to meet a deadline on some or other project."

"And you don't think that's exciting?" she asked.

He studied her, and she felt weak under his gaze. "We never really got into what you do," he said.

She felt a bout of inadequacy and said in a small voice, "I write for the *Killarney Express*."

"Oh, a journo?" Tumelo asked.

"Not a very happy one," Maki quickly added. "I've been trying to finish my crime novel for months and..."

"Writer's block?"

"The worst!" wailed Maki. "Plus community newspapers don't pay that well."

"So you won't be doing an exposé on the antics my friends and I get up to?" Tumelo smiled, but Maki could tell he'd become more cautious.

"Not unless I joined you in said antics," Maki joked in a bid to ease his concerns. It worked. Tumelo laughed out loud, throwing his head back. Maki liked to make people laugh, but she really loved seeing Tumelo laugh.

"What about TV?" Tumelo asked.

"What about TV?" Maki repeated, her stomach fluttering in nervous excitement.

"Wouldn't you like to cut your teeth writing for TV?" he probed. "I'm sure you recognised my friend from the number one soapie in the country. His boss is here. Should I introduce you?"

Maki could have kissed him. Her eyes lit up, elated, but she'd been in Joburg long enough to know that she had to play it cool. "Sure," she replied nonchalantly, although her heart was thumping loudly against her chest at a thousand beats per second.

"Follow me," Tumelo smiled, and he led her to a group of older looking women in a secluded part of the garden who were wrapped up in their own conversation and laughing loudly.

"Ladies," Tumelo said, as he and Maki approached them and they all turned to him. "I trust you're all having a fabulous time?" he asked.

"Of course," the heavily-made up ladies replied. "Monica was just telling us about her lovely protégé, Sipho."

"I would like to introduce you to one of Mzansi's finest young writers," Tumelo said. Maki blushed. Was he referring to her? The group of ladies focused their attention on her.

"Maki," she said, extending her hand to theirs. They shook hands with her while peering at her curiously, and they went round the circle introducing themselves: Monica, Sarah, Jess and Michal.

"My friend is keen to take a crack at writing for TV," Tumelo said to the group of ladies.

"Ooh, is that right?" the one named Jess asked.

"And what experience do you have?" Michal queried.

"Um, I currently write for the *Killarney Express*," Maki replied. Her nerves surprised her; she'd never thought of herself as the nervous type before.

"Oh," the ladies droned, rather bored. Maki bit her bottom lip nervously; this wasn't going very well. Then Tumelo piped up and said that she was also writing a murder mystery novel.

"Ooh," the ladies all chanted again, their faces picking up.

"Listen here, dearie," Michal said, fishing out a business card from her purse. "What did you say your name was again?"

Tumelo smiled, chuffed that his introductions had reaped benefits.

"Maki," the young woman quickly stammered. *How could she have forgotten my name already? It's only four letters and two syllables!*

"That'll be easy to remember," Monica chuckled. "Like the sushi?" The ladies all laughed. Maki had to restrain herself from rolling her eyes, and shared a quick, uneasy glance with Tumelo.

"My full name is actually Dimakatso," she said.

The laughter came to a screeching halt. "We prefer shortened African names," Sarah cooed. "Your names are all such tongue-twisters."

Maki's jaw dropped. Had she heard correctly? She turned to Tumelo but he was smiling politely. She figured it wouldn't take anything away from her to smile too. So she did, despite how much she despised the joke on her name and Sarah's comment about African names.

"Like Muthokozisi," Monica chimed in, complaining.

But you just said it! Maki thought in stark rebellion.

"Or Camagwini," Jess chipped in. "Just makes me think of linguini, then I get all hungry." The ladies laughed as though Jess had said the most hilarious thing.

"I want to divorce my husband for not buying me a Lamborghini," Sarah piped up, and the ladies were in hysterics again.

This is unreal! Maki thought. *People like this exist?*

"Here's a card," Michal continued, finally handing Maki a business card. "Call Mpho on that landline number and ask her to send you a test script, okay?"

Maki struggled to contain her excitement. "Yes! Of course," she squealed. She carefully placed the card in the back pocket of her jeans. "Thank you," she said, but the ladies had already turned back to each other, ignoring her. She felt snubbed, but Tumelo gently began to pull her away.

"Mission accomplished," he whispered in her ear.

"But they're ignoring me," Maki protested. "And what the hell was that about linguini?"

Tumelo laughed. "Does it matter?" he smiled. "You got what you wanted, didn't you?"

"Aaahhh! Thank you, thank you, thank you!" Maki threw herself into his arms.

"I'm keen on a number of ways of being thanked," he said in her ear.

Maki pulled away rather abruptly, suddenly uncomfortable. "What do you mean?" she stammered. Her decade long stint at celibacy suddenly tormented her. She was weird with sex. She was good with situations where she took the lead, which probably said a lot considering her lack of action in the last ten years, but when she had to be vulnerable and follow a man's lead? That wouldn't work. And frankly she wasn't too keen on that either. So her defences shot up.

But then Tumelo smiled a long, wide, smile. "I've been wondering how to ask you out again," he said.

Relief washed over her and she playfully punched his arm.

"Ouch!" he laughed, rubbing his arm. "Surely I don't deserve that."

"But you do deserve this," she said, leaning in to kiss him.

That caught him totally off guard, and he pulled her in close to him. Maki felt electricity ripple through her body, and when she opened her eyes, she was met with his big, radiant smile.

"Wow, well, okay then," he gushed.

"You're welcome," she smiled.

"You, young lady, are making me blush," Tumelo cooed.

"I should probably go find my friend," Maki said.

"Good idea," Tumelo replied. "Before you proceed to undress me."

Having entirely released her inhibitions, Maki let out a raucous belly laugh. As she walked around the garden looking for Tebza, she prayed that she'd find her quickly so that she could tell her all that had transpired.

Lerato walked into Pierre's, a dimly lit Mandela Square eatery, wearing a long sleeved, cleavage-exposing nude crop top with a matching high-waisted, figure-hugging mid-calf skirt. She had on long diamond earrings that drooped all the way down her neck, and beige stiletto-heeled Louboutins. When she approached the private lounge and told the hostess her name, the woman quickly checked a list of names and let her in. At the entrance of the enclosed private area, Lerato was met by another hostess who led her towards Manur's table where loud laughter emanated. Lerato was hit with a rush of familiarity as she recognised the laugh as Manur's.

As she turned the corner, the room fell silent. *I've still got it*, she thought contentedly, as all eyes had turned to her. She saw Manur's eyes intensely bore into her, and he dramatically threw his napkin on the table as he drank her in. She fixed her eyes on him and put an extra swing in her hips entirely for his viewing pleasure as she walked slowly towards him, a naughty grin on her lips.

The call of the wild, she thought, suddenly reinvigorated. *Why did I ever give this up?* Then the thought of Seputla caused her stomach to momentarily plummet. *That's why,* she thought glumly, but she lost neither footing nor focus as Manur took her hand and kissed it in adoration.

"My love," he murmured.

She grinned. "Manur, you old fox! You haven't changed one bit." In reality he had drastically lost weight and looked haggard. Clearly business wasn't going too well. He was probably in SA to check on his profit margins. As Lerato sat down she realised that the men who were seated at the table – and their dates – could not keep their eyes off her. She recognised some of them from her hey days. *Ha,* she told herself, *it's only been three months!* But three months in their line of work – for lack of better wording – was like a century; girls were replaced in a heartbeat. Lerato's confidence shot up because she knew she still commanded a room.

Mothusi, the man with his mouth most agape, extended his hand to her. Then Max, then Patrick, then her heart sank – Aubrey. She tried to regain her composure but her mouth had gone completely dry. What kind of sick and twisted game was Manur playing? She turned to him and, judging from the leer on his face, it was clear that he'd deliberately invited her here to taunt Aubrey. From what she could tell, it was working. Lerato leaned back against Manur's chest and, poker-faced, said hello to Aubrey. He was wearing his wedding band. Lerato mentally rolled her eyes without giving anything away, and sipped on expensive French champagne. The bubbles dancing on her tongue caused her to momentarily shut her eyes as all her senses reawakened. *Champagne, darling,* she thought. It was good to be reacquainted with her old friend.

Tebza shrieked in laughter. She was seated in a secluded part of the garden that had a tiny rock pool and a clear view of the full moon. The actor was seated with her on the rocks and they shared a spliff.

Tumelo led Maki to the pool and she wondered how many crevices and secret compartments this huge and beautiful garden held. Maki smelled the all too familiar sweet scent of marijuana and was surprised that her new beau was leading her in that direction. A voice that she recognised as Tebza's loudly said, "Aowa lena," and shrieked in laughter. Maki was shocked; Tebza rarely spoke Sepedi. She was keen to figure out what exactly was transpiring in that corner of the garden, and was stunned to see smoke floating up from Tebza's mouth as she handed the spliff back to the actor.

"Tebogo!" Maki yelled.

"Chomeeeeee!" Tebza shrieked, before being attacked by a violent coughing-spell.

Maki was confused. "What the hell?" she yelled. "O tsuba patji?"

The actor and Tumelo chuckled as the actor handed Tumelo the spliff. Maki was conflicted; should she join them? Then her better judgement kicked in as she regained her senses and decided not to. Not wanting to come across as an uppity snob, she decided to invite Tebza to accompany her to the bathroom instead.

"Sure," Tebza said, holding her hand up so Maki could help her stand. Maki did, and held her steady all the way to the bathroom.

"Chomi, this party is a lit-uation!" Tebogo squealed as soon as they got into the bathroom. Did you know that the actor is friends with Mandla who plays Spikiri in *Kas'lethu*, or is it Spikiri who plays Mandla in *Kas'lakho*?" Tebza asked, confused, before bursting into giggles.

Ordinarily Maki would call her friend to order, but as she stared at Tebogo in the mirror, she couldn't remember the last time she'd seen her have so much fun. And she liked it, not only because Tebza would be stuck with Tshepo for life, but also because Tebza was the sweetest person in the world and she deserved happiness. So she let her be. She tuned back into Tebza's story about the actor's rise to fame. He too was Limpopo-born like her and she loved that they had that in common.

"Sure, Tebza, but weed?" Maki laughed, as she saw that Tebza's eyes had become tiny slits in her sockets.

"YOLO, Mogwera!" Tebza screeched uncharacteristically, as Maki led her out of the bathroom.

Maki caught a glimpse of Jess and Sarah staring at Tebza as Maki led her back out to the garden, and heard Jess mumble under her breath, "How unbecoming," as she stared at Tebza. Sarah gave her a sympathetic look. The colour drained from Maki's face. Had she just jeopardised her job prospects? Thank goodness Michal wasn't with her friends, and Maki made a note to email her assistant, Mpho first thing on Monday morning.

As they stepped back into the garden, Maki saw a woman talking to Tumelo in the distance. She thought she was seeing things, but it was unmissable. The full moon shone brightly, illuminating the garden, and she saw the woman lean in and whisper something in his ear which caused him to smile a long, wide smile. Maki wanted to turn and run but Tebza had spotted the actor and was already screaming his name which caused Tumelo to turn and see them. He said something to the lady he was standing with and she took off hurriedly. As Maki approached him, he smiled a long, lazy smile, but Maki was less than impressed.

The actor leaned in to Tebza. "You good?" he asked. His intoxicated state caused his voice to deepen and it made him sound hella sexy. Maki also noticed the way he leaned into Tebza when he spoke to her, zooming in on her and shutting out everything and everyone else – unlike his friend, Tumelo.

"Awesome." Tebza smiled a slow sexy smile to the actor.

Maki did not like where this was heading. "Listen, we're going to head out," she said to the actor, and Tumelo knew that it was about what Maki had seen. Strangely enough, he didn't protest, but the actor and Tebza did.

"What?" Tebza complained.

"Already?" the actor asked.

"Afraid so," Maki replied. "Say your goodbyes."

The actor pointed at Tumelo, "I'll get your number from," then he pointed to Maki, "who'll give me your number, to give me Tebza's number, right?" By the time he was done with all the pointing he seemed a bit confused, but Maki put him out of his misery.

"Sure," she said, patting him on the shoulder.

The actor swept Tebza off her feet as he hugged her good-bye and Tebza cooed in glee. "It was so great to meet you."

"The pleasure was all mine," the actor said, in his husky, sexy, voice.

Maki couldn't help but smile. She glanced at Tumelo who was still staring at her with a small smile on his face. He parted his arms indicating that he wanted a hug too, but he didn't walk towards her. Her legs betrayed her as they approached him, and she gave him a small, cautious hug.

"That's it?" he asked, as she quickly let him go.

"Yes," she said, turning to leave. "I'll be seeing you."

In the car Tebogo cranked up the volume to DJ Sumbody's *Monate Mpolaye*, loudly yelling, "Champopo!"

Maki was in her own zone, preoccupied with the mental picture of Tumelo with his lady friend; she couldn't shake the scene from her mind. It was clear they had been flirting and that he had enjoyed it, but to do that while she was there, knowing that she could walk back out at any time – that was just disrespectful! She was glad she'd decided that she and Tebogo should leave. If they'd stayed she would have been forced to talk to Tumelo, and she didn't want to do that. What would she say to him anyway? It wasn't exactly like she was his girlfriend. Heck, they weren't even dating! She had absolutely no right to call him out on his behaviour. He'd invited her to the actor's house and she'd brought a friend. Plus there were a million other people there, so it definitely didn't constitute a date.

But he introduced me to Michal and her friends, she thought sullenly. Despite herself, she felt her insides melt somewhat. That was sweet, and it had given Maki all she'd ever wanted – a fighting chance; a foot in the door. And he'd given that to her. *But,* she reminded herself, *that didn't give him a free pass to hit on other women while she was still around.*

Maki clicked her tongue in annoyance. It must be the filmmaker thing; and the dreadlocked thing. And the overall "come hither" presence that he possessed. Damn it! If she didn't know that she was into him before, she did now. But she definitely wouldn't call him; he would have to chase after her so that she could see if he really was into her.

Tebogo was shocked when they drove into Maki's complex. "Hey! What are we doing here? You need to take me home! Tshepo's going to be worried."

"There's no way I'm delivering you to Tshepo like this!" Maki laughed. "You are spending the night here."

"Okay, then let me send him a message." Tebogo took her cellphone out of her bag and started typing. "Dear Tshepo," she started. "Nah, sounds too formal." She started again: "Baby..." Maki grabbed the phone out of Tebogo's hand. "Hey!" she protested, but Maki was already typing: "Hi Tshepo. Long night. Too tired to drive there to drop Tebza off. Will drop her off in the morning." Then she handed Tebza's phone back to her.

"You're a pro," Tebza exclaimed.

"Let's go," Maki said, wearily climbing out the car.

Manur, Mothusi, Aubrey, Patrick and Max were in the middle of a conversation, mostly led by Manur who had a childlike exuberance about him. But anyone who did business with him knew that appearances could be deceiving; Manur's childlike exuberance could quickly be replaced by a wild and fiery temper. The women who were their companions never spoke to each other; it was unnecessary. Instead, they looked pretty and sipped champagne.

Lerato's phone beeped in her bag. She looked up at Manur and, seeing that he was in the heart of conversation, decided to quickly check who the message was from, secretly hoping that it would be from Seputla. She failed to see Aubrey's eyes darting to her to check her out. Lerato smiled – the message was from Seputla, but she couldn't read it there. She excused herself and headed to the bathroom, going into a stall to read its contents. "Hey baby," she read in Seputla's voice. "Thought you'd be home by now. About to go to sleep. The party must be a real turn up. See you soon."

Lerato thought for a second and quickly typed back: "Hey baby. It's lit. I'm spending the night at Maki's. I'll see you in the morning."

Her phone beeped again. It was a heart emoji from Seputla. Lerato's stomach sank. Why was she doing this? Was this all because she was tired of cooking for her boyfriend? Her otherwise perfect boyfriend. She sent back a heart emoji and decided that she would call it a night.

But she'd already told Seputla that she'd be spending the night at Maki's, so she would head there. Besides, she could do with a bit of girl time, and she needed to remind Maki who her real G was, seeing that she had swopped Lerato for Tebza to go partying with. Stepping out of the stall Lerato saw Aubrey's date at the sink powdering her face. They made brief eye contact in the mirror as Lerato proceeded to wash her hands, but Aubrey's date continued to stare at her. Lerato glanced back at her and was hit with the feeling that she looked familiar. She'd earlier thought that it was because she was Aubrey's date, but that wasn't it. She struggled to place her.

"I have a message for you from Aubrey," the other woman said, handing Lerato a piece of paper. Lerato turned to her, indignant. "I don't want it," she snapped.

"I suggest you take it," the girl replied. Against her better judgement, Lerato dried her hands and took the note. But instead of reading it she tossed it into her handbag and, with an annoyed glance at the girl, left.

Chapter 6

. . . .

"What a night!" Tebza said, as she flopped onto Maki's bed.

"Were you going to sleep with him?" Maki asked, sitting at the foot of the bed and taking off her shoes.

"Who, me? Sleep with who?" Tebza asked.

"Your actor friend," Maki laughed. "If I hadn't dragged you out of there, would you be jumping his bones right this second?"

"What? No. He's just good fun," Tebza said drowsily, even though Maki wasn't sure that she believed her. "You know what they say about those actor types."

"What do they say?" Maki asked, fascinated.

"That their egos are too big for them to bother with being good in bed, and that they expect the woman to do all the work," Tebza droned.

"You're right," Maki nodded, "I have heard that, but what do they say about filmmakers?"

"Hmm," Tebza thought. "Tough crowd."

"What do you mean?" Maki asked, curious. "Tough to please, or...?"

"Yeah, precisely. Chomi, is this about..." she struggled to remember Tumelo's name and she clicked her fingers in a bid to remember. Maki chuckled. She hated being called "chomi" as much as Lerato hated being called "moghel" so she wasn't going to help jog Tebza's memory.

"Remind me again, chomi, who is he? Eish. I've completely forgotten."

"Serves you right for getting high!" Maki laughed.

But Tebza didn't care. "Him, your filmmaker dude. Are you worried about him being good in bed?"

But Maki quickly changed the subject. "Did you see him chatting up that girl?"

"What girl?" Tebza asked, sitting up to remove her shoes.

"That girl.... When we came back from the bathroom he was talking to another girl," Maki explained.

"Oh. Yeah, I saw her. I just thought she was his friend or something."

"I guess you're right," Maki said softly under her breath.

"No, but chomi you must make sure, isn't it?" Tebogo protested. "Clearly you like this guy, so you can't be shunning him just because he spoke to another woman."

Maki knew that Tebza was right, but she couldn't bring herself to agree.

"Yes, but doesn't that make me seem crazy? I mean, it's not like he's my boyfriend or anything," she chuckled under her breath. She waited for a response from Tebogo but was met with calm, rhythmic breathing from Tebza's end and realised that her friend had passed out mid-conversation. Maki smiled, threw the blanket over Tebza and headed to the lounge.

This whole Tumelo thing had given her enough angst to continue working on her novel. She loved when she was in a mood like this, when she'd dredged up enough feelings of inner conflict and she could purge herself on the page. Maki removed her laptop from its bag, already thinking about how to move the story forward. Then she made a cup of coffee and read what she had written so far in order to get into the zone.

She did a quick page count which she'd always promised herself she wouldn't do because it jolted her back to reality, but she couldn't help it, and she was curious. Relieved to see that she was 102 pages in, Maki let out a mild whoop, but she quickly refocused as she re-read her words, knots tying in her stomach in anticipation of the direction that the story should go.

Maki soon caught up with the last chapter, and as she got to the last couple of lines her fingers were itching to hit the keyboard to start typing. The words came pouring out of her –plot twists and emotional journeys, this was her thing! She'd taken a momentary break to think further about the next steps in Mackenzie's story when she remembered Michal's card in the back pocket of her jeans. Good thing she'd bought data, she would email Mpho first thing on Monday morning.

Maki had been typing for about an hour when the intercom rang loudly, startling her. She checked the time. Who the hell was at her gate at 2.30am? Maybe it was Tshepo who was so used to cuddling with Tebogo that he hadn't been able to sleep. Or maybe he was so insecure that he didn't believe the text that she'd sent him, even though she'd sent it from Tebogo's phone, and he was here to check on them and make Tebogo go home with him.

"Sheesh," she said out loud. "Insecure much?" Then, smiling at the memory of how much fun Tebogo'd had, she thought, *At least it was worth it.*

Maki answered her intercom, but instead of Tshepo, Sifiso the security guard told her that there was a lady by the name of Lerato at the gate for her. "Let her in," Maki replied, surprised by the super early visit. She saved her manuscript, closed the document and opened her iTunes, allowing the soft sounds of Bongeziwe Mabandla to fill the room. Maki heard Lerato's heels clicking loudly on the ground as she approached her apartment, and she unlocked the door to let her in.

"Girl," Lerato sighed as she removed her heels and plopped onto the couch.

"Where the hell have you been?" Maki demanded.

"Out," Lerato said. But Maki stared at her, demanding answers.

"I've been calling you, why didn't you answer?" Lerato retaliated.

"Arg, my phone's on silent," Maki explained. "I've been working." She checked her phone and took it off silent.

"And Tebza?" Lerato asked.

"Passed out in the bedroom. Seputla know you're here?"

"Of course, what do you take me for?"

Maki removed a frozen microwave meal from the freezer and punched holes in the top. "Hungry?" she asked without looking up.

"Starved."

With the meal in the microwave, Maki faced Lerato expectantly.

Lerato looked Maki in the eye. "I was with Manur," she confessed.

"Who?" Maki asked, confused.

"A sheik I know. He's Aubrey's friend." Lerato shut her eyes in anticipation of Maki's reaction.

"Aubrey? As in Bra Aubs? As in never in a million years going back to him? That Bra Aubs?"

"I didn't know he'd be there!" Lerato protested.

"What the hell do you mean?" Maki barked. Bra Aubs was a dark and dangerous man. It had taken all of Maki's wiles to eventually get him to leave Lerato the hell alone, now it seemed all her hard work had gone to waste!

"I was sitting at home – bored – and Seputla was at work," Lerato started. Maki stared at her, annoyed. "I swear the man works harder than the Japanese," Lerato complained.

"Maybe he's trying to save up for a future with you!" Maki yelled. "Have you ever considered that?"

"Maybe," Lerato agreed sheepishly.

"But what does this have to do with Bra Aubs?" Maki asked, impatient.

"I'm getting there!" Lerato objected as Maki stared daggers at her. Exhaling deeply, she continued. "You and Tebza had gone out and I was jealous."

"So this is our fault?" Maki asked, pursing her lips.

"If you don't let me finish you'll never know the full story."

"Fine. Say it," Maki snapped.

"So, with Seputla at work and you and Tebza out, I thought to myself: Is this what my life has become? Playing wifey to Seputla and cooking for him every night? Hell no!"

"But you're the one who invited him to move in with you," Maki droned.

"Girl, you know I have terrible foresight," Lerato lamented. "Anyway, Manur sent me a text. At first I thought it was from you and Tebza, but when I realised that it was from Manur, memories of my old life came flooding back. Girl, you should have seen me – I was at home in a tracksuit on a Saturday night, for goodness' sake!" Lerato wailed.

"So what did you do?" Maki sighed, even though the next part of Lerato's story was pretty obvious.

"He asked me to meet him for dinner in Sandton and I sent Seputla a message to tell him I'd be out with you and Tebza…"

"Why? You know how that man feels about you," Maki said, feeling Seputla's pain.

"Girl, bye. Men lie to us all the time," Lerato defended.

"But has Seputla ever lied to you?"

Lerato's heart sank. She knew Maki was right. "Anyway," she proceeded. "When I got to the restaurant Manur wasn't alone – he was with Patrick, Mothusi, Max and Aubrey, his South African business partners."

"They're business partners even?" Maki asked, despondent. "I should slap you in the face."

"But I felt so guilty when I got there…"

"No you didn't. You only felt guilty when you saw Bra Aubs," Maki replied, tired.

Okay, fine, you're right," Lerato agreed, "But then Seputla messaged me and I ran to the bathroom to read his message."

Maki shook her head in disappointment. "The life you choose to lead," she sighed.

"When I read Seputla's message I felt so guilty that I told him I'd be spending the night here. Then, when I got out of the stall, Aubrey's date was staring at me in the mirror and powdering her face. I thought she looked familiar but I couldn't place her. She told me that Bra Aubs had a message for me, and although I told her I didn't want it, she insisted that I take it."

"What was the message?"

Lerato stood up and took the note out of her bag. "I read it on the way here," she said, handing it to Maki. In big, bold letters was written: I WANT YOU.

Maki got shivers down her spine. "What the hell?"

"I know, right?" Lerato was almost in tears. "What does it even mean?"

"It means," Maki surmised, "that Bra Aubs is a typical man – a man who knows what he wants and will do whatever it takes to get it."

Lerato swallowed nervously. That was exactly what she was afraid of.

Suddenly Tebza stumbled into the room, groggy. Lerato and Maki turned to her. "Hey," she said, dragging Maki's blanket behind her. "I thought I heard voices."

"Hey, boo," Lerato said.

"Rato?" she asked, squinting her eyes, "Is that you?"

Lerato couldn't help but smile. "Are you okay?" she asked.

Tebza headed to the microwave and took out the meal that Maki and Lerato had forgotten all about. She found a fork in a drawer and began to eat. "That was the best night ever!" she droned, tired.

Lerato looked to Maki for answers. "Hangover?"

"Weed." Maki smiled.

"Weed?" Lerato shrieked, shocked. "Who are these people that you guys are hanging out with?"

Tebza was only too happy to drop the actor's name, but it didn't work – Lerato had no clue who he was. Lerato turned to Maki for answers and she was only too happy to divulge the details of the night. Maki also wanted Lerato's opinion on the situation that she now faced regarding Tumelo and the other woman.

"Start from the beginning," Lerato said, curious. She hugged a cushion and listened, as Maki told all.

"Tumelo is a filmmaker and I met him in a DVD store the day before Tebza's engagement party," Maki said. She hated talking about herself, so she made it fast. "I made a joke about his dreadlocks..."

"That explains the weed," Lerato surmised.

"Then I asked him if he wanted to go out for dinner and he agreed. But not only did he agree to the dinner that I'd asked him to, but he paid for it too."

"As he should!" Lerato proclaimed.

"Amen, girl," Tebza agreed.

"Then at the end of the night he asked for my number which I punched into his phone, but forgot to ask him to give me a missed call so I could have his," Maki added, shame-faced.

Tebza sighed and shook her head disapprovingly. Lerato was on the edge of her seat.

"So when Tebza invited us over for the engagement dinner and you laughed when I said I'd bring a date, I thought it'd be a good time for him to meet you guys..."

"But you didn't have his number so you couldn't get hold of him to invite him to the dinner," Lerato deduced.

"For someone who considers herself lacking in foresight, you sure have tons of it when you're not confronted with your own problems," Maki droned.

"Story of my life," Lerato sighed.

"Then, fun story," Maki chuckled, drily. "I found him on Facebook after hunting him down among the throng of Tumelos on there and left him a message inviting him to the engagement dinner."

"Hmm," Lerato said disapprovingly.

"Wrong move?" Maki asked, anxious.

"It just seems a bit desperate."

"It gets better. When I got to Tebza's, I realised that he had replied to my inbox but he said that he wouldn't be able to make it."

Lerato and Tebza shared a look, but Maki proceeded. "Then he called the next day to apologise for not making it and said that he wanted to take me to a party for his friend who'd been nominated for a SAFTA."

"What's a SAFTA?" Lerato asked, blank.

Tebza and Maki shared a shocked look, and Maki burst out laughing.

"South African Film and Television Award," Tebza explained, bored that Lerato had no clue who the actor was or what a big deal he was.

"Oh, so the actor is a big deal?" Lerato smiled, impressed. She offered Tebza a high five and her friend reciprocated with a mild, annoyed slap against Lerato's hand.

"So we got to the party and I met all the actor's friends." Tebza picked up where Maki had left off, which surprised Maki because she thought she was telling Lerato her story. She was gracious enough to let Tebogo have her moment to shine.

"I'm talking all your A-list actors – you name it, they were there. And I'm thinking: Yeah, Tshepo how you like me now?" Tebza laughed.

Maki and Lerato whooped at Tebza's sudden bout of confidence.

"Then the actor whisked me to the side, and I thought he was going to kiss me..."

"And you didn't stop him? Lerato asked, chastising her friend for Tshepo's sake.

"Listen," Tebza said, holding a hand up. "But he pulled out a joint instead. I was fascinated. I hadn't seen one of those since varsity days," she laughed.

"So you blazed it up?" Lerato asked.

"Like a pro," Tebza giggled.

"And that's when I found her," Maki swooped in. "High out of her mind! Speaking Sepedi even!"

Lerato fell over laughing, glad that Tebza had a good time.

"Then we went to the bathroom, and when we came back I saw Tumelo give this chick a lingering hug with a smile on his face," Maki said, studying Lerato's face for an indication of her thoughts on the matter.

"Say what now?" Lerato asked. She looked like she was ready to punch someone in the face.

"I know!" Maki quipped. "I didn't want to make a big deal out of it so I decided that we should leave, then and there."

"Good," Lerato said, pensive. "Don't let him ruffle your feathers."

"But I still want to know who the hell that chick was and why they were so happy to see each other," Maki wailed.

"And you're wondering if it's your place since you haven't known him that long and aren't even dating him," Lerato concluded.

"Exactly," Maki nodded. Lerato's worried expression caused her heart to drop. "What?" she asked, anxious.

"What are the odds that he was with her on Friday night and that's why he couldn't make Tebza's engagement dinner?" Lerato asked.

Maki's face fell. "Quite high, I suppose. But he was attentive to me the entire time I was at the party."

"Until you were out of sight," Lerato nodded, in understanding. "Out of sight, out of mind. Classic F Boy behaviour."

"What?" Tebza asked, squishing up her face.

"F Boys. They're everywhere. They normally target girls in their early twenties, but hey, who doesn't?" Lerato chuckled, wry. "Don't go catching feelings. If you do, it won't end well."

Maki's heart was thumping loudly in her chest. She hated to admit it, but gauging by her pounding heart and sudden dry mouth, it was clear that she already had caught feelings. "What do I do now?"

"Ignore him. Give him the silent treatment for a couple of days. Weeks, if you can. Show him that two can play the 'out of sight, out of mind' game. Then boom, text him a sexy pic."

Tebza threw her head back, laughing and threw Maki a look. "Do you have one of those, chomi?"

Lerato laughed too, but Maki was annoyed. Was Tebza seriously still calling her "chomi"?

Maki, Lerato and Tebza eventually all passed out in the lounge, but Maki was awakened at the crack of dawn by her screeching phone signalling that a call was coming in. Still half asleep, she reached for it and checked the caller ID, then woke right up, screaming, "It's him! It's him! What do I do?" She shook both Lerato and Tebogo awake.

"What?" Tebza asked drowsily, but Lerato sat up immediately. "Who?" she asked.

"Tumelo the filmmaker is calling! What should I do?" Maki screeched. Lerato was now wide awake. "Answer it!" she yelled.

"But you said I must ignore him!" Maki yelled back.

"F Boys are also notorious for being tons of fun," Lerato defended.

"You just want to meet him," Tebza laughed.

"That too," Lerato smiled.

"The phone's still ringing!" Maki yelled, confused.

"Answer it!" Both Tebza and Lerato yelled in unison.

In a quick breath Maki collected herself and suavely answered her phone. "Hello," she said, coolly.

"Oh," she said a second later, "hold on."

Maki handed Tebza the phone. Lerato was confused.

"The actor wants to speak to you," Maki said.

Tebza squealed excitedly and yelled into the phone, "Hey, boo."

Lerato shot Maki a questioning look and mouthed the word "boo", but Maki was amused.

"Of course we can meet for breakfast!" Tebza said, eyeing her friends with a twinkle in her eye. "Just give us an hour or two to spruce up. Later, boo."

When Maki took her phone back from Tebza she quickly checked it and noticed with a sinking feeling that Tumelo hadn't even stayed on the line to speak to her. It was the second time that he'd left her to drive in Joburg in the middle of the night and hadn't called or texted to check if she'd arrived home safely. She quickly plastered a smile on her face so that Lerato and Tebza would not pick up on her sombre mood.

"Bathong, Tebogo," Lerato scolded, fascinated by Tebza's new lease on life. "You're calling him Boo?"

With a mischievous smile, Tebza replied, chuffed. "Get ready, girls. We're going for breakfast."

Chapter 7

· ·

Freshly showered, Lerato pulled on her nude-coloured crop top that she'd worn the previous night. She was wearing Maki's boyfriend jeans, and Maki had to admit that they looked a hell of a lot sexier on Lerato than they'd ever been on her. Lerato picked up Maki's mascara too, but when Maki told her that it had dried out, Lerato disapprovingly produced her own from her "just in case" overnight make-up kit that she never left home without. All the while she lectured Maki on the importance of a lady having mascara on her at all times. She had worn her Louboutins and let her hair hang loose so it cascaded down her shoulders, completing the look with a dab of lip-gloss.

Maki was shocked when Tebza walked into the bathroom asking if she could borrow one of Maki's dresses – a dress that she was already wearing. Maki marvelled at how, on Tebza, the dress cinched at the waist and hugged her curves deliciously. She thought, depressed, that the dress did nothing but emphasise her boyish figure; she might as well let Tebza make the most of it.

While Tebza and Lerato did their make-up Maki scoured her wardrobe for something to wear but wasn't happy with anything she came up with. She wasn't even sure if Tumelo would there; if he wasn't, then all her efforts would be in vain anyway. The actor had called Tebza from Tumelo's phone and he hadn't even bothered to speak to her. Not even a mere, "Hello, how are you?" she thought, depressed.

Burdened by her thoughts and her overwhelming desire to look good, she crumpled to the floor. Tebogo walked back into the room to put her shoes on and found Maki lying in a heap. "What's wrong?" Tebza asked, quickly rushing to her.

Despite herself, Maki wailed loudly. "I have nothing to wear!"

"What do you mean?" Tebogo asked, but Maki was too emotional to answer. "Okay, show me your options," Tebogo said, trying a different tack.

Maki stood unhappily and faced her clothes. She flipped through all her hangers and turned to Tebogo. "I have none."

But Tebogo was having none of it. She cast Maki a sympathetic look and flipped through her hangers, picking out a long summer dress.

"Not in the mood for a dress," Maki replied.

"Okay," Tebogo said, focusing her attention back on Maki's wardrobe. She took out a pair of jeans and held them out for Maki to see.

"Don't feel like wearing jeans," Maki replied, dejected. "See, I told you there was nothing in there," she added, morose.

But nothing could deter Tebogo. She moved over to Maki's shelves and found a black miniskirt. "Hmm," Tebza said, impressed. "How's this?"

Despite herself Maki perked up. "Okay," she smiled. "I haven't worn that in years, but it could work."

"And to top off the look …" Tebza smiled, enjoying herself immensely. She dug deeper into Maki's wardrobe and found a plethora of tank tops with catch words written on them including "feminist", "girls rule" and "#blessed". Tebogo opted for a white one with the word "dream" written in black across the front. She threw the top on the bed, matching it with the skirt, and smiled at her handiwork. "And since we all know how you live in biker boots and sneakers, you can wear the black biker boots you wore to my engagement party and look like a biker girl," Tebogo proudly declared. "Now sit down so I can do your make-up."

"As long you don't make me look like a zombie." Maki laughed as she felt the warm comfort of her all too familiar depression lift somewhat.

"I'll make you look like a dream," Tebza whispered. She ran to Maki's bathroom and re-emerged with Maki's powder, eyeshadows and brushes. "Now close your eyes," she commanded.

"Yes, ma'am." Maki felt her insides tingling; no one had done her make-up in a long, long time.

Lerato walked in. "I just got off the phone with Seputla, he'll be joining us for breakfast," she said coolly. Then, when she saw Maki's transformation in progress, she gasped.

"That bad?" Maki laughed nervously. She hated being the centre of attention.

"That good," Lerato gushed. "Remember how Tebza did all our make-up for the Matric dance?"

"And how we used to idolise the Spice girls!" Maki replied, worried. She secretly hoped that Tebza wasn't stuck in a time warp.

"I was Baby Spice," Tebza smiled nostalgically.

"I was Posh," Lerato reminisced.

"And I was Scary," Maki recollected. The air filled with a contented silence as each of the girls visited the memories of their high school years. A moment later Tebza declared with a smile that she was done. Maki went to look at herself in the bathroom mirror and her mouth fell open at what she saw. Tebogo had blended her eyeshadows in a way that highlighted her eyes and made them strikingly piercing. "I look gorgeous!" she said in disbelief.

"Of course you do, silly," Lerato smiled. "Now get dressed so I can meet these men of yours." Lerato quickly texted Seputla to tell him that they were about to leave the house, while Maki turned to Tebza and hugged her. "Thank you," she whispered, teary-eyed.

"Anytime, my friend," Tebogo replied with a heart-warming solemnness.

***

Maki, Lerato and Tebza were feeling themselves. They were in Maki's car and had cranked the windows all the way down, singing loudly to Boom Shaka's most popular collection of 90s hits.

Maki drove, but she was hella nervous. She kept picking at her nails and biting her bottom lip in anxiety. On the surface she sang along happily while Lerato busied herself with the playlist, but she'd never been good at hiding her feelings, so it would be obvious to Tumelo that something was bugging her. Lerato, sensing her distress, turned to her.

"It'll be fine," she smiled reassuringly. "Just eat and smile a lot. You'll get through it."

Maki appreciated Lerato's coaching. "Thanks," she replied, but sadly Lerato's words did nothing for the knot in her stomach. At the shopping centre they pulled into a parking space and got out the car. Tebza did a final check on her lipstick, and Lerato thought that for someone who insisted that this actor dude was just a friend, she was doing a hell of a lot to make sure that she looked good.

"You called Tshepo yet?" she asked Tebza, linking her arm through her friend's.

"Tshepo? The guy I'm about to spend the rest of my life with?" Tebza asked sarcastically.

"Yes. Your soon-to-be-husband and father of your kids."

"Slow your roll, Lerato. Husband? Yes. Kids? Not so much."

"Whatever. Have you spoken to him today?" Lerato sighed.

Tebogo pursed her lips. "I'll call him," she said defiantly. Then, changing the subject, added: "I'm famished. Let's go eat."

As the three young women emerged from the parking lot, Maki immediately noticed that all eyes fell on Lerato. But either Lerato wasn't aware of how much attention she summoned or she was used to it, because she acted like it was the most casual thing in the world. Her looks alone commanded stares, never mind her body or sense of style. *The girl is flawless,* Maki thought enviously.

They soon found the restaurant where Tumelo and the actor were waiting, and Maki immediately spotted them at a table but the men didn't see her. Tebza and Lerato also scanned the place, and when Tebza's eyes landed on the actor she squealed in delight. The actor looked up and when he noticed Tebza it was obvious he was as happy to see her.

Suddenly Maki noticed with a sinking feeling that Tumelo's eyes were fixed on Lerato. He started with her face, then ran his eyes down her body, lingering for a moment on her chest and waist, then back up to her face. But Lerato, unaware, turned to Maki in amazement at Tebza and the actor's excitement at being in each other's presence again. Maki turned back to look at Tumelo again. This time his eyes were on her, but Maki noticed that they were downcast and didn't contain the same admiration they'd exhibited a moment before when he was taking in Lerato.

Maki and Lerato followed Tebza to their table and the actor stood to embrace her warmly. "Hey you," he smiled. "I missed you."

Tumelo stood too, but instead of hugging Maki, he extended his hand to Lerato. "Tumelo," he smiled.

Lerato took his hand in hers. "So you're the guy giving my friend sleepless nights." Maki could have screamed!

Tumelo turned to Maki and, smiling, asked, "I am, am I?"

Maki hugged him awkwardly. "Lerato's just being silly. How'd you sleep?" she asked as she sat down.

"Sleep?" the actor replied loudly across the table. "Yo! That party was a jump! Y'all left too soon!"

Tebogo took the actor's phone and punched in her number. "We can't make the same mistake twice," she said as she typed before happily returning the phone. The actor, who was obviously totally smitten with Tebza, gave her a missed call but Tebza's phone was off and he promised that he would message her later that evening so that she would have his number.

Watching Tebza and the actor's natural ease and display of playful affection, Maki shifted in her chair, suddenly awkward around Tumelo. Just then he turned to her and said, "Thanks for coming."

Maki, relieved to have some form of acknowledgement from him, smiled back and said, "Of course."

A couple of minutes later Lerato's phone beeped. She checked it and hurried out of the restaurant, returning soon afterwards with Seputla. A silence fell upon the place as the patrons and waiters all focused on them. Even Maki couldn't help but stare. Seputla was dressed in a plain white T-shirt and jeans, but she could not drag her eyes away from him. There was something about his presence that drew one in.

"What a gorgeous couple," she heard someone murmur and she was sure that she saw Tumelo's eyes fall in disappointment when Seputla and Lerato sat down at the table together. Maki smiled brightly. *Serves you right,* she thought.

Seputla introduced himself to the other guys, and Maki heard the waiters giggling and laughing as they watched the actor from where they were standing. One of the waiters who was struggling to keep his emotions under wraps approached the table and took their orders. Once they'd ordered, a happy atmosphere fell upon the table as they chatted among themselves and subsequently enjoyed the food. When they stood up to leave a waitress came running up to them.

"Excuse me," she said.

"Yes?" Lerato said, turning to her expectantly. She was used to people mistaking her for Joanne Reyneke.

But the waitress turned to the actor instead. Do you mind if I take a selfie with you?" she asked shyly.

"Sure!" The actor smiled happily. Lerato was floored. Who had Maki and Tebza said this guy was? People had stared at him all morning; she would have to Google him on the way home. The waitress strained to take a selfie with the actor, so Tebza offered to take the picture for them, while Maki, Tumelo, Lerato and Seputla watched. A couple of clicks later Tebza showed the waitress the pictures she had taken and, satisfied, the waitress thanked her and rushed off to show her friends.

"I'd like to see you again," the actor said to Tebza, "but next time with an audience of only one."

Tebza felt her stomach plummet. She would have loved to see him again too but, bummed, she held up her engagement ring for him to see.

"I'm engaged," she confessed.

The actor was visibly disappointed. "I thought that was just for show," he replied sadly. Tebza slowly shook her head. After giving her a tight bear hug, the actor told her to never stop being the lovely person that she was, and walked away.

As Tebogo stepped out of the Uber outside her house, she smelled herself. She caught a whiff of the actor's cologne on her and she suddenly got very nervous, but she decided to brave it out. She had gone out and met a nice guy who'd bought her and her friends breakfast. There was nothing wrong with that. But as she walked up to the door she knew that wasn't entirely true. Taking a deep breath and exhaling slowly, she bravely turned the doorknob and walked into her home.

Tshepo was sprawled on the couch, newspapers on the floor all around him.

"Hey," Tebogo said.

"Hey," he replied, looking up.

She went and sat next to him as he eyed her. "Where've you been?" he asked.

"Out."

"I tried calling you."

"My battery must've died," she answered nonchalantly. She looked up at him and met with his disapproving eye, but she continued. "You know I was with Maki and Lerato. You could have called me on one of their phones."

"Oh, so Lerato was with you too? But you left here with Maki." Tshepo commented, unable to hide his growing suspicions.

"What's the big deal? They're both my friends," Tebogo lamented, drained.

"The big deal, Tebogo, is that you didn't communicate with me!" Tshepo yelled, unable to hold back his anger.

Tebza fought back. "I did!" she yelled. "Maki sent you a text that I'd be spending the night at her place!"

"And yet you arrive back here at three in the afternoon in a dress I don't recognise!" he yelled.

"Wow."

"Wow?" Tshepo repeated. "Is that all you have to say for yourself?"

Tebogo got up from the couch, glaring at him, annoyed. "If you're done policing me, I'm going to take a bath."

Lerato and Seputla arrived home in stitches. "I have no idea what's gotten into her," Lerato laughed, taking off her heels and dropping onto the couch. Seputla poured them some wine and handed Lerato a glass.

"Thanks, babe," she said, as he sat down next to her.

"Where did those two meet?" he asked casually.

"At his party last night," she replied, taking a sip of her wine.

He nodded, pensive. "Last minute thing?"

"Yes," Lerato replied without skipping a beat. "Tumelo felt guilty for standing Maki up at Tebogo and Tshepo's engagement dinner party, so to make it up to her, he invited her to the actor's nomination party. Tebza and I tagged along."

"I see."

She noticed that his mood had changed and she punched him lightly on the arm. "Hey. What's up?"

"It's just odd to me that you didn't mention that it was his party, that's all," Seputla explained, taking a sip of his wine.

Lerato smiled in understanding. "We spent the night at Maki's, then he and Tumelo invited us for breakfast. We did not spend the night at the actor's place, I swear. If we had I would have told you."

Seputla smiled, reassured. She kissed him hard on the lips. "You have my affections, mister. All of them."

"Just promise me that you won't spend the night away from me again."

"I promise," Lerato agreed, then she sat back and studied him. "Who would've thought that you'd be a jealous boyfriend?" she joked, putting her wine glass on the table. "I'm going to run myself a bath. Care to join me?" she asked in a sultry voice. With a big smile, Seputla stood up and followed her.

Maki was sitting on the floor reading newspapers and eating Chinese food when her phone rang. She checked the caller ID and was surprised to see that it was Tumelo.

"Hey," she answered.

"Hey."

"Miss me already?" Maki decided she had nothing to lose by attempting to flirt.

Tumelo chuckled. "I was just sitting here thinking about how odd it is that we're the ones who brought our friends together, and yet we probably know the least about each other."

"Interesting thought," Maki smiled.

"So how about dinner?" he asked.

Maki checked the time, unsure. She wanted to get a good night's sleep since she was going to contact Mpho from *Kas'lethu* the next day to ask her for a test script, and she was already pretty anxious about that.

Tumelo sensed her trepidation. "I know it's a school night," he coerced. "I won't have you out too long."

Maki smiled and eventually agreed.

Langa Mavuso's soulful sounds filled the apartment as Lerato lay in the bath, her eyes closed. Seputla walked in with a glass of wine and stepped into the bath. She took a huge sip, then she set the wine aside and drank in Seputla's kisses instead. Things were turning steamy when Lerato's phone beeped, signalling a text message. Despite Seputla's complaints, she stopped kissing him and hurriedly checked her message. As she read it Lerato felt as if ice cold water had been thrown in her face.

Noting her tension, Seputla quickly asked, "What's the matter?"

But Lerato switched off her phone, set it aside and quickly covered. "It's nothing important, just work stuff that can wait until tomorrow."

Seputla was not convinced. "Are you sure?" he asked.

"Where were we?" Lerato whispered, ignoring his question and instead planting soft kisses all over him.

It worked. Seputla pulled her closer, having forgotten all about Lerato's cellphone. But Lerato had not forgotten; the text message from Aubrey flashed through her mind: I WANT YOU. It sent shivers down Lerato's spine. In an effort to erase it completely from her mind, she kissed Seputla harder, hoping that her fervour would eradicate the guilt that now consumed her for lying to him.

Maki sat opposite Tumelo; he had taken her out for sushi. "I hope you're not going to make any sushi jokes related to my name," she remarked while studying the menu.

"I'll only tell you what you want to hear."

She looked up at him, pensive, then cast her menu aside. "In that case, who was that lady you were speaking to when I went to the bathroom at the actor's house?"

He raised his eyes from the menu and met her gaze.

"And don't you dare say that she's your sister or cousin," Maki added. "Nobody hugs their family like that."

He silently studied her. Maki felt completely naked. Had she phrased it wrong? Come on too strong? Why the hell was he not answering her?

Eventually he emitted a slight chuckle. "I had no intention of saying that she's my sister or cousin. She's just someone I've worked with before."

"Oh, so she's a filmmaker too?" Maki probed.

"She's an editor."

"I see," said Maki quietly. He still hadn't told her who the woman was to him, and she feared that if she pressed too hard she might look more insecure than she already did.

Without taking his gaze off her, Tumelo continued. "We have slept together."

"You what?" Maki couldn't stop the words from tumbling out of her mouth, and immediately scolded herself. *Enough, you jealous freak! Just because you haven't been getting it for a decade doesn't mean nobody else is!*

"Occasionally; once in a while, here and there," he elaborated.

"I know what occasionally means," she snapped.

"And it bothers you?"

She shrugged, feigning nonchalance.

"Let's be honest here," he suggested, casting his menu aside and looking her right in the eye. "What do you want?"

Maki bit her bottom lip nervously. "I don't know," she murmured.

He smiled his long, lazy smile. "Yes, you do." He leaned in closer. "What do you want?"

Since she felt naked anyway Maki figured she might as well just say it: "I want love."

Tumelo sat back in his seat.

"And now that I've said that you want to run," she commented feebly.

"No," he smiled. "Honesty turns me on."

Seriously? Maki thought. Had she known that she would've been honest right from the start.

Seputla and Lerato woke up when they heard a loud banging on their front door. Lerato gasped as she sat up in bed and pulled the duvet up to her chest in fear. *"Was it Bra Aubs? Impossible! He didn't know where she lived, but she knew that with Bra Aubs anything was possible. Had he sent his goons? What the hell did he want?"* Lerato thought, panicking. Bra Aubs's note from the restaurant and the text message that he'd sent her earlier, flashed through her mind. She turned to Seputla but he was already halfway out the bedroom door.

"Be careful, baby," she said, before jumping out of bed, throwing on her gown and quickly rushing after him. Lerato was shocked when she heard Tshepo's voice coming from the living room. "Tshepo? What's wrong? Is it Tebogo? Is she okay?" she demanded as she ran into the room.

"Tebogo is fine," Tshepo said abruptly, pacing around the room.

"Come sit down," Seputla invited, but Tshepo continued to pace. "She came home smelling of a man's cologne."

Lerato and Seputla shared a knowing look that didn't go unnoticed by Tshepo. "Who the hell is he?" he barked. When he was met with silence, he pleaded. "Please, you have to tell me. Put me out of my misery."

Lerato went to the bedroom and returned with her phone. She had Googled the actor on the way home and had marvelled at how famous he actually was – and at the huge following that he had. Seputla had laughed at her, but now she had her search history open and she handed Tshepo her phone. He anxiously took the device and his heart sank when he saw the picture.

"The actor from *Kas'lethu*?" he asked, confused. He searched Lerato's face, and she nodded ever so slightly. Suddenly his mood changed entirely and he became violently angry. "The actor from *Kas'lethu*? I'm competing with a celebrity?"

Seputla rose from the couch. "Yo, man. Chill!"

Lerato was more worried that in his rage, Tshepo might smash her phone against the wall.

"They're just friends," Lerato said, defending Tebza.

Seputla threw her a look but she just shrugged. That had been the best she could think of. She tried to get Tshepo to calm down.

"Listen, Tshepo. Just breathe, okay. Breathe." It worked.

Tshepo inhaled and exhaled a few times, then Lerato offered to make him a cup of chai tea. Before leaving the room she held her hand out for the phone and he gave it back to her.

Lerato disappeared into the kitchen. The air was thick with tension after she'd left, neither man knowing what to say to the other. Suddenly Tshepo realised that he had barged into Lerato's apartment where she lived with her boyfriend in the middle of the night, and that they had probably been in the middle of having sex.

He eyed Seputla awkwardly, then stood up. "I'm sorry for the commotion," he apologised sheepishly as he headed for the door.

"Hey, man, you don't have to run off," Seputla said. "Have your tea."

But Tshepo was already at the door. "I've imposed enough. Thanks for the info." And with that, he was gone.

Maki and Tumelo stumbled into the lounge; he was already tearing off her clothes. She wanted to stop him but couldn't. In her head she was protesting *Take it slow!* but at the same time she was engulfed with as much as passion as he was. They fell onto the couch and made love there in a tumbled heap.

***

Tebogo felt Tshepo's eyes on her as she got ready for work. She took her time in front of the mirror, deliberately applying her make-up slowly and attentively. Since she'd been out with Maki and had given her a mini-makeover, her passion for make-up had returned to her. And if Tshepo wanted to watch, he could be her guest.

As Tshepo watched Tebogo, he noticed that she had been in much better spirits since she'd come home from her night out with Maki. *That girl has never wanted me to be with Tebogo,* he thought suspiciously. It was clear to him that Tebogo had allowed herself to become influenced by Maki. *But what the hell does Maki know about being in a relationship, let alone engaged? She's been single for ten years, for goodness' sake!*

Tebogo smirked as she felt Tshepo's eyes boring into her. She began to hum as she did her make-up, knowing that it would drive Tshepo crazy.

She was right. Tshepo quickly left the room. He couldn't stand it when Tebogo hummed. For one thing, she was always off-key, but for another, it bothered him that she was so damn happy. To make matters worse, she had taken to singing in the shower too! It was enough to drive a sane man berserk. He paced around in the living room, waiting for his fiancé to be ready for work. The previous night when he returned from Lerato's he'd woken Tebogo up and told her that he would be dropping her off at work and picking her up in the afternoon. She'd been confused at first, then accepted the idea. *Not that I gave you a choice,* Tshepo argued silently. *What I say, goes!*

A moment later he stopped pacing to see Tebogo emerge from the bedroom. She looked stunning. He angrily thought of the actor. *So you think you can take my woman away from me just because you're famous?* He had a mental image of the two of them in a boxing ring and him beating the actor to a pulp. The thought gave him immense satisfaction.

"Ready to go?" Tebogo asked coolly. She walked past him, leaving a trail of self- confidence lingering behind her in the air. Tshepo had to admit it – the girl was smoking. Even though her bum still swayed from side to side when she walked, she looked hella sexy.

It's amazing what confidence can do, Tebogo thought, as she grabbed her laptop bag from the kitchen counter. She could feel Tshepo's eyes all over her. *Men are so insecure, just the thought of me being happy in someone else's arms is enough to light a fire up his bum.* Tebogo chuckled out loud. She knew that Tshepo thought that he had her on lockdown by demanding to drive her to and from work, but truth be told, she hated traffic and Fourways traffic was the worst. Now, like the queen that she was, she would chill while he drove, and she would Uber to meet her friends for lunch. *What could be better?* she thought contentedly.

Maki's eyes fluttered open and she damn near lost her mind when she saw a dreadlocked man lying asleep next to her. "Aaahhh," she screamed, causing him to wake up too.

"Damn, Maki," he scolded.

Blushing, she apologised sheepishly. "I'm sorry, I temporarily forgot about last night."

Tumelo groaned in protest at the sleep he had now lost, and rested his head on her pillow, his eyes shut. "Forgot? Already?" he mumbled.

Maki studied him, a small smile on her face. "Good morning, lover."

Her new beau opened one eye and turned to her. "So now you remember me?"

"I said temporarily," she argued, then threw her head back laughing. Now that she remembered their night together she felt grown and sexy, a feeling that she hadn't had in a long while. "You got work today?" she asked, as she slipped into a gown.

"No talking, just coffee, please."

"Coming right up," Maki replied, a pep in her step.

Tumelo was lured to the kitchen a while later by the smell of bacon, and was pleasantly surprised to see that she'd made them breakfast. "Well, this is nice to wake up to," he smiled.

Maki handed him a cup of coffee. "To apologise for the memory loss," she explained. "And to thank you for all the meals you've taken me out to recently."

He gladly accepted the coffee and sat down to eat.

"Bon appetit," she smiled.

Tebogo was in the middle of validating a claim when her cellphone buzzed next to her. It was a message from Maki on their group chat. "Need to chat. Lots to tell." Tebogo grinned as she read the message. She was glad to know that Maki was happier, and she could tell from the tone of the message that she was.

Before Tebogo could reply, a message came in from Lerato: "Spill!"

But Maki was mum. "Lunch at the usual spot?"

"You know it," Tebza responded.

"Can't wait," Lerato's reply appeared. A moment later Tebza's phone beeped again. Lerato added. "PS don't believe the hype. Telemarketing is not all it's cracked up to be."

Tebza chuckled as she read the message and then put her phone aside, wanting to be done with the claim that she was working on so she would be on time for lunch with the divas.

After Tumelo left, Maki sat down with her laptop open in front of her. She held the business card that Michal had given her in her hand for a long time. Her email was open and ready to write to Mpho, but she had no idea what to say. After a while she finally gathered the courage to type that she'd met Michal at a party and that the producer had given Maki a card with Mpho's contact details on it. She explained that she was an aspiring writer and an avid fan of *Kas'lethu*, and would love the opportunity to write for the daily soapie, and she was thus requesting a test script. She'd pondered the word "thus" for a long time, wondering if it sounded too formal. Then when she realised that it didn't change the meaning, context or outcome of her email, she said a quick prayer and pressed the send button.

Mpho had replied almost immediately. "Hi!" She'd typed, bright and breezy, commenting that it was good to "virtually meet" Maki. Attached to the mail was a test script with very clear delivery outlines: when to return it by, past scripts to illustrate the tone of the show, and a request to deliver it on something called Final Draft, which Maki had never heard of. Fortunately Mpho had also stressed that since it was a test script the software wasn't imperative at this stage, it was only a recommendation. For now they would only be judging her script on its content. After Maki read the email from Mpho she realised that she'd been sweating, and she wiped off the sweat that had gathered on her top lip. "Doesn't sound too bad," she thought to herself. Mpho sounded like a gem, and Maki had already met Michal, so surely that put her in good stead.

She had three days to deliver the script. She realised that the requirement wasn't a full script, just snippets of different scenes that she would have to write dialogue for, hence the quick turnaround time. Thankfully she was used to the newspaper's tight deadlines, which is why she was sure she would have time to squeeze in lunch with the girls.

It turned out Mpho wasn't Michal's assistant after all – she was the Manager of the Script Department, or so it stated in her signature at the bottom of her email. That was clearly a very important role, because it sounded as if she would be the one to decide if Maki's script had any merit or not, and if she'd get the writing job.

Maki knew that she had to impress Mpho. Thank goodness she was an Mpho and not, say, a Laura. Maybe she'd be kind to a sister and relate to the pressures of being a black working woman, what with black tax and all. But Maki didn't actually have to pay black tax – she was the daughter of working professionals and sibling to well-rounded individuals with successful careers. But Mpho didn't know that, and neither did she have to. So Maki would use whatever was in her arsenal to make sure that she landed the job.

***

Maki was already waiting at the table for Lerato and Tebogo when Tebza walked in. She was shocked to see Maki there already. "The first to arrive? Is lunch on you?" she chuckled.

"Don't push it!" Maki laughed.

Tebza noted the glass of ice water in front of Maki. "I'll gladly pay as a thank you for taking me out the other night."

"And for facilitating your meeting with the actor?" Maki smiled. "You heard from him yet?"

"Nope. But getting to know him was very exciting."

Although Maki hated Tshepo, she knew she had to say something. "Exciting, Tebza? What about Tshepo?" she asked cautiously.

"There's no need to worry about Tshepo," Tebogo replied casually, but despite what Tebza said, Maki still felt a tinge of guilt. It was her fault that Tebza had met this actor person in the first place.

Just then Lerato breezed in. *Even when the girl is late she still looks so good,* Maki thought. When Lerato sat down Tebza informed her that Maki was the first one there.

"You were?" Lerato asked, her eyes widening in surprise. "Getting up before noon, nowadays!" she chuckled. "Any particular reason why?"

Maki bit her bottom lip. "I got some."

Tebza choked on her saliva and Lerato's jaw dropped in shock. "You what now?"

"With the filmmaker?" Tebza squealed.

"His name is Tumelo."

"Ooh," Tebza smiled.

"And?" Lerato enquired, curious.

"It was magical," Maki squealed.

"Well, it's about damn time," Lerato laughed.

"You two talk yet?" Tebza asked.

"Not yet," Maki replied. "But I'm sure I'll see him soon."

They placed their orders and then Lerato got serious. "In news of my own, Tshepo was at my place last night."

Tebza was shocked. "Tshepo was at your place?"

"Why?" Maki asked, although a hint of fear washed over her.

"What do you think?" Lerato said, looking Tebza squarely in the face. "He wanted to know why you came home smelling of a man's cologne."

Maki's jaw hit the ground, and Tebza squirmed ever so slightly in her chair. "Is that right?" she asked, maintaining her composure. Then she chuckled. "That explains why he's turned himself into my chauffeur."

Maki touched Tebza's hand. "Friend, this is serious."

But Tebza remained stoic. "No. What's serious is that he's jealous just because someone else is interested in me. And now he's feeling threatened."

"This is the man you're going to marry!" Lerato protested. "He threw you an amazing engagement dinner."

"Only after he proposed!" Tebza yelled, irrationally.

Well, yes, that's how it typically works, Maki thought, but she knew better than to say it out loud.

"He has not done anything for me in years, and suddenly I should toe the line because he put a ring on it?" Tebza scolded. "Ha! He can kiss my fat ass!" Then she shot Lerato a look. "And you can tell him that the next time he comes knocking on your door in the middle of the night."

Silence fell at the table – a defiant one from Tebza's end. Lerato decided to change the subject by revealing her other news: "Bra Aubs is back," she said in barely a whisper.

Maki's fork dropped from her hand.

Tebza stared at Lerato. "Aubrey?" she asked. Lerato nodded feebly. "The same obsessive Aubrey it took you months to break up with?" Tebza asked accusingly.

Lerato looked to Maki for back up, but Maki just returned her look. Clearly Lerato was on her own in explaining just how Bra Aubrey had come back into her life. She took a deep breath and started from the beginning.

Chapter 8

· ·

Lerato's Uber drove into the parking lot of the building where her office was. "Thanks," she said to the driver. As she grabbed her handbag and emerged from the car she felt shivers down her spine, as if someone was watching her. She shut the car door and, when the driver drove away, she scanned the parking lot. The young woman's hackles rose when her eyes landed on Aubrey, his focus solely on her and a steely expression on his face. Lerato knew better than to show any signs of distress, so she casually draped her handbag over her shoulder and sauntered up to him, her eyes never leaving his.

"Bra Aubs," she said breezily as she approached him. "Fancy meeting you here."

"You've been ignoring me."

"Oh, come on now," she said, attempting to walk past him and continue to do exactly what he now accused her of. But he grabbed her arm, causing her to stop in her tracks.

"You know how I hate being ignored," he said menacingly.

"Bra Aubs, I haven't seen you in so long it's hard to remember what you do and don't like," Lerato replied smoothly, ignoring the pain that shot up her arm. She turned to face him. "Now let me go," she demanded, with an alluring smile on her face. Lerato might have denied remembering that the man hated being ignored, but there was nothing about Bra Aubrey that she would ever forget, least of all how he hated being told what to do.

Despite that, he let her go. She leaned against his car. "Is that why you're here?"

Seeing that he had her full attention, he melted. "I miss you," he smiled, peering at her from behind his dark sunglasses. "And seeing you the other day did nothing for my blood pressure."

Lerato chuckled. "You mean seeing me with Manur?"

"I'd rather we kept him out of this," Aubrey smiled. "Besides, I had you first."

Lerato licked her top lip. Despite her attempts to stay cool, she was starting to sweat.

"Since you've been ignoring my messages I thought I'd come see you in person," he whispered. Leaning into her he enunciated every word: "I want you."

Fear gripped Lerato; she had to get away immediately. "Consider your message delivered," she said, turning to walk away.

Thankfully he didn't grab onto any of her body parts again. She was 30 years his junior so she was a lot more nimble than he was. If she'd broken into a small jog he would never have been able to catch her, but this time she didn't need to run. She turned back to face him and was met with his evil stare glaring back at her. Aubrey made an "I'll call you," hand gesture, putting his hand against his ear and then climbed into his car. Lerato exhaled loudly, realising that she'd been holding her breath all along, and ran into the safety of her office building.

Seputla walked an elderly lady towards the door of the gym.

"Interesting session," she said, breathless.

"Always good to keep your heart rate up, Gogo," Seputla smiled.

"Indeed," she replied, turning to leave. "See you again next week – same time, same place."

"Bye, Gogo." Despite his attempts to remain professional and helpful in every way with all his clients, Seputla was super stressed. His financial situation didn't help either. He had hoped that by moving in with Lerato his money pressures would've been alleviated, but they hadn't. He'd been able to catch up on his debts, but he still had to pay his university fees and monthly car instalments.

Getting more clients at the gym hadn't helped much either. Everything was constantly going up and working late just meant that he was exhausted and often passed out while studying. He didn't know how much he longer he could take. But in order to move up in the world he had to study, so he couldn't drop the ball. Seputla wanted a better life for him and Lerato, and he was willing to do whatever it took to get it.

As he walked back into the gym, Lisa called out to him from behind the receptionist's desk. "Hey, Seputla," she smiled, standing up so he could have a full view of her.

"Hey, Lisa," Seputla sighed.

"You look exhausted. Your new girlfriend keeping you up at night?"

Seputla was annoyed but didn't let it show. "She's doing everything she can to keep me happy."

Lisa maintained a poker face. "Does that include last Saturday?" she asked innocently.

"Last Saturday? What are you talking about?"

"I bumped into her in Sandton. At Pierre's. Didn't she tell you?" Lisa asked, batting her eyelashes.

Seputla's fists clenched as he thought back to Saturday night. That was the night Lerato had said she'd been out with Maki and Tebogo. But she hadn't mentioned Sandton – she'd said they were at the actor's house party in Parkhurst. Despite his concerns, Seputla planted a smile on his face. He knew Lisa wanted him. Suddenly he had a flashback to a night the previous year when she had lured him into the ladies' toilet and they'd had a quickie. The receptionist was smiling sweetly at him, but he saw right through her.

Nice try, Lisa, he thought. Ignoring her, he turned and walked away.

Maki sat anxiously in front of her laptop. She'd managed to read all the material that Mpho from *Kas'lethu* had sent her, all the scripts – and there were a lot – and the scenes that she would have to write the dialogue for. She was nervous; she had never written for TV before, but she wanted it so badly. There was still another day before the deadline on her test scripts, but since she'd done all the reading and the information was still fresh in her mind, she bit the bullet and began to type.

Eight hours later Maki was pacing her living room floor. It had been difficult for her to send her scripts but she knew that if she hadn't sent them she would have been up all night agonising over them, and too much finessing could lead to destruction. It wasn't like she would've been able to sleep anyway. The young writer looked at her scripts again. They seemed damn near perfect to her, but she didn't know exactly what Mpho would be looking for. After about an hour of re-reading them she got into bed and turned off the light, but instead of sleeping, she tossed and turned all night.

Tebogo was in bed, but she wasn't sleeping either; she was sitting up with her phone in her hand, and her mind racing with thoughts of the actor. Perhaps the realisation that her engagement ring wasn't for show had made him decide not to speak to her again. Maybe he felt that she'd led him on. But what was she supposed to do? She'd enjoyed his company. She ran through the memories of his party on Saturday night and tried to see if she'd done anything wrong, and was hit with the sinking feeling that perhaps she should have told him from the outset that she was engaged. But wouldn't that have been strange since they were just hanging out?

She clutched her phone tighter. *Maybe I should send him a message on Facebook like Maki did with Tumelo*, she thought. She logged into her Facebook account and searched for him, but what came up wasn't his personal page, but a fan page instead. The actor had 200 000 followers! His popularity hit her like a ton of bricks. Would she disappear into the sea of followers if she liked his page? Would he even notice? Would it bother him? She remembered that Lerato had told Maki that sending Tumelo a message via Facebook had smacked of desperation, so she fought off the need to send him a private message and put her phone on the side table as Tshepo walked in, eyeing her suspiciously.

"Who are you talking to?" he asked.

"No one," she replied, sinking deep under the covers.

Tebza was well aware that Tshepo knew that Lerato would tell her about him barging into her house in the middle of the night, and she also knew that if she raised the issue he would interrogate her to the point where she implicated herself in something that she hadn't even done. She'd been with Tshepo long enough to know his calculated strategies, so she turned off her side lamp and said good night. *I should probably tell him all about the actor and I so he can feel more threatened,* she thought spitefully, but despite the elephant in the room she closed her eyes and pretended to fall asleep.

Tshepo was livid. Tebogo was getting cocky. He'd last seen this side of her about six years before when they'd graduated from university and had spoken about their plans for the future. She was wet behind the ears and excited about her career prospects, and he had been as scared to lose her then as he was now. That was why he'd suggested they move in together. Luckily, she'd agreed, just like she'd agreed to the engagement. He'd never had to compete with anyone before for her affections, let alone an actor!

He was exasperated; he would have to up his game, and maybe take Tebogo out for a spa day or something to remind her of how romantic he could be. When Tebogo had stopped complaining about the lack of romance in their relationship he thought she'd come to terms with the fact that he wasn't the romantic type. Tshepo thought that she had finally accepted him for who and what he was – a simple Tswana man who wanted a quiet woman who would come home to cook for him every night. Eyeing her as she lay still in the bed, knowing that she was pretending to be asleep, he got into bed next to her and switched off the light. He too battled to sleep and tossed and turned all night as he had nightmare after nightmare about Tebogo and the actor living happily ever after.

Maki woke up in the middle of the night in a cold sweat, gasping for air. She'd felt as if something was choking her in her sleep. Turning on her side lamp, she looked around her room. When she realised that there was no one else in the room she laid her head back on her pillow but didn't turn off the light.

Unable to relax, Maki took her phone off the side table to look at the time and was shocked when she saw an email notification from Michal. She bolted upright, her hand shaking as she opened her email app on her phone. But the network signal was weak and her emails were taking forever to load. Gripped with anxiety, her mind ran with all sorts of situations. Had she done such a terrible job that Michal hadn't been able to sleep and had to email her to tell her how crap her scripts were? But surely if her scripts were that bad Michal would've just told Mpho to let Maki know, in a polite "don't call us, we'll call you" type of way? And why would she email her in the middle of the night?

Finally the emails finished loading and Maki opened the letter from Michal. There wasn't much to it, just a request to meet with her the next day to discuss her test scripts. Maki swallowed nervously and realised that her nightie was soaked with sweat. As she took it off and put on a T-shirt, she shook off the anxiety of how her meeting with Michal would go, switched off the light, laid her head back down on the pillow and prayed for sleep so that when she met Michal at noon later that day she wouldn't have bags under her eyes.

Lerato was sound asleep but woke up with a jolt when her phone vibrated under her pillow. She put it on silent and looked over at Seputla who was still sound asleep, then she took her phone and tiptoed silently to the adjoining bathroom.

After Lerato left their bed Seputla opened his eyes; he'd heard Lerato's phone vibrate. He hadn't been able to sleep anyway, as seeds of uncertainty had been sprouting since his conversation with Lisa that morning. As he watched her sneak off to the bathroom, it struck him that she'd never received messages in the middle of the night before, and that she usually slept with her phone on the table next to her, not underneath her pillow. Although evidence was beginning to pile up against Lerato, Seputla knew that he'd have to have concrete facts before confronting her.

In the bathroom Lerato sat on the toilet seat and quickly opened her messages folder where she was confronted with a picture of herself in a bikini on Aubrey's yacht at Hartebeespoort. The picture was accompanied by a message: "Remember what I did to you when I took this bikini off?"

Shivers ran down her spine, and without thinking she hurriedly typed, "Leave me alone!"

Her phone vibrated almost instantly with another message: "Glad to see you're not ignoring me anymore."

With that Lerato deleted the latest message from Aubrey and all the messages that he'd ever sent her, and changed his name in her contact list from Bra Aubs to Stalker. She stood and faced herself in the mirror; the fear in her eyes was unmistakeable. She needed to deal with Bra Aubrey and fast; he was getting way too bold again. Lerato sprayed herself with cold water and dabbed her face with a face cloth, all the while breathing in and out to calm her nerves. Then, convinced that she was calm, she quietly turned the doorknob and crept back into the bedroom, slipping into bed and putting her arms around Seputla's warm body.

"Mm," he mumbled sleepily, and as she kissed his back affectionately, she reminded herself of all the reasons why she was with him.

***

Maki didn't know how she'd made it across town to Michal's office without getting into a car accident. When she dragged herself out of bed that morning she had a strong cup of black coffee. She'd hardly slept, and despite trying her best to ignore them, the bags under her eyes were not going away. Then, when she'd realised that the coffee was just making her jittery, Maki had opted for tea instead. She never drank the stuff, but Lerato swore by it and had bought her an assortment of teas. When she'd opened her tea tray to take out a teabag, Maki had been overwhelmed. There was ginger and honey, chamomile, liquorice and mint, green tea and mint, mint and lemon, ginger and lemon, and strawberry and raspberry. Strawberry and raspberry had sounded the least detestable, so she'd chosen that one.

To her credit, Lerato had been right. Maki's nerves had been somewhat soothed, and Maki had chuckled that with the choice of men Lerato had dated she would need tons of tea to calm her nerves.

As midday approached Maki's nerves had started to build up again. She would have had another cup of tea but the last thing she wanted was to have to ask Michal to use the toilet in the middle of their meeting, so she'd rushed out of the apartment an hour before she was due to meet with Michal.

Maki signed her name on the clipboard that the security guard gave her and drove into the parking lot of Michal's production company that produced *Kas'lethu*. She looked around in awe as she stepped out of the car. Maki was wearing a knee-length dark blue skirt with kitten heels and a formal white shirt. She had copied Lerato and Tebza's style of work dress, figuring that if it worked for them it would work for her too, but she was very uncomfortable. Maki hadn't worn heels since her graduation and struggled to walk in them, despite the fact that the heel couldn't have been more than two inches high, but she walked to Michal's office as confidently as she could.

Maki was met with a bright-eyed girl sitting behind the receptionist's desk who introduced herself as Phumz, and Maki extended her hand to Phumz's and informed her that she was there to see Michal. Smiling, Phumz pointed to a sofa where Maki could sit and wait.

"Thulz," Phumz said into her phone, "I've got a..." she stalled, and Maki looked up to see Phumz looking at her expectantly. "Maki," she quickly said, and the receptionist said into the phone's receiver, "Maki. She's here to see Michal."

Maki made the most of the moment by looking around the reception area. Huge posters of the cast of *Kas'lethu* adorned the walls and she smiled when her eyes landed on a poster of the actor.

"Everyone loves the actor," Phumz said from behind her desk. Maki was slightly embarrassed that she'd been caught smiling at his picture. She wanted to explain but thought twice about it, as she was sure that Phumz might think that she was making up a story.

"Michal's just stepped into a meeting with the writers but she should be done shortly," Phumz informed her.

"Thank you," Maki smiled. She checked her watch. She was ten minutes early anyway, so she would use the time to imagine herself as Michal, and ask herself the type of questions that Michal might ask her.

Forty-five minutes later Maki was still waiting. She needed the bathroom and she agonised about whether she should go or not. What if Michal called Phumz and told her that she was ready to meet with her while she was in the toilet? Then again, what if she didn't go and struggled to hold it in during her meeting with Michal? The former was a better scenario, so she got up and approached the receptionist. She got a glimpse of Phumz's computer screen and was sure that she saw her quickly minimise a game of Spider Solitaire.

"Hey, Phumz, is it okay if I use the bathroom?"

"Of course," the receptionist replied. "First door on your left down the corridor."

"Thanks," Maki said, practically running in the direction Phumz had indicated. *This will have to be the quickest trip to the bathroom ever known to mankind,* she thought.

Maki emerged from the bathroom and caught Phumz looking at her apologetically.

"What?" she asked, panicked.

"Thulz just called. Michal was ready to see you but when I told Thulz that you'd quickly slipped off to the bathroom, she relayed the message to Michal who told her that she couldn't wait and went to meet with the editors."

Maki's heart literally dropped. Her mouth went dry and tears sprang to her eyes. Had she wasted an opportunity and waited to meet with Michal for an hour for nothing? As if reading her thoughts, Phumz quickly added, "She said she'll be done with the editors in ten minutes tops and asked if you wouldn't mind waiting?"

Maki could have kissed her. Involuntarily, she began to laugh. "Of course I don't mind waiting," she practically exclaimed. *I'd wait all night if I had to,* she thought, as she sat back down on the same spot on the couch which was still warm from earlier.

Half an hour later Maki had exhausted all the possible scenarios of how her meeting with Michal would go. She stifled a yawn and remembered that she'd barely slept. Just then the receptionist's phone rang. She heard Phumz say, "Yes, Thulz?" and a moment later Phumz told Maki that Michal was ready to see her.

Now? Maki thought as she broke out in a cold sweat. She wasn't ready! But she had no choice but to follow Thulz who had come downstairs to escort the aspiring writer up to Michal's office.

Lerato was eating a pepper steak pie at her desk when her phone beeped. She wiped her hands and unlocked her phone, panicking for a second when she saw that the message was from "Stalker". For a moment she wondered who was stalking her, then she remembered saving Aubrey's name as "Stalker" in the middle of the night. She read the message. Aubrey was inviting her for dinner that evening.

"No thanks," she typed back.

"Aren't you tired of playing wifey to a man who doesn't even appreciate you?"

"What are you talking about?" she retorted, annoyed. He responded that he knew she was always home alone at night, waiting for her man to get back from work. Lerato's breath caught in her throat. How the hell had he known that?

She quickly dialled his number. "I told you to leave me the hell alone!" she barked.

"I always get what I want," he replied, eerily calm.

"You're married," she said, changing tack.

"That would be a fun fact for your man to know, don't you think?" Aubrey threatened.

Lerato called his bluff. "You know nothing about me and my man!"

"Is that right?" he chuckled. "I reckon Seputla would love to know all about your sordid past."

Hearing Aubrey say Seputla's name caused the young woman to freeze. Icy shivers ran down her spine. "What do you want?" she whispered, petrified.

"You," Bra Aubs replied. "But for now I'll take dinner tonight."

Maki had finally made it into Michal's office but she still sat in there alone, waiting. She tapped her foot anxiously as she waited, and was grateful when Thulz walked in with a bottle of water for her. Her mouth had gone completely dry and her stomach growled in hunger. Maki cursed her stomach for its inappropriate timing.

A moment later Michal walked in and closed the door behind her. She was a lot more beautiful than Maki remembered, and her black hair contrasted with her green eyes, causing them to be much more striking in the light of day.

"So sorry to keep you waiting, doll," she apologised as she sat down at her desk, grabbing an apple out of her fruit tray and biting into it.

"No problem," Maki replied meekly.

"I have had quite the morning," Michal said. Maki felt as though the producer's green eyes were boring into her soul. For a moment she thought about bringing up the actor's party on Saturday night, but then decided against it. She would only say something if Michal spoke about it, and luckily she didn't.

"I read your submission," Michal began. Maki licked her bottom lip anxiously. "I must say, it wasn't as refined as I'd expect a junior writer's script to be, but it had something – a rawness that only a beginner writer could possess."

Maki felt as if Michal's words were swirling around her and she tried to make sense of them. Did she like the test script or not?

"Ordinarily I wouldn't have given a submission like this more thought," Michal continued. "And Rian didn't want me to either—"

"Rian?" Maki interrupted.

"My script editor. I met with him before I met with you, and with the amount of convincing that I had to do, you would have thought that it was up to him to hire you."

Maki was stuck on Michal's last two words. "Hire me?" she gasped.

"Rian would have to train you," Michal continued, "but you're someone I'm willing to take a chance on. Of course Rian would rather be on his yacht in the south of France than training a junior writer. He seems to think holidaying is part of his job description and not training young writers!"

Maki was still confused. "You're hiring me?" she asked, breathless.

"Of course," Michal replied enthusiastically. "I couldn't let Monica get away with bragging about her Sipho, so I'm going to hire you and get Rian to whip you into the best soapie writer this country has ever seen!"

Maki fought the feeling to leap across the table and kiss the producer. "Thank you," she squealed.

"No problem," Michal smiled, tilting back in her chair and studying Maki. "It's just that attitude that's lacking in the industry today. Gratitude. Manners. These days people are so entitled you'd think that their mothers owned their entire industry."

Maki chuckled.

"But to be a good writer you need to have tons of life experience," Michal said, leaning towards the younger woman. "Live!" she belted out, causing Maki to jump from her seat. "Explore! Travel! Initiate sex! Have sex in public! Get arrested! Live!"

Maki was shaken. How would she write for a soapie from behind bars?

"And while you're doing that, come back tomorrow to sign your contract; Mpho will have it ready. Your first writer's meeting will be this Friday morning," Michal instructed. "You do get up before noon, right? I know you journo types."

"Of course," Maki said quickly. She'd been trying to hold onto Michal's every word.

Michal stood and Maki did the same; she assumed the meeting was over.

"Don't forget to come back tomorrow to sign your contract," Michal said, shaking Maki's hand.

"C-c-contract?" Maki stammered.

Michal laughed. "Yes, tomorrow. Mpho will have it ready for you then," she confirmed, ushering Maki out of her office.

Maki effusively thanked Michal for the job and said goodbye. She was thrilled – and still in shock – but the sense of elation that she'd earlier felt was quickly replaced by exhaustion. She remembered that she'd barely slept the night before and had not only woken up before noon, but had left the house before midday too.

That evening Lerato stepped into the dimly lit restaurant and spotted Aubrey in the corner. He was disappointed to see that she hadn't dressed up for him the way that she had for Manur, and his mood didn't improve when she sat down and immediately told him that she was merely there to tell him in person to leave her the hell alone.

Despite his irritation Bra Aubs smiled as a waitress appeared and filled Lerato's glass with champagne. "You know you can't resist the good life, Rato," he snarled. "You were born for it."

Lerato sank into her seat and sipped her champagne. It was hard to argue with him when there was a bottle of champagne chilling next to her. A moment later, a seafood platter was placed on the table and she cursed herself for salivating. She eyed Bra Aubs, a small smile on her lips as she doused the mussels in hot sauce. He was going on about some or other exotic location he wanted to take her to and was promising to eat sushi off her naked body; but she just stuffed oysters into her mouth.

The older man eyed Lerato lasciviously; she was eating the seafood but its effects seemed to be manifesting on him. When she was done eating and had finished her champagne, she got up while he was mid-conversation. The young woman wobbled a bit on her feet and realised that she was a bit tipsy, but she kissed him on the cheek and bade him good night before walking to the door without a backward glance. She knew that he wouldn't dare go after her in public, so she was safe. Once she was outside Lerato took out her phone to order an Uber, and to tell Seputla that she was on her way home.

Seputla stewed angrily. He'd come home early to speak to Lerato and was surprised to find that she wasn't there. But unlike Tshepo, he wouldn't be hounding Tebogo or Maki to ask about Lerato's whereabouts. He couldn't sit still; he had to search for clues. When he opened her wardrobe all he came across were her expensive clothes, shoes, handbags and sunglasses.

No doubt bought for her by her sugar daddies, he thought angrily.

He wasn't naive – he'd known the type of life that women like Lerato lived. But he'd still allowed himself to fall in love with her, despite knowing full well that he couldn't afford that life and that someday the past was bound to come knocking. If his instincts were anything to go by, today was that day. He'd really hoped that they had built a strong enough bond between them that Lerato would be able to tell him when that happened, but it seemed he was wrong.

Lerato got out of the Uber and walked slightly unsteadily to the door. She was about to put the key in the lock when her phone beeped with a message from "Stalker": I'm willing to be patient to get what I want. In Lerato's tipsy state she didn't care – Bra Aubs aka Stalker was the least of her concerns right now. She'd had a platter of mussels and oysters and was ready to jump Seputla's bones.

"Baby," she called, as she opened the door but she was met with silence.

"Baby?" she called again. When she walked into the living room she found Seputla watching TV. "Hey, baby," she said, licking her lips seductively.

He barely looked at her. "Where were you?"

"Out," she smiled, straddling him and kissing his neck.

"With who?" he asked, pulling back from her and eyeing her, straight-faced.

"Does it matter?" Lerato put a finger on his lips to silence him as she got off the couch. "One second," she said, disappearing into the bedroom. Lerato reappeared a moment later draped in a sexy lingerie. She straddled Seputla's lap, burying her face in his neck but he didn't respond at all.

"Baby, what's wrong?" she asked, sensing that something was off.

Seputla seemed disgusted by her. Shoving Lerato off him, he reached for the remote, changed the channel and fixed his steely gaze on the TV. Her stomach plummeted, her suspicions aroused.

Is he onto me? Lerato wondered, alarmed.

Chapter 9

Maki woke up at the crack of dawn feeling more rested than she had in a long time. Then her meeting with Michal came back to her. *Was I dreaming?* Trust her to have a life changing meeting then think that she had dreamt it all up. Just to be sure, she reached for her cellphone and scrolled through her emails. Nope, there it was. Michal's 2.30am email requesting to meet with her the day before.

She threw the duvet cover aside and screamed excitedly. As she jumped on top of the bed she also remembered that Michal had said something about meeting with Mpho to sign her contract. She quickly grabbed her cellphone again and sent Mpho an email, asking her what time would be good to meet with her to sign the contract. Proud of herself because she seemed to be acing this "waking up before noon" thing, she jumped into the shower in case Mpho wanted to meet with her first thing in the morning.

When she stepped out of the shower she checked her emails. Mpho hadn't replied yet which gave her enough time for a cup of coffee. Around 9am Mpho finally emailed back, saying that Maki could come to the office at 1pm. Glum, Maki realised that she could've still been in bed, but she made the most of the opportunity and watched the news. She hadn't watched the news channel since banning it from her TV after discovering that the news exacerbated her depression. She'd taken the decision one night after she'd cried her eyes out and had an overwhelming sense of helplessness and sorrow that she felt was one of her depression triggers. But this morning with her happiness at an all-time high, Maki was relieved to realise that she could actually watch the news bulletin and not feel an overpowering sense of despair.

As Lerato stepped out of the shower she wrapped a towel around her. For the first time in months she wasn't met with the pleasant aroma of coffee. She would have to be woman enough to confront Seputla about whatever it was that was bothering him. But as she stepped out of the bathroom and called his name, it hit her that for the first time since they'd dated, he'd not only *not* made her coffee, but he'd also left for work without kissing her goodbye.

Tebogo and Tshepo sat in the car in stone cold silence. "We have to talk to each other at some point," Tebogo said, turning to Tshepo.

"What about?" Tshepo asked, not taking his eyes off the road.

"Anything," Tebogo squealed. "This silence is driving me crazy."

"Well, since you brought it up, I've been wondering when you want to talk about our wedding. Most bride-to-be's start planning their weddings as soon as they get engaged, but you haven't said more than two words about it."

He finally turned to look at her and Tebogo's face fell with the realisation that he was right. "I was just waiting for you to tell me when you'd send your uncles to my mother's house," she replied, quickly thinking on her feet.

"Save it, Tebogo," Tshepo replied drily. "What you should really be thinking about is whether you want to marry me or not."

Tebogo's chest heaved. Despite her recent behaviour, she didn't know if she could live without Tshepo. He was like her favourite pair of old slippers – soft and comfortable. And now that he'd thrown their future in her face, she was filled with a sense of dread and regret at what she had done.

When Maki drove into the parking lot she was a lot less nervous than she'd been the previous day. She even greeted the security guard and struck up conversation with him in her broken Zulu as she signed her name on the clipboard that he had handed her. At the reception desk she greeted Phumz warmly, and asked her to let Mpho know that she was there. Phumz had heard the good news and congratulated Maki on her appointment. The young writer couldn't help but beam proudly.

Soon afterwards Mpho arrived, formally introduced herself and asked Maki to follow her up the stairs to her office. Maki was struck by how beautiful Mpho was, and she wondered fleetingly if Tumelo had slept with her too, but she quickly discarded that thought. When they got to Mpho's office, the manager of the script department invited Maki to sit and told her all about the writing department. She mentioned that Maki would have an opportunity to meet the other writers that Friday in their weekly meeting which ran from 9am to 5pm.

With the contract signed, Mpho offered to take Maki around the office. First Mpho showed Maki to the director's room where she introduced her to the directors – Seretse, Lungi and Wandi. Maki noticed that Mpho called Lungi and Wandi "Lungz" and "Wandz", and it occurred to her that yesterday she'd met Phumz and Thulz.

"Funny how a lot of names around here end in a z," she joked. Without batting an eyelid, Mpho replied that it was practically office policy. Maki thought that she was joking, but when she turned to Mpho she realised that the other woman wasn't amused.

"So how come yours doesn't end with a z?"

"I simply refused to be called Mphz."

Maki laughed out loud at that; she liked this Mpho chick and, even more importantly, she felt comfortable around her in this new territory. Next, Mpho took Maki to the wardrobe department where she met Melz and Kelz, then to the art department where she met Lebz and Sanz, and finally to the editing suites where she met Thapz and Julz. Finally Mpho indicated that the tour was over, and reminded Maki about her Friday meeting. As Maki walked away, she pondered whether she would like being known as Makz and thought delighted, that it had a nice ring to it.

It started to rain just after she got home. Safely warm inside, she excitedly called Tumelo to tell him her good news, but he didn't answer his phone.

"Hey, just called to let you know that I got the job at *Kas'lethu*," she said in her voice message. "Remember how you introduced me to Michal at the actor's party? Well, I met with her yesterday and she offered me a job, so I wanted to invite you to dinner to thank you. My treat."

Content, Maki lit candles and ran herself a bath. An hour later Tumelo called and suggested that they do dinner at her place instead of going out. Maki eagerly agreed, and half an hour later he arrived at her door with pizza and a bottle of wine. The young woman chatted effortlessly as she poured them each a glass of wine, but noticed that Tumelo seemed distant and that he checked his phone a lot. Shaking off her irritation, Maki warmed up the pizza and handed him a glass of wine. Eventually when Tumelo checked his phone for the third time Maki asked if she was keeping him from something or someone more important than her.

Suddenly Tumelo began to badmouth the actor. Shocked, Maki defended the actor, and asked Tumelo how he could badmouth his friend. Tumelo yelled that the actor wasn't his friend and he hoped that Maki was happy now that she'd got what she'd wanted. Maki was completely thrown by Tumelo's outburst. As she studied him, she remembered what Lerato had said about him being an F boy. Even though she'd only heard the term recently, it was now clear to her exactly what Lerato had meant and what Tumelo was doing, so she called him out on it.

"So you only hang out with the actor to get chicks?" she asked calmly. As soon as she'd said the words Maki saw the colour drain from his face. Obviously what she'd said was true, and it seemed like Tumelo wasn't used to being called out on his behaviour.

"Um," he stammered in an attempt to respond.

"You're so fake," Maki blasted him. "I don't know if I need to remind you that I met you and went to dinner with you before I even knew that you are the actor's friend, so I didn't use you."

"Maki, I think you've got the wrong impression about me," Tumelo started to explain, but Maki held up a finger to silence him. "I'm not done," Maki quipped. "I didn't need to meet the actor to sleep with you! I slept with you because I wanted to, but now that we're done here, you may leave."

Tumelo was floored and tried to defend himself, but Maki wasn't having any of it; she stood up and opened the door for him to leave. Sheepishly he stood up and walked out of her flat, with nothing more to say for himself.

After Maki closed the door behind him, she realised that Tumelo had left the wine and the pizza. *Score!* she thought, drinking pointedly from the bottle.

While Tebogo was busy packing up her laptop getting ready to go home, Tshepo called her to say that he would be going out that evening, so he wouldn't be able to pick her up from work. Tebogo didn't know what to say. He was the one who had insisted on chauffeuring her to and from work in the first place, and now in typical Tshepo style he was going back on his word. Annoyed, she ordered an Uber, but when she started to type in the address of where she was going, she couldn't bring herself to type in her home address; instead she typed in "Parkhurst".

All the way to Parkhurst Tebogo felt like her stomach was filled with restless butterflies. She wanted to change her mind and tell the driver to take her home to Fourways despite the extra charges she would have to pay, but every time she tried to do that the words wouldn't leave her mouth. Besides, that morning on the way to work Tshepo had pretty much given her an ultimatum, and she knew that his sudden after work plans had to do with what they'd spoken about. She also knew that she had to see the actor again to know if the connection they'd had was real.

When the Uber approached Parkhurst the driver looked at her in the rear view mirror and asked where exactly to drop her off. Tebogo had no clue what the actor's exact home address was, and there was no way she'd call Maki to find out, so she asked him to take her to a coffee shop where she would devise a plan and beg her memory to return to her. Having ordered a cafe latte Tebogo began to feel very stupid for going all the way to Parkhurst without knowing exactly where she was going, but she decided to enjoy her coffee anyway before booking another Uber to take her home. As she called the waiter to ask for the bill, her phone rang – it was a number she didn't recognise. Despondent, she answered, and was shocked when she heard the actor's voice.

"Do you make a habit of going to coffee shops in your friend's neighbourhood?"

Tebogo looked around. Clearly the actor had spotted her. Her stomach flipped when she saw him seated in the corner of the coffee shop, his laptop open in front of him. She couldn't help but smile as she spoke into the phone.

"And do you often let beautiful ladies drink coffee on their own without inviting them to join you?"

He smiled back. Tebogo hung up and floated towards the actor, who stood and gave her a warm embrace.

"I thought I'd never see you again," he confessed. "I didn't contact you because I couldn't bring myself to accept just being your friend. I want more."

Tebogo blushed. "I haven't been able to stop thinking about you either, and today, instead of going home, I came to Parkhurst to look for you. It sounds silly, I know. Plus, I would have liked your Facebook page but I didn't want you to think of me as a groupie."

The actor laughed out loud. "I wouldn't have known either way – my manager handles my Facebook page. I'm more of a Twitter guy." The actor took Tebogo's hands in his. "And I'm glad you came to look for me."

Tebogo blushed again for the second time in five minutes. As the actor packed away his laptop, he invited Tebza to his house for a sundowner. She smiled and immediately cancelled her Uber.

They barely made it through the door without keeping their hands off each other. Tebza and the actor hungrily searched each other's bodies with their lips, making love like two souls that had finally found each other and connected as one. Tebogo could not remember a time when she felt more adored, as the actor was a thoughtful and attentive lover. As they climaxed together, she felt a strong sense of home.

After they made love the actor turned over on his side to roll a joint and Tebogo wrapped herself in the sheet, watching him.

"You look beautiful," he smiled.

As they smoked, Tebogo opened up to the actor, telling him that her dreams lay dormant because of her need to appease her mother by becoming a lawyer.

"I really admire you for following your dream of becoming an actor," she commented.

But the actor shocked her by revealing that acting hadn't really been a dream of his, and that writing was. That was actually what he'd been doing when he saw her in the coffee shop earlier – working on his script for a feature film.

Tebogo gasped and told him that Maki was a writer, and that she admired all artists for being able to follow their dreams. Taking a long drag on the joint, the actor studied Tebogo.

"And what do you want to do with your life? What's your dream?"

"Make-up artist and nail technician," Tebza replied shyly.

The actor smiled. It was the first time that Tebogo had ever voiced her dreams to anyone, and she hung onto his every word when he told her that she could do it, and that he believed in her.

Not in a rush to go back home, Tebza decided to raid the actor's fridge and make them something to eat. The actor went to put on some music, while Tebogo chopped up a green pepper with the sounds of Thandiswa Mazwai floating through the air.

The actor walked back into the kitchen and put his arms around her waist. "Seeing you here is definitely something I can get used to."

Tebogo melted at the warmth of the actor's embrace and turned to kiss him passionately.

"Let's watch a movie."

"Sounds great," Tebogo beamed. "I can't remember the last time I watched a movie. Tshepo is more into series."

The air became thick with tension as soon as she said Tshepo's name. Tebogo froze and eyed the actor who was clearly gutted. He walked silently back to the lounge. Tebza could not face him, so she hid away in the kitchen using cooking for them as an excuse, but could no longer hide when she had to walk into the lounge to announce that dinner was ready. When the actor didn't respond, she took in his assortment of CDs.

"Great collection," she mused, attempting to defuse the situation.

"Music is the one thing that always meets me at my point of need," the actor said melancholically.

Tebogo noticed that the actor seemed to have withdrawn from her, so she left to go and dish up for them. When she walked back into the lounge with their food, the actor had switched off the music, and put on a movie. Whilst Tebogo and the actor ate, watching the film in silence, she silently cursed herself for bringing up Tshepo's name and ruining the mood.

At the end of the night she called an Uber and to her disappointment, he didn't object to her leaving although she was hoping he would. Meekly, she bade him farewell and with a long, lazy hug, he said goodbye.

Tebogo's soul felt crushed and her knees almost buckled as she walked away from him, because she felt like a part of her had been taken away. What she didn't know was that he felt the exact same way.

Upset that the one woman he'd be willing to give his heart to belonged to someone else, the actor loudly played Gqom music in an attempt to wash out the memory of Tebogo and the ache in his heart. She belonged to someone else, and it was very clear who she wanted to be with, judging by her decision to go back to her fiancé that night.

**

At 8:45 on Friday morning Maki entered a world that was previously unknown to her. Two middle-aged white men and a younger coloured guy were seated around the table, and when she walked into the writer's boardroom, their conversation came to an abrupt halt. The men immediately introduced themselves and Maki was happy to discover that one of them was Rian, the script editor who would be training her. The other two were Greg and Mark. In an effort to ease the tension, she jokingly asked Greg if his nickname was Gregz, but he stared at her blankly, and Rian explained that the writing department was very different to the rest of the office.

Clearly, Maki thought, as she poured herself a cup of coffee, grateful for it because she hadn't had a cup before she'd left her house. A few more people walked in, and Maki was surprised to see that Mpho wasn't among them. She casually asked about this, and Greg replied that Mpho didn't attend writer's meetings. Maki thought that was strange since she held the title of Script Manager. It felt to Maki like Greg had been attempting to minimise Mpho's role.

The room settled down as everybody took their seats and Mark chaired the meeting. Ten minutes into the meeting a young man walked in, but nobody seemed perturbed that he was late, which struck Maki as odd. The man sat down and Mark introduced him to Maki as Sechaba – the cultural consultant.

To her chagrin, Rian made a joke that there had probably been a taxi strike, which would explain Sechaba's late arrival. Maki squirmed on his behalf and looked across the table at him, attempting to make eye contact to assure him that she was a "sistah" and had his back. But Sechaba didn't even bother to look at Maki as he busied himself with digging in his bag for a pen.

Lerato had happily agreed when Seputla told her that he'd be inviting his friends over to watch the soccer game, firstly because she'd never met any of his friends, and secondly because she hoped that having other people in their home would ease the tension between them. Neither of them had raised the issue in days. But when she arrived back home with ribs, wings and beers for Seputla and his friends, she was shocked to see the other guys leaving as she walked in, and Seputla staring at her with a murderous look in his eye.

"Baby? What's wrong?" she asked hurriedly.

To her shock, he threw her phone at her.

"Who the hell is Manur?" he yelled, his angry stare never leaving her face.

Lerato was struck by confusion, but then it clicked. "Are you going through my phone?" she barked accusingly.

"You've been getting texts all day," Seputla defended.

"That gives you no right to go through my phone," she spat back. "And if you must know, he's an Arabian sheik who's pursuing me."

"A what?" Seputla asked.

Lerato rolled her eyes. The man didn't even know what a sheik was. You would think that for the copious amount of time he spent studying, he would actually be learning something.

"Do you even know where Dubai is?" Lerato mumbled under her breath.

"Don't get smart with me," Seputla seethed.

Lerato paused and studied him. Now seemed like as good a time as any to tell him exactly how she felt about his small-mindedness and empty pockets. "Dubai. Do you know where that is?"

"Screw you, Lerato!"

"Oh, that's charming," she smiled. "This is an argument, Seputla – when one person makes a certain argument the other is supposed to make an opposite and stronger statement in contradiction of what the first person stated, not swear at them."

"You learn that from your investment banker sugar daddies?" he sneered.

"No, from Papa Paul," she replied snidely. "He's a judge."

Seputla stormed off to the bedroom and began to throw his stuff into an overnight bag. But arguments had always turned Lerato on, so she gave it her all, not even trying to control the flow of words that spewed out of her mouth.

"Good to finally know what you really think of me. How long have you been pretending to love me, Seputla? Since the day you moved in? Have I always just been a conquest to you? And since you know what it's like to be with me you're going to leave me? Is that what this was all about? Well, no one leaves Lerato Angela Meale, I'll tell you that for free," she chuckled, "since you can't afford anything else anyway."

Seputla took his bag and headed towards the door. Before leaving the room he turned to face Lerato. "Lisa from the gym has been hired by a guy called Aubrey to try break us up. I guess he won." Seputla slammed the door behind him.

"Lisa from the gym?" Lerato mused. Then it came back to her – Lisa was the girl who'd given her the note in the bathroom that night at Pierre's in Sandton. She screamed loudly in frustration to no one in the now abandoned home. Seputla had been onto her all along but had tried to retain their relationship because of his love for her, but like the ultimate self-saboteur that she was, she had messed it up.

Tebza didn't want to go home after work, so she called Maki. Maki didn't answer her phone, but she sent a reply back that she was in a meeting. Tebza was shocked. It was 4.30pm on a Friday – what meeting could Maki possibly be in? Tebza wanted to leave the office, so she asked Maki what time she would be done. When Maki said 5pm, Tebza replied that she was in need of some girl time and would buy them food and meet Maki at her place in about an hour. Maki replied with a thumbs up emoji and Tebogo left the office to head to the convenience store down the road. What she didn't notice was that Tshepo was parked across the road from her workplace, and that he followed her to the convenience store.

When Tebogo emerged soon afterwards with a few packets and got into her car, Tshepo followed her, happy with himself and the plan that he had hatched when he decided to stop picking Tebogo up from work. The first day he stopped fetching her he got home at 9pm, but she arrived back at 10pm. She had barely said two words to him that night; she simply had a shower and went straight into bed. That made him more determined than ever to get answers for himself, so he thought that he should follow her and figured that by doing so, he would gather enough information to be able to confront her. But to his disappointment, it seemed as though Tebogo was driving towards Maki's place, and his heart sank when he saw her drive into Maki's complex. He watched her for a moment then decided to go home, disappointed at his epic fail of catching her in the act with someone else.

When the writer's meeting finally adjourned Maki wanted to speak to Sechaba as she felt like they might've gotten off on the wrong foot, so when he went to the smoker's corner and lit a cigarette, she followed him. "Hey, Sechaba" she said breezily. "The balance of people in that room is a bit off don't you think, considering that the audience is a majority black audience. If you think about it, if the writing room was more balanced, we wouldn't even need a cultural consultant."

But the joke didn't land.

"So you're going to try to convince Michal to hire more black people?" Sechaba asked.

"Why not? Seems like we need it."

"Meaning I'd be out of a job?"

Maki back peddled.

"That's not what I mean," she cried, attempting to rescue the situation, but Sechaba continued to smoke his cigarette and ignore her.

Thankfully her phone beeped, and when she checked the message it was Tebza telling her that she was waiting at Maki's place. Maki had all but forgotten about her plans with Tebogo, but was glad that she had an excuse to leave. She apologised to Sechaba again, who had gone back to not even making eye contact with her, and dashed out as fast as she could.

Lerato bawled her eyes out. She'd never been ruled by her heart or emotions and this was exactly why. She'd only fought with Seputla and hurled all those insults at him because that's all she knew. She'd always had to fight her own battles, and it had gotten her this far. As she scrolled through pictures of them on her phone in happier times, the tears flowed effortlessly down her face, and she wondered why he hadn't fought with her as hard as she had with him.

She was stumped when the realisation finally hit her: it was because he loved her.

Maki had lent Tebogo a pair of tracksuit pants and they were slouched on the couch eating junk food and watching the movie's end credits roll. Maki switched off the TV and turned to Tebogo who intentionally avoided Maki's eye.

"Any particular reason why you won't go home to your fiancé?" she asked.

Tebogo, feeling small, finally met Maki's concerned gaze.

"I slept with the actor," she said, barely audible.

Maki tried to reserve judgement. "And?" she asked.

"I've never felt anything like it."

"You do realise that what you're doing is dangerous, right?" Maki cautioned, but Tebogo avoided Maki's gaze. "Tebogo, you're cheating on the man you're going to spend the rest of your life with. That hardly sounds like the foundation for a good marriage."

Tebogo exhaled deeply, and eventually said, "I know. I'll tell him. I'm just trying to find the strength to do it."

Lerato had no appetite for dinner so she got into her pyjamas and went to bed. A couple of minutes later her phone beeped on the side table and she quickly checked it. Her heart sank when she realised that it wasn't Seputla – it was Stalker Aubrey, but she had no heart to entertain him. She switched off her phone and, imagining her pillow to be Seputla, she hugged it tight and cried herself to sleep.

Tebogo got home after midnight and found Tshepo in bed.

"Hey," she said. "I thought you'd be asleep by now."

"Is that why you came home late?" he asked.

Tebogo knew that there was no time like the present to be honest.

"Yes," she replied. "It's not exactly like this is a happy home."

Although her words struck Tshepo, he couldn't argue because he knew that they were true.

"I know why you insisted on driving me to work and back home," Tebogo continued. "It's not like I haven't given you reason to be insecure. I haven't exactly been behaving like a woman who's about to get married."

Tshepo's ears pricked up. Was she about to confess to her lying and cheating ways?

Tebogo sighed and prepared to explain. "The guy who was supposed to join Maki at our engagement dinner is a film-maker and is friends with an actor from *Kas'lethu*. The night that Maki and I went out we went to his party." She handed him her phone with a Google image of the actor.

Tshepo silently seethed and eyed her phone angrily but didn't take it.

"Did you sleep with him?" he asked bitterly.

"No," Tebogo said shaking her head. She had been as honest with Tshepo as she could manage for the night. One little lie wouldn't hurt.

***

The next morning, Lerato arrived for work sporting huge sunglasses to hide her bloodshot eyes, but as she stepped out of the Uber in the parking lot of her office building she saw Aubrey waiting for her. She had no heart to deal with him. She was tired and had bags under her eyes and Aubrey's ego was the last thing that she wanted to nurse.

"I would've come to your place, but since I don't know where you live..." his voice trailed off.

Lerato stopped and looked him in the eye.

"Happy?" she asked.

"Immensely," he sniggered.

She walked off, but he yelled after her. "I heard your man spent the night at the gym."

Lerato turned to face him sharply. "Don't you ever talk to me about my man again, do you hear me?" she barked.

Aubrey laughed, sinister. "Easy, Lerato, don't forget who you're talking to." Lerato was about to reply that she had no illusions about who he was or what positions of power he held, and that frankly, she didn't care, but just then her stomach heaved violently and she felt like she was about to puke. Scared, she cupped her hand over her mouth and ran into the office building barely making it into the toilet stall before she violently hurled, feeling like she might puke all of her insides out.

When she finally stopped vomiting she stepped woozily out of the stall, leaning on the bathroom counter for support. She splashed her face with water, trying to recollect if she'd eaten anything that might have caused her to feel ill, but all she remembered was crying herself to sleep the previous night. An overpowering sense of missing Seputla hit her. As tears involuntarily formed in her eyes, she splashed water on her face again. A sudden thought struck her, and she studied herself in the mirror. She couldn't be. Could she?

Lerato burst through the door of her apartment. She'd told her boss that she wasn't feeling well and had picked up a pregnancy test on her way home. Anxious, she peed on the stick and waited out the dread-filled two minutes before peering nervously at the stick. Validating her fears, two bold pink stripes confirmed that indeed, she was pregnant.

Chapter 10

. . . .

Lerato paced the reception area of the gym waiting for Seputla. Lisa had sneered at her as she took her time paging Seputla to come to reception, even though Lerato had made it clear to her that it was urgent. Lisa rubbed her up the wrong way, but she had to control her emotions. This was about her and Seputla, not Lisa.

A moment later Seputla appeared and his heart dropped when he saw Lerato. For as long as he'd known her, this was the worst that he'd ever seen her. He fought the urge to run to her and hold her in his arms; his ego simply wouldn't let him.

"Hey," he said, approaching her slowly.

"Hey," she replied, letting out a weak smile. Then, aware of Lisa staring pointedly at them, she asked him if they could speak in private.

"You can speak in private all you want, honey, but I know all about your sorry little life," Lisa laughed.

They both ignored her and Seputla led Lerato outside to the parking lot.

There was a heavy silence between them as they stood face to face. Lerato had never been in this situation before, and although all she had to say was "I'm pregnant", the words refused to pass her lips.

"How've you been?" she asked carefully.

"Don't act like you care," he spat back.

Stung, she added, "I heard you've been living in the gym."

He froze. Lerato immediately realised her mistake.

"Who told you that?" he barked, studying her carefully. "Your sugar daddy, Aubrey?"

"I haven't seen him since you left, I promise," she defended.

"Don't lie to me, Lerato! We both know that I'm not good enough for you, so this really isn't about Aubrey. I love you, but we obviously can't be together! Can't you see that?"

Just then Lisa stepped outside. "Your ten thirty is ready," she called out to Seputla.

With a disgusted look in Lerato's direction, Seputla turned to walk back into the gym with Lisa, but Lerato blurted out, "I'm pregnant!"

Both Seputla and Lisa stopped in their tracks and turned around. Lerato thought that she saw Seputla momentarily melt, but then Lisa yelled, "Are you sure it's not Aubrey's?"

Lerato saw Seputla stiffen again. Despite her earlier efforts to remain calm, she bolted towards Lisa and gave her a whopping hot slap across the face.

"Shut up, you whore!" she barked at her.

"Lerato!" Seputla cried, dragging her out of Lisa's reach, who was about to smack Lerato back.

"You will pay for that, you slut!" Lisa seethed, as she clutched her face.

"Voetsek!" Lerato yelled back. She felt vindicated. That slap was the least that Lisa deserved.

"Are you trying to get me fired?" Seputla yelled, holding Lerato tight by the shoulders.

Then it hit her – she had started a fight with Seputla's colleague at his workplace. If Lisa wanted, she could press charges for assault.

"I'm sorry," she cried, throwing her arms around him.

But he pushed her away. "Go home, Lerato," he said, defeated.

Lerato didn't even try to fight the tears that flowed down her face as she watched the only man she had ever loved walk away from her, knowing that soon she would be the mother of his child.

The following day Lerato, Tebogo and Maki had gathered for lunch and Maki was happily chatting about her new job at *Kas'lethu*. She indulged and revealed all the details of how she'd met Michal and her group of friends at the actor's party, had taken Michal's business card, sent in test scripts and landed the job as junior writer. She squealed in delight, but her news was of no effect. Both her friends were silently drawn to their own lugubrious thoughts.

What else was new? she thought. For once she had good news of her own to share, and her friends were selfishly stuck in their own thoughts instead of sharing in her joy and sense of accomplishment. It was clear to Maki that both Lerato and Tebogo thought that she had no right to be happy when they obviously weren't, so she tried a different tack.

"Have you ever met a group of people who've all been given nicknames that end with a z?" she asked. "I even met a Sanz and Kelz, and their names are Sanelisiwe and Keletso!" she laughed raucously, slapping her thigh in glee. When she still got no response, she added. "I kicked Tumelo to the curb." Still no response. Eventually she hit the table angrily, causing both Lerato and Tebogo to jump. "What's wrong with you two?" she shouted.

Maki was met with even more silence, so she rolled her eyes helplessly and took a long swig of her dry, white wine.

"I told Tshepo about the actor," Tebogo finally whispered.

That got a reaction out of Lerato. She blinked her eyes in disbelief at Tebogo, then sank back into her sadness. "It's about time, babe."

Maki was less supportive. "Did you tell him that you slept with him?"

"Of course not," Tebogo cried. "You both know what Tshepo's like. If I told him that he'd begin a smear campaign against the actor on social media."

"True," Maki sighed. Then she turned to Lerato. "And you? What's with the long face?"

Lerato exhaled, gathering her strength as tears formed in her eyes.

"Babe," Tebogo gushed, concerned. She quickly took Lerato's hand in hers, searching her face for answers, but Maki looked on dispassionately.

"Seputla broke up with me," Lerato sighed.

"What did you think would happen when he found out that you were sleeping with Aubrey?" Maki asked.

"I didn't sleep with Aubrey!" Lerato yelled, defending herself.

"It doesn't matter! You entertained him!" Maki yelled back.

Tebogo shot Maki a look, urging her to have more sympathy, but Maki was angry that she had to downplay her happiness to accommodate their emotions. She sneered as she sipped her wine. "You brought this on yourself."

"And my pregnancy," Lerato whispered, "Did I bring that on myself too?"

Maki froze. An overwhelming sense of regret washed over her.

"Pregnancy?" Tebogo asked, shocked. "Babe, you're pregnant?"

Lerato nodded at Tebogo who wiped away the tears that cascaded down Lerato's face. Then she turned to Maki sharply: "And don't you dare ask me if it's Seputla's or Aubrey's."

Maki immediately felt bad. "I'm sorry," she said sincerely. After a moment of studying Lerato, she added, "Are you happy?"

"How can I be happy when the man I love wants nothing to do with me?" Lerato snapped.

"I wondered why you were having a virgin Mojito," Tebogo joked, attempting to lighten the mood.

"Does he know?" Maki enquired gently.

"I went to the gym to tell him," Lerato said. "Then I got into a fight with Lisa and he chased me away."

"Who's Lisa?" Tebogo asked.

"The receptionist," Lerato said. "And the whore who gave me the note from Aubrey at Pierre's."

Maki gasped. "The 'I want you' note?"

"Bra Aubrey hired her?" Tebogo pressed.

"Yup," Lerato confirmed, sipping her virgin cocktail. "He wanted me back that badly."

"I hope you won't be messing with him again," Tebogo warned, and she was satisfied when Lerato shook her head. "A baby is a blessing," she added with an encouraging smile.

Lerato acknowledged Tebogo's kind words and put her hand over her friend's. She looked into Tebza's eyes gratefully. "Thank you, my friend."

"What are you going to do?" Maki asked gently.

Lerato shrugged. She had absolutely no idea what she was going to do, and she didn't have the strength to think that far ahead either. All she could do was think about the moment that she was in, and in that moment, she had no idea what she would do. Tebogo got up from the table and hugged Lerato, but for some reason, Maki could not bring herself to do the same.

Back from lunch, Tebogo sat at her desk and searched the internet for an apartment. It was clear that she and Tshepo needed space. She'd lived with him for six years and had dated him for eight. What moving out meant for their relationship though, she had no idea. For one thing, she was still wearing her engagement ring, but she'd felt torn ever since he put it on her finger. She looked forlornly at the sparkling gold and diamond band, and thought that hers must have been the most spontaneous proposal ever known to mankind. Proposals were meant to be romantic, not a rushed response made in fear of losing your partner because they told you they were unhappy. She knew what she had to do, but her courage failed her dismally.

Maki sat dejectedly in the writer's room. Despite her initial excitement at finally being part of an actual writer's room on an actual TV soapie, with every meeting that she'd had, she'd felt more incompetent. Her confidence had begun to wane, and she could feel that it was about to slip completely from her grasp. She hadn't received the affirmation that she'd needed to believe that she could actually do this; instead Greg repeatedly made condescending remarks anytime she'd made a contribution to the story.

Rian hadn't yet spoken with her about the training that Michal had said he would provide, and Maki wasn't sure if she should bring that up because at the end of every meeting he was always the first to rush out.

Sechaba was no help either. What was the point of them being the only two comrades in the room if they didn't band together? But Maki knew that other than her high level of melanin, she had no other traits that linked her to being a comrade, let alone an activist. Sechaba probably saw right through her feeble attempts at friendship and loved himself enough to not allow himself to be used by her. He probably hadn't forgiven her for the crass comment that she'd made to him, and probably still thought that Maki wanted an all black writing room, which left no space for him as a cultural consultant.

Maki clicked her tongue, annoyed and lost in her thoughts. Suddenly she saw people in the room standing up, and when Rian dashed out the door she realised that the meeting had adjourned. Despondent, she packed up her laptop bag, but instead of getting into her car and going home, she decided to march to reception instead, and asked Phumz if she could please speak to Michal.

Thulz came down the stairs and warned Maki that Michal hated impromptu meetings, and that she'd told Thulz to let Maki know that she could only spare her a few minutes as she needed to fetch her son Julian from nursery school. As if Maki wasn't scared enough. How would Michal feel that Maki was there to complain about Rian and his lack of commitment to her script training? But scared as she was, Maki had to let Michal know how she felt. She timidly entered Michal's office, and sat across from her at the desk.

"Um," she stammered, barely audible.

"Speak up, darling, I can't make out what you're saying," Michal commanded.

"I'm sorry for asking to meet with you at the last minute, but..."

"I'm here. What is it?" Michal demanded. "Spit it out."

"It's just that," Maki continued softly. "I read my contract and it specified that I'm a junior writer and that I'm to receive training from Rian, the script editor."

"And?" Michal asked, impatient.

"Well, I haven't received any training from him since I've been here," Maki concluded.

Michal sighed and stood up to go. "I'll have a chat with him in the morning."

Maki remained seated.

"Is there anything else?" Michal asked, and Maki hurriedly stood.

"No. Thank you for your time."

"Well, let's go then. Little Julian hates it when his schedule is disrupted. I can't be late picking him up from nursery school."

On the drive home, Maki thought about her two best friends. Maki thought that she had done amazing things with her life lately. For one, she'd seen Tumelo for the fraud that he was and had called him out on it. She deserved kudos for that, surely? Plus she'd realised her dream of getting a full-time writing job on a soapie. It didn't get any better than that, right? Writing for a soapie had been her lifelong dream. But it felt empty. She was consumed by the feeling that even though Lerato and Tebogo had problems in their love lives, at least they *had* love lives! What did she have? A cold apartment that she went home to every night.

Then a barrage of guilt consumed her. She'd been really spiteful to Lerato at lunch. Her heart sank. She ought to check up on her, but she would do so in the morning. For now all she wanted was to curl up in bed and shut her eyes to the loneliness that consumed every fibre of her being.

Seputla stood in Lerato's lounge holding an empty box. "I'm here to get the rest of my stuff," he said, emotionless.

Lerato nodded and sat back on the couch to watch TV. After a while Seputla emerged from the bedroom. The box he held in his hands was filled with his T-shirts, shorts, socks and a headphone set. He sighed as he stood watching her. Then, without a word, he turned to leave.

"You moving in with Lisa?" Lerato asked feebly.

Seputla froze, and slowly turned back around.

"Do you care?"

"I need to know if our child will be visiting you at her place or not."

Seputla put down the box and sat next to Lerato on the couch. He softened. "So we're really going to be parents, huh?" he smiled.

Lerato welcomed his smile. It felt like a long sip of ice cold water on a hot summer's day. "Yeah," she replied, returning his smile warmly.

"How do you want to do this?" he asked.

The question shook her. Wasn't it obvious? "I thought we'd get back together," she whispered.

But Seputla sadly shook his head. "We can't do that," he replied.

Lerato was gutted. "You don't want to get back together for the sake of our baby?"

"Having a baby is not reason enough for us to get back together."

His words swirled around Lerato's head; she was extremely confused.

"I'll be there for you and the baby," he continued, "but I have to move on with my life."

Lerato felt dizzy and grasped onto the couch to steady herself. Her world was literally spinning and falling apart. But Seputla calmly got up, took his box, and left.

Tebogo managed the Joburg traffic like a pro, lost in her thoughts as she drove to the actor's house. Since they had last seen each other, Tebogo had asked the actor to be patient with her as she was still engaged to Tshepo but had feelings for him, so he had invited her over so that they could talk. At least this time he was expecting her. She chuckled again as she thought about how they'd met. Then, out the corner of her eye, she noticed a car in the rear view mirror, three cars away, that she'd spotted about ten minutes ago. Was it following her? She didn't think so, but she couldn't shake the feeling of dread that rose up in her, cautioning her to be careful.

To disguise her actual journey, she turned into a street that led in the opposite direction to the way she needed to go, and noticed that the car she suspected of following her, did the same. She began to freak out, but upon closer inspection recognised the car as Tshepo's, and that he was behind the wheel. "The man is following me!" Tebogo realised in shock. How long had Tshepo been this obsessive person? Had he always been this crazy and she'd just missed the signs?

She realised with a sinking feeling that her plans to visit the actor would have to be derailed. Tshepo would have loved nothing more than for her to lead him to the actor's house where he would confront them both. Knowing him, he would probably record the entire scene and upload it onto social media. "I will not give him the satisfaction," Tebogo told herself, resolute. Annoyed, she stepped on the accelerator and drove home to Fourways.

Tshepo was happy; he was hot on Tebogo's tail. Suddenly he realised that it seemed she had changed direction and was now headed towards Fourways. Had she seen him? Was she onto him? With a smirk he dismissed that thought; Tebogo wasn't that smart. But when he saw her head towards William Nicol Drive, it became clear to him that Tebogo was going home, so he decided to go to the local pub instead where the bartender knew him by name.

***

Michal arrived at her production office early the next morning. She already had a packed day with meeting after meeting scheduled, but she had to meet with Rian before he ruined all her plans regarding Maki. She was happy to see that Phumz had already arrived for work and that Rian was seated in the reception area waiting for her. *I run this place like a well-oiled machine,* she thought contentedly.

Rian followed her up the stairs and into the office, and a moment later Phumz stepped in with a tray of coffee for them – cappuccino for Michal and filter for Rian. Michal noticed disapprovingly that Thulz hadn't even arrived to work yet, and that Phumz was starting to exhibit the skills of a better assistant than Thulz. She smiled thankfully at Phumz, then turned stiffly to Rian.

"What's the matter?" Rian asked, stirring sugar into his coffee.

"Other than the fact that I asked you to train that junior writer, Maki, and you haven't obeyed my instructions?" Michal enquired.

Rian rolled his eyes. "That girl is thicker than a ton of bricks. She has no concept of story, narrative, plot or character!"

"And you are the expert that knows everything, aren't you?" Michal asked sarcastically. "I go to bed at 3.30am every day rewriting the crap that you submit to me as final scripts."

"Maybe if you bothered to show up to a writer's meeting every once in a full moon, you wouldn't have to rewrite the scripts," Rian pointed out.

"And who would run this ship?" Michal barked. "You? We all know you've been vying for my position for years."

Rian shifted nervously in his seat.

"Now that I have your full attention, you will train Maki Dilobetso. Understood?" she instructed.

"Sure," Rian sighed.

Michal smiled. It was clear why she was the boss around here. "And I don't want to hear any more stories of you undermining her. She is Tumelo the filmmaker's girlfriend and I've wanted him to be a part of my team for a long time." She sat back in her chair, satisfied, and sipped her coffee indulgently. "I hope I've made myself clear," she concluded, raising a commanding eyebrow at Rian.

"Crystal." Rian slurped the last of his coffee and stood to leave, defiantly slamming the door behind him.

Of all the apartments that Tebogo had viewed, the one that she was standing in was her favourite. The sun streamed in through the windows and she revelled in the light rays that caressed her skin and warmed her soul.

"I'll take it," she said decisively to the agent, Adrienne, who smiled widely at Tebogo's words.

"Excellent," Adrienne replied, clapping her hands together. She produced a lease agreement from her briefcase for Tebogo to sign, and reminded her client to email through her latest payslip, three months' bank statements and a certified copy of her ID.

"Don't you need my kidney too?" Tebogo joked, as Adrienne locked the door behind her. It seemed Adrienne didn't appreciate Tebogo's humour.

"I know it's excessive," she said, "but it's the law. Once you've been approved you'll need to pay the deposit and the first month's rent upfront."

"Sure," Tebogo agreed, shaking hands with Adrienne and leaving to get into her car.

Tebogo and Maki had agreed to go shopping that afternoon for some baby things for Lerato. They were both consumed by guilt and felt like bad friends – Maki even more so than Tebza – but they'd all been friends long enough to not stay mad at each other for too long. They had been through their highest highs, and lowest lows together and would get through this too. Tebogo texted Maki when she got to her complex, and a moment later Maki came down the stairs.

"Hey girl," Maki smiled.

Tebogo smiled. "How's it going?"

"So, so," Maki responded. "Doing what I got to do so I can do what I want to do."

Tebogo laughed. "Okay, Miss Quote-a-bumper sticker."

Twenty minutes later Maki and Tebogo were standing in the middle of a huge baby shop, clueless. "I've never been in one of these before," Tebza confessed.

"Me neither," Maki replied. "I was twelve when my older sister Tsholo had my nephew, Tiisetso."

"Let's just walk around and pick out stuff we like," Tebza suggested.

After cooing and gushing over all sorts of items and selecting baby clothes that weren't gender specific in colour, Maki pushed the trolley to the till. They had selected an assortment of bibs, booties, socks, rompers and blankets, and they felt good about their selections, but Maki's mouth hung open when she saw that their purchase amounted to a whopping R2 000.

"You were supposed to keep tabs on the prices!" she yelled to Tebogo.

"But look at how cute everything is!" Tebogo protested.

Begrudgingly, Maki took her debit card out of her wallet and handed it to the cashier, instructing her to only take off R1 000, as Tebogo was to pay the other half.

"Oh, come on," Tebogo said. "This is for your best friend, remember? The same best friend who's about to be a single mother."

Maki softened. Tebza was right.

Lerato could not control her tears as she went through the plastic bags of baby goodies that Tebogo and Maki presented to her.

"Oh my gosh, guys! Thank you so much," she gushed.

"You're welcome," Tebza smiled, putting the kettle on for tea.

On their way to Lerato's they'd stopped at the local bakery to pick up a red velvet cake –Lerato's favourite.

"I haven't even thought of stuff like this," the mother-to-be cried. With a glint in her eye, she added, "I went to the gynae today."

"You were meant to tell us so we could come with you," Maki scolded.

"I know. But a part of me didn't want to believe that it was real, you know?" she said, removing a picture from her bag which she handed to Maki. "Until I saw this."

Maki studied the picture in disbelief as Tebogo came running from the kitchen to have a look. It was a picture of the baby in Lerato's womb. Despite herself, Maki teared up.

"You're going to a mommy," she said, hugging her friend tightly.

While they enjoyed the cake and tea Tebogo looked her friends in the eyes and boldly said, "I've decided to get my own place."

"What?" Lerato screeched.

"When?" Maki asked, and quickly added, "Does this have anything to do with the actor?"

Tebogo sighed. "Yes. But I haven't told Tshepo that I'm moving out." After a huge bite of her cake, Tebza added, "Do you know that I caught him following me to the actor's house?"

Maki chuckled. "The man is incorrigible." But Lerato was not amused. "Babe, please be careful. You're playing with fire."

Guilt-ridden, Tebza was forced to agree, and promised her friends that she would be careful.

Lerato stared at the picture of the baby in her womb, forced to face her reality. "I can't afford to have this baby."

Maki gasped. "Are you saying you want to abort?"

"No," Lerato sighed. "I can't do that, and not even my sad state of financial affairs can convince me otherwise."

Suddenly, Tebogo had an idea. "Why don't you move in with me?"

Maki and Lerato turned to her in surprise. "It'll be perfect! For once I might actually enjoy cooking because I won't be cooking for Tshepo," she chuckled. "It's a small apartment, but we can make it work. And besides, I can't leave Tshepo and take all the furniture too, so you might need to bring yours."

Lerato broke into raucous, spontaneous laughter. "Babe, are you serious?" she asked, wiping away the tears that had formed in the corner of her eyes.

"Like a heart attack," Tebogo replied with a big smile.

"Aaahhh!" Lerato squealed in delight, throwing her hands around Tebza, and planting kisses all over her face. "Thank you, thank you, thank you! I don't know how much longer I could have lived here. This place just reminds me of Seputla."

Chapter 11

. . . .

The next morning Maki stepped into the writer's room with trepidation. As usual, she was the first junior to arrive and she found Greg, Mark and Rian huddled around in mid-conversation. They were obviously talking about her because they fell into an abrupt silence as soon as she walked into the room. But unlike on her first day, Maki didn't bother trying too hard to be friendly, and didn't even look them in the eye as she walked to her regular spot at the long boardroom table, took out her laptop and switched it on. *"Clearly Michal has had her meeting with Rian, and he was telling Greg and Mark about it when I walked in,"* Maki thought.

A moment later two of the other writers and Sechaba walked in on time, but surprisingly Greg didn't comment on this, and Mark commenced with the meeting. Maki was content because for once, Greg didn't make any snide remarks and if he'd wanted to, he kept them to himself.

Slowly Maki felt her confidence begin to rise, and for the first time since she'd joined the *Kas'lethu* writer's room, she voiced her thoughts on a storyline that was being discussed. To her shock, her idea wasn't shut down. In fact, Mark probed further, encouraging her to think deeper about the character's traits and motivation.

As the day pressed on, Maki began to note that for Greg the meeting was too long for him to maintain his façade because by 3pm his sourness towards her had returned. But Maki didn't care. With every comment that she'd made throughout the day she'd felt more confident, and she'd even noticed Sechaba peek at her out the corner of his eye, with a newfound admiration.

When the meeting adjourned, Rian approached Maki and told her to come back the next day as he wanted to start her on an intense training programme on scriptwriting. Maki could not contain her excitement and promised that she would be there. As she left the writer's boardroom she felt as if she was walking on air.

Tebogo knew that she had to one up Tshepo. He was still following her after work, so she'd devised a plan to outsmart him. As she stared at her plan in the bathroom mirror at work, she beamed with pride. She was wearing a long Brazilian weave that covered her forehead with a fringe, and she didn't look too shabby either. Tebogo smiled as she slid a luminous red lipstick along her lips, and completed the look with a huge pair of sunglasses that pretty much covered the rest of her face. Loving the role playing, she dabbed her new expensive perfume on her wrists and neck.

"Perfect," she smiled, studying herself in the mirror. She didn't think that even Maki or Lerato would recognise her in this disguise. Confident, she ordered an Uber, and when it arrived she sauntered out of her office with the confidence of a Victoria's Secret model. Out the corner of her eye she saw Tshepo's car parked in the same spot where he always watched from, waiting for her to leave, but she gave nothing away and stepped into the Uber. As the car drove out of the office parking lot, she looked back to see if Tshepo was onto her. He wasn't. His eyes were still fixed on the door of her office building. Tebza kicked and punched the air victoriously, causing the Uber driver to glance curiously at her in the rear view mirror. She took out her phone and beamed happily as she texted the actor to let him know that she was on her way.

Tebogo rang the intercom at the actor's house, and when he opened the door he broke down in laughter at her new look. Relieved that he wouldn't insist that she look like this every day, she explained why she looked the way she did, causing his laughter to come to a screeching halt. Lost in his thoughts, and absorbing what Tebogo had just told him – that she'd had to disguise herself to throw off her fiancé who'd taken to following her every day after work – the actor made himself a cup of tea. Tebogo was coming to recognise that this was his way of calming down. When he went to sit in the lounge with his tea, she also made herself a cup and joined him. They sat together in silence.

"Is this a game to you?" he asked eventually, unable to hide the hurt in his voice.

Tebogo was gutted. "What do you mean?"

"Getting into disguise so you can come and see your lover?"

Tebogo detected a hint of judgement. Her heart sank.

"Don't put it like that," she whispered.

"How exactly do you want me to put it, Tebogo?" the actor yelled, his voice rising angrily.

Tebogo knew better than to reply, so she averted her gaze, but he continued to stare piercingly at her.

"How do you expect him to behave when you're cheating on him but continue to go home to him every night and boldly display his engagement ring on your finger?"

The words hit Tebogo like a ton of bricks. She had not anticipated that her mission would turn out like this. Ashamed, she slowly took off her wig, but the actor glared at her.

"It's not your wig I'm worried about," he spat.

But Tebogo could not bring herself to take off the ring.

"You don't understand," she said slowly.

"Then make me," he challenged, but Tebogo shifted her gaze from his face again. "High school sweethearts?" he probed.

"Varsity," she replied. Eventually she looked up at him and was met with his icy stare.

"You do realise that actions have consequences right?" he asked softly, and she nodded meekly. "Which is why you have to leave."

Tebza was confused. "Leave?"

"You need to think long and hard about your future and who you want to be with. I refuse to keep sharing you," the actor concluded decisively.

Tears sprang up in Tebogo's eyes, but the actor just stood up and went to the kitchen. As she watched him walk away she felt as if her world had been ripped from her. Although she wanted to run after him, throw her arms around him and tell him that she loved him, she knew that he was right. He deserved better. She deserved better. And Tshepo certainly deserved better too.

**

Maki arrived at the *Kas'lethu* writer's boardroom for her training with Rian early the next morning. The confidence that she'd exuded at the writer's meeting the previous day had left her reeling with excitement, and she hadn't been able to get a good night's rest. Her nerves were shot and she was in desperate need of a strong cup of coffee. As she walked into the boardroom she found Rian already waiting for her; and she also noted that the sandwiches and coffee she'd become accustomed to at every writer's meeting were nowhere in sight.

She put that disappointment aside though when Rian welcomed her warmly and wasted no time in outlining the material that they would cover. He planned to train her on scriptwriting principles, such as story, character and plot. Struggling to make sense of what Rian was saying through his thick Afrikaans accent, Maki typed notes as fast as she could, forcing herself to keep up.

Rian, who was essentially her supervisor, had taken time out of his schedule to train her. It was not within her rights to ask him to repeat himself because she hadn't been able to make out what he'd said, so she continued to type relentlessly, but by 10am she was famished. Magically, as if on cue, Mpho walked in with a tray of sandwiches for them and Rian told Maki that they could take a tea break.

The apprentice writer approached Mpho smiling. She hadn't seen her in ages, and Mpho returned her warm smile. She gushed on about how lucky Maki was to be trained by Rian. Biting into her sandwich, Maki was confused and asked Mpho why she said that. Mpho explained that when she'd joined the *Kas'lethu* staff she had also been promised scriptwriting training, which was one of the reasons why she'd chosen *Kas'lethu* over *Jozi Lights*, another popular local soapie. But in the six years that she'd been at *Kas'lethu* it had just never materialised. Even though she'd originally joined *Kas'lethu* as a writer, after a year Mpho had been promoted to Script Manager which was just a glorified administrative position that didn't speak to her writing talents or capabilities.

Mpho related how she'd sent Michal email after email, and sometimes even text messages, but Michal had completely ignored her. Eventually the young woman found out that Michal was the type of person to ignore whatever she didn't want to deal with. In this case it was Mpho, so she had just given up. It was also around the same time that Mpho put her foot down and blatantly refused to be given a nickname that ended with a 'z'. She wouldn't be deliberately snubbed and given false expectations in her contract that weren't met, and then agree to be given a ridiculous nickname like 'Mphz'.

Maki chuckled. "Maybe they would have gone for Mphoz," she suggested, but Mpho wouldn't hear of it.

"Mphz, Mphoz, same WhatsApp group," she laughed.

Mpho told Maki that the same thing had happened with Sechaba. He had joined the *Kas'lethu* writing team as one of the junior writers but Michal had decided, upon Rian's recommendation, that they make him the cultural consultant instead. Just like that, Sechaba had been demoted from scriptwriter to cultural consultant. No one even knew what that title meant. But Sechaba had sucked it up and done what he'd had to do for the last two years.

Maki was very perturbed by what Mpho was telling her. She had a million questions, but they were all stuck in her throat.

"If you're wondering if this treatment is due to there being a million young people who would like to join the *Kas'lethu* writing team, then you're right," Mpho said, as if reading her mind. "We can leave, but trust me, we'll be very quickly replaced because of the lure of writing for a TV soapie."

Maki was gutted. She thought back to when she'd first met Michal and her group of friends. Something hadn't sat right with her then, and now she knew what it was. She stared back at Mpho, searching her face for answers. She would have expected this from Monica or Sarah, but not Michal. Maki was deep in thought. If things were as bad as Mpho made them out to be, then why had Michal taken a chance on Maki?

"Perhaps she's seen the error of her ways and wants to change?" Maki suggested.

Mpho vehemently disagreed; she'd worked for Michal for six years and knew she wasn't the type of woman to change merely on a whim. Mpho advised Maki that whatever it was that she had done, she needed to keep doing it, because clearly it had worked.

None of this sat well with Maki.

Just then Rian walked back into the writer's boardroom, signalling that their ten minute break was over. Mpho left and Maki hurriedly gulped down the last of her sandwich and prepared to resume her lesson. She wasn't sure if Mpho had told her all the background to make her feel lucky to be the "chosen one" or what, but that was not how she felt. In fact, all Maki felt was guilt, and she resolved to start using her full name from that moment on.

She re-opened her notes on the laptop, but Rian announced that he'd just received a text message regarding a family emergency and had to leave. Maki exhaled, relieved. She didn't know how she would have managed to get through the rest of the training after what Mpho told her. Concentrating, she typed up the homework that Rian had given her, which she was to send to him before the writer's meeting the next day.

Tebogo walked into Lerato's place with the announcement of good news: "We got the apartment!" she screeched excitedly, dangling the apartment keys in the air. But Lerato wasn't as excited as Tebogo had thought she would be, and admitted that even though she'd said she wanted to move out because her place reminded her of Seputla, she still had mixed feelings about it.

"It's my place, you know?" she mused. "It's the only place I've ever been able to completely let my hair down and truly be myself. My little haven that I worked so hard for, and only shared with those who are nearest and dearest to me."

Tebogo understood. "I get it," she said. "It hasn't been easy for me to get the apartment because it feels like I'm closing the door on my relationship with Tshepo, and even though I'm unhappy in the relationship, leaving him just feels so final."

The two friends sat together in melancholic silence, lost in their thoughts. Eventually Lerato looked up at Tebza. "How's it going with the actor?"

"He gave me an ultimatum to choose between him and Tshepo."

Lerato smiled. "He wouldn't have done that if he wasn't serious about you."

"That's exactly what I'm afraid of." Tebza sighed. "What if it doesn't work out? What if I throw away eight years with Tshepo and break up with him for nothing?"

"But what does holding on to Tshepo give you?" Lerato asked. "The memories of happier times? Babe, it's clear that neither of you are the same people you were eight years ago."

"Have you seen *The Notebook*?" Tebogo asked sadly.

"It's one of my favourite movies," Lerato smiled. "And don't you dare tell me that the actor is the Ryan Gosling to your Rachel McAdams!"

Tebogo nodded sadly. "There's no other way to put it. Every time I'm away from him I literally feel like I've lost my other half."

Lerato sighed and admitted that Tebogo and the actor's chemistry was undeniable.

"But, friend, it's only been a month," Tebza said, defeated. "Isn't it too soon?"

Lerato took the big sister approach that she and Maki had often taken with Tebogo during their 15 year friendship. Technically Tebogo was the baby of the group, even though she was only a year younger than them.

"Take a note from my book," she said, dabbing away the tears that fell from Tebza's eyes. "I dabbled with my past and let it affect my current relationship, and look where that got me."

Tebogo felt for Lerato and held her hand as Lerato continued talking. "I knew within a week of meeting Seputla that he was the one, but if we're not careful sometimes we can also push away that special person."

Tebogo chuckled to lighten the atmosphere. "Who knew that getting pregnant would turn you into a sage?"

But Lerato was serious. "Take it from me, babe. That earth-shifting kind of love that meets you one way and transforms you into another doesn't just happen, it's ordered from above. But you need to be able to receive it when it chooses you."

Tebogo nodded, shaken by Lerato's words.

Lerato moved forward to hug Tebogo. "It seems to me like you've already made your choice, Tebza. Now you just need to be woman enough to see it through."

Maki arrived home and dove straight into bed. All this waking up before noon stuff was taking a toll on her; she was knackered. She set her alarm to wake her up later that evening, and when it went off at 8pm she woke up still groggy, but determined to give her homework from Rian her best shot. Despite what Mpho had said, she couldn't throw away the opportunity of being trained by Rian. She dragged her body out of bed, made herself a strong cup of coffee and opened her laptop.

Rian had told her that for her homework she had to choose two lead characters and force them into a situation that would cause them conflict, and yet move both their stories forward. It had to be plausible and true to the characters, as well as emotionally-driven and relatable to the audience.

Whew! Maki thought, suddenly missing her old job at the *Killarney Express*. But her role of journalist was quickly forgotten as she thought about the best characters that she could come up with and the scenarios that they could encounter with a rival family that would lead them to conflict. Before long she was typing furiously.

At 1am Maki boiled the kettle again for more coffee. She was pumped and remembered how she'd loved writing in the middle of the night. Maki thought briefly with longing back to her crime novel. Then and there she decided that she would focus all her energy on *Kas'lethu* during the week and dedicate her weekends to finishing her murder mystery novel. The young writer still believed it would be a bestseller and would catapult her life from monotonous drudgery to stardom and fame.

Maki sat back down to add the finishing touches to her storyline, and by 3am she was re-reading it to see if it made sense.

She smiled, chuffed, as she got into bed, remembering what Mpho had said to her about being lucky enough to be trained by Rian. A few minutes later it was clear to Maki that she wouldn't sleep again that night thanks to the vast amount of caffeine she'd consumed.

To appease her curiosity, she typed Rian's name into the Google search engine and her eyes bulged out of their sockets at the plethora of links that appeared on her laptop screen. Intrigued, she clicked the first one and discovered that Rian was not only currently a script editor at *Kas'lethu* – duh – but that he'd been in the industry for a good 30 years. Most of that had been as a producer, but a little over ten years ago he had turned his focus to scriptwriting and script editing.

Maki noted, impressed, that Rian had produced some of the country's biggest blockbuster films in the nineties. She wondered why she'd never heard of him, but decided to take Rian even more seriously so that he wouldn't feel like he was wasting his time by training her. Suddenly Michal's comment that Rian would rather have been on his yacht in the south of France than training her made sense, especially when she considered all the experience that he had garnered over the years.

Her mind reeling, Maki typed Mark's name into the search engine and she noted that he too had some formidable credentials behind his name. He had 15 years in the game as a scriptwriter and had written for the country's top TV soapies and dramas. With a sinking feeling Maki typed in Greg's name and of course he too boasted decades of experience and had accolades to boot – mostly as a director, but also in the last eight years as both a script editor and scriptwriter.

"Well, then, no wonder he thinks he has the right to throw his weight around; he thinks he's earned it," she mused as she closed her laptop. But as she shut her eyes to attempt to sleep, a small part of her agreed that with so much experience under his belt, Greg was entitled to throw his weight around at least a little.

Maki noted that now she was even more intimidated and burdened with the overwhelming feeling that she had to, at the very least, try to impress the trio that were her seniors, and who boasted dozens of accolades and years of experience, among them.

Tebogo went through the routine of getting ready for work, hoping and praying that Tshepo would leave soon. Eventually he did and she exhaled heavily. She was dressed for work even though she'd taken the day off to pack up her stuff. As soon as Tshepo left, she slipped into her tracksuit and went to the kitchen to make herself a much needed cup of coffee. She had agonised about her decision all night and had barely slept. Luckily for her, Tshepo only followed her back from work, not at lunchtime, so he wouldn't know about her plans to pack and move out.

Her thoughts veered back to her conversation with Lerato. Tebza knew that Lerato was right. She had been miserable for six out of the eight years that she and Tshepo had been together. In fact, almost as soon as they'd moved in together the euphoria had worn off, and although she'd repeatedly told herself that they were just going through a phase, nobody went through a phase for that long. Tebogo knew that she could no longer hold on to the relationship for sentimentality's sake.

"Heck, I'm not getting any younger," she told herself glumly. Drowned by her melancholy, she thought of her earlier fun days with Tshepo before their careers and "adulting" had got in the way. She remembered with a smile how the thought of Tshepo used to give her butterflies in her tummy; he had won her over with his effortless charm and sense of humour. That very charm and humour had clearly worked to get her a ring on her finger, but sadly it was not enough to build a future.

Tebogo sighed and snapped out of her reverie; she had a lot to do before Tshepo came back home from work. To start with she went to the garage to fetch the boxes that she had always stored in there; as much as she may have denied it, in her heart of hearts she'd always known that this day would eventually come.

Maki walked into the writer's boardroom with bags under her eyes; she'd been up until after 3am and had to be at the

Kas'lethu writer's meeting at 9am. Despite his recent efforts to be nicer to her, as soon as she walked in Greg commented that she was in desperate need of her beauty sleep.

"Looks to me like you've gone decades without any sleep, let alone beauty sleep," Maki snapped.

The words tumbled out of her mouth before she could stop them, and even though Mark gasped, she was sure that she saw Rian give a small, impressed smile. But when she turned back to Greg his face was red with fury and he hurriedly got up and left the room. The young woman tried to gauge Greg's level of anger by looking at Rian and Mark, but they both busied themselves by fiddling on their laptops.

Oh well, Maki thought, *it's not like he could keep up the pretence any longer.* She absentmindedly poured herself a cup of coffee, and as she gazed out the window she saw Greg having a heated discussion with Michal. Her stomach sank. Were they arguing about her? Was Greg trying to get her fired?

Maki quietly took her coffee back to the table and sat down, her mind racing with anxiety-filled thoughts which didn't cease the entire meeting. She tried to keep them at bay, but she only spoke when spoken to, addressing each question in the moment. Unlike at the previous meeting, she offered no ideas of her own, and felt Greg's eyes watching her maliciously the entire time.

When the meeting ended Rian was eager to stay and give her feedback on the story that she'd sent him. Maki was shocked that he'd had time to read it already.

"I've been in the game long enough to know from the first line if a story has any merit," he said.

"Okay," Maki said, shutting her eyes dramatically. "Give it to me, but be gentle." Despite the attempt to use humour to calm her nerves, it didn't work. She opened her eyes to find Rian staring at her, a bit annoyed by her antics.

"It didn't wow me," he said, point blank.

Maki's stomach dropped. It seemed that Greg might well get his way and she truly would be fired, but not for calling him ugly – but because she couldn't write. Rian noted her obvious disappointment.

"You can't take it personally every time you receive criticism," he coached. "In this business all you ever get is criticism. If it's not from your fellow co-writers in the writing room, it'll be the audience, the producer, the script editor...." his voice trailed off.

Maki smiled. "You're talking about yourself."

"You have a talent, Dimakatso," he said, surprising her by calling her by her full name. "And if you're wondering how I know your full name it's because I took the liberty to Google you." Maki's face fell.

"Don't worry, other than a few drunken snaps on Facebook there's nothing to be embarrassed about," Rian chuckled.

Maki laughed. She never thought she'd see the day that she and Rian would have something to laugh about together. She was surprised to admit it, but the old geezer was growing on her.

"I was only hard on you because you need a thick skin to make it in this industry. I would never have been in a position to train anybody if I'd worried about who liked me or if I wasn't able to take feedback from my superiors. The same goes for Mark and Greg."

Maki's stomach dropped at the mention of Greg's name and the memory of the argument that she'd seen him have with Michal. Unaware of her thoughts, Rian continued: "Being an artist means being vulnerable to people's opinion about your work. It's inevitable."

Maki shrugged, feeling slightly appeased. Even if Greg got her fired, at least Rian had showed her some kindness, and that she appreciated.

Tebogo had rehearsed her speech a million times. She was done packing and had put her big suitcase and boxes in the boot of her car. She'd deliberately left her overnight bag in the lounge hoping that it would serve as an ice breaker, and she anxiously paced the living room floor waiting for Tshepo to return. Suddenly the door opened and she froze. Tshepo stood in the doorway and studied her; it was clear that he could tell there was something wrong. Out the corner of his eye he clocked the overnight bag.

"Going somewhere?" he asked, blasé, slowly stepping into the room.

"I'm moving out," Tebogo replied boldly, although her hands shook.

His reaction was nothing like she'd imagined. He loosened his tie, walked past her and switched on the TV. Tebogo could not believe it. Was he really snubbing her at a time like this? Maybe she shouldn't have bothered to wait for him to come home from work before telling him that she was moving out; clearly a text message would have sufficed. She shouldn't have had the decency to prepare a speech either. She should have just left when she was done packing an hour ago.

"You're going to live with him?" Tshepo asked eventually, not removing his eyes from the TV. Tebogo walked over and sat next to him on the couch.

"No," she whispered, "But we both know that things can't carry on this way. I think we both know that this has been a while coming. Without communication and trust, we have nothing." Tshepo exhaled deeply but he kept silent and fixed his eyes on the TV screen. She studied him sadly and eventually kissed him gently on the cheek before standing up to leave. As she dragged her overnight bag out of the house, she took off her engagement ring and placed it on the kitchen counter.

Tshepo didn't look up at her because he knew that if he did, the tears that had gathered in his eyes would fall uncontrollably down his face. So he fought back the tears. And fixed his gaze on the TV. Broken.

Feeling like Rian was in her corner and convinced that if Michal wanted to fire her she would have done so by now,

Maki realised with happiness that her confidence in the *Kas'lethu* writer's room was growing. That was partly due to Rian's training, but mostly due to their budding friendship, and she was happy to note that she was becoming more assured of her own voice. Not only did she trust her opinions enough to raise them, but she challenged a lot of Greg's ideas too. To her jubilation, Rian often backed her up and, on occasion, Mark did too. Even Sechaba was starting to look her more directly in the eye.

But Greg didn't back down. In the midst of a heated argument with Maki about the villain's emotional journey, he blatantly blurted out that he didn't understand why anybody took Maki seriously; after all, she'd only been given the job at *Kas'lethu* because she was sleeping with Tumelo the filmmaker and Michal wanted him to work for her.

The air immediately left the room and Maki choked, feeling the air leave her body too. Sechaba's eyes darted in her direction, judgementally piercing her from beneath his Kasi sporty hat. Maki, ashamed, fixed her gaze on her laptop, unable to look anyone in the eye.

The air lay thick with tension. Greg steely fixed his eyes on her, challenging her to argue with him, while Mark and Rian shifted nervously and stared at their laptops. Eventually Maki looked up at them. Did they think that she'd slept with Tumelo to get this job too? It was clear to her from their sudden nervous behaviour and inability to meet her eye that that's exactly what they thought.

Feeling naked and ashamed, Maki summoned all her strength, switched off her laptop and slowly left the room. As she walked out, she felt Greg's beady eye on her, beaming and satisfied that he had ultimately won.

Chapter 12

· ·

"Huu he-e, Moghel, can your booty still fit in these cheeky shorts?" Maki laughed. She was helping Lerato pack her stuff to move in with Tebogo.

Lerato looked up. "Not for much longer at this rate," she replied sadly.

Despite Maki's efforts to lighten the mood, Lerato was still burdened with emotion. "I heard that women can't stand their partners in their first trimester, so maybe that explains why you were so mean to him," Maki commented gently.

"Maybe," Lerato sighed. "Or maybe this is the universe's way of punishing me for all those married men I slept with."

Maki felt for Lerato. The only thing she'd ever judged Lerato on in their 20-year friendship was her good looks and how she'd used them for gain. Although Maki had never approved of her choices in men, she'd never judged Lerato for that because she knew that deep down the girl had a heart of gold. She sighed as she set aside the clothes that she'd been packing and sat next to her friend on the bed.

"You weren't in on it alone, babe. It's not like those men didn't know what they were doing," she said.

"But I went along with it," Lerato sighed.

"Oh, babe," Maki commiserated wiping away a tear on Lerato's face.

Lerato looked at Maki glumly. "It seems like all I ever do these days is cry."

"Crying cleanses the soul," Maki assured her, but when that didn't warrant a smile from Lerato she added. "Don't worry, we'll just call your child Dikeledi."

Lerato couldn't help but laugh.

"That's more like it," Maki smiled. "You have me, Tebza and Dikeledi."

Lerato threw her hands around Maki's neck, hugging her tight.

"Thank you, my friend," she whispered.

"Anytime," Maki whispered back.

***

Maki boldly walked into the *Kas'lethu* production office and came face to face with Thulz holding a box in her hands filled with papers and a pot plant. The poor woman was crying as she walked down the stairs and almost ran out the door. Suddenly Maki heard Michal shouting from upstairs, her voice reverberating throughout the entire office.

"And let that be the last time you ever disrespect me!" she yelled.

Maki turned to Phumz for answers. The receptionist quickly hid her smirk and turned to face Maki. "I wasn't aware that there's a writer's meeting today."

Concerned for Thulz, Maki replied, "There isn't. I'm here to see Michal." Motioning with her head in the direction that Thulz had run, she asked, "Is she okay?"

Phumz shrugged. "Thulz just hasn't been cutting it, so Michal fired her."

"Oh no," Maki gasped.

"No need to worry, I've been promoted to Michal's PA. But as you can see, I don't think now is a good time to see her."

Fired up and completely ignoring Phumz, Maki charged up the stairs.

"You had no right to fire that girl," Maki barked, storming into Michal's office.

Michal, who was on the phone, clocked Maki and spoke into the phone receiver: "Let me call you right back." She hung up and glared at Maki. "Something I can help you with?"

Maki felt her knees buckle under Michal's icy glare, but she had to solider on.

"That is no way to treat an employee," she said in a quieter tone.

"Oh, and how would you know, Miss Investigative Journalist? How's that working out for you?" Michal sneered.

Phumz walked in behind Maki.

"Everything alright, Michal?" she asked.

Michal gave a slight nod to Phumz. Maki could not stand the air of superiority. "Speaking of my investigative journalism skills, I'm still on excellent terms with my editor at the *Killarney Express*." Maki saw the colour drain from Michal's face. Feeling her adrenaline rush and blood boil, she added, "I'm sure he'd love to get an exposé about the way you run your production company, Miss Boss Lady."

"Get out!" Michal seethed.

"Gladly. I was here to resign anyway." With that, Maki whipped around, much to Michal and Phumz's shock and, with her head held high, stormed out of Michal's office.

But Maki's heart sank when she drove out of the parking lot and saw Thulz sitting on the pavement outside the security gate, sobbing. She rolled down her window and yelled, "Do you need a lift?"

Thulz didn't even lift her head, so Maki parked her car, much to the chagrin of the security guards, and sat next to Thulz.

"She got rid of me as if the last five years I've worked for her mean nothing," Thulz sobbed.

Maki took Thulz in her arms, but then Thulz's crying turned into a fierce anger.

"Do you know that I wasn't even on a permanent contract and haven't been able to get any credit to buy a car or a house?

And yet I still showed up every day and gave her my all!" she yelled angrily.

Maki consoled Thulz as best she could, and when her crying subsided, she said, "I know a good lawyer."

"Good," Thulz nodded, resolute. "As long as she addresses me by my full name – Nokuthula – then I'll be willing to speak to her."

Maki smiled. "I'll be sure to let her know."

Tebogo exhaled before knocking on the actor's door. Even though he knew that she was coming, she was filled with anxiety at how her visit would go. A moment later the actor, looking delectable in a vest and white drawstring pants, opened the door; Tebogo could not settle the nerves that caused her stomach to knot.

"Hey," she breathed.

Instead of replying he opened the door and stood aside for her to enter. Licking the sweat off her top lip, Tebogo walked into the house and turned to face him. "I did it."

The actor raised an eyebrow at her questioningly, and she continued. "I broke up with Tshepo and moved out."

In one swooping move the actor took Tebogo in his arms and pinned her against the wall. Before she knew it he had removed her clothes and was hungrily making love to her in the corridor.

When Maki walked into the *Killarney Express* offices she was hit with a bout of nostalgia as the busy-ness and smell of the newsroom engulfed her. She closed her eyes to take it all in but was violently shaken out of her reverie by a booming voice that shouted, "California roll!"

Before she opened her eyes, she chuckled. Her former boss, Andrew, was the only person she'd ever allow to associate her name with sushi, and that was only because of the rapport they'd built over the five years that she'd worked for him.

"Hey, you old geezer," she jokingly replied.

"You back to grovel for your old job?" he chuckled, walking towards her.

"Grovel? Honey, please. Maki Dilobetso does not grovel," she replied with a smile.

"So that glamorous TV show you left me for didn't work out, huh?" he asked.

"You don't know the half of it!"

Andrew took her in. *"Bathi hamba uzobuya,"* he chuckled, causing Maki to laugh out loud.

"Well, I guess they're right," she replied. "And there is no place on earth I would rather return to, but before we pop the champagne, darling, there are a few things I want to discuss with you regarding my contract."

Andrew raised an alarmed eyebrow at her. "Ooh, someone taught you to have some chutzpah."

"By the gallons," she laughed.

"Alright, then. Come this way, please ma'am."

An hour later Andrew had agreed to one out of Maki's three requests. He agreed that she would do more investigative journalism and fewer puff pieces about local politicians, but they'd argued about the second condition for 45 minutes. Eventually he conceded that he would give her a ten percent increase on her previous salary, but not the twenty that she had proposed. Her last request – to work flexi-hours and to not work on public holidays – was absurd, he said. What journalist ever took off on a public holiday?

With that, Maki shook hands with Andrew and he congratulated her on coming back home and for standing up for herself to re-negotiate the terms of her contract.

Tebogo rolled over in the actor's bed to answer her phone and smiled when she saw that it was Maki calling. "Chomi," she mused, happily.

"Tebza, I need your help," Maki said, as she opened the door to her apartment after her meeting with Andrew.

"What's wrong?" Tebogo replied, sitting up, immediately concerned.

"I quit my job at *Kas'lethu*," Maki said, tossing her handbag on the sofa.

"What? The same job you were bragging to us about last week?" Tebogo replied.

"Yes," Maki sighed. "I'm back at the paper. But that's not why I called. When I went to *Kas'lethu* to hand in my resignation, Michal had just fired her PA, Nokuthula, and I heard her yell that she wouldn't be disrespected anymore. She didn't care that the poor girl was crying. And when I spoke to Nokuthula, she'd said that she'd worked for Michal for five years without a permanent contract."

"Hmm," Tebogo said, creasing her forehead in thought. "If she agreed to those terms there might not be much she can do from a legal perspective."

"Damn it," Maki replied as she boiled the kettle for coffee.

"But she could go to the CCMA for unfair dismissal," Tebogo concluded.

"Thanks, I'll let her know." Maki hung up, pensive. If Thulz agreed to take Michal and *Kas'lethu* to the CCMA, she might have a big scoop for Andrew on her hands. She smiled in glee and opened up her own manuscript on her laptop. As she read over it, she smiled happily to herself. "Mackenzie, my old friend, how I've missed you..."

Twelve hours later Maki smiled as she read over what she'd written and her heart nearly burst with pride. She had not only finished her manuscript, but she'd also challenged herself to think of ways of getting Mackenzie into unbearable and painstaking situations that caused her to almost get caught. Just in the nick of time, though, she literally got away with murder.

"This is not half bad if I do say so myself," Maki chuckled out loud.

She saved her manuscript on a flash drive, planning to print it the next day so she could have a hard copy, and then she would email the electronic copy to a few publishers. She considered her options, and figured that if all went well the book could be in all the major bookstores by the end of the year.

Maki stretched lazily and thought of the latest turn that her life had taken. She hadn't even sunk her teeth fully into her writing role at *Kas'lethu* before she'd quit, but she doubted that she would have cut it as a scriptwriter anyway. *Why would I expose myself to constantly being criticised for my work?* She might not have been the most self-aware of people, but she knew how much validation meant to her. The lack of it made her feel inadequate, and that would lead her to compare her life to others, which was a major trigger for her depression.

In celebration of her finished manuscript, quitting her supposed dream job on a TV soapie, and getting back her old job back at the *Killarney Express* – with an increase – she poured herself a huge glass of wine and closed her eyes to take in the sweet taste of success.

Maki was about to turn off the lights to go to bed when her phone rang loudly, and was shocked to see that it was Tumelo calling. "It's eleven o'clock at night," she complained to herself. Then, when the realisation hit her that she was nothing more than a booty call, she answered, annoyed.

"Hello."

Tumelo sounded equally, if not more, annoyed. "Have you been running around Joburg telling people that you're my girlfriend?" he barked.

Maki was completely caught off guard. "What?" she yelled back, then quickly regained her composure. "You should be so lucky."

"Care to explain to me then why Michal from *Kas'lethu* called me and told me that you'd quit your job and begged me, as your boyfriend, to ask you not to write about her in the *Killarney Express*?"

Maki laughed bitterly. She should have known that Michal was behind this.

"Ah, so Michal's ego is the reason you're calling me so late making all sorts of ridiculous accusations."

"She's a very powerful lady, Maki," Tumelo warned.

"That gives her no right to treat people like trash! She told the entire writing team that I only got the job because I'd slept with you! So screw her and screw you!"

The line went silent, then after a while Tumelo said. "But you did, didn't you?"

Maki was defeated. "Goodbye Tumelo," she said before hanging up. Annoyed, she polished off her glass of wine and retired for the night.

***

Maki was spinning around in the chair at Andrew's table, sitting opposite him, as the editor hung onto her every word, impressed.

"So what do you think?" She had a scoop on her hands and she knew it.

"Write it up," Andrew said. "I've always been wary of those 'Devil Wears Prada' types and wondered how they treat their staff. Now that we have irrefutable proof let's expose the demons."

Maki laughed at Andrew's enthusiasm.

"I knew you had the makings of a good journalist the day you walked in here five years ago," he continued.

"Yeah, right," Maki chirped.

"I had to put you through the trenches," Andrew said, standing up to leave for a meeting. "I want that article in my inbox ASAP."

"It will be my pleasure."

As soon as she got back to her desk, Maki called Nokuthula, formerly known as Thulz, and was happy that the young woman seemed to be in happier spirits than when they'd last spoken.

"Have you had a chance to call the CCMA?" Maki asked after they'd exchanged warm greetings.

"Sure did," Nokuthula laughed. "And guess what? I got my job back!"

Maki was floored. "What?"

"The CCMA called Michal to validate the statement I'd made against her, and within an hour she called me, begging me to take my job back."

"That woman is incorrigible."

"Image is everything to her," Nokuthula added. "She hates being publicly humiliated."

"I hope this means that she won't be calling you Thulz anymore," Maki said.

"Not only will she no longer be calling me Thulz, but she gave me a permanent contract with a substantial increase."

"Yes, girl!" Maki cheered.

"And she'll think twice before firing me on a whim again," Nokuthula laughed before turning serious. "I have you to thank for all of this. If you hadn't taken the time to hear me out and fight for me, I'd still be at home crying my eyes out."

"You're welcome, Nokuthula."

"Can you call me Thuli?"

"Sure," Maki smiled before hanging up.

Tebza parked her car in the parking lot of her new complex, took her laptop and handbag out of the boot and walked to her apartment, filled with a sense of freedom that she hadn't felt for a long time. When she got inside she found Lerato on the couch eating ice-cream with peanut butter.

"Hey, girl," Tebza said in greeting.

"I can't believe this crap tastes so good," Lerato mused.

"Enjoy it!" Tebza said before disappearing into the bedroom to change out of her work clothes. Suddenly there was a knock on the door.

"I'll get it," Lerato shouted. She was shocked when she saw Tshepo standing in the doorway, but he was more shocked to see her, particularly because of her bulging belly.

"What are you doing here?" Lerato sneered.

"You're pregnant?" Tshepo asked.

Lerato remembered what Tebogo had told her and Maki about Tshepo following her, and figured that Tshepo must have followed Tebza to their new home.

"As you can see," Lerato nodded. "But don't get it twisted, Tshepo. I know some very powerful men who can kick your ass if you continue to follow Tebogo around." Tshepo had always had a crush on Lerato, and immediately cowered.

"I didn't mean anything by it," he defended. "I just wanted to get closure."

"Then get some closure, but leave Tebogo out of it. She has moved on and I suggest you do the same," Lerato barked before slamming the door in Tshepo's face, leaving him brooding outside.

"Who was that?" Tebogo asked, emerging from the bedroom.

"Tshepo," Lerato replied, sitting back on the couch.

"He's still following me?"

"I don't think he'll bother you again, but if he does, just get a restraining order," Lerato suggested as Tebogo sighed wearily.

Maki sat back in her chair and read her article on Michal. "*Kas'lethu*: No home for blacks" the headline declared. The young writer had always sucked at producing catchy headlines, but she knew she could count on Andrew to fix that. For her, the more important thing was the content, and in this article the content was very juicy. She'd gone into great detail about how Michal couldn't be bothered to say her African employee's names, so she'd patronisingly shortened them and given them all nicknames that ended with a 'z'. She also explained how the producer had hired both Sechaba and Mpho as writers to only reduce them to positions that carried no real significance, and how she'd breached their contracts by not giving them the training that was contractually due to them. The final nail in the coffin was that Thuli had worked for Michal for five years on an independent contract with no real benefits. Chuffed with herself, Maki sent the article through to Andrew.

As she got ready to leave for the day she remembered that she had to print out her manuscript. When she skim read over it she was impressed with her handiwork. She Googled a couple of publishing houses and read through their submission processes. Most of them required only the first chapter. Had she known that she could've sent them the first chapter months ago! Maki chose eight publishing companies and, as she emailed her work to the last one, she said a small prayer that her book would live up to the success that she knew it could.

Since moving out of Lerato's place Seputla had found himself a small apartment close to the gym. He'd invited Lisa over a couple of times to try and erase Lerato from his system, but it was no good; he missed Lerato more than ever. He even missed her cooking which he'd always pretended to enjoy even though the food would always be either slightly burnt or undercooked. He scrolled to her name on his phone's contact list and his finger hovered over the green button, in two minds about whether to call her. Fighting with himself, he decided to send her a message instead.

"Hey, I'd love to see you," he typed.

He was hesitant about sending the text but had to make a snap decision when a client approached him and said that she was ready for her session. He quickly pressed the send button, put his phone on silent and slipped it into his pocket.

Like he'd done over the last few weeks, he attempted to push Lerato as far back in his mind as he possibly could.

Tebogo laughed in glee. The actor had bought her an easel, canvas, paint and paintbrushes just like Ryan Gosling had for Rachel McAdams in *The Notebook*. As usual, she'd gone over to his place after work.

"I want to be a beautician, not an artist," she laughed, but she took the actor's face in her hands and kissed him fervently. "But I love it."

"Good, because I have no intention of returning any of it. What will your first painting be?" he asked, handing her a glass of wine.

"You can't rush creativity," Tebogo joked. "But when I decide, you will be the first to know."

She teased him for living in upper middle class Parkhurst, but he joked that he loved it because old Jewish people didn't know who he was, and the black upper middle class pretended not to know him, so it worked out great.

"I'm tired of being cooped up in the house," Tebogo said suddenly. "Let's go to the night market down the road."

"Who would get tired of all this good loving," he joked, but then turned serious as a thought struck him. "Move in with me," he proposed.

Tebogo froze, speechless.

"You and Lerato are crowded in that tiny flat, and I have more than enough room."

"So that's why you bought me the canvas."

"Precisely," he smiled. *"Mi casa es su casa."* He approached Tebogo and kissed her on the lips. "So what do you say?"

She kept quiet for a minute, then squished her face up, deep in thought.

"I don't want to make the same mistake twice and rush to move in with a man," she eventually said, careful not to hurt his feelings. "I just got my freedom from Tshepo and I realised the other day that I've never had my own place. Sure, Lerato lives with me, but she kinda needs me right now."

"Okay. So will you move in after she's had the baby?" he pushed.

Tebogo laughed. "We'll see. Now let's go out."

Lerato was documenting her thoughts in a journal and drinking a cup of tea when there was a knock on the door. She sighed and put her book aside. She'd had a barrage of feelings when she received the text from Seputla – mostly sheer longing – and had invited him over so that they could talk. She patted her hair down out of nerves and walked to the door, hoping that her knees wouldn't buckle at the sight of him.

"Hey," she said, as she opened the door and was hit with the familiarity of his alluringly masculine scent.

"Hey," he smiled back.

Lerato stepped aside so that Seputla could enter, and as he walked into the apartment, he momentarily took in her bulging tummy.

"Nice place," he said.

"Thanks." Lerato walked to the couch and sat down, and Seputla slowly followed her and gingerly sat down next to her. "Tebogo let me move in with her; I couldn't stay at our old place any longer."

The use of the word "our" wasn't lost on Seputla.

"Thanks for the text," she smiled.

Seputla couldn't help but notice how radiant Lerato was looking. As if reading his thoughts she added, "I've been journaling; it's helping me deal with everything."

"Everything?"

"Our break up," she said softly, then jokingly added, "And my new mommy vibes."

"How are you holding up?"

She sighed. "It's getting more difficult to sleep, and when I do find a comfortable position staying in it is impossible. But the baby's healthy and growing. In fact, I'm due for a check-up next week." She eyed him shyly. "Want to come?"

Seputla beamed. "I'd love to."

Suddenly she giggled.

"What?"

"The baby just kicked." Then she giggled again. She took his hand and placed it on her belly.

"I don't feel anything," he complained.

"Give it time," she replied, shutting her eyes.

Seputla thought it was weird, but he did the same. Suddenly he smiled widely as he felt his baby kick in Lerato's tummy. He looked up to see Lerato smiling at him and he smiled back in wonder as he felt the affirmation of his love for Lerato moving around inside her.

The actor and Tebogo strolled around the night market. He had his arm casually draped around Tebogo's shoulder, and she truly felt like she was in heaven. For one thing she was out of the house on a weeknight which was unheard of when she was with Tshepo, and for another she was feeling good because she'd lost a bit of weight. That was mostly due to the actor's strict diet which apparently was a clause in his contract with *Kas'lethu*. When the actor had told her some of the other clauses that were in his contract Tebogo realised how much Michal had protected herself.

Since she'd received the call from Maki about Michal's PA, Nokuthula, and her unfair dismissal, Tebogo had insisted on the actor showing her his contract. Some of the clauses were hideous. The "no weight gain" clause was one such ridiculous stipulation. Thinking of Lerato, Tebza wondered if there was a non-pregnancy clause in the lead actresses' contracts.

There'd been other demands such as mandatory publicity appearances which mostly happened on weekends that would be unpaid, and the acknowledgement that the shoots sometimes spanned 12 hours. Tebogo was pretty sure that the shooting times alone were unlawful, but when she'd told the actor that Michal had fired her PA, he had told her that he preferred to not get involved. His duties began with memorising his lines and ended with showing up to work to record them, and he had no intention of getting involved in who Michal hired or fired – as long as it wasn't him. Tebogo admired that about him; she thought that his line of thinking was very wise and that she should probably adopt it too.

Deciding to forgo the healthy option, Tebogo indulged in a caramel-drenched doughnut with hundreds and thousands sprinkled on it, but as she paid for it, out of the corner of her eye, she thought that she saw Tshepo. She blinked and did a double take, but the spot where she thought she'd seen Tshepo was empty. *My mind must be playing tricks on me.*

Still she felt an eerie sensation creep up her spine, as if someone was watching her. Tebza didn't want to mention it to the actor who was taking selfies with a group of girls, so she bit into her doughnut to ease her mind. But as the actor walked towards her, she turned and saw Tshepo staring hatefully at her from a distance. Infuriated that he was still following her, Tebogo smiled at the actor and kissed him passionately. When she looked up again she saw Tshepo charging towards her, and her heart caught in her throat. The actor turned to see what had scared her and was met with Tshepo's fist in his nose.

"Tshepo!" she screamed, and the people at the market turned to see what had caused the commotion.

But the actor was quick and threw so many punches at Tshepo in retaliation, that he was soon a whimpering and pathetic mess on the ground. A crowd had gathered and some bystanders had taken out their cellphones to record the fight.

"Stay the hell away from Tebogo," the actor barked at Tshepo, who was still on the ground, much to the crowd's amusement. Then he quickly took Tebogo by the hand and led her away from the commotion.

Tebogo insisted that they go to the nearest police station, even though all the actor wanted to do was to go home. The angry young woman was adamant that she wanted to get a restraining order against Tshepo immediately. The policeman behind the desk had been shocked to see the bruise on the actor's face, and although he tried to maintain his professional stance, when a colleague arrived for his shift, the policeman made a senseless comment that celebrities were not above the law.

The actor was livid, and it took everything in him to heed Tebogo's advice and not react to the policeman's snide remarks. It was obvious that the policeman was wielding his power over the actor and deliberately trying to rile him up. While Tebogo was busy giving her statement a policewoman asked her what she thought would happen after cheating on her fiancé with a famous actor, and then leave her fiancé for that very same actor. Tebogo rolled her eyes dismissively, but the policewoman continued prodding and sniggering, asking Tebogo if the sex was that good. Fortunately Tebogo's legal training kicked in and she managed to maintain her composure while giving her statement, much to the policewoman's annoyance.

Eventually, two hours later, Tebogo's application for a protection order was done, and Tebza and the actor finally left the police station with the police's assurance that they would hear from the court when their protection order was ready to be granted.

When they got home the actor was furious! "Your ex-boyfriend might have caused me my job," he yelled, panicking.

Tebogo put an ice-cold face cloth on his nose, but he removed it, annoyed.

"I can't go to work like this! It'll be swollen in the morning."

"I've got my make-up kit here; I'll fix it for you," Tebza assured him, putting the face cloth back on his face. "No one will know."

"How did he even know we were there?" the actor demanded.

"He must've followed me from work again. He was probably camping outside the house."

"So much for neighbourhood security," he murmured. Then he grabbed his phone which had been beeping relentlessly since they'd arrived home. His stomach fell as he saw the reason for all the notifications. "Oh no!"

"What is it?" Tebogo asked.

"Don't bother with the make-up; the whole world has seen the fight."

He showed Tebogo the video of him and Tshepo's fight; it had gone viral.

"260 000 views?" she sighed, exasperated.

"It'll be a million by the morning." When the actor's phone rang he wasn't surprised to see that it was Michal. He exhaled deeply before leaving the room to take the call. Tebogo was furious; she had a good mind to call Tshepo, but she knew that if she did she'd be playing right into his plan. Her anger would merely fuel his antics, so instead, she poured herself a glass of wine to help her deal with all the stress.

Tshepo angrily slammed the door shut, and paced the living room floor, shouting loudly to no one in particular. "What does he have that I don't have?"

He was shocked when there was a knock on his door, and when he opened it, he snarled at the policeman who stood in his doorway. "What do you want?"

"It's clear to me why you're getting into fights in public, sunshine," the policeman smirked. He handed Tshepo a clipboard and the freshly beaten man signed next to his name, before the policeman handed Tshepo an envelope.

"An application for a restraining order has been filed against you. You are to arrive at court on the date stipulated in that summons. Failure to do so will grant Tebogo Precious Seamela an automatic restraining order against you."

"You've got to be kidding me!"

"Do yourself a favour and cut ties with this girl. She has clearly moved on," the policeman advised. "Consider yourself served," he concluded, as Tshepo angrily slammed the door.

Chapter 13

Maki walked into the office the next day and saw the junior reporters huddled around a desk, watching a video on one of their cellphones, laughing and sniggering.

"Have you seen this?" one of them asked her as she walked past.

Maki really wasn't in the mood for watching silly YouTube videos with her juniors; she was more worried about whether her manuscript had been well received and if any of the publishers she'd sent it to would respond. However, to appease her colleagues, she approached to have a look.

"No, what is it?" she asked.

"The actor from *Kas'lethu* got into a fight last night," one of the reporters said. Maki's stomach sank. "Let me see." She grabbed the phone out of her colleague's hand.

"Oh no," she said, as she saw the actor punching Tshepo. She returned her colleague's cellphone and ran outside to call Tebogo.

"Babe, I saw the video," Maki said in disbelief. "Are you okay?"

"I'm fine," Tebza answered, "it's the actor I'm worried about. Michal called him in for a disciplinary meeting."

"Do you think he'll get fired?"

"I don't know, but after you told me about Nokuthula I insisted on checking his contract and it states that doing anything that brings the show into disrepute is a dismissible offence."

"Damn it," Maki said under her breath.

"The worst part is that Tshepo threw the first punch, but of course the videos online don't show that. But I've applied for a restraining order against him, so I hope he's learnt his lesson."

"Good. I hope he doesn't do anything stupid again."

Tshepo woke up at midday on the couch. He had called his boss to tell him that he wouldn't be going to work; his head hurt and his body was wracked with pain. He thought he'd heard a knock on the door which was what had woken him, so when he heard the knock again he slowly got up to answer and was surprised to see Seputla standing there.

"What do you want?" Tshepo croaked, walking back into the house.

"You don't strike me as the type of guy who has many friends," Seputla said, closing the door behind him and following Tshepo inside, "so I thought I'd come and see how you're doing."

Tshepo slowly sat down on the couch. Seputla turned to the TV and was shocked to see re-runs of Kas'lethu playing silently. He reached for the remote and switched it off.

"What good is watching that going to do?"

"Who are you – Dr Phil?" Tshepo asked lugubriously. He took the remote from Seputla's hand and switched the TV back on. Staring at the actor, he asked, "What does he have that I don't have?"

Seputla knew better than to answer that, but Tshepo added sadly, "Other than money, fame and now Tebogo?" Then he chuckled wryly and winced in pain.

Seputla handed Tshepo his cellphone with a recording of his fight with the actor.

"Have you seen this?" he asked.

Tshepo took the phone and watched in disbelief, humiliated that he'd been beaten to a pulp for the whole world to see. But then a thought struck him and he smiled slyly. "Do you think that this could get him fired off that show?"

Seputla's face fell. "I wouldn't cause any more trouble if I were you."

"Trouble?" Tshepo barked. "Tebogo left me for the actor and I'm the one causing trouble?"

"Listen, man, I know you're hurt, but..."

"Who sent you?" Tshepo interjected. "Did Lerato put you up to this? Do you know that she threatened to get some men to beat me up?"

"Lerato and I aren't together anymore."

Tshepo could not believe it. "What?" he laughed. "You knocked her up and she still left you?"

Seputla had had enough. He got up to leave before another fight ensued. "I came to help you," he said, "but you're going to have to help yourself."

Maki got home from work tired after a long day. Andrew had kept her busy, and even though he'd agreed that she wouldn't write any puff pieces she'd had to because, as Andrew said, newspapers were not glamorous and they all had to pull their weight. She hadn't been able to check her personal emails during the day, so after pouring herself a glass of wine to unwind, she opened them. Six of the companies that she'd sent her manuscript to had replied, and Maki was overcome with excitement until she realised that three of them were automated replies. The gist of it was that they had received her manuscript and that she should expect feedback from them in three to four months.

"Three to four months?" Maki yelled into the empty room. That was practically a lifetime. She opened up the other emails and her heart sank as, one after the other, they rejected her submission. One stated that she was not famous enough and had no real following so there was no guarantee that anybody would buy her book.

"Anybody? I'm sure at least one person would buy my book," she complained out loud.

She opened up the last email and, just like the previous one, the publisher stated that she had enjoyed Maki's submission but wasn't convinced that murder mystery was a big enough genre in South Africa. The dejected young woman sighed deeply and took a huge swig of her wine.

As she was about to switch off her laptop she saw that she had an email in the spam folder. Curious, she clicked on it and, to her shock, it was a reply from a small publishing house. The email stated that they were specifically looking for black, female writers who wrote niche genres, so her manuscript was the perfect fit for them. Maki's heart beat loudly against her chest. The email requested that she send them the entire manuscript as they were definitely interested. If the rest of the manuscript was as enticing as the first chapter, the mail said, then they would call her back with the good news that they would publish her book.

Maki screamed in disbelief, then forced herself to calm down as she replied to the email, thanking the publisher for taking the time to read her work and get back to her. She quickly attached her full manuscript to her email and, as she watched it load, she prayed that her wi-fi wouldn't act up. After the manuscript was attached she clicked send, and checked her sent folder at least twice to make sure that the email was gone and hadn't bounced back to her inbox.

The young writer was breathless with excitement. She didn't know what to do with herself and could not sit still, so she decided to drink one of Lerato's teas to calm her nerves, hoping that it would soothe her to sleep.

Tebogo was pacing when the actor got back home. "And?" she asked, quickly. "What did she say?"

The actor shrugged. "She suspended me."

"But what about the storyline that you're in the middle of shooting?"

To her shock, the actor smiled, not panicking in the least. "The writers will figure it out."

Tebogo wanted to scold him, but he had a glint in his eye that she was curious about.

"On my way home," he explained, "I thought about what's most important to me. It used to be my job, but for the first time in my life I have something much more important than that."

Tebogo stared at him confused. "More important than your job? What could be more important than your livelihood?"

To her astonishment, the actor took her hand in his and dropped to his knee, looking her earnestly in the eye. Tebogo swallowed, nervous as tears sprang to her eyes.

"Tebogo Precious Seamela," he said, looking at her lovingly, "would you do me the honour of being my wife?"

Tebogo screamed in delight as tears flowed down her face and she showered him with kisses.

"Is that a yes?"

"Yes! Yes! Yes!" she screamed.

The actor took out a ring box from his pocket and slipped the ring onto her ring finger.

"I love it," she cooed, mesmerised by the diamond band that had a tanzanite stone in the middle.

"I figured since I'm on a break for two months I might as well do something proactive with my time," he smiled.

"Like get married?" Tebogo laughed.

He scooped her in his arms and swung her around. "Why not?"

Tebogo swooned as it hit her that she was about to spend the rest of her life with the man of her dreams.

Maki was reading in bed when her phone rang. She rolled her eyes when she saw that it was Tumelo calling; she considered ignoring his call, but then decided to answer it so that she could directly deliver the message to him to leave her the hell alone. "What do you want?" she droned tiredly.

"Your forgiveness."

"I was about to go to sleep," she sighed.

"If that's an invitation..." he interjected.

"It's not," Maki snapped, cutting him off.

"I just wanted to apologise," Tumelo continued. "For everything."

"Fine," Maki replied. "But do me a favour."

"What?" Tumelo replied, hopeful of being given a second chance.

"Lose my number," Maki concluded, then she hung up and ensconced herself tightly under her covers, soon falling peacefully asleep.

When Tebogo woke up the next morning she checked her ring finger to make sure that it wasn't all a dream. A tear caught in her eye as she saw her ring glistening in the morning's sun rays, and the actor woke up smiling, next to her.

"Hey," he said, taking her in his arms.

"Hey, baby," she smiled in return.

He kissed her passionately, then turned to take out a notebook and pen from his bedside drawer as she observed him closely.

"What are you doing?"

"I don't know about you," he replied, "but my family observes tradition. You can't walk around with my ring on your finger and the elders know nothing about it."

Tebogo beamed. "You're writing a letter to my elders?" The gesture floored her and she was overcome with emotion.

"I want to claim you in every possible way," the actor smiled. "Emotionally, spiritually, traditionally... everything."

He sat up and wrote a letter respectfully outlining his intentions towards Tebogo, then he took out an envelope, folded the letter and sealed it shut. With a smile he handed it to her. "You're not allowed to read it," he instructed.

But Tebogo's eyes beamed in curiosity. "What did you say?"

"Just promise me that you'll deliver it as soon as possible," the actor said.

"I'll drive to Ga-Mashashane personally to deliver it," Tebogo promised.

"Good," he said, taking her in his arms and kissing her passionately. "And since I've got time on my hands, I'll come with you."

***

Tebogo had never had as much fun as she had on the road trip to Polokwane with the actor. For one thing she'd had the choice of what music to play, and she loved that the actor enjoyed a wide range of music just like she did. Along the way they sang loudly as they imagined themselves in a karaoke bar. Added to that, every time they stopped at a tollgate Tebogo had to take a picture of the actor with the cashier. She didn't mind though because she loved how good natured the actor was towards his fans.

Eventually they arrived in Polokwane and drove to the hotel where they'd booked themselves a room, but now she was alone as she drove the last 80km to her mother's house. Tebogo and the actor both knew that the initial trip to her mother's house was one that she'd have to make on her own.

As she drove she thought about the way her relationship with the actor had ignited her in the most invigorating way. To a large extent it still hadn't hit her that she was wearing his engagement ring on her finger, and that she was about to deliver a letter to her mother declaring that he wanted to pay a bride price for her. What Tebogo loved most about the actor was that she could be herself around him and he never made her feel small or inadequate. She could be her fun and crazy self, coupled with the powerful and insightful woman she'd always known herself to be. He demanded loyalty and respect, but it was easy for her to give those things to him because that is what he drew out of her.

Tebogo exhaled as she approached her mother's house. She hadn't been home in at least two years, not even for Christmas, telling her mother that she and Tshepo had wanted to establish their own traditions. That had been partly true, but the actual truth was that Tebogo and her mother didn't get along, and ever since she'd graduated from university her mother took every opportunity to tell anyone and everyone that Tebogo's success was due to her sacrifices as a single mother.

Her mother never credited Tebogo for working hard and being focused while her peers had been out partying and messing around with boys. Nope, she just believed that it was the values she'd instilled in Tebogo that had given her daughter her laser-sharp focus. And if Tebogo was brutally honest, she knew that she had her mother to thank for her success. But not for the reasons that her mother thought, rather because she wanted to be nothing like her mother. From a young age Tebogo had vowed to work hard to achieve her goals so that in her adulthood she would be nothing like her mom.

She took a deep breath as she saw her mother's house in sight, conjuring up the strength to put on the mask required to deal with her.

Seipati looked up when she heard a car hooter going off outside her house. As she rushed to the door to scold her neighbours who were well-known party revellers, her jaw dropped. She realised that the reason for all the noise was the arrival of her long lost daughter, Tebogo Precious Seamela.

"Tebogo?" she muttered under her breath, straining her eyes in the hot Limpopo sun to check that they weren't playing tricks on her.

Tebogo stuck her head out of the car window as she drove into the yard, her hooter still blaring loudly, and Seipati felt her heart plummet. Tebogo knew that she hated surprises; why hadn't she called to let her know that she was coming?

But she rushed to the car all the same and gave her daughter a big hug.

"What a surprise," Seipati said, as Tebogo returned the hug.

"It's good to be home, Mom."

Seipati roughly removed herself from Tebogo's embrace. "Good to be home? If it's so good to be home then why haven't you been home in two years?"

"Mom, can we get into the house before we fight?" Tebogo joked, trying to calm herself and avoid having her own feelings flare up.

"So an honest question would make you want to fight with me?" Seipati scolded.

Tebogo ignored the question and turned to open the boot of her car and remove some bags of groceries. "I bought you a few things."

Seipati helped Tebogo carry the grocery bags into the house. "As an only child should," Seipati commented, and Tebogo rolled her eyes as she followed her mother into the house.

Tebogo studied Seipati's face as she read the letter.

"Who is this from?" the older woman asked when she was done reading.

"A man who wants to marry me," Tebogo slowly replied.

"That much is clear, but who is he?"

Tebogo and the actor had decided to keep his identity a secret until his uncles arrived at Seipati's house for the actual negotiations. As Tebogo searched her mind for answers, Seipati searched her face.

"I'd rather not say," Tebogo eventually replied.

Seipati laughed out loud and clapped her hands once for dramatic effect. "So how do you expect me to agree to such when you won't even tell me who wants to marry you, and I know you to have been in a relationship with Tshepo for close to ten years?"

"He's an actor," Tebogo said under her breath.

"Askies?" Seipati probed. "Speak up please, I can't hear you."

"He is an actor on *Kas'lethu*," Tebogo said more audibly.

Seipati pursed her lips and shook her head at Tebogo. "Have I not taught you anything in the 27 years of your life? You are leaving Tshepo who has a managerial position in a corporate organisation for an actor? How on earth will this actor take care of you?"

Tebogo eyed her mother, hurt, but Seipati continued. "Are you ready to deal with the groupies? And having your face splashed all over the newspapers? And if he – excuse me, let me correct that – *when* he cheats on you, will you be ready for your business to splashed all over the tabloids?"

Tebogo fought back tears.

"Are you ready for your entire life to be under scrutiny?" Seipati concluded, aware of how she was hurting Tebogo's feelings, but determined to drive her point home.

Tebogo finally found the strength to speak, her fists clenched in her lap. "I have come to your house after two years; I've put my pride and issues aside and, instead of congratulating me, you're telling me that my husband-to-be is going to cheat on me?"

Seipati studied Tebogo dispassionately. "And what are those issues might I ask?"

As if it wasn't obvious! Tebogo shook her head in disbelief.

"Ma, you don't celebrate me," she said passionately. "You never have! I got the highest grades in Matric and all you were worried about was making sure that I didn't embarrass you by getting pregnant. I graduated top of my class and you weren't happy. Working in an insurance company isn't good enough for you. And now there's a man who actually loves me and wants to marry me, and your biggest concern is that it's not Tshepo."

"Tshepo recently called me in the middle of the night in tears," Seipati said, her voice strained.

Tebogo couldn't believe how much of a parasite Tshepo had become since their break up. "And what did he want?" she asked, exasperated.

"He was crying and telling me that you'd left him for another man," Seipati said, choosing her words carefully so that she did not upset Tebogo any more than she already had. "I told him to call me again in the morning, and when I didn't hear from him, I called him but he just said that you are a slut and hung up on me."

Tebogo rolled her eyes. That was classic Tshepo behaviour – always being a victim and playing the blame game.

"Did he tell you that he got into a fight with my fiancé in public and that I had to get a restraining order against him?" she asked matter-of-factly.

"Tebogo, the man is hurting."

"How did this conversation even become about Tshepo?" Tebogo yelled angrily.

Seipati held her daughter's gaze. "Are you not being unreasonable? How do you expect Tshepo to feel about you moving on so quickly without him?"

Tebogo stood up slowly, feeling defeated.

"I came home to bring you that letter, Ma. My fiancé's uncles will contact you to set up the first phase of the negotiations." She eyed her mother, hurt. "It's interesting to me that in this entire conversation you haven't even bothered to ask me what I want, and if I'm happy. Your sole concern is for someone who hates me so much that he had the nerve to tell you that I'm a slut."

Guilt stung at Seipati's heart. "I'm just trying to protect you, that's all."

But Tebogo turned around and left.

Seputla and Lerato laughed happily as they walked back into Tebogo's apartment. Seputla had bought Lerato a huge preggy pillow and teddy bear, and they were laughing about the fact that Maki had christened their baby Dikeledi because in the first trimester Lerato had cried so much. They'd just been to the gynae together and had seen the baby move in Lerato's tummy. Before going to the doctor they'd decided that they would wait until the baby was born to discover its gender, but after Lerato left the gynae's room Seputla, unable to contain his curiosity, had rushed back in to ask the doctor if they were having a boy or a girl. The gynae had been happy to share the information with Seputla.

As he plopped himself on the couch next to Lerato who was tucking into a huge bowl of choc-chip ice-cream, Seputla asked her if she'd thought of any baby names. Lerato listed a few but none of them stuck, and when the baby's father suggested only female names Lerato asked if he was trying to tell her that they were having a girl. Seputla quickly mentioned a few random boys' names as well, but he wasn't a good liar.

"So we're having a girl?" Lerato asked, her eyes lighting up.

"I'm sorry," Seputla apologised. "I didn't mean to give it away."

"It's all good. "I was hoping for a girl, but I hope she's nothing like me."

"Why would you say that?" Seputla laughed, thinking that Lerato was joking.

"Well clearly she'll be hot, because look at us," Lerato laughed. "But I've made some terrible life decisions," she added more soberly.

"Then I guess we have to give her the tools that'll enable her to make the right decisions," Seputla said, drinking Lerato in with his eyes.

"I wish it was that easy."

"Hey," Seputla said, taking her hand in his, "we're going to love the heck out of this baby." Lerato smiled warmly at his encouragement and repeated use of the word "we".

"I've given a lot of thought to the way things ended between us," he said.

"I'm so sorry about that," Lerato replied, ashamed.

But Seputla smiled. "A love like ours doesn't come around every day; I get how that can be overwhelming. And I know that I said having a baby doesn't mean that we should be together… but I've reconsidered."

Lerato's heart caught in her throat, and Seputla shyly held her gaze.

"Do you want to give it another shot?" he asked.

Lerato bit her bottom lip. "I don't want to run the risk of screwing it up again," she whispered.

Seputla averted his gaze so that she wouldn't see the hurt in his eyes. "Having this baby has forced me to see myself for who I really am, and it's hard dealing with the fact that I was such a lousy girlfriend," Lerato confessed. "I just need time to work on myself, that's all," she concluded, and Seputla nodded, hopeful that things might still work out for them.

Maki rubbed her palms anxiously against her skirt. She was meeting with Corrine, the publishing manager from the company that had expressed interest in her novel, but Corrine had sent Maki a message to say that she was running late. The young writer ordered a bottle of still water while she waited, because she feared that her nerves wouldn't be able to handle a burst of caffeine. A moment later a strikingly beautiful lady, probably in her mid-thirties, walked in and scoured the place. Maki raised her hand and the woman rushed over, fervently shaking Maki's hand and introducing herself as she sat down. Corrine ordered a cappuccino and plunged straight into business.

"So, we love your work, which is obviously why I'm here. I read your manuscript and it felt like I was holding my breath the entire time. To sum it up into one word, it was unputdownable."

Maki choked on her water. "You liked it?" she asked with trepidation.

"Of course!" Corrine exclaimed. "Loved it!"

"All I want is for my book to have a fighting chance, but I've been led to believe that there isn't much of a market in South Africa for murder mystery novels."

"Which is why our focus isn't only on South Africa," Corinne explained. "We have distributors in England, Poland, Germany and Canada, and if the book does really well we'll even translate it."

Maki was floored.

"But as I stated in my initial email to you, we're a small publishing company, and we're invested not only in the success of our books but also in the author's success. We live in a consumerist age, so our approach doesn't just boil down to book sales; we help our authors build their brands too."

"Okay," Maki replied, unsure of what that meant.

"Basically we build a marketing strategy around our authors. We build your brand, market your book and send you to book fairs and markets so that your readers can interact with you. Plus, a publicist will train you on how to interact with the media, and a stylist will be hired to style your wardrobe."

Maki could not believe her ears. "Wow!"

"The only requirement from us, naturally, is that you sign an exclusivity deal," Corinne expanded.

"Of course," Maki replied eagerly.

"And since we invest so much not only in the books we publish but in our authors too, we obviously expect a return on our investment."

Maki was slightly confused and Corinne saw that on her face.

"You will be contracted to write a novel every year for the next three years, which is the duration of your contract. Failure to do so will be considered a breach of contract and then we will reserve the right to terminate the contract."

Maki was shaken. *I knew it sounded to be too good to be true,* she thought. But all she said was, "Thank you Corinne, that is a very generous offer. Please may I review it and get back to you?"

"Of course," the publishing manager agreed with a smile, sliding Maki her contract across the table. "I know it's short notice, but we're having a meet-and-greet with all our potential authors this evening. I'll send you the address on WhatsApp; it would be great if you could join us."

"Thank you," Maki beamed.

As Corrine left, a trail of her perfume lingering in the air behind her, Maki was struck by how nice Corinne seemed to be. She was tempted to sign the contract only because of that, but then she remembered what a shark that Michal from *Kas'lethu* had turned out to be, and promised herself she would not take Corinne at face value.

Tebogo's phone rang as she walked into the lobby of the hotel, and she answered it without checking the caller ID. She was emotionally exhausted from the trip to her mother's house. "Hello?" she droned. She suspected that the call might be something urgent from work because despite the fact that she had colleagues, her boss liked to act as if Tebogo was the only one who could do her job.

"Hey, Tebza," Maki's bright and breezy voice come through the phone.

"Hey, babe!" Tebogo squealed, excited to hear from her friend. "You won't believe where I am."

"Where are you?" Maki asked, curious.

"In Polokwane. I've just come from my mom's house; I had to deliver her a letter from the actor – he wants to marry me." The line went silent. "Hello?" Tebogo glanced at her phone screen, but it seemed that Maki was still on the line.

"Maki?" Tebogo demanded.

Suddenly Maki burst into raucous laughter. "Are you serious?" she cried.

"Did you go speechless on me?" Tebogo asked, returning Maki's laughter. They both knew that Maki was hardly ever quiet.

"Are you freakin' kidding me?" Maki laughed, causing Tebogo to laugh even harder. "Dude! When were you going to tell me?"

"He wanted us to keep it to ourselves until I'd spoken to my mom," Tebogo explained.

"How'd she take it?" Maki asked, although her instincts already knew.

"How do you think?" Tebogo sighed. "She was more interested in talking about Tshepo who called her in the middle of the night crying that I'd dumped him, and then proceeded to call me a slut!"

"Typical! Listen, personally, I'm beyond ecstatic for you."

Tebogo beamed, "Thanks babe."

"There's only one snag though," Maki continued.

"What's that?" Tebogo asked, suddenly anxious.

"Lerato and I don't know any traditional wedding songs!"

Tebogo laughed. "Don't worry, girl, that's what aunts are for!"

Maki hung up, having completely forgotten that she'd called Tebogo for advice on her publishing contract. She called Lerato to share the news about Tebogo's pending nuptials and was surprised when Lerato answered the phone sounding breathless.

"Girl!" Maki squealed before she was thrown by Lerato's heavy breathing. "What are you doing?" she asked, suspicious.

"Stretching," Lerato groaned.

"Oh," Maki smiled mischievously.

"Girl, get your mind out the gutter. Nobody wants my pregnant ass," Lerato laughed. "Except of course, for my baby daddy."

Maki's jaw dropped. "He wants you back?"

"Yeah," Lerato replied nonchalantly.

"And?" Maki asked anxiously; she knew that Lerato and Seputla were perfect for each other.

"I don't think it's a good idea," Lerato explained. "For one thing I live in Tebza's flat and we all know about his financial situation," Lerato droned, but at the mention of Tebza's name, Maki interjected.

"Did she tell you that she's getting married?"

The line went silent. Then after a moment, Lerato replied, "Please tell me it's to the actor?"

"Yes!" Maki squealed.

"Thank goodness! For a second I thought Tshepo might have guilt-tripped her into taking him back."

"She's in Limpopo right now talking to the elders."

"That actor certainly does not waste time!" Lerato exclaimed.

"He's a man who knows what he wants," Maki mused. Then she got an idea. "Where are you?"

"At home – duh."

Maki smiled. "Get into the shower; I'm on my way."

Chapter 14

. . . .

Lerato was freshly showered and busy drying her hair when she heard a knock on the door. Knowing that it was Maki and eager to know what she had planned, she opened the door quickly to let her friend walk in.

"And then?" Lerato asked with a smile. Maki rarely displayed her happiness so boldly.

"What I didn't mention on the phone," Maki said, walking in with a bottle of wine for herself and a non-alcoholic sparkling wine for Lerato, "Is that, I Dimakatso Innocentia Dilobetso, have been offered a publishing contract."

Lerato's eyes bulged wide in her sockets and she screamed excitedly. "What! Babe, that's awesome."

"Which is why I'm here," Maki added. "I've been invited to an event that the publishers are hosting tonight. It's black tie."

"And you need something to wear?" Lerato asked, visibly disappointed.

"Of course," Maki said, adding with a glint in her eye: "And a plus one."

Lerato threw her arms around Maki. With Tebogo spending so much time with the actor, her idea of them having a slumber party every night hadn't quite materialised. And, truth be told, a part of the reason that she didn't want to get back together with Seputla was because then she would have to be responsible for raising their daughter. A small part of Lerato was secretly hoping to send the child to her mother in Kimberley so that Lerato could reclaim her social life. But she knew that Seputla would insist on being as hands-on as possible, what with him being the morally upright man that he was.

The mother-to-be was deep in thought as Maki poured herself a glass of wine and walked towards the bedroom, chatting about the assortment of designer dresses that she could choose from in Lerato's wardrobe. Suddenly Lerato snapped out of her reverie and followed Maki to the bedroom, her glass of wine in hand, thoroughly depressed that her beverage was non-alcoholic.

As Maki looked through hanger upon hanger of Lerato's dresses, she chatted casually about how far she, Tebogo and Lerato had come, what with Tebza about to be Mrs Actor, Lerato a new mommy and her a published author. She nonchalantly held up dress after dress against her body, lost in her own nostalgia until suddenly she heard quiet sobbing behind her and turned around to see Lerato wiping her eyes.

"Hey," Maki said rushing to her, "what's wrong?"

"Don't worry about me," Lerato answered, pretending to be okay. "I'm so emotional these days; I cry about everything."

"You're not getting out of this that easily. What's going on?"

Lerato reached for a tissue and blew her nose dramatically. "It's just, I didn't think that my life would turn out this way, you know?"

Maki nodded in understanding.

"I wasn't supposed to be a mother, let alone a single mother," Lerato cried. "And we used protection every single time so I really don't know how this happened."

"Maybe you willed it," Maki smiled.

"What do you mean?"

"I think that deep down you really want this baby but you're scared of commitment because every single man you've ever loved has let you down," Maki surmised.

"The only man I've ever loved is Seputla."

"And your dad."

Lerato froze. She often forgot how well Maki knew her. She'd pushed her dad to the back of her mind, and since adulthood she'd done a very good job of forgetting about him. But clearly she hadn't entirely let him go.

"I think that you dated all those old men because you were subconsciously looking for a father figure in them," Maki concluded.

"And that's why I pushed Seputla away?" Lerato asked, baffled.

"Exactly. For once you're not in a toxic relationship and it's unfamiliar, so you sabotaged it."

"Wow, moghel," Lerato smiled. "When did you get so smart?"

Maki threw back her head and laughed. "You're not the only 'know it all' around here. Now let's get dressed so we can go to this party."

Lerato opted for an elegant black wrap around dress that hugged her body beautifully, while Maki chose a shimmery gold number.

"Ooh," Lerato whistled after Maki got dressed. "If I was to hazard a guess I'd say you're about to get knocked up in that dress!"

Maki dismissed Lerato's joke, and when Lerato began to do her make-up, Maki took out her phone and secretly sent Seputla a message with an update on their plans for the evening. She also sent him the address where the party was being held. Quickly checking to see that Lerato wasn't onto her, Maki slipped the phone back into her bag and acted as if she'd been listening to what Lerato had been saying all along. She smiled a small victorious smile when she realised that Lerato was none the wiser, happy in anticipation of the night ahead.

In the car Lerato turned to Maki. "I'm proud of you," she said softly.

Maki was caught off guard. "What?"

"Out of the three of us you've always been the most ambitious, and now look at you –about to become an author and all."

Maki wasn't sure, but she thought she detected a hint of envy in Lerato's voice. "And out of the three of us you're the one who can handle motherhood the best."

"Yeah, right." Lerato sighed as she subconsciously rubbed her belly. A thought struck her and she turned again to Maki. "Why didn't you offer to have me move in with you?"

Maki chuckled. "Girl, you know Tebza is a better candidate to take care of you. To start with she cooks, has matching Tupperware and she changes her sheets; it was a no brainer."

When Lerato didn't laugh despite Maki's attempts at humour, Maki turned to her friend. Lerato's melancholy was not lost on Maki.

"I'm just trying to figure out what's going to happen to me when Tebogo moves in with the actor," Lerato confessed. "It'll be way too stressful to live with Seputla and a newborn baby."

Maki glanced at Lerato sympathetically. "I was thinking of going to Kimberley for a while and possibly leaving my baby there," Lerato added.

"At your mother's?" Maki asked, shocked. "I understand you need your mom, but surely she can come to Joburg for a while. You can't leave your baby there!"

"It was just a thought," Lerato sighed.

"We'll talk to Tebza when she gets back," Maki suggested. "Between the three of us we'll figure out what to do. We always do."

Lerato sighed and looked out the window as Maki drove, slightly appeased.

When Maki and Lerato got to the upmarket Kyalami venue their eyes nearly popped out of their sockets. A valet offered to park Maki's car and they walked up the stairs into the dimly lit room where soft jazz was playing and beautiful people were walking around drinking champagne. Maki took a glass of champagne and Lerato settled for juice as they took in their surroundings.

"Girl, these publishers don't play!" Lerato commented, impressed.

"They told me that they do most of their business overseas, but I didn't think it would be on this scale," Maki marvelled.

"Have you signed your contract with them yet?"

"Not yet. They have an exclusivity clause I want to discuss with Tebza first. But they literally turn their authors into rock stars; they give them a makeover and everything."

"Judging from this set up I think you should sign it. And we all know how desperately you need a makeover."

"Whatever," Maki laughed. She saw Corrine across the room, and waved at her as they walked across.

"Hey," Corrine greeted.

"I want to introduce you to someone," Maki said to Lerato, but Lerato handed Maki her drink to hold before quickly dashing off to the bathroom.

"I'm glad you could make it," Corrine said, smiling warmly.

"Thanks for the invite, even though I'm not officially a member of the team just yet."

"Have you had time to think about the deal?"

"It's all I've been thinking about," Maki replied.

"We've invited all our potential authors tonight just to give you guys an idea of what we're really about. There are a few authors here that we're hoping to sign," Corrine added. "Come with me and I'll introduce you."

Lerato emerged from the bathroom and scoured the venue looking for Maki. It was hard to see in the dimly lit room, but Maki wasn't where Lerato had left her. She cursed slightly under her breath. This was totally Maki's scene and not hers. The room smelled of intellects, plus her feet were throbbing and she regretted forcing her swollen feet into her shoes. Just then she gratefully spotted a table with snacks and headed straight there. As she reached for a baguette another hand reached for the same baguette.

"I'm sorry," she said sheepishly, as she heard the other person also apologise. Lerato looked up and saw the most beautiful man she'd ever seen. Even behind his glasses she noted his piercing eyes. He had dark chocolate skin with absolutely no blemishes, and a chiselled, masculine jawline. "I'm sorry," she repeated, blushing.

"No, I should apologise," the man said, and Lerato thought she heard a hint of a French accent. "I shouldn't be keeping food from a pregnant woman."

Lerato smiled, embarrassed, but the man handed her the baguette on a serviette. "It's all yours," he said.

"Thank you," Lerato smiled.

The man extended his hand and introduced himself, "Jean."

"Lerato."

"Pleasure to meet you, Lerato. Are you one of the authors?"

"No, but my friend Maki is. She's around here somewhere."

"Smart woman," Jean commented. "Writers are the most self-loathing creatures on the planet."

Lerato laughed. "Where are you from?" She felt at ease around Jean and bit into her baguette hungrily.

"Cote d'Ivoire," he replied. "Have you been?"

"No," Lerato replied.

Staring at Lerato with his striking eyes, Jean added, "I'd love to take you some day."

Lerato felt her insides burn with desire. It was a feeling that she hadn't felt in a while, and she was impressed that even in her condition a man could still set her on fire. She was about to reply flirtatiously when, out the corner of her eye, she thought she saw Seputla standing in the doorway. She blinked and did a double take; the dim light in the room must have been messing with her. She looked again. It was definitely Seputla. He was standing in the doorway watching her interaction with Jean very keenly, and he seemed unimpressed.

"Excuse me," she said to Jean, before walking towards Seputla.

"Hey," she greeted, surprised to see him.

"Didn't mean to interrupt your conversation," Seputla replied, unable to hide the jealousy in his voice.

"We were just talking," Lerato explained. "What are you doing here?"

"Maki invited me."

"Of course," Lerato answered, unsurprised. Suddenly there was an awkward silence that Lerato had never had with Seputla before. "Can we talk outside?" she suggested.

"Sure," Seputla said, leading the way.

Corrine had led Maki over to two very good looking young men. Maki introduced herself as they shook hands with her, one introducing himself as Puo, and the other as Robert. Maki found Puo rather striking but gave nothing away. She cast a small, inconspicuous glance at him while Corrine was speaking to them, and was startled to find his eyes firmly on her. Maki couldn't help but emit a small giggle. She turned back to focus on Corrine, but her mind was muddled as she tried to piece together what Corrine was saying. Feeling Puo's eyes on her, Maki looked up again to meet them and felt herself blush. He smiled a small smile at the effect he was having on her.

Maki was shaken out of her daydream when she heard Corrine excuse herself and Robert as the two of them walked off, with Robert asking how long it would take to get his book out. Maki and Puo remained glued to the spot, with Maki blushing and Puo smiling at her.

"You an author too?" Maki eventually asked, then cursed herself inwardly for her feeble attempt to start a conversation. *Of course he's an author that's why he's here, stupid!*

"Hoping to be," Puo replied. "They made me an offer but I haven't signed yet."

"Me too," Maki exclaimed, noticing with much annoyance that her voice sounded unusually high pitched. "I can't decide if the exclusivity deal is a good thing or not. I mean, what if I get started on book number two but then get writer's block or something?"

"I know, right? It's a lot of pressure to produce a book a year."

A comfortable silence fell upon them, and after a moment Maki looked up at Puo. "I'm going to do it." Puo turned to her surprised, and Maki continued. "I've got nothing to lose, right?"

"I guess," Puo said, smiling and feeling at home in the company of his new friend.

Seputla led Lerato to a bench in a secluded part of the garden. "I've been doing a lot of soul searching," Lerato said, as she sat down next to Seputla. "The most soul searching I've ever done in my entire life."

As Seputla watched Lerato he took one of her feet in his hands, removed her shoe and massaged her foot.

"I'm scared," Lerato continued. "One minute I'm scared that this will actually work, then the next minute I'm scared that it won't. Maki pointed out to me earlier that the reason I'd dated all those older men was because I was searching for a father figure. You see, my biological dad abandoned me when I was nine years old. The worst part is that I have memories of him. As a result of that I've never let a man love me, and I knew that the married men I dated could never break my heart because they never had it in the first place."

Seputla studied Lerato carefully as she spoke.

"But you do," she added. "Loving you is the scariest thing I've ever done in my life." Seputla took Lerato's hands in his, gently drew her towards him and gave her a sweet and endearing kiss.

Maki was walking in the garden with Puo, and threw her head back in laughter as he told her tales of his life growing up in Botswana. Suddenly she remembered Lerato and excused herself to make a call, but Lerato's phone was on voicemail.

"Damn it," she muttered under her breath. Next she dialled Seputla's number. He answered after a couple of rings.

"Hey, have you seen Lerato?" she asked, slightly panicky.

"Yes, she's with me," Seputla answered.

"Okay, good. Where are you? I'm on my way."

The actor lifted his eyes from the menu to look at Tebogo. She had been in a weird mood ever since she'd come back from her mother's house. At first he thought that it was because she'd found him swimming with a group of girls in the pool, but as he studied her he could tell that something deeper was bothering her.

"You never told me how your trip to your mom's went," he probed gently.

"The less said about that the better," Tebogo answered, not removing her eyes from the menu.

"That bad?"

"My mother is toxic. She always makes me feel so inadequate," Tebogo explained. The actor nodded, happy that they were finally getting somewhere.

"Most parents are like that," he commented.

"Really?" Tebogo asked in disbelief.

"Absolutely," the actor replied. "I'm a 30-year-old actor. Unless I start to work behind the scenes there really are no career prospects for me in TV."

Tebogo listened intently. "I've never thought of it that way."

"And do you think my mother ever lets me forget?" the actor laughed wryly. "Our parents are from an era where they could not reinvent themselves. Choices were limited back then, and if you made a choice you stuck to it."

Tebogo nodded, finally understanding. The actor had given her a new perspective on her relationship with her mother.

"Thanks," she smiled. "I needed to hear that."

Maki spotted Seputla and Lerato sitting on a bench and was again struck by how good they looked together. She chuckled as she said, said under her breath, "Dikeledi's parents."

"Hey guys," Maki greeted them cheerily as she and Puo approached. They were so lost in each other that they jumped with a start at her greeting.

"Hey," Lerato smiled, aiming a questioning eyebrow in Puo's direction.

Seputla extended his hand to Puo and introduced himself, but Lerato glared pointedly at Maki.

"This is Puo," Maki replied to Lerato's glare. "He's an author too."

"Nice to meet you, Puo," Lerato said, and Maki prayed that her friend wouldn't say anything to embarrass her.

"You look like you're ready to go," Maki said to Lerato.

"Seputla can take me back if that's okay?"

"Okay, cool," Maki said, "I still need to go back in and chat with the publisher." Maki drew Lerato in for a hug. "Thanks for coming with me," she said.

Lerato squeezed her back tightly. "Thanks my friend, for everything."

Tebogo was seated on the bed as she watched the actor pace back and forth, talking on the phone with his uncle, trying to get him to agree to go and see Tebogo's mother about his intentions to marry Tebogo. But the actor's uncle seemed to have a lot of questions that the actor clearly hadn't anticipated.

"I've known her for a few months," he said into the phone, exasperated. "Yes, I'm sure she's not after my money," he added, then threw Tebogo a look which caused her to giggle. "Because she has her own," the actor said, pacing again. "I understand," he eventually said, before hanging up.

"Sheesh," he cried, as he threw himself on the bed. "You'd think that they never want to see me married."

Tebogo stroked his bald head gently. "They just have the best intentions for you, that's all. For all they know I'm a scam artist who wants you for your millions."

The actor laughed. "If I had millions I would gladly give them to you. I suspect you'd build a better home for us and our kids with them anyway."

The actor's comment caused Tebogo to have a sudden thought.

"Have you thought about how you want to do this?" she asked.

"What do you mean?"

"Your uncle brought up a good point. Do you want to get married in community of property or out of community of property?"

The actor sat up. "I know your intentions for me are pure. I've thought about leaving *Kas'lethu* for so long, but I've become accustomed to the financial security and have put my dreams on hold. If I were to take the leap I know that you would stand by me no matter how much money I had or didn't have."

Tebogo studied the actor. "And how do you know that?"

"I've talked to God about you," he replied.

Tebogo was floored. "You've what?" She knew that the actor meditated every day, but she never thought that it was about her.

The actor smiled. "Every day since the day I met you."

Tebogo kissed him hard, emotional at the generosity of his character and his uninhibited display of his intentions for her.

Maki walked towards Corrine who was chatting with two young ladies.

"Hey, Maki," Corrine said brightly when she saw her. "I'd like to introduce you to Stacey, she runs our publicity department, and this is Maggie – our stylist."

Maki extended her hand to the ladies. "Nice to meet you," she said with a smile.

"I hope you're enjoying the party."

"I am, thanks Corinne," Maki replied. "So much so that I'm going to accept your offer."

Corrine clapped her hands together. "Excellent!"

"Welcome to the family," Stacey added.

"Thanks," Maki mused.

"I can't wait to get started on your novel," Corrine commented. "Let's meet up ASAP so you can give me a copy of your signed contract."

"Sure," Maki agreed. "And thanks again."

Maki looked around for Puo, and when she didn't see him she headed to the bar for a much needed glass of wine. She was stirred with a mix of both trepidation and excitement. As the bartender handed her the drink, Maki turned and saw Puo walking towards her. "Hey," she said. "You're looking at SA's next murder mystery novelist."

"Well done, that's awesome."

Maki sipped her wine, searching her brain for something to offer for inspired conversation, but her thoughts were interrupted by Puo who announced that he was leaving.

"What?" Maki squealed, disappointed.

"I have an early flight," Puo explained.

"Business trip?" Maki probed, then chastised herself for being nosy.

"No, I live in PE."

Maki was bummed. *Of course you do,* she thought.

"But I was hoping that we could stay in touch," he added, suddenly shy.

Despite herself, Maki blushed. She watched as Puo took a business card out of his pocket and handed it to her. "Those are my details."

Maki smiled, slightly disappointed. She took the card from his hand and sipped her wine as she watched him walk away.

Lerato and Seputla had barely made it through the door of Seputla's apartment before they'd stripped each other of their clothes. She hurriedly removed Seputla's shirt and took in his comfortingly familiar scent, while hungrily searching his body with her lips, but when he took off her dress she felt naked and exposed, and immediately stopped kissing him.

"What's wrong?" he asked, concerned, but Lerato just hung her head, avoiding his eye. Sensing that she was self-conscious because of her bulging belly, Seputla gently kissed her tummy. Tears welled up in Lerato's eyes as he looked up at her lovingly and took her in his arms, carrying her to the bedroom where he made love to every inch of her.

***

Tebogo was having breakfast with the actor when his phone rang. He checked the caller ID and looked up at Tebogo, surprised.

"It's my uncle," he announced. Tebogo's breath caught in her throat as she stared at him with wide eyes.

"Malome?" the actor gulped nervously when he answered the phone, and Tebogo watched anxiously. "Yes, Malome."

Tebogo tried to read the actor's body language to figure out what was going on. Nervously he looked back at her.

"Okay, Malome," the actor said before hanging up.

"What's up?" Tebogo asked nervously.

"They want to meet you," the actor replied, and Tebogo bit her bottom lip, petrified.

Chapter 15

An hour later Tebogo was dressed in a long skirt and head wrap, and she and the actor were on their way to his mother's house in Seshego. As he drove she was uncharacteristically quiet and wrung her hands nervously.

"They're going to love you," the actor encouraged warmly.

"And if they don't they won't let us get married," Tebogo whispered, feeling hollow inside.

"Then we'll elope," the actor suggested with a smile.

"Yeah, the papers would love that story," Tebogo replied, but was happy that she felt a bit lighter. "What do you think they want to say?" she asked, her anxiety building up again.

"They just want to suss you out, make sure your intentions are clear, see what kind of background you come from."

Tebogo exhaled deeply as the actor pointed to a house in the distance.

"That's the house."

The young woman sat up to take it in, but she was even more anxious when she saw that there were cars parked in the driveway. Clearly the actor's whole family was expecting them. The actor drove into the yard, parked the car, turned to Tebogo and asked: "You ready?"

Tebogo wanted to scream "No!" but instead she exhaled deeply and, bracing herself, replied, "Let's do this."

As they walked into the house, Tebogo prayed that she would make a good impression. There were two men in the lounge and they stood up to greet and hug the actor as if he was their prodigal son. The actor introduced his uncles to

Tebogo, and although she was polite and kept her head bowed low, she sensed that the elder uncle, Malome Masemola, was not as eager to meet her. Malome Makgoromecha, on the other hand, boisterously shook Tebogo's hand and declared himself the chief negotiator. He was immediately chastised by Malome Masemola who reprimanded him and told him to hold his horses. From what Tebogo could gauge, Malome Masemola took himself very seriously.

"I've heard about you, young lady," he said in a gruff voice, sizing her up.

Tebogo shook his hand. "All good things I hope," she offered with a meek smile.

"That remains to be seen," Malome Masemola replied.

"Where's Mom?" the actor asked hurriedly, but suddenly a woman's voice was heard coming down the corridor, singing in a high soprano at the top of her lungs.

"Makoti ke dinako," the sharp voice sang the traditional song, welcoming Tebogo to the family, and Malome Makgoromecha who, upon closer inspection, Tebogo suspected to be slightly inebriated, joined in boisterously.

"Wa jika jika makoti wa gana na?" Malome Makgoromecha loudly sang off-key.

The actor laughed and turned to see his mother, Mam' Melita walk into the lounge, mid-vibrato. Malome Masemola was visibly annoyed by all the antics, but the actor smiled widely at his mother and gave her a huge hug.

"Hi Mom," he said lovingly.

"Hi, son," the actor's mom said, before turning to Tebogo.

"Woo, what's this?" she asked, peering at Tebogo. "Is this what you've brought us, son?"

Tebogo froze. *Doesn't she like me?* she thought, panic-stricken. Mam' Melita's personality was too much for her to handle, but the older woman continued unhindered, as if intent on making her more nervous.

"A daughter? A daughter-in-law? The actor, nephew of Masemola, Matlhomola, may his soul rest in peace, and

Makgoromecha! You've brought us a whole entire daughter-in-law?"

Tebogo stood glued to the spot, unsure of what to do, but suddenly Mam' Melita pulled her in and enclosed her in a huge embrace, causing Tebogo to gasp for air.

The actor laughed and clapped his hands together, but Malome Masemola was annoyed and broke up the drama.

"She's not your daughter-in-law yet," he said, his voice gruff. "Melita, take her to the bedroom with you so we can talk as men."

"Sure, Semo!" Mam' Melita chuckled. "Come this way," she said to Tebogo, taking her by the hand and leading her out of the lounge. "The actor's aunt is waiting for you this side."

Before Tebogo could respond, Mam' Melita had a firm grip around her wrist and was leading her down the corridor. She took one last nervous look at the actor who sat stoically with his uncles. Their eyes briefly met and he smiled encouragingly at her but, unlike him, Tebogo's demeanour portrayed no stoicism; her heart beat loudly against her chest, as she was practically pulled along to meet her fate.

Michal walked into the production office feeling particularly rejuvenated after spending a morning at the spa. Phumz stood up as soon as Michal walked in, and Michal smiled at her. Phumz had taken her demotion back to receptionist quite gracefully, but for some odd reason – and very much unlike her – Phumz had a scowl on her face this morning.

"Pull yourself together, darling," Michal complained. "That's no way for a receptionist to look. You are the face of this office, for goodness' sake."

Phumz handed Michal a newspaper. "Have you seen this?" she asked, concerned.

Michal, thinking that Phumz was being overly dramatic, took the newspaper out of her hand and looked at the headline: "*Kas'lethu*: Where slavery runs rampant." Michal's blood ran cold as Phumz stared at her, searching her face for answers. "Get my publicist on the line," she demanded and marched upstairs to her office, the newspaper firmly in her hand.

Mark, as was his usual morning routine, walked into a coffee shop and ordered a cafe latte, then browsed through the newspapers on the stand while he waited. A headline on the cover of the *Killarney Express* grabbed his attention. Shocked, he grabbed the newspaper and hurriedly read the story while waiting for his coffee.

"Several staff members have complained about unfair treatment..." he muttered under his breath.

"...And have accused Michal Scott, the daytime soapie's executive producer of making promises in their contracts that have not materialised," Greg read as he pored over the article online.

Nokuthula walked into Michal's office with her boss's daily cappuccino and heard her barking instructions to the publicist on the phone.

"Do a press release ASAP! Organise a press conference if you have to. I will not have people thinking that I'm racist!"

Nokuthula placed the coffee on Michal's desk and smiled a small smile that gave nothing away, knowing that she was part of the reason that the revolution had been televised, or in this case, newspaper-vised.

Thanks, Maki, she thought, as she sauntered out of Michal's office.

Mpho, who was seated in her office, giggled with glee as she read the well-written article. Maki had cleverly put together the information that Mpho had given her.

"Two staff members were hired as writers but were soon asked to fill other positions that did not include writing for the daily soapie," she read out loud.

Sechaba beamed as he read the article. "The two staff members, who refused to be named, now work in positions that are not what they were hired for. They were coerced into agreeing to these positions because they thought that they had value, but have learnt over time that their new positions hold no real weight."

Sechaba put the newspaper aside and let the truth of the words sink in. He knew that one of the employees mentioned in the article was him, and for the first time in a long time he felt a sense of affirmation.

Rian finished reading the *Killarney Express* article and suddenly saw that it was written by Dimakatso Dilobetso.

"Well, I'll be damned," he said with a smile. "The girl has what it takes after all." He had written Maki off as lacking in chutzpah, a trait that every writer worth their salt contained. And a trait that he now admired fiercely in Maki.

"Take that, Michal," he said, satisfied as he reclined in his chair, taking an indulgent sip of his coffee.

***

Tebogo was seated on the edge of the bed surrounded by the actor's mom, Mam' Melita and two other women that she assumed were the actor's aunts. Soon it turned out that one of the ladies, Mamoreki, just ran a tavern next door because Mam' Melita ordered her out and told her that they were conducting family business that had nothing to do with her. Mamoreki didn't budge, insisting that she'd lived next door to Mam' Melita long enough to be considered family, but when Mam' Melita told her that the neighbourhood kids were devising ways of breaking into her tavern to steal her booze, she quickly scurried off, cursing the kids at the top of her voice. That left Tebogo with Mam' Melita and a lady that Mam' Melita introduced as Aunt Petunia, Malome Masemola's wife.

Tebogo swallowed nervously in anticipation of the conversation that was about to take place, but Mam' Melita immediately produced a traditional Sepedi outfit from her wardrobe and draped it around Tebogo. Aunt Petunia, unimpressed, burst Mam' Melita's bubble and reminded her that Tebogo had not yet been accepted into their family.

"But she will be," Mam' Melita argued petulantly. "You and Masemola are the same, always telling me what to do and ruining my fun with your rigid rules."

"Those rules uphold our traditions," Aunt Petunia declared, before turning sternly to Tebogo.

"Now, young lady, care to tell us what your intentions with the actor are?"

"Um," Tebogo stammered. "To love and uphold the actor," she shared nervously, then lambasted herself. *Why does it sound like I'm saying vows already?*

"How much do you make?" Mam' Melita asked flippantly.

"Excuse me?" Tebogo asked, stunned.

"I need to know if you're after my son for his money or not."

"Ma, I make my own money. I have my own car and a flat, and I work in the legal department of an insurance company," Tebogo replied in a small voice.

"Hmm," Aunt Petunia replied, impressed. Tebogo sighed with relief that the strict aunt had found something about her to like.

"And is your mother raising your children while you play wifey to my son in Johannesburg?" Mam' Melita asked, as Aunt Petunia smiled.

"I don't have any children."

"Stand up," Aunt Petunia barked.

Stunned, Tebogo stood.

"Turn around," Mam' Melita instructed, and Tebogo dutifully turned around. Mam' Melita and Aunt Petunia nodded, impressed at her sizeable child-bearing hips.

"Okay, sit down," Mam' Melita ordered, and Tebogo sat.

"You do realise that if you're lying to us we will find out, right?" Mam' Melita barked.

"Yes, Ma," Tebogo replied, keeping her head low as a sign of respect.

"And you know that I, as the elder of this family, will be the one to induct you into our ways and customs?" Aunt Petunia asked, scrutinising Tebogo.

"Yes, Aunt Petunia," Tebogo replied, feeling small.

"Where are you from?" Mam' Melita asked.

"Ga-Mashashane."

Mam' Melita and Aunt Petunia shared an impressed look.

Mam' Melita smiled. "I always knew that my son would bring us one of our own."

And finally Tebogo allowed herself to smile a small smile of relief.

Malome Masemola stared the actor down, the air thick with tension. The younger man nervously rubbed his hands together, his earlier confidence replaced by anxiety as he waited for his uncle to say something. Bored by the silence, Malome Makgoromecha who was seated in the corner, emitted a drunken hick and loud burp, followed hastily by an apology. Malome Masemola silenced him with a steely, ice cold stare. Malome Makgoromecha collected himself and Malome Masemola focused back on the actor.

After a long while he finally said, "Son, you do understand the intensity of marriage, don't you?"

"Of course, Malome," the actor replied solemnly.

"Shouldn't we be talking about how many cows we are giving to this girl's family?" Malome Makgoromecha offered, but Malome Masemola turned to him angrily.

"Hey, shut up, wena man!"

"There you go again," Malome Makgoromecha complained. "Treating me like I don't matter and talking to me with no re-spect!"

Annoyed, Malome Masemola decided that the best way forward was to ignore Makgoromecha and focus on the actor.

"I know that with every decision one makes in life there will be challenges," the actor expanded. "I expect marriage to be the same."

"And you will love this girl no matter what?" Malome Masemola asked.

"Yes, Malome," the actor said. "I've been on a mission these past few months to improve every area of my life. That led me to dig deeper within myself, and I've challenged myself to be the best man that I know I can be. It was in that space that I met Tebogo. I know that God has brought her into my life for a purpose."

Malome Makgoromecha laughed loudly and slapped his thigh.

"And the devil?" he asked. "Don't you think that the devil can bring her into your life? Let me tell you something son, women are from the devil, and if you are not careful, they will ruin your life! They will turn your life upside down and leave you with nothing!"

The actor resolved to keep his cool, and turned back to Malome Masemola.

"She complements me and helps me with my shortcomings. Plus she celebrates my competencies and abilities."

"That's good son," Malome Masemola said. "Those are good qualities to look for."

"Ha!" Malome Makgoromecha exclaimed. "Wait until she empties out your bank balance! That is the reason why I drink morning, noon and night, my boy! Women! Basadi. The spawn of the devil. Mark my words. If you ever come back here to tell us that you want a divorce, I will remind you of these very words."

The actor swallowed anxiously. He was reminded of the saying that in a drunken man's words lay the truth.

Malome Masemola noted the actor's nerves. "Are you sure you want to do this?" he asked solemnly.

The actor nodded, resolute. "I am," he replied, trying his best to ignore his sudden bout of nerves.

For the first time in ages Lerato had decided to sleep in. Whilst staying with Tebogo she'd felt compelled to wake up at the crack of dawn which was when Tebogo woke up. Even though Tebogo insisted that she go back to sleep, once Lerato was awake it was impossible for her to fall back asleep. It felt good waking up in Seputla's bed; for one thing his bedsheets smelled of him, and for another, the smell of coffee ran through the apartment. She wrapped herself in his gown and went to the kitchen where he'd not only made coffee, but brunch as well.

"Hey," she said, feeling coy. For some reason she had become incredibly shy around Seputla lately. *Must be all the hormones,* she reasoned, or the fact that since she'd fallen pregnant she felt exceptionally vulnerable which was completely foreign to her.

"Hey, you," Seputla smiled. "You were out for the count, so I thought I'd let you sleep."

Lerato noted that he was in his gym clothes. "Are you going to the gym?" she asked.

"Just came from there. I told my manager that I was taking the day off. With all the overtime I've been working lately I think I deserve it."

Lerato smiled.

"And you deserve for me to be here to take care of you," he concluded.

Despite herself, Lerato blushed, and she mentally scolded herself.

"Last night was awesome," Seputla said smiling in her direction.

And just like that she was blushing again. Lerato laughed out loud, deciding that it was impossible to fight her body and the display that her hormones were putting on, despite the way she felt betrayed by them.

"Yes, it was," she agreed with a smile.

Seputla handed her a cup of coffee. "I can't drink that," she said, "Too much caffeine."

"No worries. Tea?" Seputla asked, holding up a box of mint tea.

"Yes, please."

"I hope you don't mind that I brought you here. I didn't think it would be appropriate to do what I did to you last night in Tebogo's flat," Seputla said with a wink at Lerato.

To prevent herself from blushing again, she quickly changed the subject.

"Speaking of Tebza, did I tell you that she and the actor are getting married?"

"So soon?" Seputla asked, and off Lerato's nod, continued, "How's Tshepo taking it?"

"I don't think he knows."

"I didn't tell you that I went to go see him, neh?" Seputla asked Lerato, handing her a cup of tea.

"Thank you, babe," she smiled. "Why did you go see him?"

"After the video of his beatdown went viral I thought he could use a friend, but of course he insulted me," Seputla responded, causing Lerato to emit a huge belly laugh.

"That video was hilarious!" she said, but Seputla looked at her disapprovingly. "Did I tell you that he was stalking Tebogo?" Lerato asked. "The one time he followed her all the way to our place and was shocked when I opened the door. He's always had a crush on me so when I told him that I'd send men to beat him up if he carried on, I thought he'd gotten the message. Clearly he hadn't. What the actor did to him was a long time coming."

Seputla laughed. "Wow. Classic."

"Enough about Tebogo and her love triangle," Lerato said. "What about us?"

Seputla's heart started thumping loudly against his ribs. "Us?" he asked nervously in anticipation of what Lerato was about to say.

"After last night —" Lerato started, but Seputla cut her off.

"You made it clear that you want to take it slow," he said.

"You certainly didn't take it slow last night," Lerato smiled, and Seputla laughed loudly.

"I want to be there for you and the baby," he said. "As your man and as our baby's full-time parent."

Lerato was sure that she was going to cry buckets of tears. There was nothing that she wanted more, but she could not bring herself to say the words because she feared hurting Seputla again. Eventually she looked up at him. "No pressure?"

With a disappointed sigh he forced himself to agree. "No pressure."

Maki tried her best to do her make-up the way she remembered Tebogo doing it, but when she inspected herself in the mirror she sighed, disappointed. It wasn't terrible, it just wasn't great. She was about to FaceTime with Puo, and for some reason she was hella nervous.

"He's just a friend," she reminded herself in a bid to calm her nerves. "And it's just a casual phone call."

As she dialled his number the nerves came rushing back, but amazingly they instantly calmed when he answered and she saw his face light up her screen.

"Hey," he smiled warmly.

"Hey," she smiled back. "Just thought I'd check in. How was your trip back to PE?"

"Terrible," he groaned. "It was raining so there was tons of turbulence."

There was a moment's silence and then Maki told him her news: "I'm meeting with Corrine in about an hour to give her my signed contract."

"Good for you," Puo replied, then he noticed her angst. "Hey, you'll be fine; don't stress."

Maki smiled widely and was about to thank him, when suddenly she heard a woman's voice yell, "Puo, you home?"

Puo yelled back, "I'm on the phone," before turning back to Maki, but Maki was frozen.

"Are you married?" she finally managed to say.

Puo chuckled. "No, that's Nancy, my daughter's nanny."

"Oh," Maki smiled, relieved. "You have a daughter?"

"Yes, she's six. Her name is Cece."

"And her mom?" Maki was unable to prevent the words from tumbling out of her mouth.

Puo sighed. "She died. Three years ago."

Maki's heart went out to him. "Oh my goodness. I'm so sorry to hear that!"

Puo gave her a small smile. Suddenly Maki heard the sound of a little girl's voice yelling, "Daddy!" Again Puo yelled back, "I'm on the phone, sweetheart!"

Maki's heart was broken for Puo. She didn't know what to say, so a brief silence filled the air.

"It's tough," Puo admitted, "but we're soldiering on."

"Let me not keep you from her," Maki whispered, suddenly feeling emotional.

Puo studied her for a moment. "Thanks for the call," he said, then hung up.

Maki stared at the blank screen for a while.

"You're welcome," she muttered to herself, crushed.

Eventually Tebogo was led back into the lounge by Aunt Petunia and Mam' Melita. She felt her knees buckle at the sight of the actor; she was happy to be back in his presence and away from the interrogation of Mam' Melita and Aunt Petunia. He smiled warmly at her, but before Tebogo could sit down Malome Masemola instructed her to go make them all tea.

The actor stood hurriedly to his feet. "I'll help you," he offered, but Malome Masemola cut him off.

"You need to be here for the next part of our discussions," the elder commanded.

Despite the order, the actor quickly grabbed Tebogo's arm and led her to the kitchen.

"I'll just show her where everything is," he said before exiting the room. When they reached the privacy of the kitchen, Tebogo threw herself into his arms for a much needed embrace.

"Your mom and aunt are relentless," she said, then burst into a fit of giggles. It had suddenly dawned on her that they were indeed getting married.

"And?" the actor probed. "They weren't too hard on you were they?"

But before Tebogo could reply, Mam' Melita stuck her head into the kitchen. "I hope you two aren't kissing in my house," she reprimanded. Tebogo studied Mam' Melita's face, unable to tell if she was serious or joking. Just then Malome Makgoromecha yelled loudly from the other room that he hoped that they weren't naked and having sex, causing Tebogo to blush profusely.

The actor merely laughed. "You'll get used to him," he chuckled.

"Come back into the lounge, son," Mam' Melita said. "Making tea is not that hard. Tebogo will figure it out." The actor gave Tebogo a quick reassuring wink before leaving the kitchen with his mom. The young woman exhaled deeply and turned on the kettle.

"Signed, sealed, delivered," Maki said, sliding her contract across the table to Corinne.

"Excellent," Corrine smiled, clapping her hands together. She paged through the contract, and when she was done looked up at Maki. "Welcome to the team. I'll sign this and send you a copy via email."

"Thank you," Maki beamed.

"Are you ready?"

"Ready as I'll ever be."

"Good," Corrine said standing up to leave. "Your manuscript will be sent to our editor and design team today. I'll send you the editor's notes within the week and you need to implement them ASAP. I should get book cover ideas from the designers a few days after they've read the book."

Suddenly Maki felt nervous; after Corrine left she decided to order a glass of wine to celebrate her publishing contract. While waiting she looked around the restaurant and saw the *Killarney Express* on the newsstand; she rushed over to read it.

"Oh my goodness," she whispered as she read through the cover article, her article –

the exposé on *Kas'lethu*. As she read it she felt her heart flutter anxiously against her chest, shocked that she had been so brazen.

Exhausted, her mind and emotions swirling, Maki got home and plopped tiredly onto the couch. She was shaken out of her pending slumber when she got a message notification from the bank showing that a sizeable chunk of money had been deposited into her account.

"What the...?" she exclaimed, sitting up in confusion. Almost immediately another message came in. It was Corrine informing Maki that all their authors get paid a percentage of their fee upon signing their contract, and that the money that had been deposited into her account was an advance for her first book. She jokingly added that Maki shouldn't spend it all at once, and ended the text with a smiling emoji. Maki's heart beat rapidly in excitement. When the realisation hit that she was about to become a fully-fledged author, she threw her legs in the air and flailed them about exuberantly as she squealed in delight.

Tebogo found a tray and cloth in the cupboard, along with an expensive China tea set consisting of teacups and saucers, a sugar bowl and dainty side plates. Luckily she found biscuits in another cupboard. When she walked back into the lounge,

Mam' Melita was impressed, but still she exclaimed: "Those biscuits are for guests!"

"We are guests," Aunt Petunia offered.

"No, you're family," Mam' Melita replied. "There's a difference."

Malome Makgoromecha sat up at the sight of refreshments. "Start over here, sweetie," he said hungrily, but Tebogo served Malome Masemola first, bowing respectfully as she held the tea tray and he poured himself a cup of tea. She heard Malome Makgoromecha curse her under his breath. After she'd served everyone, including Malome Makgoromecha, Malome Masemola invited her to sit down with them, even though she didn't have a cup of tea.

"We have decided," he said, pausing to slurp his tea loudly, "that we will go to see your mother tomorrow morning."

Tebogo's heart beat so fast that it felt like it would leap out of her chest. "To-to-to-morrow?" she stammered, causing everyone to look up at her.

Malome Makgoromecha laughed loudly. "What? Too soon?" he bellowed.

Tebogo looked to the actor who willed her with his eyes not to embarrass him.

"No, of course not," Tebogo replied quickly. "I'll let her know that you are coming."

"Good," Malome Masemola replied. Unable to meet the actors' gaze, Tebogo kept her head low, fixated with a spot on the floor.

After showering, Lerato put on one of Seputla's oversized T-shirts and flip flops. She walked into the lounge and found Seputla reading a book, but when she walked in he looked up.

"I could get used to seeing you in my clothes every day," he mused.

Lerato blushed briefly and sat down on the couch next to him.

"You know you don't have to go, right?" he said softly. Lerato melted inside; she wanted nothing more than to stay. "Besides, what are you going back to?" he added. "An empty flat?"

Lerato briefly met Seputla's eye, feeling the strong urge to stay with him, but knowing that it was best that she go.

Seputla put his book aside. "Lerato," he said taking her hands in his and waiting for her eyes to meet his before continuing. "I want us to raise this baby together. I want you in my life – as my partner, not as a booty call or someone I occasionally sleep with. You're carrying my child, for goodness' sake!"

Lerato averted her eyes, silent.

"I know I can't afford the life you want, but I'm working towards getting there. And I want to be with you when I get it," he pressed.

Lerato bit her bottom lip nervously.

"I'm scared, Seputla," she finally said.

"There's nothing to be afraid of," Seputla comforted. When he saw that she was still unsure, he squeezed her hands. "Nothing."

Lerato swallowed nervously. "I want us to raise this baby together too," she whispered.

"So why fight it?" he asked with a shy smile. "Are we're on?"

Lerato managed a small, coy nod and Seputla broke into a wide smile as he quickly took her in his arms. She hugged him back and sighed, comforted by the fact that Seputla, the love of her life, was back in her life.

The actor and Tebogo walked into their hotel room in Polokwane and tiredly threw themselves onto the bed. Tebogo was stressed out about the actor's family meeting Seipati but didn't want to say anything to her fiancé in case she talked him out of marrying her. The young woman finally managed to calm the swarming nerves in the pit of her stomach but just when she felt that she was about to pass out, she suddenly felt like she was going to throw up. She quickly held her hand up to her mouth and bolted to the bathroom where she hurled violently into the toilet bowl.

The actor appeared in the doorway. "Tebogo, really?" he asked, unimpressed. "Are you that scared of committing to me?"

Tebogo was unable to answer, so he sat next to her and rubbed her back even though he recoiled at every hurl. After a while the hurling finally subsided and Tebogo stood up, rinsed her mouth and splashed cold water on her face, holding onto the sink for balance.

"It's not marrying you that scares me," she finally said. "It's your family meeting my mother."

"Aren't you being a bit dramatic? She can't be that bad."

"You don't know my mom," Tebogo replied, dabbing her face with a towel. "She might embarrass you, then call the entire neighbourhood to come and see that there's a famous actor in her house."

The actor wrapped his arms around Tebogo. "As long as she agrees to letting me marry you, that's all that matters."

Tebogo chuckled and shook her head. "You say that now."

The actor kissed her lightly on the forehead. "Give her a call and tell her to expect us."

"Thanks, babe," Tebogo said, leaning in for a kiss, but the actor drew back.

"I think you ought to use some mouthwash first before you bring those lips near mine," he joked as he headed out the bathroom.

After the actor's reassurance Tebogo had fallen into a deep sleep, but was woken in a frenzy at the crack of dawn by the violent shrill of her cellphone. Disorientated, she took her phone off the nightstand and checked to see that the actor was still asleep. Thankfully he was, and she tiptoed to the bathroom, her phone plastered to her ear. "Lerato, why are you calling me so early?" she whispered but Tebogo's whispering was contradicted by Lerato's loud reprimand.

"Moghel, why didn't you tell me that you're getting married?" Lerato screamed loudly.

"It's five in the morning," Tebogo croaked sleepily.

"I know. I couldn't sleep," Lerato explained. "But you're always up at this hour, so what's the problem?"

"I'm hella nervous, babe," Tebogo said, shutting the bathroom door behind her. "The actor's family is going to see my mom today about asking for my hand in marriage. I met his family yesterday and they put us through the most."

"As they should," Lerato laughed. "You've known the actor for all of two minutes."

"I guess," Tebogo replied. "I should be grateful that they're willing to have the conversation in the first place, right?"

"Exactly," Lerato agreed. "And since this means you'll be leaving me permanently in the flat..."

"I'm so sorry about that! Of all the times to abandon you!"

"Don't worry about me, girl – Seputla and I are back together."

Tebogo let out a loud scream. "I'm so happy!" she shrieked. "You two belong together. Just be nice to him, please."

"Girl, I learnt my lesson," Lerato confessed, "and that's part of the reason why I called.

His place is tiny. When you get back I presume you'll move in with the actor. I still have to convince Seputla, but I was thinking of getting him to move in with me at your place?"

"Of course." Tebogo agreed. "But truth be told I don't want to move in with the actor until the traditional ceremony."

"So we'll have our slumber party after all?" Lerato asked.

"Yes," Tebogo smiled. "And then when I move in with the actor, maybe Seputla could move in with you."

"Sounds great," Lerato said.

"You and Seputla should take over the lease and change the name on the paperwork. I'll ask the agent to run it past the owner."

Lerato smiled. "That's brilliant, thank you."

"It's the least I can do."

Chapter 16

Seipati had woken up at the crack of dawn which was unusual for her, and had started to clean her house. She had to admit that a small part of her didn't believe that Tebogo was getting married.

"There's no way she can get anyone to agree to marry her so quickly after breaking up with Tshepo, let alone an actor!"

She put on the kettle to make herself a cup of tea, knackered from the effort that cleaning required. As she removed a mug from the cupboard, Seipati was startled by the sound of a car driving into her yard, and she rushed to look out the window. "My goodness!" she gasped. An elderly man, a middle-aged man and the actor from *Kas'lethu* stepped out of a luxury German vehicle. She blinked numerous times; were her eyes deceiving her? So Tebogo wasn't lying after all! The actor from *Kas'lethu* really and truly wanted to marry her! She quickly sent a text message on her phone that read: "Come quickly! And dress to kill!"

Seipati pocketed her phone, put the mug back in the cupboard and stepped outside onto the stoep to welcome her guests.

"Good morning," she smiled widely, shaking each of their hands exuberantly. Tebogo's mother was stunned when the middle-aged man grabbed her and roughly forced her into an impromptu embrace.

"Makgoromecha!" The elderly man scolded.

The middle-aged man let her go, apologising profusely. "Apologies, maiden, I'm not accustomed to such beauty."

Taken aback, Seipati rubbed her palms against her skirt. "Okay," she said slowly, then turned to the actor expectantly.

The elderly man spoke up. "We are the elders of the actor's family. Are you the mother of Tebogo Precious Seamela?" he asked.

"Indeed I am," Seipati answered, surprising even herself with her mild-mannered tone and posh English.

"It's a pleasure to make your acquaintance," the elderly man continued. "As you can imagine we are here on quite a serious matter."

Suddenly Seipati felt uneasy. *I hope Tebogo isn't pregnant!* she quickly thought. Then she scolded herself. *Of course she is!* Now it made sense – why she had left Tshepo so quickly, and why Tshepo had called her a slut. *Why didn't I think of this before?*

Her thoughts were interrupted by the actor saying that he had found a flower at this very residence. Despite herself, Seipati was charmed and could see what Tebogo saw in him. The elderly man spoke up again and introduced himself as Masemola, before asking if they could discuss the matter in the house.

"Of course," Seipati quickly replied, gesturing for them to proceed. As her guests entered the house one by one, she noticed with glee that her neighbours had stepped out of their homes and were staring into her yard curiously. Seipati smiled a small victorious smile to herself. She hoped that John would arrive soon so that between the two of them they could milk this actor guy for all he was worth.

Maki walked into the office still lost in her own thoughts about Puo and his situation and wondering when they would speak again. She was startled by the sound of applause and was surprised to see that all her colleagues were on their feet, applauding her.

"What the...?" she gasped, utterly shocked. A few of the younger and more enthusiastic junior writers even threw in a few whoops for good measure as Maki walked to her desk, blushing furiously. Suddenly Andrew bolted out of his office and an immediate hush fell as he yelled across the room that he wanted to see Maki in his office right away. As if floating on air, Maki walked towards her boss's office.

"If you think that I'm going to applaud you too, that's where you're mistaken," Andrew quipped in a dry tone as Maki shut the door behind her.

"Oh, come on," she smiled as she plopped into a chair. "Even you can admit that article was pretty kick-ass." She studied his face and saw the corners of his mouth turn upward ever so slightly. "You know you have it in you to praise me," she joked. "You know you want to. I can see it on your face."

But suddenly he turned stern again. "Whatever, California Roll. Listen, I have a story that I want you to investigate."

"Me? Investigate a story?" Maki squealed excitedly.

"Did I stutter?"

"It's just that I'm so used to you giving me puff pieces that I never thought this day would ever come."

"When you returned to us you handed me an exhaustive list of your copious demands, remember?" he asked, straight-faced.

"Of course I remember."

"And since your colleagues think so highly of you, who better to give this story to?"

Maki restrained herself from jumping up and dancing. Two back-to-back cover stories? She allowed herself a mild yelp, trying to contain her excitement.

"You up for the challenge?" Andrew asked, eyeballing her.

"Of course!"

"Good," Andrew replied, giving her a piece of paper with some details and phone numbers on it."

But with her still seated, he barked, "You better get to it!"

Maki stood hurriedly and headed out of his office, but before she left the room he yelled out: "California roll!"

The young writer turned back abruptly. "Yes?"

"Good job," he smiled, and Maki beamed with pride.

Seipati walked into the lounge carrying a tea tray and cookies and humbly served her guests. Silence fell upon them as she sat down and eyed the men. "I don't want to lie," she started, "but I am rather taken aback by all of this."

"We understand that this is overwhelming," Malome Masemola replied, "but we assure you that we come with only good intentions."

"I don't doubt that at all," Seipati explained. "It's just that I'm serving you my tea and have warmly invited you into my home..."

"Did your daughter not tell you to expect us?" Malome Makgoromecha asked, biting into his cookie and causing a few crumbs to tumble down his chin.

"Oh, she did," Seipati answered, "I just think that I've been particularly lenient to you in the interest of protecting your privacy, considering your son's affluent stature."

It dawned on Malome Masemola and the actor and they shared a look. "We didn't mean to disrespect you, madam," Malome Masemola said, taking a wad of cash from his blazer pocket and placing it on the table. "Forgive us."

Not wanting to appear too keen, Seipati casually eyed the money. Just then they were interrupted by a knock on the door.

"Pardon me," she said, standing up and tucking the wad of cash into her ample bosom. "It sounds like Tebogo's uncle is here. Let me get the door."

"Good," Malome Makgoromecha mumbled. "These matters should be handled by men anyway." Luckily Seipati had already left the room and didn't hear Malome Makgoromecha's comment towards her, but the actor and Malome Masemola called him to task.

"If you're not going to be respectful then you might as well leave," Malome Masemola scolded.

"This woman is going to milk you dry." Malome Makgoromecha warned, "Mark my words."

"So what? It's my money!" the actor protested, then kept quiet as a tall and serious looking man in a scotch blazer, chino pants and fedora hat walked into the room. His height was quite intimidating, and the three men quickly took to their feet.

"Everyone, this is Tebogo's uncle, Uncle John," Seipati introduced the new arrival. As they shook hands the actor could not help but notice that Uncle John and Tebogo looked nothing alike. Still he kept quiet and let Malome Masemola do the talking.

"It's a pleasure to meet you, my good man," Malome Masemola started.

"Indeed," Uncle John replied, sitting down. "I always knew that my girl Tebogo would do us proud. She's always been of upstanding character; a girl with great morals."

"Correct, Uncle John," the actor replied. "In fact, that is why we are here today."

"She's not pregnant, is she?" Seipati blurted out. A cold silence fell upon the room as all eyes stared at the actor.

"No," the actor replied indignantly, "she's not pregnant."

"And how long have you known her?" Seipati asked icily.

It was not lost on the actor that Seipati had turned much colder since Uncle John's arrival.

Safety in numbers, he thought, but he replied politely, "Not that long, Ma. But she is someone I want to spend the rest of my life with."

His smile was quickly wiped off his face when Seipati pressed him. "You haven't answered my question."

"Two months," the actor replied.

Malome Makgoromecha whistled under his breath as he took a flask from his pocket and poured some of the brown liquid into his now empty teacup, much to the amusement of Uncle John.

Seipati chuckled, wryly. "And what makes you think that I would entrust you with my daughter after only knowing her for two months?"

Uncle John stepped in. "Please, Seipati, let me handle this."

"Yes!" Malome Makgoromecha agreed loudly. "Let the men handle this business, please woman! Have you no respect for our customs?"

"Excuse me?" she exclaimed, turning to look angrily at Malome Makgoromecha, but he merely shook his head at her disdainfully.

"You see," he said pointing at her with his teacup. "She's getting worked up already."

Seipati scowled at Malome Makgoromecha. "Sies, you drunkard."

"Come, hold me by the ears and kiss me," Malome Makgoromecha joked, chuckling at the look of utter repulsion on Seipati's face. "By the end of the day we'll be family anyway."

Highly annoyed, Malome Masemola cast Malome Makgoromecha a death stare that silenced him immediately, but it was the actor who spoke up authoritatively. "The qualities that you described your daughter as having are qualities that I have too. I live my life under public scrutiny, and even though I'm a young man of 30 years old, I'm sure you've never read any scandals about me in the tabloids."

Uncle John and Seipati shared a look.

"The life of an actor isn't easy, but Tebogo grounds me," the actor continued. "She brings out the best in me. And when you've been around people who only want to take from you or have the worst intentions for you, it becomes pretty easy to see the one whose intentions are pure. Tebogo is all that to me and so much more."

Despite herself, Seipati was moved. And she wasn't the sort of woman who gave in easily to emotion. "Well then, take her. You can have her."

"She is not a commodity to have, Ma," the actor corrected. "I love her."

Malome Masemola beamed proudly at his nephew and turned to Uncle John seriously. "R50 000," he said. Uncle John and Seipati shared a look and giggled.

"Tebogo is a highly educated young woman," Seipati told them. "She holds an LLB degree from the University of the Witwatersrand." She failed to mention that the law degree had been paid for by a bursary, but that was privileged information.

"And did we mention that she is without child?" Uncle John added. "We are giving her to you pure."

But Malome Makgoromecha piped up once again. "As a point of order, chief, in our culture it is frowned upon if a woman enters marriage without at least one child. How are we to know that her ovaries haven't dried up?" He chuckled and added, "Not that you would know, since you have us here negotiating with a woman."

Seipati fumed.

"Please pardon my uncle," the actor apologised profusely before Malome Makgoromecha hurled more insults in Seipati's direction.

Uncle John definitively proclaimed, "R100 000!"

The air in the room suddenly stilled, and Malome Makgoromecha clutched his chest.

"From 50 to 100 000?" Malome Makgoromecha gasped, unable to control the Sepedi that tumbled out of his mouth. "Aowa lena. La gafa?"

The actor swallowed. He hated feeling like Tebogo was up for auction, but clearly Uncle John and Seipati were aiming for a high bid, and he had no one to blame but himself for taking Malome Makgoromecha to one of the most important days in his life.

Malome Masemola cast the actor a look, and the actor gave a discreet nod. "Agreed; R30 000 will be in your account by the end of this week," Malome Masemola said to Seipati. She beamed, despite trying to downplay her elation at the huge sum of money that she had just acquired.

"You like things, neh, sweetness?" Malome Makgoromecha commented, eyeing Seipati slyly. "I can practically see the dollar signs dancing in your eyes."

Seipati cleared her throat and collected herself, turning serious again. "Pleasure doing business with you, gentlemen," she said, standing up to accompany the men to the door. Malome Masemola and the actor respectfully shook hands with Uncle John and Seipati, relieved that they'd completed their business before Malome Makgoromecha caused them more humiliation by bursting into his well-known, off-key, drunken Sepedi hymns. But as Malome Makgoromecha turned to leave and bid Seipati goodbye, he puckered his lips for her to kiss him, which caused Uncle John to kick him out forcefully.

***

Tebogo hadn't been able to calm her nerves; she'd endured a whirlwind of emotions over the past few days and she feared that they were catching up with her fast and uncontrollably. She'd been summoned by Mam' Melita and Aunt Petunia to cook lunch for the men so that they would have food after the negotiations. Considering how stressed she was, it was a wonder that she hadn't burnt any of the food. Although ordinarily she would've found it incredibly invasive to have someone hovering over her while she cooked, on this particular occasion Tebogo was grateful for Aunt Petunia's beady eye that had kept a close watch on her.

She was busy setting the table when she got a text from the actor to say that they were on their way back. Worried that they hadn't been gone long enough, she was tormented by dread-filled thoughts. Had her mother been rude to them? Had she kicked them out? Had she told them about Tshepo and failed to recognise the actor as the man who wanted to marry her?

Tebogo was so engulfed in her thoughts that she forgot to use a cloth to take the lamb casserole out of the oven and burnt her fingers.

"Ow," she squealed, fighting the desire to curse. She ran to the tap and ran cold water over her scalded fingers. *Get it together!* she scolded herself, exhaling deeply to try and reduce her anxiety, but it was at that precise moment that Mam' Melita walked in with a quart of beer and laughed at her.

"This is why I never got married," she laughed loudly. "Look at you, squirming and panicking about whether or not you will be my daughter-in-law."

Tebogo swallowed hard and fought back tears, as Aunt Petunia eyed her sympathetically. "Don't worry your pretty little head about how the negotiations are going," she said reassuringly. "Masemola is the best negotiator ever. He will have your mother eating out the palm of his hand."

The young woman felt slightly appeased. Hopefully Malome Masemola had been able to handle Seipati. She nodded her appreciation to Aunt Petunia, picked up a cloth, removed the dish from the oven and hurried to finish setting the table.

A moment later Malome Masemola drove into the yard and Mam' Melita banished Tebogo to the kitchen to pour the men juice so that they could gossip about how the negotiations had gone without Tebogo hearing their conversation. Tebza poured the juice as quickly as she could, and when she returned the room was silent; even Malome Makgoromecha was quiet, which was unusual.

Tebogo sadly concluded that the negotiations hadn't gone well. Nervously she searched for a clue on the actor's face; at first he looked downcast, then suddenly he broke into a wide smile. Tebogo was confused until Mam' Melita belted out an ear-shattering ululation and the actor excitedly scooped his fiancé up in his arms. The negotiations had gone well, he told her, and they'd reached a sum that they'd all agreed on. Tebogo realised that she'd been holding her breath the entire time, and now she exhaled in relief while clutching onto the actor tightly.

"Are you serious?" she whispered in his ear.

"Break it up, you two," Malome Makgoromecha yelled. "Makoti, we're famished. Let's taste this food of yours that we paid hundreds of thousands for."

Tebogo's eyes bulged and she looked to the actor. "Hundreds of thousands?" she mouthed to him. Much to her relief he shook his head, and she asked everyone to come through to the dining room. Of course, Malome Makgoromecha was the first to head towards the table filled with a delicious spread in the adjoining room.

Mam' Melita hugged her son, proud of the man that he had become. "You're about to become the head of your own household, my boy," she said proudly.

Tebogo waited for Malome Masemola to walk past before shyly calling his name. When the elder turned to face her, she said in a solemn, soft voice. "Thank you, Malome Masemola." To her surprise, he wrapped her in a huge bear hug, and warmly said, "Welcome home, daughter," as the actor looked on, a lump in his throat.

Maki eventually arrived home after a long day's work of re-searching her investigative story. She was tired but she didn't want to mess up this massive opportunity. She unlocked the front door, took off her shoes and bra and flopped to the couch. Just as she started to unwind she was shocked to hear a knock on the door and even more shocked that it was Maggie, the stylist from the publishing company, who had arrived to style her cupboard.

"Um," Maki stammered, embarrassed that the stylist hired to turn her wardrobe around, had found her at her most un-flattering.

"Don't worry about it," Maggie smiled. "We wouldn't need stylists if we were snatched every hour on the hour, now would we?" With a wink in Maki's direction, added, "And that's where I come in."

But Maggie's words did nothing to soothe Maki as she led her to the wardrobe, filled with dread at what the woman would think.

Back at the hotel Tebogo and the actor could finally relax and talk. "Can you believe it?" he said, turning to Tebogo. "We are well on our way to being Mr and Mrs." Unable to contain herself, Tebogo threw herself on top of the actor and flooded him with kisses.

"What's that for?" he asked as he came up for air.

"For being you," Tebogo replied breathless. "For everything."

"Your Uncle John drives a hard bargain," he chuckled.

Tebogo squished up her face and disentangled herself from the actor's arms. "Who?"

"Your uncle," he said, slowly. "John."

"I don't have an uncle named John," Tebogo replied in confusion. "My mother has two sisters and they both live in Thaba Nchu." Suddenly the realisation hit her. "Did my mother deceive you?"

"Tebogo, why didn't you tell us before?" the actor asked in surprise.

"I didn't know that she'd pull this stunt! Oh, my gosh! I'm so sorry," she whispered. "Do you think this nullifies the negotiation?" she asked in a small voice, but the actor pulled her back into his embrace.

He did his best to restrain himself, but eventually let loose with a loud and unexpected laugh. "You know what? I have to give it to your mom. She pulled the wool over all our eyes."

Tebogo managed a small smile. "You're not angry?"

"From now on we tell each other everything, even if we don't think it's important, okay?" he smiled gently, kissing her on the forehead.

"Okay."

"And we don't need to tell the elders. What matters is that your mom got what she wanted, and so did I."

Tebogo exhaled and fell asleep on the actor's chest. Drained.

Maki was less than impressed. Maggie had left just before midnight after analysing her wardrobe and compiling a look-book of pictures with styles that Maki should invest in. Maki could tell that Maggie had conducted herself with as much restraint as she could as she tried to find diplomatic ways of telling her that she had no style and that her clothes were aged and ill-fitting. In short, Maki was in desperate need of a makeover. As if she didn't know any of that already.

However, to make matters worse, the publishing company wouldn't pay for the new look that they insisted Maki obtain – it all had to come out of her own pocket. She thought glumly that she really should have asked Tebogo to go over her contract before signing it.

She had thought that after Maggie's scrutiny and input she would be looking like an Instagram model this morning, but alas she was dressed for work in her regular jeans, sneakers and T-shirt. She grabbed her laptop bag, handbag and keys and was headed out the door when her cellphone beeped signalling a message. Maki was elated to see that it was from Tebza on their Divas WhatsApp group, telling her friends that she was on her way back from Polokwane, and summoning them for an urgent lunch and catch up session.

"Hell yeah!" Maki hurriedly typed back before rushing out of the house to get some work done so that she would be able to slip out at noon for a much-deserved and long- awaited lunch with her girls.

Maki's phone beeped again. It was message from Lerato, on their Divas WhatsApp group. "You know this!" it read. Maki rushed out the house.

Seipati had hardly slept. After the actor's family left the previous day, she had given John a small amount of the money that she'd coerced Masemola to give her, with a promise to send him more when the R30 000 cleared in her account at the end of the week. Her mind was reeling with plans for the hundred gees. She wanted to extend her house, upgrade her kitchen, get new furniture for the lounge and her bedroom, and pave the driveway. She couldn't remember when she'd last had more control of her life. Unfortunately Tebogo's monthly stipend didn't match the all-time high cost of living.

"My baby girl was always cut out for more," she told herself, as she headed to the kitchen and switched on the kettle. She was annoyed when there was a knock on the door and, assuming it was John, she thought angrily that she would put him properly in his place. He had already sent her three text messages with his banking details.

"Okay, John!" she yelled, as she yanked the door open. But her frown turned to a wide smile when she saw it was her neighbour from back opposite, Gladys, holding two quarts of beer. Gladys was upset that Seipati had not told her anything, and that she'd had to hear from Seipati's next door neighbour, Joyce, that Seipati had been entertaining famous people in her house.

"Out with it, girl!" Gladys loudly exclaimed, before giving Seipati a high five and cracking open a beer with her teeth.

The tea could definitely wait. Seipati fetched two glasses from the kitchen cupboard, revelling in a heightened sense of importance at being in-laws with a famous family who drove around Polokwane in German luxury vehicles, and whose son would soon officially be her son-in-law.

Tebogo and the actor had set off for Joburg at the crack of dawn to avoid all the fanfare they'd encountered on the way to Polokwane, what with having to take pictures with the cashiers at every toll gate. But back in the sanctity of their home, Tebogo watched the actor pace the room as he spoke to his personal banker, discussing how soon he could have the rest of the money needed to finalise the magadi.

Lost in her thoughts, the young woman watched her fiancé, determination etched on his face and in every stride that he took across the room. A bubbling sensation emanated from the pit of her stomach at the realisation that all this was for her. She'd never put a price on love, but in this moment she knew that the actor loved her, and watching him now was a complete turn on.

She snapped out of her reverie when he hung up abruptly, frustrated that he could only get his hands on the thirty grand that he'd promised Seipati, and that his banker would have to get back to him later about the rest.

"Kante, how much did you agree to give my mom?" Tebogo asked. For her, and especially for Seipati, R30 000 was more than adequate. Anything more than that and Seipati might just become a delinquent to society.

The actor slumped onto the couch, his head in his hands. "I shouldn't have told you that," he mused.

Tebogo slipped onto his lap and wrapped her arms around his neck. "We said no secrets, remember?"

"This has to be a secret though, babe."

"Okay. So the R30 000 is like a first payment, right?"

"Yes," the actor confirmed.

"So why are you frustrated about the rest?"

"Because I want you, and I want all of you. Now." the actor answered hungrily.

Tebogo laughed. "Fair enough," she said kissing him light-ly on the lips. "Except your banker doesn't know when he can get the rest to you, right?"

"Correct."

"So," she suggested, "why don't we wait to hear back from him, and when he gets it together we can use that as an opportunity to not only pay the full amount but also have the traditional ceremony on the same day?"

The actor's face lit up in glee. "So instead of paying the full amount and then organising the traditional ceremony, we would have the ceremony on the same day as the magadi is finalised?"

"Correct," Tebogo announced.

The actor stood with Tebogo wrapped around his waist and spun her around happily. As she threw her head back and screamed, the actor ploughed her with affectionate kisses.

"Now you know why I love you," he smiled, as Tebogo laughed raucously.

Chapter 17

Maki was seated at her desk, typing furiously on her laptop when her phone rang.

"Hello?" she answered distractedly. She stopped typing when she realised that Corrine was on the other end of the line. "Hey, Corrine," she brightly greeted her publisher.

"Hey, Maki, I just wanted to check in and see how your initial meeting with Maggie went."

Maki felt a pang of anger coil up her stomach. Should she let Corrine know how small Maggie made her feel, not only because she showed up unannounced after hours, but also because she then proceeded to tell Maki that the new clothes would have to come out of her own pocket? She sighed and took the plunge.

"Thanks for checking in with me, Corrine," Maki started. "Yes, I did meet with Maggie. She recommended some great clothes and styles for me, but she also mentioned that I'd be footing the bill for the clothes."

"Well, yes, that was made clear in your contact," Corinne confirmed. "We just feel that you should be as invested as we are in your brand and image. Don't you agree?"

Maki was silent for a moment and her unhappiness was clear to Corrine.

"The styling process doesn't work in isolation, Maki, and I understand that clothes are an integral part of a person's identity and that your style has been a part of who you are for a long time. But trust me, once you've met with our branding specialist and you have a more holistic view of what we want to do with you and your brand, I assure you that you will feel a lot better."

"Thanks," Maki managed to squeeze out.

"Listen, I get it," Corrine continued. "This is a new process, and I should have done a better job of inducting you into it, but trust me, in the end you will see that it was all worth it."

"Okay," Maki sighed, feeling better. "Thank you," she added before hanging up. She reclined into her chair and shut her eyes momentarily, in a sense feeling her autonomy being stripped away. But for once she allowed herself to let go of her own ideals and surrender to the belief that someone else saw potential in her that she didn't see, and would help her unearth it. Scary as that was.

Tebogo had fallen asleep in the actor's arms on the sun bed and was rudely awoken by her screeching cellphone. When she answered it was Lerato yelling at her that she was already at the restaurant and that neither she nor Maki had showed up. Tebogo leapt up – despite the actor's groggy moans – and assured Lerato that she'd see her in twenty minutes tops.

Lerato hung up, annoyed, and ordered her food. In her first two trimesters she hadn't been able to keep any food down, but she was heading into her third trimester and her appetite had returned with a vengeance. She scrolled through her Instagram feed as she waited for her friends to arrive. Just after the waiter placed a double cheese burger and fries in front of her, she looked up and saw a woman bearing a striking resemblance to Maki walk into the restaurant. She did a double take and, upon closer inspection, realised that it was Maki.

Her jaw fell to the ground.

"What the...?" she shrieked, as Maki rushed over to her.

"You didn't know that it was me, neh?" Maki smiled as she sat down.

"What did you do to yourself? Who did your hair? You look fantastic," Lerato screeched.

Maki blushed; for as long as she'd known Lerato, she'd never paid Maki any compliments. After her chat with Corrine earlier Maki decided to swing by the salon and straighten her thick mane of an afro. She too was shocked by how voluminous and sleek her hair was, even though she knew that by the end of the day it would recline back to its natural coils. She'd also bought an A-line, mid-calf skirt that she had been eyeing but was doubtful would do anything for her boyish figure. Even though she was wearing it with sneakers and her usual T-shirt, if Lerato's reaction was anything to go by, clearly Maggie knew what she was doing.

"Just a little something my publisher recommended for me," she smiled, eating a chip off Lerato's plate.

"Corrine?" Lerato marvelled.

"Girl, these people pay me to look good. They had a stylist come over just to create a look-book for me," Maki laughed.

Lerato smacked Maki's hand away as she tried to take another chip off her plate.

"I've been trying to upgrade you for years!" Lerato complained. "But this Corrine of yours comes in, gives you a few tips and you take them?"

"Don't be jealous," Maki laughed. "And maybe if you didn't use the word 'upgrade' it would have worked, hmm?"

Lerato and Maki didn't notice Tebogo walk into the restaurant; it was only when they heard a loud gasp next to them that they realised Tebogo was standing there, her eyes glued on Maki.

"Dimakatso?" she laughed, as she sat down, taking a strand of Maki's hair between her fingers. "Babe, you look incredible!" she screamed.

As soon as she sat down the entire staff of waiters emerged from the kitchen singing, "For she's a jolly good fellow," carrying balloons and a huge cake, and headed towards their table.

Tebogo's mouth fell open. Lerato watched her closely to gauge her friend's reaction.

"I didn't know what people sing in restaurants other than 'happy birthday', so I hope this will do," she laughed.

Tears sprang up in Tebogo's eyes. "You did this?" she asked, and Lerato nodded and smiled.

"Maki would have been in on the surprise too had she not been getting all dolled up," Lerato added, laughing.

When the staff reached their table they put Tebogo's cake on the table and released the helium-filled balloons to float above their heads. Written boldly on the cake was: "Congrats Mrs Actor!"

"Why didn't you tell me you were organising this?" Maki hissed at Lerato, "I could have helped."

Lerato just shrugged and blamed her forgetful preggy brain. As the staff headed back to their posts in the restaurant, Tebogo wiped the tears from her eyes. "Thank you," she smiled to Lerato, rubbing her friend's belly which had grown since she'd last seen her.

While Maki ordered her meal from the waiter, Lerato turned to Tebogo. "Did your friend tell you that she has a ridiculously good looking boyfriend who is also an author?" Lerato concluded with a mischievous wink in Maki's direction. "His name is Puo."

"No!" Tebogo scolded, whipping her head round to Maki. "Who is this Puo?"

"No one," Maki said, using a piece of hair to shield her face from her friends.

"She's lying," Lerato laughed.

Maki was quick to change the subject. "And you, Mrs Actor, only telling us that you're getting married after you're already in Polokwane?"

Tebogo screamed in excitement and quickly placed her order. She turned back to Maki and Lerato. "I must tell you about the actor's mom, Mam' Melita and his hilarious Malome Makgoromecha."

"I have a better idea," Lerato suggested. "That slumber party we've been putting off? Tonight is the night."

Tebogo screeched again in delight, screaming, "Girls night!" while Maki clasped her hands together excitedly.

"Bring your alcohol, make mine non-alcoholic, and I'll see you at six o' clock," Lerato instructed with a smile on her face as Maki and Tebogo whooped in glee.

It hadn't taken much for Tebogo to convince the actor that she'd be going to the slumber party. They'd pretty much spent every waking moment together for the past two weeks, so he understood. Before she left he'd pulled her in for a long and sexy kiss with the promise of more upon her return. Blushing and gasping for air, she blew him a kiss and left in her onesie pyjama outfit.

Lerato had lit candles and was in a sexy lacy nightie when Maki arrived. Maki had tied her hair up in a bun in an attempt to prevent the imminent shrinkage and was in an oversized T-shirt and shorts. Lerato clicked her tongue, amused at how short-lived the makeover had been, but Maki, pouring herself a huge glass of wine and filling her side plate with snacks, reminded Lerato that there wouldn't be anybody at the slumber party either than her and Tebogo so there was no need to impress. Just then Tebogo arrived and the trio was complete.

Lounging around, Lerato hugging her preggy pillow, Tebogo looked Maki in the eye and asked about Puo. Maki exhaled and, with a sad expression, told Tebogo that Puo was a writer that she'd met at her publisher's event. "He's from PE, is a widower and has a six-year-old daughter," she concluded.

"Wow," Tebogo exclaimed.

"Yeah – I finally meet someone and he has baggage heavier than Lerato right now."

Lerato shot Maki a look. "Well, you're not getting any younger," she snapped back.

"Plus, I've only spoken to him once since we met and I'm the one who called," Maki added morosely.

"Eish," Tebogo sympathised. "That does say a lot, right?"

Lerato cast Tebogo a look. "How long did you wait for the actor to call you after you met him?" she asked pointedly.

"You mean other than the time he called her from Tumelo's phone and Tumelo completely ignored me?" Maki chuckled.

Tebogo rolled her eyes. "That filmmaker dude is a complete and utter douche bag."

"F Boy," Lerato added sipping her non-alcoholic champagne, "like I told you."

"But to answer your question," Tebogo continued, "we didn't speak for a long time. I was in complete agony, to the point where I almost messaged him on his Facebook account."

"Again, like I did with Tumelo," Maki replied, wryly, taking a long sip of her wine. "What am I, the classic 'how not-to-date' guide?"

Lerato threw her head back in laughter as Tebogo sighed. "To be honest," she said, more seriously. "I had to realise that there was nothing I could do to get the actor to like me, despite my feelings for him. Plus I was confused about Tshepo. So the one time Tshepo didn't pick me up from work like he'd said he would, instead of going home I Ubered to a coffee shop in Parkhurst in the hopes of going to the actor's house. Only I didn't know where he lived and I was too proud to call you and ask you. But by some miracle he was at the coffee shop too."

"And the rest is history," Maki sighed.

"All love stories are different," Lerato concluded, "but ultimately you need to listen to your heart and trust that it won't lead you astray."

"Like you and Seputla?" Maki asked, rolling her eyes, her annoyance at being "the single one" surfacing.

"It wasn't easy," Lerato replied, irritated by Maki's childish eye-rolling. "I'd practically cursed him out, and you know how proud he is."

"My point is that with your looks you would have found someone anyway," Maki snapped.

Tebogo gasped, shocked, and Maki turned to her, "Just like you with your curves; no man can resist a thick girl."

Maki chuckled as she polished off her wine, but Lerato and Tebogo exchanged a look, stung by how unaware Maki was at how she'd offended them.

"Is that all you think I have to offer in a relationship?" Tebogo asked Maki, hurt.

The penny dropped for Maki as she met Tebogo's eye.

"Clearly there's resentment that you harbour towards us just because you're single," Lerato quipped, "but if all you do is attract assholes, then don't take it out on us."

Maki sighed and bit her bottom lip. The truth of her inadequacies had finally erupted. A part of her was slightly relieved that her friends finally knew how she felt, but another part of her resented the fact she'd held their looks against them.

She got up stubbornly, "I have to use the bathroom."

Maki splashed cold water over her face and fought the sensation to run her fingers through her hair lest she disrupt the last bits of straightness that her hair would experience again in a long while. She sighed as she stared at herself in the mirror, fighting a barrage of thoughts, most of them centred on guilt and self-loathing.

Tebogo, and even Lerato in her own way, were the kindest people she'd ever known, which was why she'd been friends with them for so long. She'd just shown her friends her ugly side, but that was a side that she lived with every single day. She wished she could get her friends to understand that she hadn't meant anything by her comments and that she truly appreciated her friendship with them. Truth be told, other than Tebogo and Lerato, she really had no one else in her corner, and the last thing she wanted to do was sabotage that.

For once she couldn't hide behind Mackenzie from her novel, or any other characters that she'd written before. And as she stared at her face in the mirror, it suddenly occurred to her that she'd hidden behind her characters all her life. She had lived vicariously through them. No wonder she had false expectations of people. After splashing her face again, then wiping it dry, Maki headed back to the lounge.

Lerato and Tebogo sat in an icy silence, waiting for her.

"I'm sorry," Maki said meekly.

"You don't have to apologise if that's how you really feel," Tebogo commented, visibly hurt.

"But it's true, you guys," Maki replied defensively. "Don't act so naive – you know I'm right."

Lerato sighed and finally relented. "I've been telling you to get a makeover for years. This has nothing to do with how we look; it's all a reflection of how you feel about yourself."

"You know what I've been through with Tshepo and you're hating because I found happiness?" asked Tebogo, the hurt in her voice audible.

Maki turned to her, pained. "Sorry, Tebza."

Lerato smiled a long, lazy smile. "Let's prank call Puo," she suggested.

Maki turned to Lerato sharply and then smiled when she realised her friend was joking.

"Like we used to do in high school to the guys we liked?" she laughed, glad that the tension in the room had dissipated somewhat.

Tebogo cast Maki a long, silent, look. "Your problem is that you don't see how beautiful you are. Even with a makeover."

Suddenly Lerato screamed and Maki and Tebogo ran to her side as she clutched her tummy.

"What is it?" Tebogo asked, worried.

"Are you okay?" Maki checked.

"Yeah," Lerato said managing a small smile. "It's just a bit of gas, and the baby's kicking."

Maki's eyes shot open. "What?" she asked, then suddenly felt squeamish. Lerato took Maki's hand and placed it on her tummy while Tebogo watched enviously. Suddenly

Maki squealed in delight and moved her hand quickly out of Lerato's grip. Lerato took Tebogo's hand and placed it on her belly.

"I don't feel anything," Tebogo complained. "What's it supposed to feel like?"

"Like a tiny little tadpole fluttering in my belly," Lerato answered patiently.

Tebogo grew impatient. "I hope the actor and I have a baby soon."

"I still can't believe you're getting married," Maki said.

"You're not going to blow my face up in another jealous rage, are you?" Tebogo asked.

"No," Maki said remorsefully. "And anytime you want to give me that makeover, I'm game, since Maggie, the stylist from the publishing company only gave me a look-book."

"That's the thing I love about the actor," Tebogo said. "When I told him my dream he went all out and encouraged me. He even bought me a canvas."

"For painting?" Lerato asked.

Tebogo laughed and moved her hand away from Lerato's belly. Clearly the baby was tired of being felt up.

"For artistry," she replied.

Maki studied Tebogo closely before pensively asking her, "How did you know that he was the one?"

Tebogo shrugged. "He makes me laugh."

Maki shook her head. "Tshepo made you laugh in the beginning too."

Tebogo was quiet for a moment, then replied, "He makes me feel safe."

A comfortable silence fell among the friends and eventually Maki turned to Lerato. "I suppose you're going to tell me that Seputla makes you feel the same way?"

Lerato nodded and yawned dramatically. "If you guys don't mind, Seputla will be here any minute."

"Are you kicking us out already?" Tebogo laughed in disbelief.

"Girl, this baby has me sleeping by 8pm every night without fail, and you seriously don't expect me to sleep alone this far along in my pregnancy, do you?" Lerato asked with a hint of mischief in her voice.

"Besides, you ditched her for the actor," Maki smiled at Tebogo.

"Precisely," Lerato said.

"Now we know why you're wearing those sexy pyjamas," Tebogo laughed.

"And here I thought we'd stay up all night like we used to," Maki sighed, as it finally began to dawn on her that their lives had evolved and were nothing like their varsity days.

Chapter 18

· ·

The day of Tebogo and the actor's traditional ceremony had finally arrived. Seipati was relieved that they had decided to keep the ceremony small as it would be held at her house, and the less people she had to cater for, the less money she'd have to part with.

Seipati had gotten up at the crack of dawn again, ordering the men in her yard to hurry up and finish paving the driveway as her guests would be arriving soon. She was dressed to the nines in a knee-length, figure-hugging skirt paired with a blouse and blazer, despite the sweltering Limpopo heat, and was inspecting each and every tile, making sure that it was laid to her satisfaction. Content, she smiled at the construction supervisor as she signed off on the work the builders had done on her driveway. When she handed the clipboard back to him, she saw John walking through the gate, also kitted out in his best Sunday garb.

Seipati let out a low whistle. "Hmm, so this is how you dress when you come to see me give my daughter away?"

John chuckled. "Our daughter, remember?"

"No one can know about that, or you'll sabotage our whole plan," Seipati hissed impatiently.

"I held up my end of the deal, but for some or other reason I'm still sitting with a mere R5 000 in my account when you promised me ten," John reminded her.

Seipati pursed her lips angrily at John. "We both know that the full figure is only being delivered today, so please keep it together."

"I'll keep it together when there's R10 000 in my account!"

"If you don't keep your composure you will only dream of the R20 000 that's coming your way," Seipati barked.

John took a step back, pensive. "You're treading on thin ice, Seipati," he warned.

Seipati knew how to turn on the charm when she'd pushed too far, and she gave him an alluring smile. "I promise you, Big John, once today is over, you and I will both be smiling all the way to the bank."

Unable to resist her allure, John smiled and was about to lean in for a kiss when Modiegi, Seipati's older sister from Thaba Nchu, sweaty and dressed in an apron, poked her head out from the back of the house and yelled at Seipati to come and sort out a crisis regarding the food.

John turned sharply to Seipati. "You didn't tell me she was here!" he protested. "She's not going to ruin things for us, is she?" John dabbed his perspiring forehead with a handkerchief.

"I know how to handle my sister," Seipati said with a smile, but John was not reassured.

"Handle her," he warned. "And she'd better not get a cut from my share."

Seipati quickly pecked John on the cheek. "Don't worry, I got this," she assured him before turning to walk to the back of the house. "Coming, sis," she yelled. And with a coy wink in John's direction, she swung her wide hips generously, fully aware that John was enjoying the view.

In Seipati's bedroom Lerato and Maki were beautifully dressed in Sepedi traditional attire, and Lerato was mercilessly squeezing Tebogo into a corset. Maki, impressed by the way Tebogo had done her make-up, inspected herself in the mirror.

Tebogo gasped as Lerato cinched in her waist. "Lerato you're squeezing me too tight," she complained, but Lerato was merciless.

"You're not planning to get married again are you? Suck in your stomach! You know today's pictures will be splashed all over tomorrow's newspapers."

Maki laughed and studied her reflection in the mirror as Lerato tied up Tebogo. "Girl, you have such a talent for doing make-up. As Mrs Actor I think you should quit your job at the insurance company, or at least do make-up as a side hustle because I look hot."

Tebogo laughed as Lerato helped her get into her outfit.

"Shouldn't you be helping the pregnant lady get the bride-to-be ready for her big day?" Lerato scolded Maki, exasperated.

Maki sauntered over. "I was just admiring myself, that's all."

Lerato and Tebogo shared a look. Ever since Maki had aired her views on Tebogo and Lerato's looks, her self-confidence had shot up.

"How's the new book coming along?" Tebogo asked Maki.

"All I have is one sentence. The pressure is real," Maki complained.

"You know what you need?" Lerato said. "A new working space. Your flat is uninspiring. I bet the book would write itself if you had an ocean view."

"I'll only go to PE at Puo's invitation, not a moment sooner," Maki chuckled.

To her elation, in recent weeks Puo had contacted Maki regularly and had told her that the school holidays were the toughest times to be a normal adult as he had to entertain his daughter. However, he promised that once school opened up again he would have more time to get to know Maki better. Maki was surprisingly relieved that their "getting to know each other better" stage was done via phone calls and FaceTime, as it forced her to take her time in getting to know Puo. For Maki that was generally unheard of. She was the type to get intimate right away, but she liked the feeling of being pursued and the random romantic gestures that Puo made, like sending her flowers at the office and reading her *Killarney Express* articles online. Puo was her biggest cheerleader yet, and she blushed at the mention of his name.

Mamogolo Modiegi had a deeply ingrained scowl on her face. "Yes, Modiegi?" Seipati asked rather impatiently.

"What is John doing here? This is a family matter," Modiegi barked. "And don't you dare tell me he's part of the negotiations."

Seipati rolled her eyes. Modiegi had always been such a party pooper. Clearly the only way to keep her in line was to include her in the deal. "He's the chief negotiator. You know what Pedi men are like."

"You can't lie to Tebogo's in-laws," Modiegi commented disapprovingly.

"They are neither Tebogo's nor my in-laws yet," Seipati replied curtly, "but they will be soon if you keep your mouth shut. And if today goes well, who knows – I might cut you a piece of the pie."

"You want to buy my silence?" Modiegi replied with a smirk.

"Call it what you want." Momo had just appeared behind Modiegi and Seipati wanted to quickly wrap up the conversation before her other sister caught wind of it.

Momo sauntered over to her sisters. "What are you two whispering about?"

"We're out of spices for the meat," Seipati quickly replied, but Modiegi let the cat out the bag.

"Your sister is bribing the actor's family."

"Mm, this sounds spicy," Momo replied. "How?"

"John is fronting as Tebogo's uncle."

"I want in," Momo quickly said.

Modiegi rolled her eyes. "Of course you do."

"How much have you agreed upon and what is our cut?" Momo demanded.

Seipati sighed. She hated having her money distributed between so many people, but she had no choice. Besides, she needed Modiegi at the festivities; she certainly wasn't going to cook for all the people arriving today. And Tebogo would definitely have blown her cover if her aunts weren't there.

"R5 000 each," Seipati replied, annoyed.

Modiegi shook her head at Seipati, as if reading her thoughts, and Momo threw her head back and laughed raucously. "You've got to be kidding me," she said. "I make that in a day."

"R10 000 and that's it!" Seipati conceded.

"Pleasure doing business with you," Momo smiled, as she walked back towards the house.

Seipati turned to Modiegi, who hadn't taken her eyes off her sister throughout the negotiation. "Please, sis, don't mess this up for me," Seipati pleaded rather desperately, but Modiegi just glared at her silently.

Lerato, with Maki's help, had finally managed to fit Tebogo into her corset, and the bride-to-be was now beautifully tucked into her traditional Sepedi fishtail wedding outfit. Just then, Mamane Momo opened the bedroom door and rushed in. She got teary when she saw Tebogo. "Moghel, you look beautiful," she gushed.

Tebogo laughed. Her mom's younger sister, Momo, was her favourite aunt, and Mamane Momo calling her "moghel" was typical of her nature. She related to Mamane Momo as a sister, and whenever her mom had bothered her, Tebogo would always run to her other aunt, her mom's older sister Mamogolo Modiegi, because only she could call her mother to order. Mamane Momo always cracked jokes at Seipati's expense, though, much to Tebogo's delight. At every family function Mamogolo Modiegi would be working the pots and bossing everyone around. Everyone being, of course, Seipati who would invariably be hiding out somewhere with a quart of beer in her hand, or Mamane Momo who was the self-proclaimed family "slay queen", which was why she had joined Tebogo, Lerato and Maki in the bedroom. She was there to do their hair. Two hours late. And after they were already dressed and had done their make-up.

"But Mamane, we were expecting you two hours ago," Lerato complained.

"Mamogolo Modiegi is a slave driver. She had me manning the three-legged pots; can you believe it? But don't you worry, my beauty, Mamane Momo is here now and she will sort you out fast fast." Tebogo's aunt set up her hair products, blow dryer, combs and brushes on the dresser. "Phela, my niece is getting married to a famous actor!"

Maki was the first to get her hair done. As she sat down in front of Mamane Momo, Maki wondered how the woman was able to see anything past her heavy eyelashes.

Tebogo looked at the time anxiously. Her phone had been confiscated by Seipati at the crack of dawn, and she hadn't spoken to the actor all morning, so she didn't know if he and his family were on their way or not.

Lerato noted Tebogo's anxiety. "Moghel, o sharp?" she asked.

Tebogo creased her brow, worried. "Shouldn't the actor and his family be here by now?" she asked. "Can I use your phone to call him?"

"No way!" Mamane Momo shouted. "That man is coming here to pay magadi for you and you want to check how far he is?" Tebogo's aunt laughed loudly while effortlessly rolling strands of Maki's hair around the curling iron. "Don't ever show a man how desperate you are, even when he is about to marry you. Chill, babe! He'll be here."

Lerato turned to Tebogo. "She's right."

"Ouch, Mamane!" Maki yelped. Mamane Momo had burnt her ear.

"Get out of my chair, wena, if you're going to scream like a little girl," Mamane Momo retaliated. "Next!" she yelled at Lerato, as Maki stood up and Lerato sat in the chair with some trepidation.

"Mamane, you are aware that I'm heavily pregnant, right? If you burn me I might just go into labour."

Suddenly Mamane Momo became emotional. "You girls have grown up right before my very eyes. Lerato, you're about to be a mom, and you, Tebza ngwana, are going to be someone's wife. A whole, entire, wife! Ha!" Mamane Momo eyed Maki in the mirror as she inspected her burnt ear. "And you, Miss Journalist? Too busy working on your career to find love?"

Maki blushed slightly. "Well, there is someone ..." she started.

"Good!" Mamane Momo yelled zealously. "You don't want to end up like me — a famous hair salon owner who was so focused on making money that she didn't make time for love. Now look at me. Wherever the wind blows, I'm there. But I'm all alone. It's not worth it, moghel."

Mamane Momo had done so much talking that Lerato hadn't noticed she was done with her hair. Even if she did say so herself, she was impressed.

"Glad you like it," Mamane Momo said as she caught Lerato eyeing herself in the mirror.

"Thanks, Mamane," Lerato said appreciatively.

Mamane Momo beamed at her niece, proud. "You're next, Makoti."

Outside, Seipati was happy with the progress. The marquee was set up and, despite her earlier stand-off with Modiegi, she was almost done with the cooking. The decor lady, Mokgadi, was bossing around her staff as they put the finishing touches on the traditional Sepedi decor. She was taking it all in proudly when she saw her neighbour, Gladys, saunter into the yard trying very hard to conceal her inebriated walk.

"Is this your perfect wedding?" Gladys yelled loudly, laughing at her own joke. Mokgadi cast Gladys an annoyed look, but Seipati welcomed her neighbour warmly.

"They must first get married, ao, Gladys!" she said, before emitting a hearty laugh.

"So, tell me, how do you feel about Tebogo marrying a famous actor?" Gladys asked.

"To be honest, at first I was against it. I always thought that Tebogo would end up with Tshepo. He had grown on me."

"The fat guy she was with for twenty years?" Gladys chuckled.

"Ten years, wena! But yes, him," Seipati confirmed. "I wasn't sure about this actor guy, but then I thought about it some more. The actor is famous, and that means he will do anything to uphold his clean image."

Gladys squinted suspiciously at Seipati. "Meaning?" she asked, an evil smile spreading across her lips.

After Seipati's chat with Modiegi and Momo earlier, it was clear that she'd have to resort to other means to get what was due to her for raising Tebogo. "Meaning that any news publication will gladly pay me if I give them a scoop about the actor," Seipati whispered to Gladys.

Gladys clapped her hands once in shock. "You wouldn't!" she exclaimed.

"What's my name?" Seipati smiled.

"Tjo!" Gladys replied. "You are ruthless!"

"That's exactly what my daughter gets for not coming home for Christmas two years in a row," Seipati replied, resolute. "She completely abandoned me!"

Suddenly car hooters were heard in the distance and everybody looked up. Mokgadi started panicking when she realised that the actor's family representatives were arriving.

"Oh goodness, they're here!" she squealed. "Sello! Hurry up with those flowers! And Solly, that cutlery isn't going to organise itself!"

Sello and Solly, who were already working quickly, continued to hurry along, as Mamane Momo emerged from the house ululating loudly. Seipati immediately shushed her.

"Momo, will you keep it down? For once, please just keep it together."

Mamane Momo just laughed at Seipati. "You've always loved money too much. That's why you don't have any. You love it, but it doesn't love you. Besides, the bride's aunts are always the welcoming party, and you know how Modiegi is, so that leaves just me."

John approached Seipati and led her to the house. "Let's go inside, your sisters have got this," he whispered in Seipati's ear. It did nothing to calm Seipati's nerves, but she smiled at John and whispered in his ear, "Let the games begin."

Seipati's neighbours emerged from their homes to witness the fanfare. Tebogo's mother had been sure to tell them all about the day's event, but in true Seipati style she hadn't invited any of them except for Gladys, of course, who had always been there for her and who had never gossiped about her. Seipati's next door neighbour, Joyce, had laughed at her and told Seipati that no matter how hard she tried to associate herself with the actor and his family, she would never be one of them. But Seipati didn't care; her daughter was marrying into a well-to-do family, and that made all the difference.

Mamogolo Modiegi emerged from the back of the house dressed in her Sunday best and joined Mamane Momo at the gate; the younger sister was now singing Setswana traditional wedding songs. As the elder of the family Modiegi had to uphold their traditions, so she shushed Momo harshly while maintaining a permanent scowl on her face. Seeing that it was Modiegi silencing her, Momo halted her song abruptly as Malome Masemola, Malome Makgoromecha and the actor emerged from the car.

Mamane Momo gasped at the sight of the actor. "He's even more good looking in real life," she muttered under her breath.

"Motlagomang, didimala!" Mamogolo Modiegi reprimanded her sister.

"Welcome to the Seamela residence," Mamane Momo announced, her voice suddenly husky.

But before any of the actor's uncles could respond, true to form, Mamogolo Modiegi barked at the men. "Who are you?"

Malome Masemola, Malome Makgoromecha and the actor didn't miss a beat.

"We are from the actor's family. We are here to finalise a matter regarding the actor and a daughter found to be at this residence," Malome Masemola replied confidently.

Mamane Momo raised an impressed eyebrow, and Malome Makgoromecha who had not taken his eyes off her since they'd arrived, smiled at the youngest sister. When Momo looked up and found Makgoromecha's eyes on her, she blushed slightly.

"I have no idea who you're talking about," Mamogolo Modiegi replied, unimpressed, despite Mamane Momo's chastising eye.

But Malome Masemola nodded to Malome Makgoromecha who rushed back to the car and re-emerged with an expensive bottle of whiskey. Bowing his head low, he gave it to Mamogolo Modiegi who accepted it. Her scowl remained on her face as she inspected the bottle disdainfully.

"I don't recognise you either," Mamane Momo said suddenly, and Mamogolo Modiegi smiled slightly. Finally her youngest sister was catching on. At that, Malome Masemola removed a thick envelope stuffed with cash from his blazer breast pocket and handed it to Mamane Momo who hurriedly took the envelope and inspected the contents. She was happy to see that it was stuffed with R100 and R200 notes. She gave a small, impressed nod to Mamogolo Modiegi who then unlocked the gate.

Mamane Momo once again burst into ululations and a traditional wedding song, and was joined by Sello and Solly who had halted their decorating to witness the proceedings at the gate. Some of the neighbours also joined them in song, but Joyce maintained a disapproving and envious glare. Mamane Momo sang and danced her way to the house, followed by Mamogolo Modiegi, Malome Masemola, Malome Makgoromecha and the actor who was suddenly feeling very nervous.

In Seipati's bedroom, Lerato and Maki had their eyes fixed on the events at the gate, but they vehemently prohibited Tebogo from doing the same, saying that it would bring her bad luck. The poor young woman was pacing relentlessly.

"Okay, they've been welcomed in," Maki reported back, a smile on her face.

"Can't you at least go to the kitchen so you can hear what's happening in the lounge?" Tebogo pleaded.

"Of course not," Maki laughed, but Tebogo didn't find it funny.

"Put your investigative skills to good use for once," she lamented, but Maki was unaffected.

"Not today, boo."

"Don't worry, this is just a formality," Lerato reassured Tebogo. "They'll be done in about an hour."

"Tops," Maki agreed.

Tebogo sat on the foot of the bed. She didn't know what was worse to deal with — the fact that she didn't know what was going on in the lounge or that she hadn't spoken to the actor at all that day.

Chapter 19

Malome Masemola, Malome Makgoromecha and the actor sat opposite John and Seipati in the lounge. Tebogo's mother and "uncle" were poker faced. Mamogolo Modiegi and Mamane Momo followed them and also sat down, the air thick with tension. The actor kept his head low, sweat gathering profusely on his forehead. Meanwhile Malome Makgoromecha's stare never left Mamane Momo's face, causing her to also, shyly, keep her head low.

"It's good to see you again," Malome Masemola started.

"The pleasure is ours," Seipati replied curtly.

Mamogolo Modiegi and Mamane Momo shared a look, and Mamogolo Modiegi discreetly shook her head at Seipati.

"To begin our meeting, and to thank you for welcoming us into your home once again, we've brought you a token of our appreciation," Malome Masemola continued, as he removed another envelope stuffed with cash from his other blazer pocket. Mamogolo Modiegi eyed the envelope enviously and inwardly cursed herself for only accepting a bottle of whiskey. She began to reconsider Seipati's offer.

"Thank you, my good sir," John hurriedly said, taking the envelope out of Malome Masemola's hand and quickly stuffing it into his own pocket.

Mamogolo Modiegi sat up abruptly in her chair and cleared her throat. "There is something I would like to bring up as a matter of urgency," she said, but Seipati quickly intervened.

"I agree Modiegi, we should get the girls from the bedroom so that our groom-to-be can identify his maiden before we finalise today's matter," she quickly said, giving Modiegi a warning look. Modiegi was annoyed by Seipati interrupting her, but she let her have her way. Mamogolo Modiegi sat back in her chair, eyeing John disapprovingly.

"Speak up, please," Malome Masemola said to Mamogolo Modiegi. "That is why we are all here."

Modiegi just smiled stiffly at Masemola and turned to Momo. "Get the girls."

The actor shot Mamogolo Modiegi a quick look. It was clear that she'd been about to oust Seipati and John as fraudsters and he was relieved that she hadn't; that would destroy everything.

As Momo left to go to the bedroom, Seipati smiled for the first time since the actor's family had arrived, albeit a plastic smile.

"You must excuse my sister, Modiegi. She is catering for us today so she must be overly concerned about the lunch," she offered.

Malome Masemola visibly relaxed. "Oh, well, thank you for your concerns, Modiegi. I'm sure whatever you have prepared for us today will be delicious."

Mamogolo Modiegi raised an eyebrow at Malome Masemola. "I'm sure," she said, then turned again to Seipati and John, icily daring them to provoke her.

Suddenly Mamane Momo's loud soprano was heard in the corridor singing yet another traditional wedding song about young maidens leaving home for good to take care of their husbands. A moment later she walked back into the lounge, followed by Tebogo, Lerato and Maki, who held each other by their waists and walked in a straight line into the room, their heads covered by blankets, and their feet bare.

"Aha," Malome Makgoromecha said excitedly. "Finally something to liven things up a bit."

Seipati clapped her hands, also excited. "You know what this means, right?" she asked the actor.

"Yes, Ma," he replied nervously.

"Pick your maiden from these three ladies' feet," Malome Makgoromecha said.

"Okay, Malome."

The actor stood and studied the ladies' feet intensely, walking up and down and scratching his chin, deep in thought. Tebogo and Lerato were fair complexioned, while Maki was a bit darker so it was easy to rule out her feet. It was a choice between the pink nail polish and the red. He thought about it for a moment longer, then pointed at the feet with the red nail polish.

"These ones," he said.

"Are you sure?" Mamane Momo asked.

The actor nodded, and Mamane Momo took the blanket off the lady whose feet the actor had chosen, revealing a smiling and pregnant Lerato.

"Hello," she said in a small voice.

Malome Makgoromecha laughed raucously at the visibly dejected actor. Mamane Momo ushered Tebogo, Lerato and Maki back to the bedroom, and the actor sat down heavily.

"You don't know your wife-to-be's feet?" Seipati teased, a smirk on her face.

"It's the nerves," the actor defended.

"Nevertheless, I think that knocks off a good R20 000 from the agreed price, eh?" Malome Makgoromecha suggested.

John almost leapt out of his chair. "Good to see that you're sober today, buddy, but that's not going to happen. Your son chose the wrong feet. If anything, we should charge more."

"There's no need to be dramatic," Malome Masemola said calmly. "We've come in peace, with the intention of upholding our traditions and customs, isn't that so?"

Seipati and John gave a small nod.

"And that's exactly what's going to happen," Mamogolo Modiegi piped up. Seipati and John gave Mamogolo Modiegi a sharp stare but the eldest sister ignored them.

"What was the agreed price upon your initial negotiation?" she asked Malome Masemola.

"R100 000," Malome Masemola replied. "R30 000 was deposited four weeks ago with the intention of making the final payment today."

Mamane Momo, who had just walked back in, sucked her teeth dramatically.

"I see," Mamogolo Modiegi said. Momo shot Modiegi a look; she could tell that this was not headed in a good direction.

"You have been nothing but kind and gracious to us," Mamogolo Modiegi continued. "I don't know that we have been the same."

Seipati, John and Momo squirmed.

"You came here with good intentions, and we will do the same," Modiegi said. "Give us an extra R20 000 and we'll call it a day."

"What?" Seipati yelled, ignoring Mamogolo Modiegi's look. "R20 000, Modiegi? You have no idea of the blood, sweat and tears I put into raising Tebogo as a single woman! My daughter is a lawyer today because of me."

"No, she is a lawyer today because of the bursaries she's been afforded all these years," Mamogolo Modiegi replied calmly.

"Bursaries?" Malome Masemola said, latching on. "You gave us the impression that you paid for all of Tebogo's schooling."

"I raised her all by myself," Seipati insisted.

"That doesn't make her your meal ticket," Mamogolo Modiegi declared before turning to John, looking him up and down in disgust. "And certainly not yours either."

Mamane Momo knew better than to intervene. Besides, she already had the envelope she'd been given earlier at the gate. But John could no longer contain his anger. "Let's be civil about this," he said between gritted teeth. "R50 000, gentlemen. Besides, these women shouldn't even be here."

"Let's not get into who shouldn't be here," Mamogolo Modiegi smiled at John, causing the man to sink back into his seat sheepishly.

Malome Makgoromecha turned sharply to Mamogolo Modiegi. "What do you mean by that?" he asked.

"R40 000?" John offered helplessly.

"R20 000" Mamogolo Modiegi replied, resolute.

Malome Masemola extended his hand to the eldest sister. "We have a deal, my sweet lady. R20 000 it is."

Suddenly Seipati sprang to her feet, ululating loudly before Mamogolo Modiegi could disrupt her plans any further. "Good to know there will be a wedding here today, ladies and gentlemen. If you will excuse me, I need to attend to the bride."

Seipati shook hands with Malome Masemola and the actor, but as she stretched her hand to Malome Makgoromecha, he pulled her in for an unwarranted hug. After disentangling herself from him, she nodded to the men and hurried to the bedroom. John bolted from the room, furious.

Mamogolo Modiegi, smiling widely, hugged the actor, welcoming him to the family, and invited him, Malome Masemola and Malome Makgoromecha to the marquee for refreshments.

In the bedroom Tebogo was hysterical. "I can't believe he chose your feet instead of mine! Doesn't he know what my feet look like? You're pregnant for goodness' sake!"

"But I'm carrying very well," Lerato replied, "and my feet are only a little bit swollen."

"That doesn't matter, he should have chosen my feet!" the bride-to-be wailed.

"Do you know what this means?" Maki asked.

Suddenly the bedroom door opened and Seipati walked in.

"Mom, how did it go?" Tebogo asked anxiously.

"Modiegi ruined all our plans," Seipati replied, annoyed.

"What do you mean?" Tebogo demanded. The colour drained from her face and her tummy suddenly tied in knots, anticipating the worst.

"Doesn't matter," Seipati replied. "Freshen up your make-up and come join us outside for the gift exchange."

Lerato, Tebogo and Maki shared a look. "Gift exchange?" Maki asked slowly. "So the wedding is carrying on?"

"Did I stutter?" Seipati asked, annoyed.

"Hold on," Tebogo said, clutching her head, and slowly making sense of the situation. "The plan that Mamogolo Modiegi disrupted was of you extorting money from my husband and his family?"

"Yes, so hurry up. I want them to eat and go," Seipati replied impatiently. "I want them gone by sunset."

Lerato, Maki and Tebogo screamed and jumped up and down excitedly, while Seipati looked on, annoyed. "Oh, shut up," she scolded.

"No, Mom," Tebogo replied, looking Seipati square in the eye. "That is my husband and his family you are talking about. And Mamogolo gave you exactly what you deserved."

Seipati recoiled in shock. Tebogo had never spoken to her like that before. Maki and Lerato looked on, impressed with Tebogo for standing up to her mother. "And, for the record, we will be here for as long as we want to be. Today is about me and my husband."

Tongue-tied, Seipati turned and left the room abruptly, slamming the door loudly behind her, while Lerato, Maki and Tebogo resumed their excited screaming.

***

Eventually Tebogo, Lerato and Maki emerged from the bedroom, led out by Mamogolo Modiegi who had loosened up considerably, and Mamane Momo who, true to form, was singing loudly. Tebogo walked at the back of the group and kept her head low. Mam' Melita and Aunt Petunia had arrived shortly after the morning's meeting and were seated in the marquee with Seipati, Malome Masemola, Malome Makgoromecha, the actor, and Gladys, who kept nodding off. John had disappeared after the negotiations and when Malome Masemola and Malome Makgoromecha asked where he was, Seipati had sheepishly said that he wasn't feeling well. But both uncles knew that it was because the negotiations hadn't gone his way.

Tears flooded the actor's eyes, and as he watched Tebogo exit the house he beamed proudly at his wife. Mamane Momo, it seemed, had gone and caught feelings for Malome Makgoromecha, because she didn't take her eyes off him while she sang. Seipati noted the chemistry between Momo and Makgoromecha and turned to Makgoromecha disapprovingly, but the actor's uncle just tipped his hat at Seipati and gave her a small, mischievous wink.

Tebogo's aunts and friends entered the tent, and Tebogo sat on the straw mat as Aunt Petunia, who was in her element and dressed to the nines, stood to make a speech. Aunt Petunia welcomed Tebogo to the family and remarked that, in the short space of time that she had known her, Tebogo's character had made a good impression on her. Mamane Momo ululated loudly in celebration, causing Gladys to wake up with a start and yell, "Give it to him, girl!" causing Lerato and Maki to chuckle.

When Aunt Petunia was concluding her speech, Malome Masemola joined her, and as he stood proudly in front of the gathering, it was clear that he relished his title of family elder. After Malome Masemola blessed Tebogo and the actor's union, Mam' Melita stood, loudly singing her own version of a Sepedi traditional wedding song. Gladys happily joined in, although they were both off-key and nobody else could sing along.

When Mam' Melita reached the straw mat, she looked at her son warmly and jokingly chastised him for bringing them a daughter-in-law that he'd only known for two months. Malome Makgoromecha laughed loudly and agreed with Mam' Melita, but then, to Tebogo's delight, Mam' Melita turned to her and smiled warmly, adding that she could see why her son wanted to marry her – she was genuine and warm-hearted which spoke volumes about her character, especially when you considered the actor's profession.

Tebogo melted; she had no idea that Mam' Melita felt that way about her. The actor smiled at Tebogo and his mother. Wrapping up her speech, Mam' Melita spoke about how much the actor and Tebogo had in common, including that they were both only children which meant that she was expecting grandchildren from them in less than a year. That declaration caused loud ululations from Aunt Petunia, Mamane Momo and Gladys, who again yelled, "Give it to him, girl!" causing everyone to laugh.

As Mam' Melita headed back to her seat, Seipati stood up and, plastering a smile on her face, she turned to the guests and delivered a heartfelt speech about all the hardships she'd faced when raising Tebogo on her own. She jokingly added that Tebogo was full of surprises, like this sudden wedding, which raised a giggle from everyone. Next, Seipati became emotional and faced Tebogo. Much to Tebogo's surprise, her mother heartily congratulated her on choosing a good man and getting married. She had never seen her mother exhibit so much emotion, and she also teared up before standing to give her mother a warm hug.

After the speeches Mam' Melita and Aunt Petunia handed out blankets as gifts to Mamogolo Modiegi, Mamane Momo and Seipati, as well as to Lerato and Maki, but Mam' Melita wrapped her blanket around Tebogo's shoulders as a symbol of acceptance into her family. Tebogo's aunts also handed out blankets to Malome Masemola, Aunt Petunia, Malome Makgoromecha and Mam' Melita. Similarly, Seipati covered the actor's shoulders with a blanket, and then the gift ex-change ended with vibrant ululations from both families.

As Mamane Momo led the procession out to the street, Gladys walked right beside her, singing loudly so that the uninvited neighbours could see her. Some of the neighbours ululated and sang along while others took pictures and recorded the proceedings on their cellphones, but Joyce, Seipati's next door neighbour watched everything with an envious scowl.

As Gladys and Momo led the procession back to the marquee Mokgadi, Solly and Sello began to serve lunch.

Tebogo was shocked when she suddenly noticed Tshepo's car parking in the street and was even more horrified to see him walk into the yard. Tebogo, Lerato and Maki shared a look, and the actor whispered angrily to Tebogo, "What the hell is he doing here?"

"I don't know," Tebogo replied, irate. "Get rid of him!"

Mamane Momo, who had seen the shocked looks on the faces of Tebogo, the actor, Lerato and Maki, turned to see the cause of their alarm. Her jaw dropped when saw Tshepo. She nudged Modiegi who hadn't seen him; she was just as confused about why Tebogo's ex was there. Meanwhile Seipati looked like a deer caught in the headlights.

"Looks like I got here just in time for lunch," Tshepo announced loudly.

Seipati swallowed nervously. With all the drama from the morning and John leaving, she'd forgotten to text Tshepo to tell him not to come anymore. She cursed inwardly and kept her eyes glued to the ground.

"Who are you?" Malome Masemola barked, while Malome Makgoromecha, Aunt Petunia and Mam' Melita shot a questioning look at the actor, who stood up.

"You're not welcome here," he barked at Tshepo.

"But I come bearing gifts," Tshepo replied drily.

"You haven't answered my question," Malome Masemola replied angrily.

"He's my ex." Tebogo said urgently, causing Aunt Petunia and Mam' Melita to shoot her a questioning look.

"Ex being the operative word," the actor said before turning back to Tshepo. "Get out."

"How did you even know about today?" Tebogo asked, confused.

Seipati finally looked up; gathering all her courage, she said, "I invited him."

Tebogo shot her mother a furious look. "You what?" she seethed.

"I'm sorry," Seipati replied hurriedly. "It was before I changed my mind about the actor and, to be honest, ngwana'ke, I just wasn't sure that the actor was the man for you. But after our chat in the bedroom earlier I realised how much you love him, and that he truly is the right man for you."

"Wow," Lerato said under her breath.

Tebogo cast an apologetic look to Malome Masemola, Malome Makgoromecha, Aunt Petunia and Mam' Melita. "I'm sorry," she said. "I was engaged to Tshepo before I became engaged to the actor. We dated for eight years."

The marquee fell silent. Even Mokgadi, Solly and Sello stood quietly in the wings, watching curiously to see what would happen next.

Seipati turned to Tshepo. "You have to go."

Tshepo ignored her, and producing a bottle of expensive whiskey, approached the actor. "I brought this for you," he said.

"Keep it," the actor snapped, but Malome Makgoromecha spoke up loudly, "Not so fast, son. Bring that over here."

The actor, Tebogo, Malome Masemola, Aunt Petunia, Mamogolo Modiegi, Mamane Momo, Seipati, Mam' Melita, Lerato, Maki, and even Gladys, were shocked at Malome Makgoromecha's betrayal for a bottle of whiskey.

Tshepo shot Tebogo a chuffed look, puffed out his chest and approached Malome Makgoromecha boldly to hand him the bottle of whiskey.

"Hmm," Malome Makgoromecha said as he took the bottle from Tshepo and studied it. "This is good stuff."

"Thank you, sir," Tshepo replied.

Suddenly Malome Makgoromecha shot Tshepo a murderous look, sending chills down the younger man's spine. "Now voetsek," Malome Makgoromecha sneered, bringing loud ululations from Mam' Melita, Mamogolo Modiegi and Aunt Petunia, who shot to their feet. Mamane Momo, Lerato and Maki began singing a Setswana traditional wedding song about the actor being the conqueror. Tshepo sheepishly slunk away. Seipati, who was still seated in her chair, looked up at Tebogo feebly, and was shaken to the core when she met her daughter's fuming eye.

A little later Maki's phone rang and she was delighted to see that it was Puo calling. She couldn't wait to fill him in on everything. As always, he was face timing her; it had become their mode of communication.

"Hi, love," she greeted him, after slipping around the side of the house.

"Hey, baby," Puo smiled, sending the butterflies in Maki's stomach flying around in a flurry. "How's the wedding?"

"You won't believe what just happened. Tshepo, Tebza's ex showed up."

"What?" Puo yelled.

"Tebogo's mother invited him."

"You've got to be kidding me," Puo laughed in shock.

"He was so proud, he even brought a bottle of whiskey," Maki continued. "We got rid of him, but of course, Malome Makgoromecha took the bottle before telling him to voetsek!"

Puo laughed loudly. "I think I like Malome Makgoromecha."

"He is quite a character," Maki conceded, then turned serious. "I miss you."

Puo smiled. "I miss you too."

"I should get back to the wedding."

"Okay, I'll call you later."

And, as was their ritual, they both kissed the screen before hanging up.

As Maki turned the corner of the house, she saw Tebogo immersed in conversation with Aunt Petunia and Lerato, and the actor speaking with Malome Masemola and Mam' Melita.

Malome Makgoromecha had had enough festivities for one day, and sat under the marquee taking it all in. As he watched, he poured himself a healthy dose of the whiskey that Tshepo had brought. Mamane Momo approached him, her eyes fixed on him and a steady swing in her hips. "Sweetness," Makgoromecha called out, "fancy a glass?"

"After all that drama, make it a double," Momo replied as she sat down next to him.

"The nerve of that boy," Makgoromecha complained as he handed Momo her drink.

She took a long, luxurious sip, then eyed him coyly. "I didn't come here to talk about Tebogo's ex."

"Is that right?" Makgoromecha smiled. "So what did you come here to talk about?"

"You," Momo replied. "And how you haven't taken your eyes off me all day."

Makgoromecha chuckled. "My eyes haven't encountered a pretty thing like you in a long, long time."

Momo melted. Her parents had always insisted that they have a good education, so she'd always fancied a man who had a good command of the Queen's English. She and Modiegi had a great education, but Seipati had moved to Limpopo with Tebogo's father after she'd married him as a teenager, and he stopped her from finishing high school. Momo believed that was what sent their mother, Moipone, to her early grave.

"I don't come around here too often," Momo continued." My sister moved here years ago and decided to stay after Tebogo's father died."

"And if I invited you around here?" Makgoromecha enquired, hanging his head low and peeping at her from under his fedora hat, a sly smile on his lips. "Would you come here more often then?"

"You'd have to put in a lot of work to get that to happen," Momo replied flirtatiously. "I'm a woman of a certain class. I need to be pursued."

Makgoromecha took a long sip of his whiskey, as he contemplated accepting Momo's challenge. "I know all the top places in Polokwane," he eventually replied. "If you visit me, your wish will be my command."

The day's festivities were drawing to a close and the actor and Tebogo were deeply engrossed in conversation with Malome Masemola, Aunt Petunia and Mam' Melita, while Mamogolo Modiegi thanked Mokgadi and her team for the impeccable work they had done. Seipati slowly approached Tebogo and gently pulled her away, asking to speak to her daughter privately. The actor cast Tebogo an understanding look as she walked off to the side to speak to her mother.

"I'm sorry," Seipati began feebly.

"For?" Tebogo asked, hurt, but pretending to be okay.

"I haven't been the best of mothers," Seipati continued. "The truth is, I took out my grief of losing your father on you."

Tebogo shifted uncomfortably and stared at her mother, shaken by her vulnerability. "That was twenty years ago."

Seipati shrugged helplessly. "I was young when I fell in love with him. I didn't get a chance to finish school, and that's why I always pushed you so hard and took the credit for all your hard work. He was an artist, and I guess that's why I resented the actor so much. I was afraid."

Tebogo felt a surge of compassion for her mother, but maintained her steely gaze. "So why did you invite Tshepo here?"

"I did that about a week ago and I totally forgot to tell him not to come. I've bullied you all your life and I'm sorry."

Tebogo cast her mother a long look. "Thanks for organising today," she eventually said.

Seipati exhaled and smiled. "Of course."

"But I love the actor," Tebogo continued, "and if you ever get up to any shenanigans that involve him, you will never see me again."

Seipati swallowed and nodded slowly. "Of course, I understand."

Tebogo smiled a small smile at her mother and extended her arms. "Hug?" she offered, and Seipati threw herself into her daughter's arms.

***

Exhausted, Maki drove into Lerato and Tebogo's complex.

"I'm so glad I don't have to move or look for a new place so close to giving birth," Lerato yawned.

Maki, who'd been uncharacteristically quiet, turned to Lerato and smiled.

It was the day after Tebogo and the actor's traditional wedding and she had driven all the way from Limpopo while Lerato chatted non-stop.

"You heard from Puo lately?" Lerato asked.

"Sure," Maki replied.

Just then Maki's phone beeped, signalling the arrival of a text message. She quickly checked her phone.

"Is that him?" Lerato asked.

"Don't be so nosy," Maki complained, before stuffing her phone into her shirt pocket.

Lerato sized Maki up. "Your phone has been beeping all the way from Polokwane. Who are you talking to?"

Maki smiled. "Like I said, none of your business. And you could have driven too. It's silly to think that women who are eight months pregnant can't drive. Some women even drive themselves to the hospital when their water breaks," Maki continued as she drove into an empty parking spot.

"Good for them. And I see what you're trying to do."

Maki side eyed Lerato. "What?"

"Changing the subject so you don't answer my question about who's been blowing up your phone. Don't think that I forgot just because I have preggy brain."

Maki laughed as she stepped out of the car.

"You got the key?"

"Yes," Maki replied, dangling Lerato's apartment key in one hand and locking the car with the other.

"Good, let's go – I need the bathroom."

"I love that the actor's family is accepting Tebogo into the family today and that they kept both ceremonies so small and intimate," Maki said as they walked up the stairs.

"Aside from the pics we took there wasn't even a photographer," Lerato added. "It made it all feel so special."

Suddenly Lerato grabbed the key out of Maki's hand. "Sorry, girl but I've got to go," she said hurriedly. As Lerato did her best to hurry up the stairs, Maki walked right behind her keeping up with her pace.

When she finally reached their apartment, Lerato unlocked the door and turned on the lights. She screamed loudly in fright when she saw Seputla standing in front of her holding a huge teddy bear and pink balloons.

"Surprise," Seputla yelled, but Lerato screamed again, scared. She turned to Maki, "Is this who you were talking to the whole way here?" she asked.

Her friend beamed and nodded proudly. "Welcome to your baby shower!"

Lerato just looked down as a warm liquid trickled down her legs.

"Girl, did you just pee on yourself?" Maki asked, disgusted.

But Lerato, frozen in place, shook her head. "I think my waters just broke."

***

Tebogo ran down the hospital corridor as fast as she could. She finally got into the maternity ward and sprinted to the reception desk, but out the corner of her eye she saw Maki pacing in the waiting area, and ran to her.

"Hey," Tebogo said, breathless, "I came as quickly as I could."

Maki gave Tebza a quick hug. "How is she?" Tebogo asked, panicked.

"She's been in there for more than eight hours! Nobody's telling me anything. Surely they would say if something was wrong, right?"

"I'm sure they would," Tebogo replied reassuringly as she led Maki to a chair.

"Is it normal for it to take this long?" Maki asked, concerned.

"Your guess is as good as mine."

Suddenly a nurse walked towards them and both Maki and Tebogo leapt to their feet.

"How is she?" Maki asked quickly.

"I believe congrats are in order, aunties," the nurse said, smiling.

Maki and Tebogo shared a look. "She's here?" Tebogo gasped.

"She's been here for about an hour; she's even had her first bath and meal already," the nurse added.

"Can we see her?" Maki asked.

"I'm afraid not," the nurse replied.

"What?" Maki demanded, restraining herself from cursing at the nurse, considering how long she'd been waiting to meet the baby.

"Only family can go in right now," the nurse continued, "but if you stick around for the next twenty minutes you could go in when the visiting hour starts."

Maki almost fainted and Tebogo burst out laughing as the nurse smiled and walked off. The young author flopped back into the chair. "I was about to curse her out," she laughed.

"Let's go grab a bite to eat," Tebza suggested. "It looks like you need it."

When visiting hours started Tebogo and Maki walked into Lerato's hospital room and saw Seputla holding the baby in his arms, a huge grin on his face. Lerato was in the bed, looking worse for wear.

"Hey, Rato," Maki gushed, as Tebogo ran to take the baby, but Seputla moved protectively away.

"Seriously?" Tebogo chuckled. "Okay, fine if I can't hold her then at least stand still so I can see how gorgeous she is."

"Hey friends," Lerato said, slowly sitting up in the bed.

"How're you feeling?" Maki asked.

"Exhausted. If this is an indication of how the next few months of my life are going to be then thank goodness Seputla is back in my life."

"Hey!" Seputla protested lightly.

Tebogo sat down. "Okay, fine, I'm sitting," she said to Seputla. "Now give her to me." Seputla gently and trepidatiously handed Tebogo the baby.

"She's so cute! What's her name?" Tebogo gushed.

"Medupe," Lerato smiled, and Maki noted that she had never seen her friend appear more radiant.

"Medupe," Maki repeated.

"Medupe Reatlegile Meale," Seputla said with a smile at Lerato.

Tears gathered in Tebogo's eye. "She's gorgeous."

Chapter 20

....

One year later:

"Dearly beloved, we are gathered here today to bear witness to the Holy Matrimony between Bokang Letsoalo Moeletji, otherwise known as 'the actor' and Tebogo Precious Seamela."

Seipati and Mamane Momo, who were seated in the front row, smiled and Mam' Melita and Aunt Petunia wiped tears from the corners of their eyes. Beside the actor stood two of his friends, Ofentse and Oatile who were also actors, and beside Tebogo stood Maki and Lerato.

Lerato glanced at Seputla who was holding a sleeping baby Medupe in his arms. His eyes were fixed on the mother of his child, and he smiled sweetly as she looked at him, causing her to blush.

"If there is anyone here who knows why these two should be not be married, please speak up now or forever hold your peace," the priest continued.

Apart from the click of the photographer's camera, the room fell into a hush. Tebogo licked her lips nervously, but the actor who was staring solemnly into her eyes squeezed her hands reassuringly.

Suddenly the church doors burst open and a bright light filled the room. Tebogo gasped as she squinted, struggling to see exactly who it was that had disrupted her wedding, and the entire congregation turned and did the same. Maki cursed under her breath when she realised who it was.

"Sorry," the new arrival said, out of breath.

The priest spoke up. "Just in time, son. If you know of any reason why Bokang and Tebogo should not get married, then please let us know."

Puo swallowed nervously; he hated being the centre of attention. Maki felt for him, and Tebogo cast her a questioning look, but all Maki could do was shrug apologetically.

Puo held up his hands. "No objection whatsoever," he said, and practically dove into a pew so that the attention could be diverted from him.

"Good," the priest smiled before turning back to the actor and Tebogo. He asked them to repeat after him as they exchanged their vows, and when they were done, Mamane Momo and Mam' Melita burst into loud ululations. The actor and Tebogo slid their rings onto each other's fingers, and finally sealed their marriage with a kiss, which caused their guests to erupt into joyous song.

After the ceremony the guests mingled and sipped champagne in the garden as the bride and groom took photos with their families. Maki spotted Michal in the distance and her tummy did an involuntary anxious flop. She was nervous about seeing her ex-boss again because of the exposé that she'd written for the *Killarney Express* on *Kas'lethu* where she'd practically called Michal racist. She approached the producer with trepidation.

"Hey, Michal."

"Hey to you too," Michal replied stiffly.

Maki summoned her courage. "I owe you an apology…"

But before she could continue Michal held up her hands and shook her head. "No. I'm the one who owes you an apology," she said, much to Maki's surprise.

"Despite how much I loathed what you wrote about me, every last bit of it was true," Michal sighed. "Except for the racist bit – I'm not racist. I guess I just gave in to the notion that for a TV show to be successful the writers should have years of experience even if they didn't represent the people they were writing about. Worst of all, I was letting those experienced writers get away with not training the newbies." Then with a small look Maki's way, she added. "I fired Rian."

"You what?" Maki asked.

"And Greg and Mark resigned shortly afterwards."

"Woah!"

"They didn't like the changes I made to the team after I fired Rian, so they left."

"What changes?" Maki asked.

"Well, for one thing, Sechaba is a senior writer now. And I have an all black writing team – you know, for the culture," Michal smiled in an attempt to lighten the mood.

But Maki didn't find the joke funny. She spotted Puo in the distance. "I'm sorry, but I see someone I need to speak to," she said to Michal before turning to walk away.

Before she left the producer grabbed Maki's arm. "So will you come back?" she asked.

"Excuse me?"

"I revised my staff's contracts, and I was wondering if you wanted to rejoin the team."

Maki sighed and gently removed her arm from Michal's grip.

"I don't know, Michal. I've moved on." But when she saw the desperation in Michal's eyes, she added, "I'll think about it," before heading off towards Puo. He broke into a huge smile when he saw the writer.

"Hey, wedding basher!" Maki laughed.

"I'm so embarrassed about that," Puo said.

"That was quite the entrance! Your timing was impeccable."

"I should apologise to Tebogo and the actor," Puo continued.

"Don't worry, I'll speak to her for you," Maki offered. "I'll just tell her your flight was delayed or something."

"It was," Puo said as he wrapped his arms around Maki. "It's good to see you," he added before gently kissing her on the lips.

"Dimakatso Innocentia Dilobetso!"

Maki whipped around and saw Mamane Momo heading towards her. She quickly removed her arms from around Puo's neck as Mamane Momo came charging towards them.

"Who is this man that you're kissing in broad daylight?" Momo demanded.

"Um, Mamane Momo, this is my boyfriend, Puo," Maki stammered, embarrassed at being chastised for her bold PDA.

Puo extended his hand to Mamane Momo. "Hello Mamane Momo," he said politely. Mamane Momo just looked him up and down.

"So you're the pretty boy my niece's bestie hasn't been able to shut up about?"

Puo chuckled. "I don't know, am I?" But when Puo saw that Mamane Momo was less than impressed, he added, "I would hope so."

Momo crossed her arms and sized up Puo. "And what exactly are your intentions for our Dimakatso?" she asked.

"Mamane!" Maki scolded, embarrassed, but Mamane Momo broke into a wide grin.

"Just playing with you," she laughed. "It's good to see you sweat."

Maki exhaled and mouthed the word "Sorry" to Puo who smiled in understanding.

Mamane Momo turned to Maki. "The photographer is looking for you; we're done with the family pics so it's time for the bridal party to take their pictures." But Maki stood glued to the spot.

Momo glared at her.

"Hello, maid-of-honour, that means you!"

Maki cast a nervous look at Puo.

"Don't worry, your man is in good hands," Mamane Momo smiled. "I'm sure we'll find lots to talk about."

Maki's stomach flipped anxiously, but when she turned to Puo he gave her a reassuring wink.

"Tsamaya!" Mamane Momo pressed.

Maki knew that she couldn't argue with Mamane Momo, so she lifted her dress up to her knees and sprinted across the garden, anxious about Mamane Momo and Puo's pending conversation.

Maki found Tebogo having her make-up retouched and Lerato standing with Seputla and baby Medupe, while the actor was chatting to his groomsmen.

"Hey, babe," Maki said to Tebogo. "Sorry about that commotion with Puo earlier."

"You mean when my heart stopped because I thought your man might object to my marriage?" Tebogo asked.

"Girl, that only happens in movies," Maki laughed.

But when Tebogo didn't laugh, Maki elaborated. "His flight from PE got delayed. Besides, what good reason would he have for stopping your wedding?"

Tebogo shrugged. "You never know."

"Are you serious?" Maki laughed, then wiped the smile off her face when she realised that Tebogo was serious.

Tebza had been under a lot of strain since her traditional wedding to the actor. As soon as the story had broken to the media there'd been tons of articles written about them, and most of them didn't put her in a good light. Added to that, some of the actor's ex-girlfriends had crawled out of the woodwork, claiming to still be in relationship with him.

Despite the actor's constant reassurance, it had all been too much for her to handle. Part of her wondered if that was why he'd been so eager to marry her as quickly as he had – before she could really find out what she was getting herself into and change her mind.

Maki studied Tebogo's expression. "Girl, are you good?" she asked, causing Tebogo to snap out of her reverie.

"Sorry, my friend," she sighed.

"Do you want to talk about it?" Maki probed, but the make-up artist interrupted them.

"All done," she said, breezily, causing Tebogo and Maki's conversation to come to an abrupt end.

Tebogo smiled stiffly to the woman. "Thanks." Then she turned to Maki, "Let's get these shots done so we can get some real shots," she laughed in an attempt to lessen the tension.

But as Tebogo headed back to join the actor, Lerato, Ofentse and Oatile for the photographs, Maki studied her and reminded herself that Tebogo battled to speak up when faced with challenges, so she promised herself that she would speak privately to her before the end of the night.

When the photos were done Maki sped off to look for Puo.

"Where are you running off to?" Lerato asked.

"I left Puo with Mamane Momo," Maki replied anxiously.

"You better run," Lerato laughed as Maki took off.

When she eventually found Puo she was glad that he was standing by himself at the bar. "Hey," she said, out of breath. At that he turned and wrapped his arms around her, giving her a big kiss. "I'm guessing your conversation with Mamane Momo went well?" Maki asked, conflicted about him kissing him in public again.

Puo smiled mysteriously.

"Wipe that smirk off your face and tell me what she said!" Maki protested.

Puo shrugged. "Nothing much."

"Nothing much?"

"She told me that she liked my suit and went off to talk to that guy."

Maki looked to where Puo was pointing and saw Mamane Momo seated on Malome Makgoromecha's lap, wrapped up in raucous laughter. She was confused. Mamane Momo had said nothing much? That was unlike her, and gave Maki even more reason to be concerned. Feeling Maki's eyes on her, Mamane Momo raised her glass to Maki and smiled. The young woman turned back to her boyfriend.

"Actually, she mentioned that she wouldn't be outdone by a thirty-year-old child, and that is when she went to sit in his lap," Puo laughed. "Although it doesn't seem like that man minds at all."

Maki burst out laughing. "That's Malome Makgoromecha," she said.

"Oh … now it makes sense."

"Those two are peas in a pod," Maki smiled as Puo drew her closer to him again.

"So, since it seems as if we have Mamane Momo's blessing …" he started.

Maki's heart raced against her chest. *He's not about to... is he...?* she thought, panicked. Maki's eyes darted around the room and Puo was taken aback.

"Are you okay?" he asked.

Maki quickly disentangled herself from Puo's embrace.

"Tebza needs me," she yelled, before racing off in the other direction, leaving Puo very perplexed.

Maki ran to the room that she, Tebogo and Lerato had been using to change in, and found Lerato helping Tebogo into her second dress.

"Where have you been?" Tebza yelled.

"And why am I always the one helping Tebogo?" Lerato scolded.

"Sorry, guys. It's hard managing a new relationship and being focused on my maid-of- honour duties at the same time," Maki apologised.

Lerato grimaced at Maki. "It's not that new."

"But it's always been long distance and over the phone, and now he's here," Maki elaborated. "And I think he wants to marry me."

Lerato squealed and Tebogo's eyes widened in shock. "He better not propose at my wedding!" she protested.

"Are you serious?" Lerato pressed.

"I'm not sure," Maki answered, squishing up her nose.

"What do you mean you're not sure?"

"His exact words were, 'Now that we have Mamane Momo's blessing...'"

"Oh my goodness!" Tebogo yelped.

"What else did he say?" demanded Lerato.

"That's it," Maki lamented. "I bolted out of there before he could finish."

Tebogo and Lerato shared a look. "So you don't actually know if he wants to marry you?" Lerato asked, annoyed.

"I know it was serious," Maki replied. "Either way, I'm not here for it."

"Why?" Tebogo asked. "You've always said you want a good guy."

"I know. But at what cost, Tebza?"

"What do you mean?"

"Marriage is where good relationships go to die," Maki answered defiantly. "No offence."

Tebogo turned to Lerato to back her up, but Lerato dropped her head guiltily.

"You agree with her?" she asked, and Lerato gave a brief nod.

"We're not stuck in the dark ages, my friend," Lerato explained. "Look at Seputla and I – we're a family and we're happy."

"And if you break up it will affect Medupe," Tebogo argued.

"It would affect her worse if we were married and got a divorce," Lerato replied.

Tebogo deflated in disbelief. "Wow."

"It doesn't make us any less supportive of you," Maki consoled, but her words were wasted on Tebogo. "I'm just a commitment-phobe, that's all," Maki shrugged. "I always have been."

"Just be careful that you don't push away a good man," Tebogo cautioned.

"So it's always going to be all or nothing?" Maki asked.

Tebogo nodded. "Commitment is."

Maki sighed and eyed Tebogo cautiously. Softly she said, "I saw your expression earlier when you were talking about the actor. Marriage is not all it's cracked up to be, neh?"

"Oh, so now you're punching holes into my marriage?" Tebogo snapped.

"I'm only asking because you tend to keep things to yourself. And I care."

Tebogo sighed and darted a look at Lerato.

"Wait. She knows?" Maki asked, pointing at Lerato.

"You should be more punctual with your maid-of-honour duties," Lerato defended.

"You're not regretting any of this, are you?" Maki probed, wide-eyed.

"No," Tebza replied. "I just feel like I could've been better prepared."

"For the groupies?"

"And the negative press," Tebogo continued.

"But it doesn't change the way you feel about the actor, right?" Maki pressed.

"No," Tebogo replied, her voice rising in emotion, "Of course not."

"Okay, that's good. And babe, you're brave – braver than I could ever be."

"Clearly," Lerato chuckled.

"Just because marriage petrifies me and isn't for Lerato, doesn't mean that it's not for you."

"I know," Tebogo said. "I've always wanted to get married."

"And you and the actor are perfect for each other. You're just not used to all the attention, that's all. But trust me, after a while all those vultures will get bored and move on to someone else," Maki reassured her friend as she wrapped her arms around Tebogo.

"Yeah, you journalists are so flaky," Tebogo smiled.

"It's the name of the game, boo."

Lerato checked her watch. "We better get back out there before they send a search party for us."

Tebogo turned to Lerato. "And as for you, take it one step at a time – you never know what the future holds." Lerato embraced Tebogo warmly, and Maki threw her arms around both of them for a group hug.

As the sounds of DJ Kent filled the reception area and the bridesmaids and groomsmen danced their way into the beautifully decorated room, Puo smiled encouragingly at Maki, but Maki consistently averted her gaze, petrified of looking in his direction. Eventually she managed to steal a glance and found Puo looking at her perplexed, so she gave him a sheepish grin, before quickly looking away again.

All the cast and crew from *Kas'lethu*, including Phumz, Thuli, Melz, Lebz, Julz, Sanz, Thapz, Seretse, Lungz, Wandz, Sechaba, Mpho and Michal whipped out their cellphones to record the festivities, and the actor and Tebogo's friends and family took to the dance floor as the room filled with exuberant celebration.

Puo slowly approached Maki. "Hey," he said. "You okay?"

"Yeah," she smiled, then she took him by the hand and led him to a quieter part of the room. "I'm sorry about earlier. I had to go and help Tebogo, since it's her wedding and all."

"Okay," Puo replied slowly as he continued studying her. "Are you sure you're okay?"

"Yes!" But Puo wasn't having it. He crossed his arms and studied her. "Okay, fine," Maki snapped, then took a big sigh. "Earlier..."

"Before you left me hanging," Puo probed.

"Before I left you hanging," Maki continued, "you said, and I quote, 'Since Mamane Momo seems to have given us her blessing'..."

Maki looked up at Puo hoping that he would rescue her and finish off the sentence, but he continued studying her. "Yes?" he pressed.

"I thought you were going to ask me to marry you," Maki finished off, embarrassed.

Puo remained unmoved. "And that's why you ran away?"

Maki nodded.

"Is the idea of marrying me that repulsive to you?"

Maki gasped. "No! It's not marrying you that would be the problem. It's just marriage itself."

"I see," Puo replied. "So marriage is something that you are totally averse to?"

Maki suddenly felt stupid. She wasn't going about this the right way and she felt incredibly childish. "We just haven't spoken about what we want, that's all," she eventually replied.

"It was presumptuous of you to think that I was about to ask you to marry me," Puo chuckled, and Maki was relieved that the moment had lightened, but she furrowed her brow at him.

"So you don't want to marry me?" she asked, slightly offended.

"Like you said, we haven't discussed it," Puo replied. "But now that I know it's off the table, how about you move in with me instead?"

Maki's jaw dropped and tears sprung to her eyes. "What?"

"Well, not just me, but Cece too," Puo added.

"Does she know?" Maki asked.

"It was her idea," Puo smiled. "She can't stop talking about you, and she seems to think that, thanks to you, I've been in a much better mood than I have been since her mom died, so..."

"So she wants us to be a family?" Maki smiled, touched. But then a panic-stricken thought crossed her mind. "Wait. Do you want this too? Or are you only doing this for Cece?"

Puo shrugged. "I like you. A lot. And after meeting Mamane Momo I really thought about what she said and what my intentions are for you."

Maki's heart beat loudly in her chest. "And?"

"I don't think that this will be a short-lived thing, it's just that I'm scared that..."

"...That it might not work," Maki concluded, and Puo nodded.

"I have the exact same fear," Maki said gently, as Puo wrapped his arms around her.

Just then Lerato hurried over. "Girl, they're about to start the speeches!"

"Okay," Maki said, and as Lerato ran back to the bridesmaid's table, she said to Puo, "I guess we'll just have to take our time." That left Puo wondering if she would move in with him and Cece or not, but either way he was relieved that they'd had the conversation.

After some heart-warming speeches from Malome Masemola, Mam' Melita, Mamogolo Modiegi, Seipati, Lerato, Maki, Ofentse and Oatile, Tebogo squealed in delight as the sounds of Beyoncé's *Single Ladies* filled the room and she headed to the dance floor, swirling her bouquet in one hand, and yelling at the single ladies to come and catch the flowers.

Mamane Momo was the first to leap out of her seat, gyrating her way to the dance floor and singing at the top of her lungs, much to everybody's amusement, and Mamogolo Modiegi's embarrassment. Maki and Lerato sullenly joined the group of ladies on the dance floor which included Thuli, Phumz and Julz. Maki eyed Mpho questioningly, but she gladly whipped her up her left hand to show Maki her wedding ring.

Lerato turned to Maki. "If I catch it I'm giving it to Mamane Momo." But as she looked across at Seputla and Medupe a warm sensation filled her. For the first time since Medupe had been born, she thought about the possibility of the three of them being a legal family, and she was unable to deny the heart-warming feeling that imbued her.

Maki broke Lerato's reverie, as she laughed loudly. "If I catch it, I'm burning it!"

Unhappy that her mom and Mamogolo Modiegi were still in their seats, Tebogo dragged them to the group of single ladies on the dance floor. The actor also dragged up his mother who complained, but seemed excited at the thought of perhaps catching the bouquet.

"Okay, ladies, are you ready?" Tebogo yelled as she turned away from them, swirling her bouquet in the air.

Mamane Momo shouted, "We're ready, Tebza ngwana!"

Makgoromecha encouraged her loudly from the side-lines. "It's yours, baby, it's yours!"

Momo yelled back even louder: "I know it's mine! Now keep quiet, you're distracting me!"

"One, two, three!" Tebogo yelled before throwing the bouquet into the air.

Mamogolo Modiegi stood stiff as she eyed the bouquet and was shocked to see that it seemed to be heading in her direction. But suddenly Mamane Momo leapt up and grabbed the bouquet mid-air, while still singing along to the pop song.

Makgoromecha leapt to his feet, applauding loudly. "That's how you do it, baby!"

There was much less fanfare as the group of single men took to the dance floor, and as Malome Makgoromecha stood to join to the circle of men, Malome Masemola loudly chastised him. "Where do you think you're going?" he asked.

Makgoromecha proudly answered, "I'm going to get my garter."

Aunt Petunia also reprimanded him, well within Mamane Momo's earshot. "You're not a single man!" she rebuked, causing Mamane Momo to stare at Malome Makgoromecha questioningly.

"I'm divorced!" Malome Makgoromecha protested.

"Separated," Malome Masemola intervened. "It's not the same thing."

"It's been a year!" Malome Makgoromecha argued.

Mamane Momo squinted angrily at Malome Makgoromecha. "You're married?" she barked.

Malome Makgoromecha sighed. The actor was about to throw the garter and clearly he was going to miss his opportunity. He turned to Mamane Momo. "According to them," he said, pointing at Aunt Petunia and Malome Masemola.

"No, according to the law," Mamane Momo retaliated. "You led me on!"

"We were just having fun, baby," Makgoromecha defended himself.

Momo left him hanging as she stormed over to Modiegi and Seipati's table.

As the DJ spun tracks and the guests took to the dance floor, Lerato approached Seputla.

"You look exhausted," he said.

"Thank goodness you're here," Lerato smiled. "I don't know how I would have coped without you."

Lerato took Medupe in her arms. Even though her daughter was now a year old, she still couldn't get used to her beauty and the overpowering protectiveness she felt for her. According to the other mothers that Lerato had spoken to, that feeling never went away. She leaned into Seputla for a kiss, and thought about how grateful she was for her small, yet complete, family.

Maki looked around the room but couldn't see Puo, so she decided to go out to the garden for some fresh air. Suddenly she heard his voice, and it sounded like he was on the phone. "I miss you too, sweetheart," he said, "But I'll be home soon."

Maki approached him and heard him say, "I love you too," into the phone. "I have to go now," he added, hanging up.

Puo sighed as he hung up, watching Maki. And as she neared him, he wrapped his arms around her and kissed her forehead. "What am I going to do with you?" he asked.

"I just need time," she replied. Then, when she sensed a shift in him, she added. "I don't even have matching Tupperware."

Puo laughed as Maki wrapped her arms around him, closed her eyes and rested her head on his chest, comforted by his warm embrace.

***

Maki stood at the podium looking out at the crowd that filled the room. Her sister, Tsholo, had driven from Kimberley with her nephew, Tiisetso, to support Maki at her big event. Alongside them in the front row were the actor and Tebogo who held hands as Tebogo wiped away some proud tears. Seated behind them were Lerato and Seputla who watched Maki in awe. Maki felt a great sense of accomplishment as she saw Corrine, Maggie and Stacey also seated in the crowd.

In her speech Maki told everyone about her journey to becoming a published author. She was sad that Puo hadn't been able to attend her first book launch, but thanks to Maggie she looked gorgeous in an ankle length black evening dress that was embellished with tiny crystals, causing her to literally dazzle the crowd.

Maki had to admit that she missed Puo, and ever since he'd asked her to move in with him and his daughter, Cece, she'd agonised about it over and over again, constantly weighing up the pros and cons of both options. As she neared the end of her speech, she looked across the crowded room that was filled with friends, family, a photographer and journalists.

One of the journalists raised a hand and asked the author what was next for her; just then Maki heard a shuffling at the door. As she looked up to see what the disturbance was, she was stunned to see Puo discreetly find a seat at the back of the room. When he sat down they made eye contact, causing Maki's heart to catch in her throat. The journalist snapped Maki out of her reverie when she repeated her question.

Without taking her eyes off Puo, Maki announced happily, "I'm moving to PE," and Puo's face split wide smile, causing Maki to do the same, and Tebogo and Lerato to loudly whoop in elation.

After Maki's speech she introduced Puo to Tsholo and Tiisetso. Maki's sister interrogated Puo about why he thought Maki was the one for him, while Tiisetso joked about how long his aunt Maki had been single, causing Tsholo to add that the entire family had been worried about her. But Maki was floating on cloud nine and was not concerned about Tsholo interrogating Puo or Tiiseto's comments.

Lerato, Seputla, Tebogo and the actor approached them, congratulating Maki on her decision to move to PE. Lerato asked Maki what had convinced her to make the decision, and Maki simply shrugged. "The heart wants what it wants."

Corrine approached the group and joked that, had it not been for her, Puo and Maki would have never met, even though Puo had turned down their offer to publish his book. Happy at the direction their relationship was going, Puo took Maki in his arms and kissed her affectionately.

Medupe ran around Maki's flat as Lerato and Tebogo helped her pack up her belongings. "The heart wants what it wants, huh?" Lerato commented, casting a sidelong glance at Maki.

"You know it's true," Maki laughed.

But Lerato wasn't entirely convinced. "No, seriously," she probed. "Why did you decide to move to PE?"

"Writing books with an ocean view," Maki laughed, causing Lerato to laugh too.

"I knew it!"

"Plus I can't wait to be a mom to Cece," Maki acknowledged. Since she knew that moving to PE had been Cece's idea, she couldn't wait to officially move in with her and Puo.

"Are you broody?" Tebogo asked.

"Just a little," Maki added. "But not enough to get me knocked up just yet. And you?"

"Medupe makes me broody, but that man works too hard for me to consider having a baby with him just yet. Besides, we want to enjoy our marriage, you know? Travel, see the world..."

"Girl, I hear you," Lerato laughed.

Maki sighed. "Whoever thought that our lives would change so much in a year?"

Lerato raised her hand. "I did!"

"That's because you were pregnant!" Tebogo laughed.

"Do you remember the night of the engagement party that Tshepo organised?" Maki asked, causing Tebogo to cringe.

"That feels like a lifetime ago," she said softly. "All I remember about that night is how unhappy I was, and how trapped I felt."

Maki turned to Lerato. "I knew even then that you and Seputla would end up together."

"Before I almost messed it up by messing around with Manur and Bra Aubrey was sending me 'I want you' notes.

"Imagine!" Tebogo said, rolling her eyes.

"Whatever happened to Bra Aubs?" Maki asked.

"He continued tracking me down at work, and when my preggy belly started showing, he was disgusted by the fact that Seputla, in his words, had 'ruined' me, and I never saw or heard from him again.

Maki shook her head. "Typical."

"But look at you now," Tebogo smiled. "Mommy and all."

"Do you guys remember that I'd lied and said Tumelo would be my date but I didn't even have his number?" Maki laughed. Tebogo and Lerato also burst out laughing.

"That was the night before I met the actor at his party," Tebogo added.

"And the rest, as they say, is history," Lerato smiled.

"You know what?" Maki asked, pulling a bottle of vodka from the cupboard.

"Uh-oh," Tebogo laughed.

"Uh-oh is right," Maki quipped, as she poured the vodka into three glasses. "I keep this here vodka for special occasions, and this, if I do say so myself, is a special occasion."

"Here here!" Tebogo and Lerato shouted in unison as Maki handed them their glasses.

I'd like to propose a toast," Maki continued, raising her glass. "To friendship!"

"And love!" Tebogo quipped.

"And trips to the coast," Lerato yelled exuberantly, with Tebogo and Maki echoing after her, "Trips to the coast!"

"To somersaults," Maki added proudly.

"To somersaults," Tebogo and Lerato yelled after her, and Maki continued, "In the hailstorm!" The three women clinked their glasses loudly as they shouted in unison: "To somersaults in the hailstorm!"

*** End ***